SHIFTING SANDS

Shifting Sands

M.R. Hennecke

One World Publishing
4901 W Grace Street
Tampa, FL, 33607

ISBN: 1499209401
ISBN 13: 978-1499209402
Library of Congress Control Number: 2014907704
CreateSpace Independent Publishing Platform
North Charleston, South Carolina

To Derek:
For never a dull moment.
For loving me.
You are my muse.

The ride continues.

Acknowledgements

It takes a community to write a book. Thank you to my husband, for making sure that once the fun part of writing is finished, the book actually sees print. To my three loving daughters, thank you for reminding me how to be a kid. Thanks to C. Piccone, and F. Weiss, for your tireless patience in reading and correcting the manuscript. C. Piccone, you brought my characters depth, and F. Weiss, you were right—the climax begged for flames. Thank you to my Muslim and Coptic Egyptian friends who helped me keep my setting true to life.

This book may strike a cord with some. While I have done my best to present a realistic scenario within a fictional setting, I apologize in advance for any inaccuracies. I have lived in Egypt, but I am not Egyptian. I cannot climb into the Egyptian persona like a native. What I can do, however, is to identify and strip away—one by one—the western filters through which we view Egyptian political and religious headlines. Only as we begin to see without these impediments do we come to understand the motives that color events in the Middle East. Understanding is always a good beginning.

...whenever any of the monks [or any Christian] in his travels shall happen to settle upon any mountain, hill, village, or other habitable place, on the sea, or in deserts, or in any convent, church, or house of prayer, I shall be in the midst of them, as the preserver and protector of them, their goods and effects, with my soul, aid, and protection, jointly with all my national people; because they are a part of my own people, and an honor to me....No one shall bear arms against them, but, on the contrary, the Muslims shall wage war for them...And by this I ordain, that none of my nation shall presume to do or act contrary to this my promise, until the end of the world.

- The Prophet Muhammad, in the *Achtiname of Muhammad*

Preface

This book was completed in 2012. When I first took to the keyboard, the idea of a Muslim fundamentalist group in Egypt bombing a Coptic church in Egypt seemed a stretch. Before I finished the book, a bomb tore apart a church in Alexandria, killing 23 Copts and wounding 97 more in a New Year's service in 2011. It was only the beginning. By some estimates, as much as half of the Coptic population has left Egypt.

And yet there is hope. After the Saints Church bombing, something remarkable happened. When the Coptic parishioners returned to their church, a ring of their Muslim neighbors encircled it, holding candles and praying, making sure their Coptic brethren could safely return to worship. It is those Muslims, and the vast majority who are like them, who are the heart and soul of the true Egypt.

I

My house never smelled like fresh baked bread.

I lay tangled in a sheet, my eyes closed. This couldn't be happening again. *Oh, please, don't let this be happening again.* Maybe some strange mood had taken over my mom, and she had done a complete 180 from overworked, overstressed, hyper-career mom into the fresh-bread type.

But the sounds were wrong too. I heard doors slamming, footsteps above me, a dog barking somewhere. I never heard sounds like these in the bedroom of my quiet house in suburban Florida.

Oh, God, I thought, my heart racing. *Not now of all times. I have SATs to think about.* I fought a wave of nausea. I opened my eyes.

And shut them again. This was not the bed I had climbed into last night. Where were my sky blue walls? My yellow surfboard with the mirror set into it? Where were my little maple desk and the corkboard frame with pictures of my favorite movie stars?

With resignation, I opened my eyes again and surveyed a small bedroom with white walls and white furniture. I lay on the top bunk in a corner of the room, my body covered by a white sheet under a tattered homemade quilt in shades of pale pink and baby blue. On the wall opposite the bunk bed stood a white dresser. A large white-framed rectangular mirror hung over it, with overlapping photos and postcards tucked into every corner—smiling faces and sunny places mostly. From one photo, a dark-haired girl who looked a bit like my friend Sandra feigned mock horror from the seat of a Ferris wheel. Only it wasn't Sandra. A free-standing closet filled another corner—again, white—and a clean white night table beside me with a lamp and a cheery pale yellow lampshade. Under a window at the end of the bed, a white desk brimmed with stacks of neatly piled textbooks, a binder, a pink cup with a half dozen sharpened pencils, and a pink backpack slung over the chair. Everything was eerily tidy. I thought of my own desk at home in Florida, its surface cluttered with candy and magazines, a statue of a black poodle like the one I used to have, a set of three stone elephants given to me by my friend Charlotte two birthdays ago, a magnetic box of paperclips and a cell phone holder shaped like a chair.

I sat up slowly. A delicate lavender floral nightgown floated around me as I moved. If the room wasn't enough of a clue, the nightgown gave it away. I was a girl. What a relief.

I peeked warily at the bottom bunk. A similar quilt lay rumpled in the bed below, with a little face buried in a pillow. A messy stream of ebony hair flowed over a plain white cotton pillowcase. It was hard to tell, but I put her about the same age as my little sister at home—eight. On the floor by the edge of the bed lay a creamy-skinned doll with long, tangled dark hair. The bedraggled doll must have fallen during the night. The girl and the doll were a matched set.

I leaned back against the wall and pulled my arms across my chest. Without thinking, I popped a fingernail into my mouth and began chewing. It tasted odd. I pulled the fingernail out and stared at the neatly trimmed tip. No one had ever chewed this nail before. An involuntary shiver shuddered through me.

So who was I this time? I knew from experience that I needed to gather clues immediately from my surroundings. The little girl dozing beneath me would wake up soon, and I'd have to fill the shoes—so to speak—of the body I was in.

I was a tidy girl, and from the look of the desktop, I probably took my studies seriously. Judging by the old floral quilt in shades of baby blue and pink, the lacy nightgown, the bare whiteness of the room and the vase of frayed red silk roses on the dresser, my new self had absolutely no taste. Everything here reeked of sweet and girly. If this were my room, I'd have painted the walls neon green, tossed out everything with a flower on it and introduced something fun. Maybe a huge black and white canvas of the Eiffel tower on a foggy morning or an oversize print of a zebra. Anything but flowers.

As if to confirm my judgment about taste, I looked at the wall above my pillow where a huge, foot-tall ceramic crucifix stared mournfully down at me.

This crucifix was unlike anything I'd ever seen before. In my church at home, one wall of the sanctuary displayed a sad, gentle-eyed Jesus, serenely draped over a cross—a distinctly PG-rated messiah. Not so, this one. The Christ figure above me now wore a deathly gray pallor and a gash across his abdomen that oozed painted blood. More blood seeped from beneath his crown of thorns, and iron nails protruded from his bloody hands and feet. His gruesome form hung from an ornate, gold-painted cross, gaily decorated with tiny red, purple and yellow silk flowers. Christ's brown eyes, half closed in agony, bored deeply into mine.

Wherever I was, I was far, far from home.

I covered my eyes with my hands and drew a long, ragged breath. I had shifted again.

II

My name is Molly, and I'm a shifter.

At least, that's what I call myself. Every year or two, for no reason I know of, I shift into someone else's body. I'm lucky it happened in the night this time, because I've woken up in strange places without time to adjust. I nearly drowned once when I was sitting in chemistry class one minute and swimming in the Gulf of Mexico the next.

I've never met another shifter, but they're out there. Right now I'm in this girl's body, and she's in mine. It's always a swap. That makes her a shifter too.

I could be anywhere. No country seems to be off limits. I never have any idea how many days, weeks or even months I will be forced to live in a strange body. I've shifted for as few as three days and as long as three months.

Without opening my eyes, I went over a mental checklist. One: Get the address in case I get lost. Two: Locate some cash. Same reason. Three: Find a best friend and keep him or her close. Four: Email Mom. Tell her to send me the SAT prep tests.

I took two deep breaths to slow my racing heart then pulled my hands away from my face and looked down at myself.

Creamy, mocha-colored skin covered fine-boned arms that tapered off into delicate hands with neatly filed, unpainted nails. It was a far cry from the pasty white skin I normally woke up to. My own skin never tanned. It had two settings—pale and sunburned. I slowly peeled off the quilt and quietly lowered myself to the floor. The little dark-haired girl didn't move. I walked to the dresser mirror.

A pair of wide, deep brown eyes stared back at me, set into a delicate, heart-shaped face. Shiny black hair fell to her waist in a tangle of loose waves. She was about seventeen. My age. I always seemed to shift into girls my own age.

I took a step back and turned sideways. I pulled the fabric of the nightdress tight to see what kind of body I'd shifted into.

Slim figure, tiny waist, curvy, long shapely legs. This kind of body could easily grace the pages of *Vogue Magazine.*

Huh! This girl was gorgeous. How cool was that? Maybe this would be fun.

Back home, I had long curly strawberry blonde hair—more strawberry than blonde. Full and shining, it could turn heads. Unfortunately, my hair rarely looked its best. Most of the time, as soon as I stepped out the door into the Florida humidity, it sprang into frizz. I had condemned it to life in a ponytail.

My Florida body was also different from this one. I liked that body. It was muscular and lanky, shaped for endurance sports. My shoulders were sinewy and strong, and my curves were the kind that come from training. I took pride in the line of my quads and the power of my calves. I'd earned those lines. Still, I longed for a tiny waist, and it was my lifelong ambition to achieve a B cup.

I turned to the closet and felt like I had regressed to my Barbie doll days. What fun to dress this body up! I imagined a closet full of smooth fitting jeans, cute little skirts, simple, snug-fitting T-shirts and some big silver hoops to peek out from behind these long lustrous locks.

I pulled open the doors of the wardrobe to receive my second shock of the morning since shifting. Half of the closet was filled with little dresses and blouses, all a child's size eight. I ran my fingers through white and pink lace tops and knee-length dresses with smocking on the top. All very sweet—perfect for an eight-year-old. Unfortunately, my side of the closet was pretty much a larger version of the same, infused with loud splashes of color. Knee-length dresses and skirts hung side by side, all in the brightest possible patterns. I saw floral patterns, broad geometric patterns, polka dots and stripes, and every one of them was glass-shatteringly loud. I pulled one dress out, a bold print of purple and black flowers. I groaned inwardly at its shapeless lines, and the thin shiny black plastic belt sewn onto the back of the dress. Who would wear clothes like this?

Not a single pair of pants. Not a single item in denim. I'm no fashion diva, but I know what to wear. To be forced to wear these clothes would be a nightmare. I wouldn't be caught dead in a single outfit in this closet.

But then again, I wasn't me.

Dismayed, I surveyed the disastrous closet more closely and selected the least offensive dress I could find: a white dress with puffed sleeves and hot pink dots all over it. I scrounged through some of the drawers that lined one side of the closet and found the appropriate undergarments, put them on, and then slid the dress over my head. I looked in the mirror and despaired as all those lovely curves vanished into the nothingness of the dress.

I decided that the girl in the polka dot dress was a headband kind of a girl because headbands are what little girls in polka dot dresses wear. I opened a dresser drawer and was immediately rewarded by a selection of about twenty headbands. I chose a pink one that more or less matched the dress I had on and began to hunt through the bottom of the closet among the selection of incredibly boring black flats.

"Aren't you going to school today?"

I had been so lost in my thoughts that the innocent little voice broke into them like a canon. I shot up out of the closet.

"Uh—yes. Of course. Why?" My new voice was startlingly high. A soprano to my usual alto.

She swung her legs over the edge of the bed and surveyed me from bleary eyes. Her hair stuck out in improbable directions, framing a perfect, creamy, heart-shaped face. The face and the hair were just a backdrop for those huge dark-brown eyes, lined with impossibly long black lashes. I stuck with my previous estimate—she was about eight.

"You're not wearing your uniform."

"I know. I was just trying this on to see if it still fits," I improvised.

She flashed those brown eyes at me, not convinced.

I scanned the room. Uniform? I didn't see anything that looked remotely like a uniform. I pretended to continue evaluating the dress in the mirror, and my eyes found the photos tucked into its frame. Interspaced among the numerous colorful religious postcards and stickers—a faded Mary with baby Jesus on a cloud, a pencil sketch of Jesus reading to the little children, Jesus with a blind man—were photos of my new self with friends. In one of them she—or was it me? Pronouns were confusing. One of us had my/her arm around another girl. The girl was shorter and squatter, a touch plump with an effusive smile and perfect teeth. A long braid ran down her back, and she wore dangling feather earrings. Very Cherokee. Their heads were bent together, and they both clutched binders and textbooks. More importantly, they both wore identical white blouses with gray skirts.

I turned and opened the bottom drawer on the large-clothing side—the one drawer I hadn't opened yet. Eureka. There, neatly stacked, were about a half dozen identical white blouses and gray skirts. I pulled off the pink polka dot dress, tossed it over the desk chair and began to change into the blouse and skirt.

The little girl stared at me the whole time.

"What's the matter with you?" Big Brown Eyes asked.

I smoothed a section of the bed beside her and sat down. She scurried up next to me and sat with her legs tucked up underneath her, examining me like some kind of science exhibit. I felt an immediate, overwhelming affection for her.

"Nothing's the matter with me," I said and instinctively pulled her close then gave her a squeeze. "Why do you ask?"

"You're Magda...." she said, and paused cautiously, looking up at me, "... but you're not."

Oh great. I hadn't been in this body more than a few minutes, and I'd already blown it.

It was vitally important that I become—what was her name? Magda. What kind of name is that? Anyway, I had to have her tastes, follow her routines, learn her mannerisms and do the things she would do. I had to pretend I knew the people she knew and try not to say too many things that were out of character. If I messed up, I could really screw up her life. I could make her friends and family hate her, ruin her reputation or have her branded a slut. I could fail exams that would change her life.

I hoped that wherever Magda was in my Florida body, she would have the same consideration.

I looked back into the curious eyes, reached out and smoothed her tousled hair. "Everything's fine, honey. You're right though. I'm not feeling myself today. It must be a bug. I feel a bit stuffy-headed and confused today."

An idea struck me. "I know. You like playing games, right?"

She sat back smugly. "Sure!"

"Let's make this morning fun. Pretend I'm a robot. I'm completely under your control. I can't do anything without you telling me to. Your mission is to get me ready for school. You have to tell me everything I have to do to get ready. Tell me everything I should do and everything I should know—right down to where my toothbrush is. Okay?"

"Okay," she answered. "Like I should tell you that you look funny in my headband?"

"Yes," I laughed, "Did I really put your headband on? Sorry. Told you I was out of it." I pulled the headband out of my hair and handed it to her.

"Okay!" she said, thrilled to have someone willing to play so early in the morning. She hopped down from the bed.

"Get my skirt and blouse," she instructed.

I put on my best robot face and looked at her blankly.

"In the drawer," she added.

Nothing.

"In the drawer in the wardrobe—under my dresses," she said, smiling.

I heard and obeyed. Using my best robot walk, I marched rigidly to the closet. I bent over and pulled out a small gray skirt and white blouse. Then I stood, still facing the closet, holding them, frozen.

"Give them to me," she giggled.

I turned and did so.

She got dressed, and the morning progressed smoothly this way. It proved a great way to find the bathroom without opening the wrong door.

We brushed our teeth together, and she instructed me to put my hair in a tight ponytail.

"No, no, at the *back* of your head!" she said, laughing, when I tried brushing it over my right eye.

She finished my look with a plain gray headband (blah!) and a pair of white pearl earrings (yawn). I looked just like the Magdas staring back at me from the photos.

"Wait!" she said. "You can't go out without your lucky bracelet!" She ran over to the dresser, opened the top drawer and pulled out a little silver chain. A dozen silver charms, each a different stylized cross, hung evenly spaced around it. I gave her my wrist and she clasped it. When I dropped my hand to my side, it made a lovely tinkling noise.

"Okay, boss, looks like we're stylin'," I said. "What do we do next?"

"Breakfast," she said. "I'm starving."

"What do robots eat for breakfast?" I asked.

"Whatever Mom makes for you. It's Wednesday, so—eggs. Then Mom yells at us because we're running late. Then Layla comes and drives us to school. But first, you have to give me braids."

This I could do. I took the plain, white plastic brush on the dresser and began running it through her long hair. She didn't look at all like my own little sister who had long blonde hair and blue eyes, but in other ways they were exactly alike. I felt a pang of longing for my Gabrielle. What had I said to her the last time I saw her? I think I berated her for talking constantly about ocean life. I wanted to finish my homework last night, and she kept interrupting me with this or that fact about the sunfish. Did I know they were born only 1/10th of an inch long and grew to fourteen feet? I did not. Did I know they ate algae and jellyfish? I did not. I felt pang of regret that the last thing I said to her was to stop talking.

How many days or weeks would it be till I saw her again? I wondered if the real Magda was at my house right now, running Gabrielle's pink My Little Pony brush through her hair and separating the strands to braid them.

I knew that wherever the real Magda was, she was in a much, much better situation than I was. Only two people in the world know I'm a shifter: my mom and my sister. Mom figures, in hindsight, I probably started shifting when I was two. That's when the child psychologists started. She says I was a normal, well-adjusted kid and then, like the flick of a switch, one day I was crying all the time, acting like I didn't know her. I wouldn't answer to my name. My beloved blankie was no comfort. The four-story houses I loved to build with my red and blue wooden blocks collapsed after two stories. More shocking still, I started to do things I shouldn't have been able to do. At a friend's piano, I played a competent "Twinkle Twinkle Little Star" even though I'd never touched the black and white keys before. Then a week later, another switch flipped in the middle of breakfast and I flew out of my booster, sending a bowl of oatmeal flying. I ran into her arms and wouldn't let go of her for an hour.

When I got older, I could talk about my experiences in other people's bodies. I would talk about the excruciating heat, muck and the bugs in the rice paddies, or another time about pouring and stretching maple syrup on the snow, so it would freeze and turn into candy. I spoke of these things like other kids talk about their day at school. I once told my mom when I was upset that if she put a little shot of tequila in my juice, it might help me calm down.

The psychologist didn't last long after I started talking because once hallucinations were involved, the psychologist referred me to a psychiatrist. Only psychiatrists can prescribe medication. There's really only one diagnosis for clear and vivid hallucinations about working in rice patties and stretching maple syrup, and that's schizophrenia. The psychiatrist prescribed little pink pills that were supposed to make the hallucinations go away. I hated them. They made me tired all the time. I probably should've stopped talking about my shifting, but I was mad that no one believed me, so instead I redoubled my efforts to convince everyone I was telling the truth.

Shortly after the pills started, I shifted again. I was six, and I was gone for two months. I came back from a summer in rural England bursting with stories. I'd been a country vet's daughter named Claire and traveled to farms with the vet almost every day. I spoke of muddy rural roads, driving on the wrong side of the road and a great motorway called the M4 that went all the way to London. I described what it looked like to watch a calf birth, taking particular interest in how much blood is involved and the way blood smells like rusty metal. I stuck out my right arm to demonstrate how, if the calf won't come out, the vet puts his whole arm inside the mother just so. Then I gradually twisted my wrist to show how to straighten the calf out, so it could move down the birth canal.

The pills did not seem to be preventing the hallucinations.

The Florida me, I later learned, started another "episode," as Mom called them, two months previously. I apparently woke up one morning terrified and for three days wouldn't leave the bedroom. I insisted on being called Claire and repeatedly requested, without raising my voice, that I would like to be taken back to Farnborough, please. After a week, Mom got me to go to school where I sat in a corner and spoke to no one, except to tell the teacher on my third day that Tom, a rotund red tabby cat that frequented the school playground, was not a boy and needed to be brought inside to have her kittens. The next week, Tom deposited six tiny kittens in the crawlspace under the stairs.

Then there was the incident with the pool. One afternoon, I fell into the pool and sank straight to the bottom. Mom had to pull me out, call 911 and resuscitate me. After three and a half years of lessons, I suddenly didn't have the slightest clue how to swim.

Mom, at her wit's end, didn't know how to handle me. It was a horrendously bad year all around. Mom was expecting Gabrielle, and just before she started her third trimester, we got the call that my dad had been killed in a car accident while on a business trip in Houston. The shock put Mom in the hospital for two days, and she almost delivered Gabrielle thirteen weeks too soon. We were on our own. When Mom returned home, Grandma told her she should stick with the schizophrenia diagnosis and give it more time, but Mom said her instincts told her the diagnosis was wrong. She changed psychiatrists.

The new psychiatrist agreed that the diagnosis for hallucinations was schizophrenia, but then he told her something she didn't know: that hallucinations were the only symptom I displayed that fit the diagnosis. He told her that true schizophrenics can't show a range of emotions. I was capable of the full rainbow of emotions, from terror to sadness to hugs of joy. He said true schizophrenics don't produce a set of "non-existent skills," like suddenly being able to play the piano. He explained that true schizophrenics find it difficult to connect with other people. I showed all the signs of seeking love and closeness from family and friends. The list went on and ended with the fact I lacked what the psychiatrist called *genetic loading* for the disease, meaning it didn't run in the family—something schizophrenia almost always does.

That left my frazzled mother without a diagnosis. Some brief discussion ensued of something called Dissociative Identity Disorder, better known as Multiple Personalities, but the psychiatrist said while it was possible to find a couple of doctors who claimed to treat it, the vast majority consider such a diagnosis the stuff of great fiction and nothing more.

Sherlock Holmes once said that when you have eliminated the impossible, whatever remains, no matter how improbable, must be the truth. Mom was forced to consider the only remaining possibility: the possibility I could shift.

Now when I shift, my Mom and Gabrielle know. Magda would be welcomed as soon as she put the wrong clothes on, screamed when she looked in the mirror or couldn't find the bathroom. It was almost certainly her first time shifting—no one who shifted into my body had ever done it before. She would be asked to go to school for me and take good notes but not run track meets—I made a mental note to email Mom to ask Magda to take detailed notes in my SAT prep sessions next week. Magda would not be allowed to pet my bird Kiwi, a Green Cheek Conure who bit everyone but me, and was the only one who unerringly recognized me the minute I shifted back. I love that bird.

For Magda in Florida, there'd be school on weekdays when Mom was working, weekends on the beach and in Disney World, and Mom would take extra days off from her real estate agent job whenever there was some event—say a major exam, or any exam at all in French—that she didn't want Magda to attend for me. On those days they might visit the aquarium or go for a walk in the Brooker Creek Preserve. It used to bug me that Mom would take days off for my shifters but almost never for the real me. She said she was doing it for me—to keep my shifter from messing things up. When I got back, Mom would have to work doubly hard to make up for the time she took off.

The coming weeks would be stressful for me as I tried to blend into Magda's life without attracting psychiatrists. I also knew this was not going to be an easy period in Magda's life. I had a theory about my shifting; I always shifted for a reason. Either something in that person's life needed fixing or some major, life-changing decision had to be made. One time I shifted into the body of a girl who was hanging out with a group of friends experimenting with drugs. She valued being a part of that group but she had to do drugs if she wanted to be with them. I shifted into her body during a pivotal moment in her life. Saying no was easy for me because I didn't feel any pressure to fit in with those people. Through me, she said 'no' in a firm and confident way then found a group of friends who rewarded her for her decision. I shifted in and out of her body in a week. Another time I shifted into a girl who needed to talk a friend out of committing suicide. That shift took two months. I never got to just blip into someone's life, see the sights and go home.

For me, the coming days or weeks would be full of anxiety and stress as I pretended to be a girl I wasn't and then help her deal with a life-altering situation or decision. For Magda, if she accepted her situation, this would be kind of like the ultimate exchange student experience.

I parted Magda's sister's hair down the middle and plaited first the right side, then the left. I twisted the two long strands of braid in the middle and used a little bowl of bobby pins on the dressing table to pin the braids into a knot. It was Gabrielle's favorite hairstyle, and she made me do it for her all the time.

"Cool," Big Brown Eyes said, appraising herself in the mirror. "This is new. I love it." Her eyes turned to watch me in the mirror as I put the brush away.

"Where'd you learn to do it?" she asked.

"I saw it in a magazine."

She stared at me in the mirror, but her eyes looked right through me.

III

"Magda! Maraya!" I heard a stern, motherly voice calling. "Get out here, girls. Right now. Your breakfast is getting cold, and it's nearly time to go."

Maraya! I had a name for Magda's sister. Magda and Maraya. Unusual names, but they flowed together. I followed Maraya to the kitchen.

A plump woman of average height, her back to us, bustled about the kitchen. Her black hair, slightly peppered with gray, was pulled up into a severe bun. When she turned to set two plates on either end of the table, I saw the inspiration for Magda's beauty—the high cheekbones and well-proportioned face, but here the execution was harder, more chiseled, and dark circles underscored her eyes. Her clothing, predictably, hung shapelessly over her—a simple gray skirt to just below the knees with a matching blazer over a plain white blouse and a pair of sensible, one-inch black pumps. A gold chain with a cross framed her throat, her only adornment.

"*There* you are, girls," she said with a note of exasperation. "Layla will be here any minute, and none of us have eaten. Sit down; let's pray." She flipped two more steaming plates of eggs on the table, where a bowl of fresh pitas waited. I cringed inwardly—I hate eggs—but the scent of the pitas more than made up for them. Freshly-baked pitas? What a revelation. They come from a bag.

I chose the chair across from Maraya and nearest the wall, underneath a niche which housed a painted statue of the Virgin Mary cradling baby Jesus. At one end of the table sat their dad, a dark-haired man, tapping away on a smartphone. The mother sat down at the opposite end and pulled her chair in. The father laid the phone aside, and we all bowed our heads.

"Our heavenly Father," Magda's father began in a soothing baritone, "we thank Thee for this food. Feed our souls on the bread of life and help us to do our part in kind words and loving deeds. We ask in Jesus' name. Amen."

"Amen," we echoed. There was a rush for the cutlery at the center of the table.

"There's an admin meeting before patient hours today," Magda's mother said. "They've specifically requested all the doctors attend, so I'm not going to be able to escape it this time. I'll just be an hour or so late getting home, God willing. Magda, you come home with Layla like normal, but Maraya I've emailed your teacher that you'll be going home with Nadia. I'll pick you up there on my way home."

Fresh bread and a doctor too?

"Nadia? Do I *have* to?" Maraya whined. "She's so annoying. I always have to play what *she* wants, and she just plays baby games all the time."

"Yes, darling, you have to. You're her guest, and you'll play what she wants you to. It's polite. It'll only be an hour or so," she said firmly between bites.

"How come when I'm the guest I have to play what the hostess wants me to play, and when I'm the hostess, I have to play what my guest wants to play? I never get to play what I want. It's not fair," she pouted.

"Life isn't always fair," their mother replied. "The hostess should always be looking out for her guest's interest, but when that doesn't happen, it's impolite to say so."

Maraya sulked.

"So what's else's on the agenda for you two today?" Magda's dad asked, his relaxed manner a stark contrast to Magda's mother's agitation. His black hair thinned at the temples, and his mustache had long ago given over to gray. A set of small, black wire-rimmed glasses gave him a scholarly look. He wore a dark gray business suit, white shirt, navy tie, and he glanced up from his phone as he spoke.

What was on the agenda? Trick question. I had no clue. Shifting was like being in a play; only I was the only one who didn't know the script.

"Oh, nothing." I said, opting to hide behind universal teenage non-answer. Maraya, however, forgot about her sulk and proceeded to gleefully fill in any conversational gaps.

"I can't wait to get to school. Mary said she's bringing me a Wee Pets bracelet—the kitty one!—it's the only one I don't have. Plus we have PE today and we're playing four-square. It's going to be the best day *ever.*"

Magda's dad's eyes started to glaze over around the words, Wee Pets. I smiled to myself. Maraya had used the exact phrase Gabrielle used to describe any generic good thing. It was always either the best or the worst day ever. No in-betweens.

"Well, that's great," he said, taking a sip of thick black coffee and then returning his full attention to his phone, his brow furrowed.

I faced my plate of eggs. Reluctantly, I loaded my fork and put it in my mouth. To my surprise, they were delicious. I guess I shouldn't have been surprised. I was, after all, using Magda's taste buds, not mine. I began to scoop the eggs up with enthusiasm, and my mind wandered to the real Magda at my house who would have to make do with corn flakes. If Mom or Gabrielle remembered to show her the cupboard.

Brrrrriiiing! Brrrriiing! the doorbell sounded urgently, and I shoveled down the rest of the egg without tasting it. Magda's mom called out that Layla was here, threw Maraya's backpack over her little shoulders and pushed us to the door.

"Goodbye, Mom! Goodbye, Dad!" I said.

"Come straight home after school Magda!" Magda's mom shouted down the hallway.

I threw open the door and there stood Layla. I recognized her immediately from the photo on the mirror. She was plump, but she wore her extra curves confidently. Her hair was pulled back in a low, wavy ponytail, festooned with a full red silk hibiscus flower. Her ears dripped with a cascade of golden flowers, and her right arm was decked out with three inches of colorful bangles of various shapes and sizes. Where Magda wore plain black leather flats, Layla's flat black shoes were shiny patent leather, and a coiled black zipper adorned each like a flower. I couldn't say for sure I liked what she was wearing, but this girl had style. She exploited every gap in the school uniform code to its fullest, and I respected her for that.

She reached through the doorframe and gave me a squeeze.

"Hi, Amazon girl," she said jovially. The top of her head came to my nose.

"Good morning Uncle Cyril, Aunt Ireney," she called into the kitchen.

"Good morning, Layla," Magda's mother answered.

Layla bent down and gave Maraya a hug. "You ready for another ride in the belly of the lion?"

"Magda says your car's more like a dying horse," Maraya answered. Layla shot me a dirty look.

"Don't listen to her. My car is a fierce and powerful lion, and it will navigate the streets of this jungle city and deliver you safely to school," she said as the door of the apartment slammed shut behind us, and we walked down a narrow staircase to a small foyer with white marble floors and a wall with eight brass mailboxes. Layla pushed open a set of double doors, and I braced myself as we stepped out into a world I couldn't possibly have prepared for.

IV

The heat hit like a physical blow. I'm from Florida and I knew heat, but I'd never felt anything like this before. Florida heat is a thick, humid blanket that gently envelopes and saps energy like a hot bath. This dry heat seared the skin like a hot grill. It burned my lungs and made me short of breath.

The sun, white-hot, reigned free in a cloudless sky. The contrast from the darkened hallway made me step backwards and throw an arm up over my eyes.

In the same instant my nose was confronted by a putrid, sickly-sweet smell that made the eggs in my stomach contemplate a return voyage. I scrunched my nose and with squinty eyes, and I searched for the source of the stench—a big old dumpster on the corner to the right brimming with black plastic bags, loose cans and bits of refuse. I noted with astonishment a gray swayback donkey that stood in front it, hitched to an old wooden cart. The donkey glanced placidly at me and then looked away again, bored. Its head hung down and its ears drooped. A filthy old man in torn brown pants and a black T-shirt hefted bag after bag of trash from the dumpster into the cart.

Where in the world was I? Layla and Maraya pushed on down the narrow paved street, oblivious to my amazement. I struggled to keep pace. Rows of chipped concrete fences about three feet high lined both sides of the street in front of small, three and four-story apartment buildings like the one we had just left. It was a gray, concrete, urban landscape. A bit of green poked out over a fence, a small triumph for nature. I could hear the hum of traffic somewhere nearby, but this street was quiet. A single teenage boy passed us on the opposite side of the street, his hands deep in his jeans pockets, the black cords of a set of earbuds extending from his ears into a back pocket. He didn't look up.

We walked along the pavement of a narrow, aging street with no sidewalks, forcing us to weave around parked cars until we came to a small red one. I don't know much about cars, but Layla's did not live up to her lion analogy. A boxy Toyota, it didn't look like it could make it around the block. The other cars parked around it looked no different.

I realized, belatedly, that Layla had been talking to me as we walked. ". . . can't believe Annalisa doesn't like Ramy anymore," Layla whined. "He's all she ever talked about for months. Remember how I had to practically force Ramy to go over and talk to her at the church picnic? I mean, really, I was performing a public service, so she'd stop whining about how much she liked him and *do* something about it. She was driving us *all* crazy. Then he finally starts talking to her, and now she doesn't want anything to do with him. Honestly, he's a pretty good catch . . ."

And so it went. Layla kept up a steady stream of talk, and my input was apparently not required. Even Maraya appeared cowed into silence by the verbal onslaught. We climbed into the car. The story about Annalisa continued, morphed into something about some kids she babysat for, then moved on to history homework. I interjected the odd word of agreement or sympathy though I don't think she really noticed.

Layla started the beast and off we went. I felt every bump of the rough roads. The traffic picked up quickly until we were in the midst of a dusty, throbbing, organic mass of cars. This definitely wasn't Florida. My heart quickened as I realized this couldn't be anywhere else in the U.S. either. Soldiers stood on the street corners and wore heavy camouflage fatigues in the oppressive heat while looking uniformly bored. No traffic lights regulated the flow of cars through crowded intersections. In the intersection ahead, a harried solider stood in the middle of the sea of vehicles gesturing wildly this way and that in an attempt to direct traffic. Only the few cars within eye contact slowed to obey him.

The noise was ceaseless. Cars accelerated, braked and honked in a constant chain of automotive chatter. Layla drove on, completely unmoved by it all. She kept up a constant stream of talk as she aggressively maneuvered the car from lane to lane through the chaos.

Foot traffic picked up as we entered a commercial area. Men lumbered along on the sidewalks. Some dressed in business suits like Magda's dad; others wore jeans and button-down shirts. A few wore those floor-length cotton dresses like you see in pictures of—

Omigosh—I was somewhere in the Middle East.

But wait. How could that be? I'd woken up this morning under a huge floral crucifix, I'd said grace, I wore a Christian bracelet, and Layla talked about church picnics. This part of the world is Muslim. My eyes furtively scanned the horizon for some evidence one way or another. Sure enough, I saw a distant silver dome with the Muslim crescent moon on it. This had to be the Middle East.

What Middle Eastern country had Christians too? I racked my brain for some shred of useful information. I always paid close attention in history class. I figured it was a good idea to learn as much as I could about other countries since I could wake up in one at any given moment. Last year, we studied the Arab-Israeli conflict, so I should know this. Was I in Israel? The Holy Land has lots of Christians. But Israel has lots of Jewish people too, and I didn't see any of those black yarmulke caps they wore.

So where the heck was I?

I surveyed the women for more clues. Most wore those Middle Eastern type, loose flowing dresses that touched the ground. Many were black, but I saw blue, green and a dark red too, and the ladies all wore them with some kind of scarf over their hair then pinned the scarf under the chin. Quite a few women wore conservative Western clothes like Magda's mother. Of those, some covered their hair and some didn't. Layla hit the brakes as a woman in a full-length black dress with a black headscarf stepped out in front of our car, a laundry-sized basket balanced confidently on her head, her hands loose at her sides. The woman's eyes swiveled to glance at us, and her head turned slightly, but her face registered no expression and she kept walking.

I ruled out Saudi Arabia and Afghanistan, strict Muslim countries where the streets would be full of *burqas*, those full dresses with the gloves and veils that allow just a tiny screen for the women to see the world through.

"Magda, are you listening?" I hadn't a clue where the conversation had turned. I rewound my memory. Layla had just said something that ended with, "Don't you just hate that?"

"Oh, yeah, sorry, Layla," I said distractedly, "I'm just a little slow this morning. Yeah, I know what you mean; it drives me nuts too." This seemed sufficient. She plowed on cheerfully about PE and how we were going to have to run laps and get all sweaty and what that would do to her hair.

It occurred to me that we weren't speaking English. Not Layla and not me. I didn't have a name for this language, but it was definitely not English. Even though Magda had left her body, I knew there would still be, well—sort of "resonances" of Magda left behind in her body. The most obvious of these was speech. The way I think of it, language is so much a part of a person, so engrained, that it stays with the body. Magda, in my body, would speak perfect English as well. Or my version of English anyway.

The billboards lining the street showed me an alphabet with long, vertical strokes. It was so easy to read; it was definitely Magda's first language. It's funny really—I could tell that when Magda said the word *etneen* it meant two, but I couldn't tell what language it was. Yet.

Most of the resonances I would pick up from Magda would be less engrained. I would sense them only now and then, like unexplained whiffs of emotion out of nowhere. These feelings would clue me in when I met someone Magda felt about intensely. I had felt a strong positive resonance immediately when I looked down at Maraya in her bedroom. I'm sure that's part of the reason I connected with her immediately, and I would have even if I didn't have my own little sister back home.

If Magda felt only passing or ambivalent emotions about someone, I wouldn't be able to pick up on them. This too gave me information. For example, the warm glow I felt at first sight of Layla told me she was probably not just a friend, but a close friend.

We had only been in the car a few minutes when Layla pulled down a small, quiet side street and came to a stop. She gathered up her things and clamored out of the car while Maraya hopped lightly out of the backseat and dragged her backpack behind her.

I threw Magda's pink backpack over one shoulder and winced inwardly as I picked up her laptop in its pink canvas case. Being seen with a pink backpack was hard enough, but a matching pink laptop case was almost too much to bear. I tucked in beside Layla. As we headed toward the gaping front doors of a large brick building, the mass of uniformed humanity grew thicker. This was going to be tricky. How was I going to figure out my classes? My locker combination?

"Hey Magda!" a little wisp of a girl, about a head shorter than me, fell in beside us. She was slim. No, scrawny is a better word. With a long narrow nose under bushy eyebrows. Her hair was tucked back in a sunny yellow scarf. The scarf had to mean she was Muslim. No one wears a headscarf for a fashion statement. So Muslims and Christians hung out together in this school. Cool.

"Hi, Layla," she said, peering across me.

"Morning, Aisha," Layla replied, brightly.

"Morning," I added.

"Say, Magda," Aisha began, "have you got the answers to the questions on chapter eight in biology? This whole concept of amino acids has me totally confused. That and I was doing my community service in Giza till nearly eleven last night. There was an accident coming home on the 6th of October Bridge, and we were stuck in traffic for an hour. I fell asleep on my computer. Can you help me real quick?"

On the bright side, I now knew where I had to be first period. And, as it happens, I was pretty strong on amino acids. Actually, I sailed through all of my classes. The counselors back home described me as "strongly academically gifted." Not having to struggle through class work, on top of everything else I had to adjust to, really helped. Still, I hadn't a clue what the homework was.

Then I remembered. Last night before bed, Magda had been Magda, so the homework was probably done.

"Sure, no problem," I ventured. "I just have to get to my locker. I'll help you out when we get to class."

Yeah! Double whammy. Aisha would walk with me to my locker, where I hoped Magda kept her class schedule, and then to my first class.

"You're the best," she replied with a grateful sigh. "I'd never get through bio without you."

We turned down a long corridor of lockers, one row on the bottom and one on top. Layla and Aisha stopped suddenly. Layla began flipping open a combination lock on an upper locker while Aisha waited for me.

"Oh, dang," I improvised, suddenly. "Layla, I think I sprained my thumb last night. Can you open my locker for me?" Crap, I'd been doing so well this morning and then I came out with a lame excuse like that.

Layla stared at me oddly. I couldn't meet her eyes.

"How did you sprain your thumb? Your brain, I could understand that, but your thumb?"

"It's kind of embarrassing. I was leaning back on my chair and it tipped over. I twisted to break my fall, and I must've landed on it wrong."

"Okay, now that I can believe. For a minute I thought you were going to tell me you'd taken up sports or something," she said. She leaned over to the locker next to hers, and I watched as she twirled the dial, first left to 40, then right to 4, and left to 8.

"You're lucky I'm here," she said. "And that you've had the same padlock since the sixth grade." The locker fell open, and Layla stood aside.

I surveyed the contents, which proved that Magda was a total neat freak. Relief flooded through me. The locker looked sanitized. There was a little green shelf in the middle, and she had textbooks and binders stored above and below, each with neatly typewritten labels. Affixed to the door was a long pink cloth organizer with a series of pockets in it. Out of those pockets poked a brush, some pens (all identical), some neatly sharpened pencils, another gray headband, a calculator and a couple of magnets with pictures of singers or movie stars I'd never seen before. There, neatly taped on the door of the locker below the organizer, was a list of all of her classes, including the teacher's name and the classroom number. Thank goodness for nerds.

I paused for a moment to picture poor Magda as she opened my locker in Florida. I try to keep everything in order for potential shifters, but it's hard. I'm not naturally neat, and it'd been more than a year since I last shifted. I guess maybe I had also started to hope I was finished shifting and could live a normal life. For the last few weeks, I had reverted to throwing things in wherever they fit. I taped my schedule to the locker when school started in August, but it was February now. It fell off the door a couple weeks back, and I shoved into the back of the locker. It lay crumpled back there somewhere. Probably. How was Magda going to figure out my life? I needed to email Mom first chance I had.

I hurriedly pulled together the textbooks that corresponded with my morning classes and slammed my locker closed, clicking the combination lock back in place. Aisha waited patiently, chatting with Layla, and jumped to attention as soon as my locker slammed shut. I gathered we were running late.

We skulked into the back of the classroom, in the manner of clandestine students sharing homework answers everywhere, and I flipped open my binder to the last page where the answers to chapter eight were neatly laid out in clear and precise English. English! So classes were taught in English. Interesting. Aisha poured over them intensely then threw herself into the seat next to me, flipped open her binder and began scribbling furiously as the last students fell into their seats and the buzzer rang.

"Open your textbooks to chapter eight, everyone," boomed a tall, middle-aged man with deep acne scars. He wore running shoes with his brown khakis and a black polo shirt. Only an American would wear running shoes with dress pants, and a slight Bostonian accent confirmed my cultural diagnosis.

I resisted the instinct to relax and drift through the class. Magda obviously excelled at this class, and I knew I could be in her life for days or even weeks. I owed it to her not to blow her grades. If I paid attention to the assignments and put a little effort in, I should be able to keep her marks up.

My only minor panic was when, at the end of class, I couldn't remember what came next. Then I discovered that Magda had neatly taped the same class schedule that was in the back of her locker inside the front of every binder. Again, I thanked my luck for her obsessive behavior.

Her next class was Arabic. Well, this confirmed the language we were speaking, anyway. I would have to tread carefully in this class. Sure, I had Magda's language skills, but I didn't have her memories about Arabic grammar, and I didn't know anything about Arabic literature. What if I was asked a question about some Arabic version of *Macbeth* that Magda's class was halfway through reading? They'd think something was seriously wrong with me. And how would I catch up?

I was going to need a smart friend, I decided, as I walked into the classroom and selected a seat near the back. Did Magda already have a friend who might be strong in Arabic? I glanced around. A boy was settling into the desk in front of me, smiling and making eye contact.

I'd have had to have been brain-dead not to notice this guy. His white uniform shirt stretched across a broad chest, and the tightness of the short sleeves accentuated toned biceps. With his latte-colored skin, dark, short-cropped hair and coal eyes, he might've just slipped off the polo pony in a Ralph Lauren ad. Mmmmm. I noted the plain silver cross that hung around his neck. A Christian, like Magda.

He didn't say anything, but I was pretty sure there was a connection here. I checked the recesses of my mind for any resonances of emotion from Magda when I looked at him. Nothing. No strong emotions, good or bad. The warm tones of his Arab skin contrasted with the bleached white of his shirt deliciously. Was he interested in me? Er—I mean—in Magda? And, back on task, could he be the one to help me with Arabic? I suddenly realized the class was underway, and the teacher spoke.

"Mark!" the dark-haired teacher with distractingly long sideburns said sternly. Apparently, our brief inattention had not been missed by the sideburns. I mean teacher. "Would you please review for the class the importance of the book *Zaynab* in Egyptian literature?"

Close call, he could've picked me. I sat back in the chair and popped a fingernail in my mouth. It tasted bad, but I was getting used to it.

Mark fumbled with his papers, chose one, and read in a clear baritone in Arabic, "Despite the structural flaws of the novel, including the division of the focus on Zaynab and Hamid, and a letter which is unashamedly Haykal's own words merely summarizing the events so far, the novel is hugely important in beginning the era of the modern Arabic novel. It is groundbreaking in its use of vernacular language and characters as well as its liberalizing political dimension."

His answer satisfied the teacher. Mark glanced quickly back at me. A small smile played on his face. Probably, he just wanted to see if I was paying attention. I most certainly was.

I smiled shyly, held his gaze intentionally just a little too long then looked quickly back to my notebook, but the invitation had clearly been left. I tried to return my attention to the class discussion, but I was keenly aware of his glances in my direction.

We read a chapter of the book, students taking turns doing the reading, with frequent interjections by Mr. Sideburns to delve deeper into what the author tried to achieve. I pulled off Magda's turn at reading. The words flowed from my tongue as effortlessly as English.

Our homework was to write an essay on the transition of Arabic literature from the classic to the contemporary period and draw examples from *Zaynab* by comparing and contrasting a book or books of classic literature of our choice. Seriously? I had to try to keep Magda's grades up while I was in her body. I could probably manage her marks in everything else, but I hoped vehemently that she sucked at Arabic. I needed the bar to be low.

The bell rang, and I gathered my books and stood. Mark had already disappeared into the crowd. How was I going to get a chance to ask this guy if he could help me with my Arabic?

I squeezed through the door into the hallway and merged with the flow of foot traffic. Miraculously, Mark slid into place by my side.

"I thought that class would never end," he said.

"You and me both," I replied conversationally. There was an awkward pause.

"You ready to hit the track?" he said.

"Yes." I replied, with feeling. "I can't wait." PE was next. A good run would let me vent some steam.

Mark looked surprised. "Is that sarcasm?" he asked.

Drat. Layla had said something about Magda not doing sports, hadn't she?

"Maybe. It's just that I feel a bit sick of Arabic right now. I need to stretch my legs."

"Yeah. Well, at least it's not so hot today," he said. "Yesterday was killer." I wondered what he considered to be hot, if today was an improvement to him. "Track and field season starts today!" he said, enthusiastically.

Then he checked himself, evidently feeling he'd made a mistake.

"At least I bet you're glad volleyball season is over," he added, glancing at me. "How's the wrist?"

"Fine," I said, glancing at them both, reflexively. Come to think of it, the right one was pretty sore. I guess Magda hadn't mastered the overhand serve. "I'll get 'em next year," I said.

He snickered. "Maybe you should stick to academics. You kick butt in math, science, Arabic—pretty much everything that involves opening a book. Your talents lie there."

Oh, boy. Magda was good in Arabic? How could I ask him for help with that lead in?

Frankly, I hadn't even decided for sure that I should ask him. It did seem pretty clear that Mark liked me—I mean Magda—and I was pretty sure he would help. But I didn't want to lead him on if Magda wouldn't want me too. But *man* he was cute. My pulse quickened at the thought of spending some time alone with him.

I made up my mind. Ultimately, I didn't have a choice, did I? I needed to keep Magda's grades up. I could be in this body for weeks. He was the only one I knew in Arabic class, and it seemed clear that he was a top student.

"Say, Mark," I said, struggling to find the words as we walked. "I wanted to talk to you about my academics. Actually, I've been having a tough time in Arabic lately, and I'm really concerned about keeping my grades up. Do you think you might be able to tutor me a bit? Maybe help me with the essay we're supposed to do?"

He tripped. I mean, he literally fell over his own feet, nearly dropping his books in the process. His jaw fell open, and he looked at me in astonishment. Apparently, this move on my part was not expected.

"Magda," he said, "You're an honors student in Arabic. You've earned the top mark in our grade two years in a row. Stealing it from me, I admit. Last week, I heard Mr. Hussein tell you that when he read your assignment on dialogue, *"the skies opened up and the sun shone through."*

Crap. I was that good?

"I know it looks odd," I fumbled. "It's just that . . . well . . . this *Zaynab* book isn't coming easily to me." That last statement was more honest than he could know. "I've sort of hit a wall. I thought maybe if we went over it together, it would help."

"Of course, I'll meet with you. Magda. I've been asking you out and suffering rejection since kindergarten. I never realized all I had to do was impress you with my Arabic. How's Thursday after class?"

"Thursday's perfect," I said. "But, Mark . . ." He stopped and turned to face me, just outside a door with a stick figure of a boy on it. "It's not a date. It's just Arabic, okay?"

He looked at me long and hard then broke into a grin. "On my honor. Just Arabic." His right hand thumped his chest across his heart, and he laughed, turned and disappeared into the locker room.

I hunted for the girls' changing room, found it, and slipped inside.

Great! I had some Arabic help. And whether I liked it or not, I was pretty sure Mark saw it as something more than just tutoring. Oh, well. He was really cute. Thursday. Wonder when Thursday is?

I felt oddly confused. Okay, not so oddly. Confused was a pretty normal state today. I felt warm pleasure in the delight I'd just given to Mark, but also worry. Had I been too forward for this country, whatever country it was? Maybe girls weren't supposed to approach boys like that. I knew in many Middle Eastern countries, boys and girls kept separate, and their roles were very traditional. If Mark had been asking Magda out for years, there was probably a reason she hadn't gone out with him before. Maybe Magda wouldn't be thanking me later.

Still, I needed the help, and Mark was clearly willing. And now I stood in the middle of the girls' locker room with absolutely no idea what to do next. I had no clue what locker was mine; I had no Layla, Mark or Aisha to lean on. I put my books down on the bench and pretended to flip through them while I waited for someone to recognize me or to see someone I recognized.

Two girls walked in, side by side, arms wrapped tightly around their binders. They were average height and build, and both wore headscarves, one blue and one gold, which the girls had tucked into their uniform shirts. They turned their heads toward me and, in unison, gave me a scathing look.

The blue-headscarf girl had a finely chiseled face, which might have been beautiful if she wasn't so slim. Instead, she had a hollow-cheeked, bony look. Her lips turned down slightly in a permanent sulk.

The gold-scarf girl stood out. Who would've imagined anyone could be so stunning in a shapeless uniform, her head half covered? Granted, her skirt was hiked up, and I suspected her uniform shirt had been altered to flatter a little. But it wasn't really necessary. She had high, perfect cheekbones, a clean bold jaw line, and her skin had the light bronze, lustrous, polished look of a goddess. If she were a photo, I'd have sworn she was airbrushed. Her perfectly shaped brows were a deep brown with golden tones and delicately overlay a set of almond-shaped eyes, ever so slightly turned up at the outsides, giving them an exotic Arabian princess look. It was an otherworldly beauty. Every sway of her hips showed she knew it. The expression she wore proved the only ugly thing about her.

I tried to resume flipping through books on the bench as I feigned disinterest, hoping the girls would pass.

"Hey, Magda," the golden scarf said, slowing down as she came closer, "try to keep up in track this year. Coach Roberts said he's gonna have to find new timers 'cause the ones he's got don't count high enough for you." She laughed, a coarse rough sound at odds with her looks. Like this was the most original joke ever.

The other one giggled harmoniously.

A flash of white-hot anger coursed through me. Who were these witches? Without pausing to consider my remarks, I heard myself say softly, "The only thing *you* could ever run and get first in is a bathtub."

Bull's eye. Why didn't these quick come backs ever occur to me in my own life? Okay, I confess, I plagiarized that one. Gabrielle read it to me out of a joke book yesterday. Yesterday . . . a lifetime ago.

Both girls stopped and broke into feigned hysterics. Golden Girl slapped her thigh and laughed exaggeratedly, "Oh, Magda, honey, I didn't know you could be *so* funny! Now if only you could run as fast with your feet as you do with that forked tongue," she said bitingly. They disappeared around a bank of lockers, still giggling.

Layla materialized at my side.

"What were you *doing*?" she whispered urgently. "Do you have a death wish?" Layla already wore her PE clothes. She must've been changing in one of the many curtained rooms along one wall. Apparently remembering my lame hand story, she dialed another number and a locker swung open, revealing a stack of three neatly folded pairs of navy shorts, three gray T-shirts on top and a row of socks. A wire shelf was set inside, creating another level above the clothes with deodorant, a mirror, brush and lip gloss. It was *so* Magda's. Was it normal that Layla knew all my combinations?

"Fatima could *kill* you on the field today, you realize that. Were you, like, trying to make her mad or what?"

"Layla, I don't know," I said. "She just—she made me mad. What's her problem, anyway?"

"Serket has a problem with everyone. She's not prejudiced. She hates everyone who doesn't adore her, regardless of race, religion or shoe size," she said.

"Serket?" I asked, without thinking. It wasn't an Arabic word. I would've understood it.

"Hello?! Serket? Egyptian gods and goddesses in grade seven history? The deification of the scorpion?" I must've looked blank. Layla rolled her eyes in frustration. "Serket's always shown as a beautiful woman with a scorpion on her head. That's Fatima—beautiful but venomous. Remember how Demiana thought she'd make Fatima mad by calling her that? But then Fatima decided she liked the nickname because Serket stuns the unrighteous. But you know all this. What's up with you anyway? You're in la-la land today."

"Serket. Of course," I said. "I just heard you wrong. I think I'm getting a cold. My ears are ringing." I sniffed for effect as I unclasped Magda's lucky bracelet and tucked it into the locker. I reached in and pulled out a pair of shorts and a T-shirt which matched Layla's. Layla stood waiting, her arms folded across her chest.

I glanced down at the crest on the front of the T-shirt in my hand. At last I knew where I was.

V

Emblazoned on the T-shirt was a crest with a flag of red, white and black stripes, a golden eagle in the middle. The words, "The Cairo American Academy," boomed above the flag.

Cairo—in Egypt. I was in Egypt. Egypt!

Did many Christians live in Egypt? Apparently so. Because I was clearly in an American school in Cairo where Muslims and Christians learned together. Egypt! Land of the Pharaohs. Pyramids and camels, Moses and the Red Sea. How cool was this?

Pacing the room, Layla blathered about Fatima and how she had nearly reduced Aisha to tears in the cafeteria yesterday when she re-enacted one of Aisha's 'fainting spells' in which poor Aisha fell into the arms of some kid named Radwan, who's pimples apparently oozed on contact. I ducked behind a curtain and threw on the T-shirt and shorts and a pair of white tennis shoes I found in the back of the locker. I wracked my brain for what I knew about Egypt. I'd studied it in geography—when was that? Eighth grade maybe?

Oh, wouldn't it be wonderful to see the pyramids! And the tombs of the pharaohs, and hieroglyphs and statues of ancient gods—who were they? I remembered Isis, and the sun god, Ra. I was in the land of Cleopatra too. What was that story? Something about sneaking into Caesar's tent wrapped up in a carpet. Why? And Mark Antony, Caesar's General, who later became her lover. Then she had to commit suicide and did it by snake bite. Snake bite!

More importantly, what did I know about Egypt today?

I knew the main religion was Muslim and the government was a democracy. At least, as I recall, it was a democracy in name, but my class agreed it was really a dictatorship because it held elections with only one name on the ballot. Did Islamic terrorists live in Egypt? I had no idea. If they did, could Egypt's Muslims live peacefully in the same country with Christians? I thought again of Aisha with her sunny yellow headscarf. Apparently, they could.

And what about women? All I knew of women in the Middle East was a vague impression of Saudi Arabia and Afghanistan, places where many women covered themselves in veils, weren't allowed to drive and were discouraged from going to school. But Magda's mom was a doctor, and Magda was going to an expensive-looking private school.

As I emerged from behind the curtain, it occurred to me that a school called the Cairo-American Academy was probably full of foreigners. Come to think of it, way too many blonds and light brunettes scurried through the school hallways compared to what I saw on the streets outside. A school like this would've been set up by Americans for American and European kids living here, but some locals would come too. In a country like Egypt, only the wealthier families would be able to afford it.

I closed my locker, lost in thought.

"Let's get out there and get this class over with," Layla said dismally, and I followed her out into the bright Egyptian sun.

We walked out onto a large, open track, not unlike any track in Florida. I've seen most of them. Track was my sport. I trained year-round and specialized in the 100m sprint and hurdles. I took fifth in the state last year in the sprint and seventh in hurdles. I wasn't headed for a career in track or anything, but I was good, and I got better every day. What I loved most about the sport was the release of getting out there and running. I loved the sensation of speed; the feeling of pushing my body as far as it would go. It was freeing.

I sure didn't expect such a beautiful track here. Egypt was a desert. How did they come up with such a large expanse of green? The field was split up into all the usual track stations. Sprinters blocks dotted one side of the track, staggered across five lanes, and a 100m hurdles track filled the remaining lanes. A high jump station occupied the grassy middle of the track and off to one side, a long jump pit lay raked and ready for use.

A short, middle-aged man in a school uniform with rippling muscles and thick thighs stood in the middle of it all and blew his whistle. Kids began to gather around him.

"Everybody number off," he shouted in a booming baritone. "Numbers one through four," he spoke the word *four* like it had two syllables. I pegged him for southern American, maybe from Alabama or Georgia. "Go!" he pointed to a small boy with knobby knees who obediently shouted, "One!" and the kids began numbering off in a clockwise direction.

Layla winked at me and elbowed me away. I think she wanted us to split up so we might land the same number. No luck, I drew team four, and Layla three.

"Okay, everyone. When I blow the whistle once, start your event," the coach boomed. "When I blow it twice, change events. We move in a clockwise formation. After hurdles you leave the circle for high jump and long jump. You got that?" He assigned team four the 100 meter sprint, and five of my team headed for the starting blocks. Three of them I didn't know—two girls and a guy. And there was Mark. He slid into place beside me.

"So I hear you ticked Fatima off in the locker room," he said. "Pretty brave. They say you said you could beat her in track. What's up with that?"

How did this stuff get around so fast?

"Ummm—I'm pretty sure I didn't say that." We took positions behind the starting line.

"Then what *did* you say?"

"I don't know. Something about a bathtub."

"A bathtub?"

"I think I said the only thing she could run and come in first was a bathtub. It wasn't really all that funny."

"You got guts!" Mark laughed. "Especially since track is *her* sport. Challenge her in English, not track."

"I didn't challenge her in anything," I said. I put my left foot forward to touch the line, my right foot back, assumed a crouching position and tensed, waiting for the whistle. Mark looked at me curiously.

"Yeah, well, I guess she's saying you did," he said. The whistle blew.

Instinct took over. I burst out of the block, kept my head low for the first fifteen meters and pumped as hard as I could. Then gradually, I brought myself up to full height. I settled into a relaxed, cycling gait. When I passed the eighty-meter mark, I began reaching for the finish and pushed my legs as hard as they could go.

I stumbled across the finished line. My heart was pounding, and I felt like throwing up. I was in fourth place, behind Mark and two of the girls.

Fourth place? In a group like this I should've beaten the girls easy, and the guys maybe, depending on their fitness and skill levels.

Then again, I never felt this bad after a single 100m dash. Magda was in lousy shape.

Mark, the clear winner, circled around and caught up with me as he panted and grinned. "You been holding out on us? You been practicing?" he wheezed. "You nearly kept up with us there. And you beat Marianna."

"Yeah, well, I'm thinking about turning over a new leaf. It's never too late."

His gaze lingered over me, taking in the bits of me that were heaving the most. On Magda, I supposed, sweating probably looked good. The double whistle blew. Hurdles.

When we reached the hurdles, I began counting my paces back from the hurdles to the block. Mark was staring at me like I was crazy, but I didn't care. I was going to give this event my best shot. I couldn't help it. It was the Molly in me. I couldn't stand to suck at track.

I thought maybe hurdles would be better than sprinting because hurdles take more skill. I had to deal with Magda's body, but I could still contribute some skill.

The single whistle blew.

I came out of the blocks strongly enough—for Magda. I felt like an accomplished pianist trying to play on an out-of-tune piano. I had all the skills to succeed but Magda's body wasn't capable of doing what I wanted it to do.

My timing was a little off for the first hurdle—her natural gait was much longer than mine. I pulled my right leading leg up straight and vertical in front of me and let my other leg sweep around, angling the foot to the side to keep from topping the hurdle. I managed to get through all the hurdles without knocking over any, but again I came in a dismal fourth.

I bent over, my hands on my quads, and gasped for air. The heat wasn't the problem. As hot as it was, Magda's body was acclimatized. It was just not *my* body! Magda's limbs were longer than mine, her muscles weren't toned, and she had the cardio-fitness level of a peanut butter sandwich. I couldn't push her any harder, and her recovery time was agonizingly slow.

I also suffered from lack of muscle memory. Athletes use two types of memory; one is in the head, the other in the muscles. I could remember all the things I had to do for a great race, but Magda had no muscle memory. It was like reading all the elements of how to make a good jump from a textbook and trying to put them together for the first time.

I made a decision. I might not be able to do great things for Magda's Arabic, but I could do something for her. I was going to get Magda fit. I would tone her muscles, introduce her muscle memory to some track skills and build her cardio fitness, so she could just feel *good* when she exercised instead of exhausted. I was probably going to screw up a whole bunch of things in her life in the next few days or weeks or months, but by getting her fit, I could give her something back.

In high jump and long jump, I felt all knees and elbows. Jumps were not my events. I'll admit to some relief when the coach told us to go shower and change, and we all headed back to the locker rooms.

Mark sauntered over and offered me his water, which I gratefully accepted. The luster of perspiration made his latte skin gleam.

"Okay. Tell the truth. You've been moonlighting at the track at midnight. What's going on with you? You hate track, and you're lousy at it. Or at least, you were last year."

"I don't know. I watched it a lot on TV last summer when I was bored," I said. "And I've decided to get fit."

Just then Layla, panting, reappeared at my side. She tugged her shirt down over her full, round figure.

"Oh, God," she said, dramatically. "I was in Fatima's group. I spent so much time eating dust I need to floss."

Mark laughed and was swept up in a group of guys exiting toward the boys' locker room. Layla closed in on me.

"What are you doing?" she hissed, for the second time today. "Have you undergone some kind of personality change or what?"

"Uh—I just tried to..." Oh, no. What had I done now?

"You've been hanging with him all period. And you were *sharing* his water."

Since when was sharing water a come-on? Right, this was Egypt. Guess the rules between guys and girls were different than in Florida.

"Well—I was—thirsty. He had water," I floundered.

"I thought you didn't want to lead him on," she said. "You were drinking his water! That's like practically dating."

"Layla, it's nothing. I was just being nice. And I was thirsty. He offered. I drank. It's not one of the seven deadly sins."

"Whatever," she said, moving huffily in front of me.

Whatever? Seriously? I didn't get what was wrong with the whole water thing, but I knew one thing for sure, I needed Layla. I couldn't have her mad at me.

"Layla—wait up. I'm sorry." I wasn't quite sure what I was sorry for, but it seemed like the thing to say.

We walked in silence and tension for a moment. Then she breathed. "It's okay. Just don't tease him, okay? Besides, don't get greedy. You get all the guys."

I gazed at her with her cherub face and cute hair, the red hibiscus still in her ponytail. I looked down at me/Magda, my shirt stuck to my body. I could feel my hair damp against my face, and my headband, unfortunately, still in place.

I got all the guys?

VI

Layla waited by my locker when I came back at the end of the day. I followed her out. I was pretty sure the silence that spanned between us was uncharacteristic.

"Where's Maraya?" I asked as we skipped down the front steps of the school and turned a corner toward her car. Weren't we supposed to bring her home too?

"I don't know," she said tersely. "Lower Division got out half an hour ago. Didn't your mom pick her up today?"

"Oh, right." I said. I should've known that Maraya didn't ride home with us. Magda's mom had said that Maraya would be going home with Nadia today. I changed the subject.

"Have you got much homework?"

"Not much. I couldn't believe Mrs. Bazzi though. I mean, I guess I should believe it since she always does it, but she just gave us a new chapter today and already there's going to be a test..." And Layla was off and talking again. It didn't take much to kick start her mouth.

Layla's little car pushed its way through the streets of Cairo, and I soaked in the sights, sounds and smells. The traffic inched along, as heavy as earlier, but the sidewalks and cafes had exploded with people since morning. On one corner, a dozen men smoked *hookahs*—two-foot tall, blue and red colored-glass bottles with gold painted trim and long cloth tubes snaking out the top. The men lounged on cushions and plastic chairs and inhaled languidly from the tubes. Sweet lavender smoke from the *hookahs* wafted into the car as we passed. Some of the men wrapped their heads in white turbans while others wore red-checked scarves that draped over their heads and shoulders, even in this heat.

The smog and fumes of the street quickly overtook the lavender as we rode past. Loud, whiny music blared everywhere. From shop front to shop front, the wailing notes overlapped, mixing with those that poured out of the sea of dilapidated black and white taxi cabs around us. The sound was tinny, and each tune struggled to stand out above the others—each winning for a moment as we passed it and then succumbing to the next. The everywhereness of the music gave a sense of celebration to the sea of people milling about.

A young male soldier on a street corner stood surprisingly alert and astute given his uniform of long trousers, long-sleeve shirt and red beret in the glaring sun. He smiled quietly at some inner thought and sported his rifle casually across his body by a strap around his neck. I don't know guns, but this was not the polite kind of gun one would see a Florida sheriff wear on the "crime-doesn't-pay" public-speaking circuits through local public schools. This was the kind of rifle I associate with serial-killing rampages. Yet, here were these young, handsome men on almost every street corner, deadly weapons haphazardly slung across their backs as I might sling a purse over my shoulder on the way to the mall.

When I got home, Magda's dad looked up from where he sat, tapping away at a laptop from the coach. "Hey, you're home! Praise, God," he said. "How was your day?"

"Great. Thanks. Yours?" I stuck with my strategy of talking as little as possible. One nice thing about shifting as a teen is that adults don't expect much more than one word answers.

"Good, good," he said, and returned to his work. Whew. One conversational hurdle passed.

Magda's mom chopped cilantro on a cutting board beside the sink. Maraya hunched over the kitchen table and did homework. When I came in, Magda's mom smiled at me and touched her cheek expectantly while she gave a quick stir to something in a black fry pan. I trudged over and gave the cheek a kiss. "How was your meeting, Mom?" I ventured. An important rule when shifting is to direct conversation to others as much as possible.

She continued chopping. "My meeting? Oh, my meeting! It was fine, *habibtee*," she said, using the Arabic word for *darling*, "As fine as these things can be. The clinic is hiring three more doctors, but we have no new offices. And there will be a new accounting system, but they're not sending us anyone who knows how to use it. Craziness," she said then shrugged her shoulders in defeat. "*Malesh*," she said, meaning *it doesn't matter*. "It's in God's hands."

I went straight to the bedroom. Before tackling my homework, I found Magda's school email account on her laptop and sent off a quick note to Mom.

Hey, Mom. How's everything there? I guess you've figured out by now I'm in Cairo. It's dirty and loud and busy and dusty and hot. I'm enjoying my family. Magda's in lousy physical shape, but I love Magda's little sister, Maraya. I hope I'll get to see the pyramids. Is Magda doing okay? Mom, this was a really lousy time to shift. I've got SATs in six weeks. Can you send me all my prep tests? And make sure Magda takes really good notes in all the prep sessions? My GPA can't fall below 4.0 or I'll never get into international affairs at Hopkins. What am I going to do about the college tour we planned in Washington for spring break? I better be back!!! Love you, Molly.

I pressed the send button then immediately went to my sent items mailbox and deleted it. Then I set about doing my homework, which was a long drawn-out process fraught with the frustration of having to hunt for calculators, rulers and textbooks. Magda was tidy, but it still took time to poke through all her drawers and shelves.

Magda's mom called us for dinner at eight. Breakfast had been around a small table in the kitchen, but this meal was more formal. We sat around a small, dark walnut dining table on chairs with blue seats, hand embroidered with little pink roses and white magnolias. Each spot was set with a lace placemat, cutlery and a white cloth napkin.

In Florida, at least in my house, a home-cooked meal was a rarity. We ate a lot of take-out, and the foods we chose were usually things like bread, pre-packaged meat, deli-chickens, microwavable vegetables and grab-and-go fruit. Everything was eaten at the kitchen table, and if Mom put out paper napkins, company was coming. I was a bit nervous sitting down to a formal meal of boiled green peppers stuffed with rice.

I picked up my fork and knife then quickly set them back down again. Heads bowed around the table, and Magda's father said grace. I waited and then picked up my fork and knife when he did, noting he didn't swap the knife and fork into opposite hands as Americans do. I'd have to eat with my fork in my left hand. Tricky.

"Ireney, *habibtee*, this looks delicious!" he cooed, as his knife bit into the flesh of the pepper.

I eyed the pepper suspiciously. Steam rose up from the rice, and I could smell onion, mint and cilantro. I scooped a little rice out first, not trusting my right hand with a knife. I slid the fork into my mouth. It tasted weird, then not so strange, then pretty good, and a moment later I decided it was amazing. The dish stimulated my tongue from every angle, working my mouth into a symphony of flavor. I carefully sawed off a piece of pepper without disaster. Heaven. I made a note to tell Mom about this. Then again, never mind. Neither of us could ever make this.

The peppers were served beside a salad of chopped tomato, mint, cilantro, little hot peppers and onions, all coated with oil. Beside a bowl of hummus for dipping, rose a mountain of wholewheat pita bread, much like the bread served at breakfast. I tried not to overeat, but I was famished after my day of athletics and left the table stuffed.

I felt pretty satisfied with my first day in this body. I only said a few things wrong, and I think I got away with them. The Mark/Arabic thing weighed on my mind, but really for a first day in someone else's body, things had gone pretty well. No one was on to me. Not that it was even remotely possible that someone would think I wasn't Magda. Body swapping? I mean how ridiculous is that? But they might think Magda needed institutionalizing. Or I could get her into trouble through my own ignorance, fail her classes, screw-up her friendships, that sort of thing. Those were the real worries. Nope, so far so good, I thought. I hoped Magda was doing as well with my life, in her hands.

Maraya and I helped with the dishes, and I wondered at Magda's mother's energy preparing such a meal after a long day at work. Now she settled into a large, stuffed couch in the living room, opposite a matching one in which her husband sat, his fingers tapping a laptop keyboard.

She picked up a worn black leather Bible, folded her legs up beside her and said for the third time, "Now to bed with you, Maraya."

"Okay," Maraya acquiesced. Her face drooped like a dying blossom. She gave each of her parents a kiss on the cheek before walking slowly, head bowed and feet dragging, toward the bedroom.

"I'm going to go finish my homework and then head to bed too," I said.

"Okay, *habibtee*," Magda's mother said, proffering a cheek for a kiss. "Good night and God bless." I gave Magda's dad a kiss as well. Before I went to my room, I ducked into the kitchen and grabbed two large cans of chickpeas from the cupboard and took them to the bedroom.

"What are you *doing*?" Maraya asked from the bottom bunk as I hefted the cans and began a set of bicep curls. She lay on her back, an open book propped up on her knees.

"Getting in shape," I said as I pumped.

A long pause. Her eyes narrowed. "Magda would never do that."

I bristled at her sentence structure and chose to ignore it. "And yet it appears I am doing that. I've decided to get in shape."

"Magda would never do that," she repeated, without taking her eyes off me. "She says our souls are what matter. Our bodies are just tools. They aren't important."

"Maraya, why are you talking to me like that? Like I'm some kind of alien and not your sister?" I asked, shifting my grip to do hammerhead curls.

Maraya put her book down, sat up, crossed her legs Indian style and looked at me intently.

"I'm not stupid," she said accusingly. "You don't act like her. You don't move the same. And you didn't know what clothes to wear this morning. And there's something wrong with your eyes. You aren't Magda. I don't know who you are."

VII

I put the cans down and plopped onto the bed beside her. Busted. I'd actually been busted.

No one has ever nailed me. I've screwed up pretty badly on previous shifting experiences, but who would ever dream the person they looked at wasn't really the person they saw? Yet this little girl had seen straight through me like some kind of psychic.

What was I going to do? I could either admit she was right, or I could deny it. Pretty simple. Which would it be?

"You're a pretty clever girl. You know that?" I said, stalling.

Silence. Her eyes bored into mine, unflinching.

Unable to meet her gaze, my eyes searched the floor. I sighed heavily. "Let's say you're right. Just imagine that it was possible, for a little while, to trade bodies with someone else. Like if I was say—a girl from a totally different country, and I woke up this morning in your sister's body. Your sister would wake up in mine. What would you think of that?"

She paused for another long while then looked up. "So who are you? And where's my sister?"

This presented a unique opportunity. I'd never confided in anyone while shifted. Shifting was my Great Big Secret. I found that I really wanted to tell her. Maybe it was selfish of me. It was certainly a huge risk. Maybe I wanted to because she was so much like my own little Gabrielle that I felt the need to reach out to her and connect. What a relief it would be to share my secret! And, I thought, more concretely, it would be such a big help to me to have someone to talk to and ask questions about how Magda would behave and what people do in Egypt.

Besides, Maraya was only eight. If she ever said anything, no one would believe her.

I fixed my eyes on some far off place and drew a deep breath.

"My name is Molly. I'm from America. That's where your sister is right now-"

Her eyes grew wide with shock.

"Oh, honey, she's okay! Don't worry. Your sister's fine. Let's see—with the time change it's probably D-block in my school, so she's in biology. I think bio will be a breeze for her," I said. "I really hope she blows the socks off Dr. Edgar and makes me look great."

She regarded me warily. "Go on."

"I have a little sister too, back home," I said. Instinctively, I reached out and took her hand, pulling it close and holding it in both my hands. "Her name is Gabrielle, and she's a lot like you. She doesn't look like you, but I bet you two would be *best* friends if you ever met. And I bet when Magda sees Gabrielle, she misses you. Just like I miss Gabrielle when I see you."

Her eyes softened. I guess when you live in a world of tooth fairies and Easter bunnies, body swapping doesn't sound all that far-fetched. Which reminded me—I pulled both of my legs up onto the bed, crossed them like hers and put one hand on each of her little shoulders to look her straight in the eye.

"You know, this is really important. Both for me, here, and Magda, in my body. It's really, really, super important that you don't tell a soul that you know we've shifted. That's what it's called when we change bodies like this. Most people can't do it, and they wouldn't believe it if you told them. They'd think you were crazy. They'd think *I* was crazy too if they looked at me closely right now. It would ruin everything."

"How do you do it? Can't you just shift back?"

I dropped my hands.

"No, honey. I can't. Shifting is kind of like—well, it's like a virus, I guess. I catch it once in a while like you catch a cold. Or maybe it's some new gene I carry. Either way, I can't control it. Neither can your sister."

Her eyes started to well up with tears.

"No! No, we *will* change back, sweetheart. I just don't know when. It's something that just—happens. I have sort of a theory about when it will happen—but I haven't shifted enough to say if it's for sure."

"So when do you think it will happen?" she asked.

"Well—I've noticed that every time I shift into a new body, something major happens in that person's life. I think I have to help Magda get through some kind of tough situation. And I think maybe we've switched because I'm in a position to help her in a way that she might not be able to help herself. Then, when the situation is over, we'll switch back."

"Is Magda helping you too? I mean, like, in America?"

"Maybe." I thought about this. I couldn't see any big dramas impending on my own horizon, except the whole SAT testing process, and I certainly didn't want a shifter writing that test for me. Who knows what would happen if a shifter wrote it? The test results might show I'd make an outstanding nuclear physicist or some other thing I totally didn't want to be. I wanted to join the diplomatic corps someday, and that meant I needed to get into a good school for international studies. Like John Hopkins. "Or maybe she just gets to hang out a while and go to Disney World. You know I live just an hour and a half outside of Disney World?" Mom and Gabrielle always took the shifters there.

"What if she's going to help you, and you're just hanging out here? Magda's really smart you know. She never needs help with *any*thing."

I hadn't really thought about that possibility. Every time I shifted, big things happened where I was. Big things didn't ever happen to my body at home. But who's to say the problem wasn't mine this time? I mean—mine in Florida? I'm not sure which prospect I liked better. Disaster here, or disaster there.

"I suppose you could be right. Maybe I'm just here to hang out. With you. You know what? I think that'd be pretty all right. I hope that's it. And I do get the feeling your sister is pretty smart. Maybe she'd be better at my life than me." I tried to say it with conviction, but I didn't really believe it. There was always something I was supposed to do when I shifted.

Maraya nodded. Apparently, this made perfect sense to her. She lay back down, pulled her knees up and picked up her book again. I returned to my bicep curls.

"You know," I said while I hefted the cans, "it'd be really helpful to me if you could tell me more about Magda, so I can act more like her and not make people suspicious. What's she like?"

"I dunno. She's nice."

"Okay," I said at length. "What kind of nice?"

"Sort of quiet—nice."

"She's shy?"

"I guess. Not so much with me. But with other people. She let's them talk."

"That's really helpful. Does she have hobbies?"

"She studies a lot. She's super smart. I wish she'd be a vet, like me. I'm going to save the animals. But she wants to be a doctor, like Mom."

"Those are both great jobs. Does Magda have a boyfriend?"

"No! She wouldn't be allowed. I think she wants one though."

"Why?"

"She and Layla always talk about boys. It gets really boring." As if to emphasize her point, she yawned deeply. She put the book on the bedside table and pulled the covers up to her chin.

A long silence stretched between us. Eventually, I set down the cans, changed into the lavender night gown, switched off the lamp and climbed up into the bed. I thought Maraya had fallen asleep when I heard a voice from beneath the covers.

"How long do you *think* you'll be in my sister's body?"

"Well, the longest I've ever shifted was about three months. Once it was only a couple of days," I said.

She digested that. "I guess I could get through a couple of days, anyway."

"Gee, thanks."

VIII

It's amazing how much damage one can do to a muscle group with two cans of chickpeas. I'd done a pretty thorough upper body workout, stressing biceps and triceps, but also some chest presses and lower back exercises and some front and side ab crunches. I hadn't slept well either. My mind swirled like a storm cloud over a turbulent sea.

In my dreams I'd been Molly again and was home with Gabrielle. We swam in the backyard pool and played a game. It might've been Marco Polo or underwater hide and seek. Gabrielle was "it." Every time I surfaced, Gabrielle tried to talk to me, but when she spoke, I couldn't understand her. It was like a different language flowed from her mouth. I tried so hard to understand. She wanted urgently to convey something, but it was gibberish to me. I was surprised all over when I woke up, and I was Magda again.

I felt a pang of regret leaving the dream, leaving Gabrielle. I missed her. I missed my mom. My insides tightened. I recognized stage one of an emotional meltdown. Been there. No time for that. I needed to focus. There was something I needed to do here. I needed to figure out what it was, do it, and then I could go home.

I checked my computer while I dressed and found a note from Mom.

So sorry you've shifted again, hon. We miss you already. Magda arrived smoothly. I wasn't sure she was a shifter until she bowed her head at breakfast, and I realized she was expecting me to say grace! She burst into tears when I told her she could tell me who she really was. She seems to be a nice girl. I told her about your theory that you shift to fix something in someone else's life, but she says she can't think of anything in her life that might need fixing. She asks that you take care of her grades. She wants to study medicine in London, but she's also going to apply to some American schools. She says if you look in her locker at school you'll find a white binder named SAT prep tests. You can use those, but she's already filled them all in. I found your tests on your computer (what were they doing in your French file?), and I've attached them. We'll take care of things here. Good luck. Love, Mom.

I downloaded the attachment, saved it to my desktop and deleted the message.

The morning routine was much the same today, and I glided through it a little more gracefully than the day before. Layla wore her hair pulled into a ponytail over her right shoulder, a purple scarf knotted at her neck. Her eyes were lined with purple and—was that purple mascara? Where did she find this stuff?

"Say, girl, you're on your own today after school," Layla announced as we pulled away from the apartment building. Maraya was strapped into the backseat. "I've got a speech arts club competition. I'm doing a dramatic duo entry with Demiana," she said. Speech arts struck me as something Layla'd be a natural at. "You good taking a taxi?" I had no idea if I was good with taking a taxi today. I had already let two of my rules slip: I didn't know my address and I wasn't sure I had money. I'd have to do a thorough search of backpack and locker. I looked out the window where a half dozen cabs slogged through traffic around us. I craned my head around but didn't see a single bus. Taxis must be what carless kids used to get around.

First period was Spanish. How strange to learn Spanish in a school in Cairo. I guess the Americans here would have to transition back to American schools eventually, and they'd need to keep up their Spanish. I was grateful. I'm good at Spanish and at languages in general. Maybe it has to do with the shifting. I've lived in a few different brains and spoken different languages in them. Perhaps there's some residual memory there. Who knows?

Aisha sat next to me in Spanish class. She wore a yellow headscarf again, this time pale yellow with big white daisies. She couldn't have been more than five foot two and ninety pounds, yet her tiny presence felt oddly comforting.

As we pulled out our books she whispered to me, "So I hear you and Mark are going out." It was a statement, not a question.

I nearly choked.

"What?! Where did you hear that?" I asked.

"I don't know," she said evasively. "The girls were talking. Apparently you're hanging out with him now. And studying together."

"It's okay," she added. "I think you make a cute couple."

"We're *not* going out, okay?" I said. "He's going to study Arabic with me on Thursday night."

"Magda. You're brilliant in Arabic. You've been brilliant in Arabic since kindergarten. You were writing poetic stanzas like Naguib Mahfouz while the rest of us were still writing our letters backwards. You wanna hang with him. It's okay. He's nice. He's probably the hottest local Christian boy in the school and smart too. Your family will be thrilled. At least, if they're okay with the dating thing. I thought Christian families were the same as us. Are you really allowed to date before you're engaged?"

Engaged?! My mind was doing mental gymnastics trying to compute the growing dimensions of this mess I was getting into.

"Listen," I said, mustering as much force as I could without sounding angry. "We're *not* going out. I know this is hard for you to believe, but I really do need help with the stuff we're doing in Arabic class right now. Maybe I've plateaued or something, I don't know. I wanted to think through my essay with someone, and he sits beside me and gets all the answers right."

"I guess," she shrugged. She didn't look convinced. "I don't think Layla'll buy it though." She turned her attention to the teacher at the front of the class. A youngish Hispanic woman with long dark hair waved her hands around emphatically and said something in Spanish. I watched the teacher without listening.

Layla? Why would Layla care? Then, slowly, realization washed over me. Of course! Layla liked Mark. How stupid of me. That's why she reacted that way to the shared water bottle yesterday.

Oh no. If word had gotten to Aisha about our study date, word would have gotten to Layla. If Aisha didn't buy my Arabic story, would my best friend? Yikes! What was I going to do? Which was more important? Should I give up the Arabic help and forego the good grades? Or risk my relationship with Layla for a good grade?

My eyes followed the teacher around the room, my expression glazed. She was going over el pretérito imperfect—the imperfect tense. Scribbled across the whiteboard was the sentence, "Yo caminaba cada día." *I used to walk every day,* my head automatically translated. The teacher dissected the root verb and explained the conjugation. She taught as if the language was communicated with both pronunciation and hand motions in equal parts.

The class was about two years behind my level at home. I was free to think about my dilemma. What would Magda do? Magda wouldn't have gotten into this mess, because Magda was brilliant at Arabic.

Three hours and two periods later the bell rang for lunch, and I still hadn't decided what to do.

The lunchroom was a long narrow room jammed with tables and benches which overflowed with grey and white clad students. My head throbbed from the noise. A buffet lined one wall. I coasted down the cafeteria line up, grateful to see some familiar items amongst the ethnic fare. I wasn't in the mood for experimenting. I chose a ham and cheese sandwich and a carton of milk. I looked around for familiar faces. I spotted Layla sitting alone a couple of tables from where I stood, her back to me. I braced myself and sat down beside her.

Silence.

"Hey," I said, hopefully.

Silence.

Okay.

"It's not a date, okay?"

"Doesn't matter to me what you do. He's not my boyfriend," Layla spat.

Well, at least we were talking.

"Layla, he's not *my* boyfriend either. I just wanted some homework help. But I'll tell him I changed my mind if it makes you feel better."

She turned and faced me.

"Magda. I don't care what you do with Mark. Maybe I do kind of like him, but who he sees is up to him. This isn't about me or even about

Mark." Her voice was cool and increasingly venomous. "It's about you being a total and complete hypocrite. And don't look at me like Miss Innocent. You know exactly what I'm talking about. You're being two-faced and not just to me." She picked up a plate of barely-touched pita and hummus and a bottle of water and began throwing them angrily onto her tray. Then she turned, looked me in the eye and said in a quiet hiss, "Do you think he's not going to notice?" I stared at her in shocked incomprehension. She stood abruptly and added, "I thought I knew you, but apparently I don't. Now if you'll excuse me, I'm going to the library."

"Layla—"

She turned on her heel, took her tray full of uneaten food to the nearest garbage, dumped the whole tray in, and stormed out. A few heads turned to her, then to me, then pretended to be absorbed in today's rice pilaf.

I stared after her in amazement. I *thought* we were speaking the same language. What on earth was going on? A hypocrite? I stared down at my tray, put one elbow on the table and stuck a fingernail in my mouth. *Do you think he's not going to notice?* I heard her say. What was Mark going to notice?

"What was that all about?" said a tall blonde girl beside me in a thick British accent. I looked up in surprise, then recognized Fiona. She had sat with us yesterday and seemed to be part of Magda and Layla's friends circle.

"I wish I knew," I breathed.

She took a bite of a cookie and swallowed it in that noiseless way only the British can do. "Boy trouble is my guess. It's always boy trouble. I've lived in England, Holland and Beijing. It doesn't matter where you live. It's always boy trouble."

I sighed in surrender and unwrapped my sandwich.

Funny thing with the sandwich. I love ham and cheese. It's my favorite. Comfort food. In Magda's mouth though, the sandwich was tasteless. Her tongue preferred the spicier local fare. I washed the bite down with some equally bland milk and ate my lunch. It would be two more periods before I began to understand what was going on.

IX

I looked forward to English class even though I wasn't sure what an English class in an American school in Cairo would teach. If the curriculum was geared to native Egyptians—about half the school—it would probably be taught as an English-as-a-second-language class and focus on grammar fundamentals. If the class targeted the fluent English-speaking foreigners, it would be about Shakespeare or Edgar Allen Poe. Either way, I figured I could do pretty well for Magda. No matter how bilingual Magda seemed to be, English was not her first language. As a native speaker, I should be able to make her shine in this class.

"The bell has already rung, people," a too-slim lady in ill-fitting black dress pants and a shapeless cream blouse said in a Jersey accent. "Let's get a move on!"

I entered the classroom in a slipstream behind Fatima and her shadow, whose name I had overheard was Baysaan. I wasn't in the mood for another conflict, so I did my best impression of the invisible woman. Fatima headed for the far back corner, and I took a sudden hard left as I made for the other corner. I totally did not see him standing there until I careened full force into him, sending the books and papers in my arms flying.

I leaned over and scrambled after the papers. He bent down and helped. "Hey, I'm really sorry," he said.

"It's okay, nevermi—," I glanced up, and nothing in my life or Magda's would ever be the same again.

My chest contracted. The air sucked out of my lungs. My head was light.

I had never felt anything like this.

It's one thing to fall in love slowly. I've fallen for a boy or two before, and maybe I've even been in love once. It's supposed to be this slow building of anticipation and excitement, the thrill of each chance meeting growing into something warmer, better, until one day you find your mind completely occupied by the other person, and you wouldn't have it any other way. That's how falling in love works.

But this? This was love by train wreck. An entire locomotive had just slammed into my brain, my heart—my lungs. I may have stopped breathing.

Magda was in full-throttle love with this guy, and all the resonances of him trapped in her mind shook free and came crashing down on me, laying me mentally flat. This was unbearable love. It wasn't the kind of love you wondered about—like, "am I in love?" She lived for this guy. As Molly/Magda, I suddenly felt a desperate need and longing for this—this—complete stranger. Somehow, I resisted the urge to throw my arms around him even though it was the only rational thing to do.

I felt his arms grip my shoulders, but not in a loving embrace. He held me firmly, looked me earnestly in the eyes and shook me.

"Magda!" He was saying. "Magda? Are you okay? Magda, breathe!"

Right. That's why my head felt light. I made a conscious effort to finish exhaling and remembered the mechanics of inhaling.

"It's—I'm—I'm okay." I lied. "I just had the wind knocked out of me."

Unfortunately, he believed me because he released his hold on me and stepped back to reestablish a polite distance between us. I had a hard time not staring at him as he shuffled around to finish gathering my things for me. Unmoved by our collision, the rest of the class continued settling into desks.

"You look like you saw a ghost," he said softly as he passed the books into my arms. He used a for-your-ears-only voice and spoke without making eye contact. Then, still softly but more urgently, "Am I so frightening now?"

Frightening he was not. I couldn't stop staring.

His face was all hard angles—square forehead, strong, square jaw, straight, angular nose. Set in the middle of all that hardness were the softest eyes. They were dark chocolate melting into a light honey brown center, framed by eyelashes far longer than necessary on a man. His hair was short and wavy, tossed in an unruly mess. When he straightened up, he looked tall for an Arab, and his build was slim but solid, A-framed and sinewy, without an ounce of fat.

It was all too much. I sat down at the nearest desk with a thud.

"No, no! Not frightening at all," I said, forgetting to speak softly. So much for my fantastic English skills. I couldn't think of anything else to say.

And the class, inconveniently, began.

"*Carpe Diem*, people!" the Jersey accent enthused. "Let's seize the day! Now if you'll open your books. . . "

I stayed in the seat I had landed in, and he took a seat two desks in front of me and one row closer to the middle. I really can't remember much about the class. Some grammar, I recall, but also a book. Yes, it was *The Great Gatsby*. I suppose the class was geared to both types of student—the English native and the students who were newer to the language. One of those mixes that usually disappoints everyone.

I spent a lot of time staring at the back of his head and trying to piece together what was going on.

So this was my hypocrisy.

Here I was, by everyone else's judgment leading Mark on, while truly being in love with someone else. Layla must know how Magda felt about this guy—whatever his name was. Hadn't she said yesterday that I was being greedy—that I get all the guys? And today she called me two-faced. If Magda loved this guy while carrying on with Mark, then I had definitely behaved that way.

Yet why hadn't this guy sat next to me? If Magda felt this strongly about him, they must have a relationship. You just can't build up this level of emotion wishing for something that isn't reciprocated. Could you?

Had they broken up? Breaking up can sometimes amplify your feelings—make you feel like that person is so much better than they were the day before. But wait. Maraya said that Magda wasn't allowed to date. So it wasn't a breakup.

In my head, I replayed the crash scene we'd had a few minutes ago. *"Am I so frightening now?"* Why would Magda think he was frightening? He must've done something horrible.

I felt guarded and confused when the bell rang and uncertain of what my actions should be. I gathered my books up slowly, hoping to be the last to leave.

He gathered his books up slowly too and glanced back at me a couple of times. Eventually, we were the last two in the room.

He slipped into step beside me as I made my way to the door. Then he walked just slightly behind me as if we weren't together and spoke to me under his breath.

"Why aren't you answering me?" he said, urgently.

Answering him?

"I—I don't know what to say," I said, with more truthfulness than he could possibly imagine.

"Say anything you want—but say *something*," he pleaded. I paused, desperately seeking something non-committal to fill a sentence with. When I didn't rush in to fill the silence, he finished impatiently, "I'll talk to you tonight," and he turned away. I watched him disappear into the crowd and felt a huge, gaping, emptiness reach in to fill the space he had just occupied.

I didn't think it was possible to bottle up so much emotion in one body. The school day was over, and I needed to go home. I needed a taxi, according to Layla, and I didn't know how or where to find one. I didn't even know what address to ask for. I'm not sure I'd memorized the route by car. And I needed to think. Or maybe just to curl up in a corner and cry.

I didn't know how Magda would deal with a moment like this, so I did what Molly would do. I went to the PE lockers, dumped my books inside, changed into my PE clothes and hit the track running.

The rhythm of my feet on the hard ground soothed me. Putting pressure on my body released my mind. I circled the track once to get into the right mindset. Then I circled it again. I should've run that track ten or fifteen times to achieve exhaustion, but the combination of Magda's fitness level and this heat wasn't going to allow that.

By the fifth time around, sweat poured off my face, and I kept having to wipe it on my shoulder. My hair was soaked and matted. A wave of nausea swept over me—a sign that my workout was done. I slowed my pace to a walk and the nausea passed. My heart rate slowed and the tension in my shoulders eased.

I had been so wrapped up in my own personal therapy that I was completely surprised when Mark caught me up. His lean, muscular frame filled out a navy soccer shirt with the school name on the back and the number 21. I had been only vaguely aware of a group of guys playing soccer in another field. He must've been among them.

"Magda!" he shouted, and I stopped and turned.

He matched my pace.

"Wow," he said, looking me over. "You look like you've been swimming."

"Yeah, well, thanks. You're pretty sweaty yourself," I said. The soccer shirt was drenched, and he shook his head sending beads of sweat flying. I laughed as I cringed and took cover.

"Thanks!" he said.

"So I waited for you after class," he said. "I thought you wanted to work on your Arabic."

Arabic. Thursday! Who knew.

"Oh, God, Mark. I'm so sorry. I lost track of the day."

"Do you want to go over it now? I mean—after your shower," he asked.

I laughed, "You won't take me as I am?" I regretted the words instantly. I wasn't supposed to be flirting.

"Girl," he said, "I'll take you any way you come. But you'll be wanting me to shower for sure," and he bent his head as if to shake it again.

I laughed and pulled away, and as I did I saw What's-His-Name—my electric shock from English class—walking back with the other guys on the field. They all laughed and tossed a ball around, but he walked apart, his eyes on Mark and me. He looked away when I saw him.

"How about if I come to your house tonight? Would your father permit me to take you to the Greek Café? We could go over our Arabic and drink coffee. It'd seem less like work."

My eyes trailed unwillingly back behind me. Hadn't he said he'd talk to me tonight? He'd probably call on my cellphone. I didn't have to stay home just for a phone call though. I could take my phone with me. I'd just excuse myself when his call came and take it in the ladies' room. I needed to study with Mark. I couldn't possibly understand the significance of a book like *Zaynab* in Arabic literature just by reading it. I needed someone to put it in a cultural insider's perspective. Keeping the study session in a public place like a café seemed like a good idea. A place away from the school might even be kept secret from my classmates. This could work. And I wouldn't do anything to make Mark feel like it was a date. After all, it wasn't. It was just Arabic.

"Su-re," I said. My voice betrayed my hesitation, but he didn't pick up on it.

"How's eight?"

"Eight's fine. Oh, and Mark—" he had turned to head toward the showers, "It's just about Arabic, okay? Nothing else."

"You bet," he said, smiling widely. He wasn't very convincing.

What was I doing?

X

I showered and put my uniform back on, carefully clasped on Magda's lucky bracelet and ran a brush through her raven-black hair before tucking the glossy mane into a plain ponytail holder, à la Magda. I ruffled through her locker looking for makeup and didn't find any. She probably didn't wear it. I gathered up my books and headed back to my locker where I pulled out my Arabic text, my computer and some other books I might need.

I searched though Magda's backpack and eventually found a small leather purse with tacky, brightly scrolled flowers all over it. I unzipped it and pulled out a driver's license. I wondered briefly why she didn't have a car if she had a license. Neatly printed beside a photo of Magda in a pink headband was an address. I now knew where home was. Reaching in again, I extracted three worn bills in shades of red and brown—a ten, a twenty and a fifty. Ten, twenty and fifty *what* I wasn't sure, but it should be enough for taxi fare home.

I emerged from big main doors of the school into the relentless Egyptian sunlight. The street in front of the school lay quiet, but the intersecting street on the left buzzed with traffic. On the corner, a requisite soldier stood with his rifle thrown over his shoulder. He eyed me up and down professionally, without making eye contact. Just past him I could see four badly beaten-up black and white taxis, idling. No other major buildings bordered the area besides the school, so I guessed these taxies served the school. A boy in the Academy's grey pants and a white uniform shirt disappeared into the passenger seat of the first taxi in the row as I got closer.

Before I came within reasonable shouting distance, one of the taxi drivers cried, “Taxi, right here, taxi waiting for you,” he gestured to his taxi with both arms as if I might not have noticed it otherwise. An older man with a ring of gray hair circling his head, he boasted an easy smile, which revealed only half a dozen, crooked, broken teeth.

The boxy little black and white Lada behind him hailed from a previous generation, probably in communist Russia. The paint was scratched and pocked and the front bumper sagged on the right. Grey duct tape held the left rear window in place. I slid into the cracked vinyl back seat and told him the address.

“What’s the matter with you today, Miss Magda?” his brow creased with concern as he looked back at me in the rearview mirror. He pulled out into traffic glancing back at me while he drove. The car shook as it gathered speed, but the driver remained at ease.

“Oh, nothing’s wrong. I’m so sorry. My mind is somewhere else,” I said, feeling more confident now that I would get home safely.

“For a minute I thought you didn’t know me! My heart was breaking!” His hand thumped his heart and his face bore a wounded expression. “You and me, we’re both Copts. Both Christians. We stick together, we Copts, eh?” he said over the wail of the cab’s radio.

Copts. Short for Coptic. The name jarred my memory back to grade eight Middle Eastern History. The Coptics were an orthodox Christian religion. I noticed then that his car was covered in images of Jesus and Mary. Bright religious stickers covered every available inch of the dash and glove box. A long, thin red and gold rug spread out under the windshield, and a beaded rosary hung from the rearview mirror.

“Yes, sir,” I said, nervously. The less said, the better.

“We have to stick together, us Christians, in a world of Muslims, eh? They take everything from us, yes? They forget this county was ours before it was theirs,” he said. He was clearly winding up for a rant. “We are the original Egyptians,” he said, gesturing broadly with his left hand and looking intently at me in the mirror. His right hand loosely gripped the steering wheel. “We became Christians when Jesus himself fled here to escape King Herod. We witnessed Christ himself, God bless us! And we lose Christians everyday because it’s easier to be Muslim. Easier to get a taxi if you're a Muslim driver. Easier to get a shop. Everything is easier if you're Muslim. Everything but the afterlife."

"I suppose so," I said tentatively. I wondered if Copts were really treated this way in Egypt or if he was a bit paranoid. I leaned strongly toward the latter, but I figured I should definitely agree with him wholeheartedly while in his cab.

"They are all hypocrites," he said. There was that word again. "Look at them!" he waved his hand floppily at a group of about twenty men, most in those dresses—the word *galabeya* flitted into my mind. Some also wore scarves loosely wrapped around their heads, and a few dressed in western clothes. They kneeled together on the sidewalk, heads bowed, hands by their ears, all facing the same direction. In front of the group, one man kneeled and repeatedly prostrated himself and led the recitations.

"They kneel and face Mecca five times a day, reading passages from the Koran and praying for forgiveness for their sins. Then they get up and go to work and lie and cheat and steal until the next prayer call. Hypocrites! All of them! God save us."

"Hmmmm," I said. I wasn't sure how to take this guy. Is this how most Christians here felt? Magda's parents and Layla weren't anything like this guy. A few moments later, he pulled to a stop, and I recognized the street. His meter, an old black box with a cracked glass cover, left only and outline of where numbers should have been. They weren't lit up. "How much is the fare today?" I asked, gesturing at the meter.

He looked at me oddly. "You forget the fare? What's the matter with you? You hit your head in school or something? Every meter in Cairo is broken! We have to put them in. It's the law. But if they work, then we can't negotiate. So we break them. It's five pounds. Same as always."

I handed him the fifty, and he made change.

"You remember," he said in parting. "We Christians, we stick together. God bless you," and he peeled away from the curb.

The apartment smelled of fresh garlic and lemon. A pot of lamb stew cooked on the stove. My stomach grumbled approvingly. Magda apparently loved lamb stew. Heaven.

"Hi, Mom! Hi, Dad! Anyone home?" I called.

"Hi, *habibtee*," A masculine voice crooned from the master bedroom, across the hallway from Magda and Maraya's room. "Be there in a second."

"In the bedroom!" a high-pitched voice called.

I kicked off my shoes, tossed my heavy pack down on the kitchen floor and pulled out my computer. Then I remembered who I was. I picked up the shoes and backpack, carried them into the bedroom and put the shoes in the closet. When I returned to the kitchen, Magda's mother was at the stove, stirring a pot. I plopped my computer down at the kitchen table, pulled out *Zaynab* and began catching up.

After a few moments, Magda's dad came in. This morning he had left in a dark suit and tie, but now he wore khakis and a white button-down white shirt. With his arms crossed and brow furrowed, he stood in the doorway.

"Mark called."

My heart kicked into high gear. "He did?" I asked.

"Weren't you expecting him too?" he asked. His left eyebrow raised.

"Well, yeah," I faked.

"He asked if he could have permission to take you to the Greek Café to study Arabic together," he said gravely.

"Oh—yeah, that."

He eased into chair at the opposite end of the kitchen table. Magda's Mom shifted nervously as she stirred the stew. Oh, God. I could sense a lecture coming.

"Magda, *habibtee,* you're seventeen now," he said. "We've spent a lot of time talking about universities but not so much time talking of husbands. Most of your girlfriend's parents will be choosing husbands for them soon. Some will be marrying after graduation next year.

"As you know, your mother and I believe there's wisdom in accepting the guidance of your elders in your decision about whom to marry. God speaks to us through many means. But if you should fall in love, then that is the voice of God also. You know very well that your mother and I were the first in both our families to marry for love. Nowadays, marrying for love happens more often, especially among the well-educated, but in our day it was uncommon," he winked at Magda's mother, and she smiled warmly and blushed while she stirred. "We don't want you and Maraya to have to go through what we went through with our families. We have always said you and Maraya may marry for love, if you choose to. But you should also listen to the wisdom of your parents and family too. Does that make sense?"

"I guess," I said, struggling to mask my shock. Parents choosing husbands? Was this the Middle East or the Middle Ages? Or both?

"Now. About Mark. We think Mark is a fine young boy. He's adored you since preschool, so we know he's patient, and that's a virtue. He comes from a fine family and has a very bright future after he completes his studies. Your mother and I think he would be a fine match for you, and we're happy to see you show an interest in such a good Christian boy."

There was a very long pause. He didn't seem finished.

"Obviously, we don't approve of dating of any kind until you are engaged. Boys and girls with all those hormones in close proximity is folly. But we do realize that if you are to marry for love, you need to get to know each other. Studying together in a well-supervised environment might be acceptable . . ." he said as if this were some huge concession.

This lecture moved faster than the speed of thought.

"Dad—I'm not asking to marry him," I interjected. His face darkened at the interruption. "I mean—I don't know. I'm not really thinking that far. I really want to meet with him, but at least for now it's just about Arabic." I said. Weren't those the words every parent was looking for? That I'm putting my studies first?

His brow furrowed then he continued as if I hadn't spoken. "I would rather you met here at home, but since cousin Peter runs the Café, he'll keep an eye on you both. I don't really like the situation, but I realize times are very different than they were in my day," he said. "I expect you to go straight there and straight home. Peter will text me when you arrive and when you leave. Be back by eleven." His knuckles tapped the table conclusively, and the chair scraped the floor as he stood sharply and left without waiting for a response.

This meeting with Mark was feeling more and more like a bad idea.

XI

The doorbell rang at precisely eight o'clock.

I wore a simple colorful dress and tied my hair up in a disinterested ponytail. Mark may be my (Molly's) type, but he wasn't Magda's. I mustn't lead him on—at least not anymore than I already had by apparently agreeing to the locally, barely-acceptable version of a *date*. Was it even a date? I think I was actually being *courted*.

Man, was I stupid.

Maybe I should call the whole thing off right now. I should tell him I don't feel well. Send him home. Wait for the call I was expecting from What's-His-Name. But I'd have my phone with me. There was nothing to miss.

Besides, bagging out now wouldn't be fair to Mark. He really was a nice guy. Plus, there was the Arabic thing. I really did need his help, and there wouldn't be another opportunity like this to study together away from the prying eyes of our classmates. I braced myself and waited for Magda's dad to call me from the front hall.

"Magda! Mark is here!" he shouted.

I approached and smiled politely. Magda's dad and mom stood together in the hallway, their arms tucked around each other's waist. Mark wore a white cotton shirt over jeans. His hair was neatly combed back, his cowlick gelled into submission. His eyes lit as I stepped into view.

"Come straight home now, all right? Eleven o'clock," Magda's dad said to the two of us. He wore a stern expression, but a warm light shone behind his eyes.

"Yes, sir," Mark said.

I steered Mark out the door as quickly as I could.

He drove a white Honda Civic. Darn. I tried hard not to like him, but here was another point in his favor. The Civic is one of the cutest cars in the known universe for teen budgets. I was saving up for one in Florida.

This one was pretty scratched up on the outside, but I couldn't see actual dents. I took that as a sign we might make our destination safely. He guided me around to the passenger door and leaned over to open it.

It didn't budge. He moved in a little closer and applied more force. Nothing. His face turned red.

"Dang! Oh, I forgot," he said. "Hang on. I mean—wait right there." He started toward the driver's side then paused and added as an afterthought, "Please."

He raced around the car, slipped inside and reached across to pull the door open. I started to get in.

"No! I mean— just wait," he said. I stood there awkwardly while he opened the driver's side door again, raced around the car and held my door open for me.

"I forgot the handle was broken. Sorry," he said, grinning and slightly out of breath.

I smiled, feeling a little uncomfortable with his performance. He was treating me like—like a lady, I guess. This was new. And kind of cool.

I looked down at the passenger seat. Three Arabic books sprawled across the seat.

"Oh! Yeah, right. Sorry," he said again. He reached past me and tossed the books unceremoniously in the backseat. They formed a third layer of things already there, on top of a gym bag, some running shoes, a couple of binders, a half dozen empty water bottles and some questionable socks in a little too close proximity to a box of granola bars. The passenger seat, however, was spotless and looked freshly vacuumed. For my benefit, I wondered?

This guy was clearly the anti-Magda. Her room was neat as a pin. Her locker was immaculate, her binders labeled, even her backpack didn't have any pencils and change clinking at the bottom of it. Except for the obvious effort where the passenger seat was concerned, I was pretty sure Mark was a pig. I felt an immediate bond with him. I— Molly—also lived like this. Well, maybe he took the point a bit far with the socks and the granola bars, but still, his behavior felt—homey. A little disgusting, true, but real. I could relate to this guy.

We didn't talk much as we drove. Mark rolled down the windows, and the cool evening breeze flowed through the car, a welcome relief from the day's heat. The city swarmed around us, busier than I had ever seen it. Evening was when Cairo came to life. In the day her streets were almost as solidly packed with people as they were now, but they were different then. Those were serious people. Seriously working, seriously not working, or just seriously withstanding the intense afternoon heat.

By night, it seemed every last man woman and child roamed the streets enjoying the cool air, laughing and haggling, drinking tea or smoking water pipes. Warm light spilled out of every shop. We passed dozens of jewelry shops, storefronts selling fresh fruit and vegetables and clothing shops that sold eclectic mixes of linens, western men's cotton dress shirts, *galabeyas* and running shoes. Lots of running shoes. Interspersed among the stores were smoke shops, cafés and *shawarma* stands with their spits of beef or lamb turning slowly under warming lamps.

More women roamed the streets at this hour. Many of them wore colorful galabeyas and scarves, but a number of them also had their heads uncovered revealing long black hair, usually curly, either tied back or braided. A lot of couples, many with children underfoot, ambled slowly along, but also knots of men and groupings of women huddled over tables of wares.

Hadn't these people ever heard of television? Shouldn't they be home on their couches at this hour on a Thursday night? An energy buzzed through the streets that suggested people were just gearing up, not gearing down as they would be in Florida.

I began to wonder how Mark was going to find a parking spot in this massive jumble of slow-moving cars and people when he fixed on a small space between two cars several lanes to the left. I wouldn't have dreamed of trying to squeeze into it, but when he saw it, he tapped his horn a couple of times to warn nearby traffic and then dove headfirst into the tiny opening. The surrounding cars braked to let him in. They were forced to since he was coming anyway. He threaded across three lanes that way then positioned himself parallel to the car in front of the space. Peering out the back window, he tapped the horn one more time in warning, slipped the car into reverse and shot deftly into the spot.

In the States, this behavior would've been shocking. Horns would have blared and tires screeched in reaction to such recklessness, but here no one waved a fist or raised an eyebrow. I took a small moment to be thankful that I had not shifted into the body of an Egyptian taxi driver.

Still frozen in the passenger seat in awe of it all, I realized Mark was already out of the car and racing around the other side to open my door for me. I obliged, of course, by popping the door open first, so he could finish the job.

I resolved then and there I was never going to get behind the wheel in this country. I wouldn't be a danger to anyone particularly, but I'd probably end up driving around all day with my turn signal on waiting in vain for someone to open up a spot and let me move into the next lane.

Getting out of the car, I saw that only about six inches separated Mark's car from the cars in front and behind. How did he *do* that?

Weaving among the people who crammed the sidewalks, we walked about two blocks through the thriving market district. Mark guided me with a hand on the middle of my back, barely touching me, except to nudge here and there. The crowd parted effortlessly. No one bumped or pushed me like I might have expected on a busy New York street.

The Greek Café was western-style, perfectly at home on a street in Tampa or Chicago or Los Angeles. White laminate floors gleamed beneath glossy black-painted chairs and tables. A single pink carnation stood in a clear glass vase in the center of each table.

A shiny black serving counter, lit every couple of feet by hanging pendant lights, ran along the back of the café. A row of colorful bottles of liquid coffee flavors lined a shelf on the wall behind the barista. A large whiteboard listed several trendy lattés, espressos and pastries and also announced the day's special—caramel latté with a vanilla twist.

Mark guided me to a table near a window in the front. Little alarm bells went off in warning inside my head.

"How about *that* table?" I said, pointing to a table in the back near the washrooms. "It looks quieter," I said. The truth was, I was afraid he was putting me on display.

He shrugged, and we settled into the table near the back. I immediately began unpacking my books to set the tone for a working meeting.

He asked me what I wanted, and I ordered a chocolate fudge latte. I am a firm believer that chocolate solves most problems. This meeting was not a time to forego any help chocolate might offer. I declined a pastry. This was business.

Mark made his way to the counter to order. A tall gangly young man in a white apron waved and winked at me from behind the counter. Cousin Peter, I presumed. I waved back.

Mark returned with two lattés, neatly crafted to create heart-shaped swirls in the frothy milk. We spent the next three hours studying Arabic under the watchful eye of cousin Peter. I can't imagine what Mark must've thought about the questions that "clever" Magda asked him, but I was determined to get on top of this. If Mark was surprised by my lack of knowledge, he didn't show it. I became thoroughly immersed in the conversation. Mark showed intelligence and expressed well-reasoned opinions.

Zaynab was a love story about an unhappily married woman pursued by two desirable men. A distinctly western-style romance, the story takes on Egyptian society and culture and defends love for its own sake. In one scene, Zaynab, the heroine, has taken a lover and struggles with guilt. "How can she flirt with these men?" I asked Mark. "How can she even put herself in that situation? The Muslim religion puts a lot of value on the sanctity of marriage."

"Sure, it does," he replied. "And the book is clear that she risked her reputation. But her lover Haykal argued that God is merciful and would recognize that she was miserable in her marriage. God would take pity on her, he says, not punish her. Haykal is bending religion to suit his own desires. People do it all the time."

"What do you mean?"

"Well," he rubbed his ear thoughtfully. "You know how in the news they say that radical Muslims are threatening to bomb Coptic Christian churches?" I disguised my shock at this and nodded gravely as if I knew about the threats. He continued, "Well, these crazy guys are arguing that Christians are infidels—which means, technically, that they're spiritually ignorant to the point of being a threat to Islam." He leaned forward, and his eyes shone intensely. "That's ridiculous! For well over a thousand years we've all lived peacefully together, and now, all of a sudden, this lunatic bunch of radicals looks at the very same Muslim holy doctrines that supported all those years of peace and says, 'Oops, sorry! Our mistake. We wrongly interpreted *jihad*. It's not about a personal struggle to improve ourselves. It's a call for a holy war against Christians,'" he said. "You see? Religious doctrine is always open to interpretation."

"Do you think they'll really do it? I mean, are you worried they could bomb our church?"

"Of course I'm worried about our church! I worry about all the churches in Cairo. We have some of the oldest churches in the world. And the climate here has preserved them like nowhere else. I'm as worried as anyone about our churches. I'm going to be an architect one day, God willing. I've already started working on my portfolio. I'll show you sometime. I hope I can get into Oxford, or at least Rotterdam. Only I'm not going to build boring, old concrete apartment buildings. I'm going to renovate and restore our great churches. Churches are art, Magda. They're art, architecture, religion and history all in one package." He sat up tall, leaned forward and began to use his hands as much as his lips. "I love the ancient intricate alter screens and glossy inlayed marble panels. I love what old floated stained glass does to the light in a room, and I love the medieval feel of a massive wrought iron chandelier lit with candles. Old Cairo has dozens of awesome churches with relics that date from the 1200s. The Church of St. Sergius and Bacchus can trace its history to the time of Christ. To lose a single one of those masterpieces would be tragic!

"Our own church is one of my favorites. I love it's skillful blending of old and new," he went on, speaking of wood and stone with reverence bordering on awe. "We have traditional interlocking wood panels behind the pulpit, but in the center is a modern mosaic. The stain glass windows remind me of Marc Chagall's work. I saw his art in a church in Paris once. Then there's the Bible in the northern side chapel. You just can't replace things like that."

"Oh! The Bible. It'd be a shame to lose that." I was fishing. What Bible?

"Did I ever tell you I'm related to the deacon who pulled it out of the water?" he asked.

"No. You didn't."

"Well, sort of," he shrugged. "A second cousin twice-removed or something like that."

"Tell me about it. I bet you have family stories no one else knows."

"Not really. It was 1976, and he saw it floating along the Nile right near the church. It was so close he could reach it, and he did. A huge old Bible from the 1800s. Who knows how it could even float? And there it was, open to the prophecy of Isaiah where it says, 'Blessed be Egypt, my people.' Everyone says it's a miracle. I don't know if it's a miracle, but it's definitely a sign." He looked solemn a moment and then shrugged.

"Anyway, I didn't mean to get so far off topic. I just wanted to say that these clashes between Muslim and Christian in Egypt? They have to stop. The way things are going, it's just a matter of time till lives—and churches—are lost. It's madness. No—it's heartbreaking."

The clock on the wall ticked over to 10:45 p.m., and I never would have noticed if Mark hadn't reminded me that he'd promised to have me home by 11. As we gathered up our things, I glanced at my phone. No calls.

We made our way into the street again. The air was cooler now, the street even busier than before. All the stores were still open, even a little grocer selling melons, oranges and figs to late night shoppers.

We pushed through the throngs to Mark's car. He repeated a series of similarly bold maneuvers back into traffic where the little Civic became one with the fast-moving river of automobiles. Little honks permeated the night air, more as conversation than warnings, while the mass of humanity ambled slowly along the streets, the odd man or woman darting madly across traffic. The noise and activity began to let up only as we entered the residential neighborhood where Magda lived.

Mark parked the car, but instead of hopping around to open my door like I had come to expect, he stayed rooted in his seat and fiddled with the keys still in the ignition. A seed of panic planted itself in my gut.

Oh, God. He wasn't going to try to kiss me, was he?

Still toying with the keys he asked, "Magda, I enjoyed tonight. May I call you again?" He looked up at me. "Maybe without the Arabic?"

There it was. Right there on the table. I took a deep breath and gathered my thoughts.

"Mark—" I said tentatively, "I enjoyed tonight too. You're a really neat guy, and I have fun with you. I feel very—well—natural with you. That's why I asked for your help with this. I'm not really sure how it became so much like a date though. I really just need your help in Arabic right now. You were really there for me. You've been a friend, and that's what I really need at the moment. Thank you."

His eyes returned to his keys, and he stayed silent a moment.

"That's about the nicest rejection a guy could ask for," he said, dejectedly.

"Mark, I'm sorry, I—," I stammered.

"No. It's okay. You want a friend. I'll try to settle for that," he said. Then he seemed to make a decision. He dropped the keys and turned to look me in the eye.

"Well, if Arabic is how we're going to communicate, I'm going to be the best damn Arabic tutor this school has ever seen. Call me anytime," he pulled the keys out of the ignition and came round to open my door.

How could you not like this guy? He was a gentleman even in rejection. He was witty, fun, smart, gorgeous and a good person, and with all that going for him, he wasn't full of himself.

How could "What's-His-Name Who Didn't Call" top this?

XII

Gabrielle visited in my dreams again. We played Marco Polo in the pool in our backyard, just the two of us, gliding through the water in silence. I stopped on the pool stairs, listening intently. Something felt wrong. The silence was too complete. The air conditioning unit beside the pool, with its near-constant hum, lay silent. My beloved bird Kiwi didn't squawk from his post beside the chair on the patio. No wind rustled through the trees in the forest behind the pool. With a sudden sense of foreboding, I opened my eyes within the dream. Gabrielle was gone.

I searched the pool and the patio, as my panic built. From the front of the house, tires screeched on tarmac. Dread gripped me. My feet pounded the grass as I sprinted between the houses, and arrived in the front yard just in time to see a white van disappear around the corner, Gabrielle silhouetted in the rear window.

I raced down the street after the vehicle but for some odd reason I carried cans of beans in my hands, and they slowed me down. Beans? I tried to go faster, but my legs felt thick and heavy. The van shot away. Why didn't anyone hear me screaming? My heart pounded, and it was so darn hot.

Hot? I shouldn't be hot. Florida's February air is cool, and I was soaked. Slowly, I pulled myself out of the dream. The sun broke through the crack between the white lace curtains of Magda's window and warmed my cheek. I had thrown my covers off and was bathed in sweat. It was Egypt in the morning.

My heart rate slowed, and relief flooded through me. Just a dream.

On the nightside table, the clock read nine-thirty a.m. on a bright and sunny Friday morning in Cairo.

Nine thirty a.m.! My heart rate shot into the stratosphere.

I threw my feet over the edge of the bed, ran to the closet and flung it open. The bottom bunk was empty, unmade. Why would Maraya get up and leave without waking me? I pulled out a clean pressed uniform shirt and skirt and quickly began dressing. Why hadn't anyone woken me? My hair would have to settle for a headband today, since I had no time even for a ponytail. I crammed the books on my desk into the backpack. Throwing it over my shoulder, I emerged from the bedroom and hurried down the hallway toward the kitchen.

The hallway ended at a junction. The living room lay before me, the kitchen through an open doorway to the right. Magda's dad reclined in the living room in a big over-stuffed gold chair, his slippered feet on an equally over-stuffed footstool, a laptop cradled in his legs. Magda's mom sat at one end of a matching gold over-stuffed sofa, while Maraya sprawled out on the other end of the sofa wearing pink pajamas and absorbed in a TV across the room which blared *Sponge Bob Square Pants* in Arabic.

Three jaws dropped in unison when I entered the room. Maraya clasped a hand over her face as she tried unsuccessfully to mask her laughter. Soon Magda's mom and dad laughed too.

How could this be? Last night was Thursday night. I knew it. Today was Friday. Was it a holiday or something?

Maraya was the first to pull herself together.

"It's Friday, silly!" she said. Like that explained everything.

I tried to smile and join cluelessly in their mirth, like someone who had been caught in a big funny joke, but to tell the truth, I felt totally deflated. The anxious dream, the challenge of school, the whole thing with Mark and What's-His-Name, Layla's frustration with me, and just the struggle to figure out how things were done from moment to moment, all hit me at once. I missed my Florida family and my Florida life. I missed my iPod and toast and peanut butter. Tears threatened to burst through my false smile, and I turned sheepishly to head back to my room before I broke down in front of Magda's family.

The others must've registered the mood change. Magda's mom left her Bible and followed me down the hall into my room.

She closed the door behind us, and I sat on the bed, preparing to be chastised for all my strange behavior. Instead, she settled in beside me, put an arm around me and pulled me close. She smelled like roses, and my head fit naturally into the crook between her head and shoulder. This little affection was too much. Tears burst through my weakened defenses. She pulled me into a big hug. The tears poured down my face and my body shook. I cried until my head ached. Slowly, the shaking subsided and my shoulders drooped, my tears spent.

She held me wordlessly until the worst was over. When I began to pull away, her hand smoothed my hair.

"What's on your mind, honey?" she asked, her voice soft and kind, not demanding.

What could I tell her? What did she *think* bothered me? Could I twist what was really going on in my head into normal teenage stuff?

"I don't know, Mom," I ventured. "I'm just not feeling myself lately," I said. How's that for an understatement? "I've been feeling a lot of emotions lately. And—" I searched for something more substantial, "—and having a lot of bad dreams."

Her brow furrowed. "Sometimes God speaks to us in our dreams. What did you dream?" she asked.

"Just about my little sister," I said, truthfully. "I keep dreaming that something's going to happen to her. Last night I dreamt that she was taken away from me while I wasn't looking," I said. I tried to choose facts that might make sense to her, without actually lying.

"Hmmm. That's a tough one. Do you have any reason to be worried about Maraya? Has she been behaving oddly? Anything at all?" she asked, her voice edged with concern.

"No, no! Not at all. I can't think of any reason for it."

"Well then, let's concentrate on the other things that might be worrying you," she said. "Did something happen with Mark last night?" she asked.

"No, he was a perfect gentlemen. I'm just not sure I'm interested in him the way you want me to be," I added.

She sighed heavily and slid back a little to face me.

"It's a lot of pressure, darling, I know. Just remember that you don't have to decide your heart in a single day. Your father and I would never force you into a marriage you didn't want. We married for love, and so will you. If we pray, God will show us who you're meant to be with. I hope you won't dismiss Mark too quickly though. You two are more alike than you may think. Remember, love is patient. You must give it time to grow," she said.

Other times love hits you like a bolt of lightning out of a clear blue sky, I thought, knocking the breath out of you. I decided not to mention this.

"I guess so," I acquiesced. A silence stretched between us.

"You've been working hard, honey. You're worrying me. All this running and lifting weights and the late nights with your school work. I tell you what. We don't have much going on today. Your father has work to do, and I have some shopping. Maraya will play at Allison's today. Take the day to rest and catch up. Curl up with a good book, or invite Layla over. Go shopping or something. I'll manage the cooking and cleaning without you. Would that be a good idea?" she asked hopefully.

Time alone with a computer was exactly what I needed.

"Love you, Mom," I said.

"I love you, Magda," she answered. She touched my cheek worriedly and left.

Time alone with my computer was a Godsend. I needed to rest, regroup, research and plan. I booted up my laptop while I changed into a white sweat suit from the bottom of Magda's closet. In the kitchen I gathered provisions: a bunch of grapes, a glass of water, some pita and a piece of melon. Then I sat down at the desk and turned myself over to the great and wise master of so many of life's mysteries: Google.

I first researched Egypt. Mostly a Muslim population, I learned, but the country also has the largest Christian population in the Middle East. Different sources told different stories, but the Christian population seemed to be between 10 percent (government estimates) and

20 percent (Christian estimates). The vast majority of Christians were called Coptic Christians, or Copts.

C-o-p-t-i-c I plugged into the Google search field. Wikipedia offered an answer. Copts were an orthodox branch of the Christian religion with a rich heritage that stretched back to the earliest days of the New Testament. When King Herod heard that a new king had been born, he ordered his soldiers to kill all male babies under two. An angel appeared to Joseph in a dream and warned him to escape with his wife and child into Egypt. Joseph bundled the family up and they fled.

The Bible doesn't say anything about what the Holy Family did in Egypt or how long they stayed, but the Egyptians say he walked their soil for seven years. Sacred places scattered throughout the heart of Egypt claim the Holy Family stayed there. Holy caves proliferate where Jesus is said to have slept, holy wells where he is said to have drank, even holy trees where he is said to have rested. The local Copts protect and honor these sites reverently.

After Jesus was crucified, according to Wikipedia, the Apostle Mark came to Egypt and started the Coptic Church. In Egypt, he is Saint Mark. The main language throughout Egypt at the time was called Coptic, and the religion spread like desert sands. Egypt was solidly Christian until the Arab Muslims conquered it in the seventh century and a gradual conversion to Islam began.

What were Muslim/Christian relations like today? I knew only what I had seen with my own eyes: they studied side by side at school. The Cairo American Academy definitely had a Coptic clique, but that was probably just kids hanging together because they had something in common. Friendships extended beyond these cliques. Aisha was Muslim, and she and Magda got along like hummus and pita. But the cabbie yesterday implied that Muslims and Copts didn't get on at all. Maybe the rest of Egypt didn't operate the way the school did?

I thought about Mark. Magda's parents seemed so excited to see Magda gravitating toward Mark. Was it because he came from a nice family? Or was it because he was Christian? Understanding how these two religions lived together was going to be a vital part of fitting in here.

Google was of two minds on the Muslim/Christian relations issue in Egypt. Some official-sounding sites said Muslims and Copts existed side by side in peace and harmony. Others said that they got along well on the surface, but the surface hid government persecution of Christians that was officially denied. These latter sites claimed the Egyptian government had to treat Copts fairly or the American government would stop sending aid money, so the government hid its persecution and appointed a few token Copts to meaningless ministerial positions.

I thought of Mark last night and his worries about bombings of Christian churches. Did terrorism groups operate in Egypt? I googled Al Qaeda. The group behind the bombing of the World Trade Center in New York wasn't very active in Egypt, but its influence was growing. The Muslim Brotherhood starred as the real player in the fundamental Islamist space in Egypt. Most Egyptians shunned them as extremists, but their political power grew. The group denounced violence officially but was still dogged by rumors they couldn't control some factions of their party. The most violent behavior in Egypt, however, was not attributed to them. Splinter groups that came and went took most of the blame for local terrorism. Al-Gama'a al Islamiyya, for example, entered the tomb of the Pharaoh Hatchesput in Luxor in 1997 and gunned down a busload of tourists in a 45-minute reign of terror that devastated Egypt's tourism industry for years. The group had since faded into obscurity.

I spent more time reviewing Egyptian history and reading what I could to learn about manners, etiquette and general social behavior from tourism websites.

Hours passed, and my thoughts turned again and again to What's-His-Name. He had said we would talk. I reached in my backpack and checked my cell phone for, like, the hundredth time. Nothing.

I scanned the contact list. Layla, Aisha, home, Magda's dad's mobile, her dad's office, her mom's mobile, her office, some other names I knew from school like Verana and Demiana. I didn't know his name, and I couldn't just start randomly calling down Magda's contact list. Besides, all the names seemed to be girls' names. He would've called by now if he really wanted to talk to me. He had seemed so sincere at school. Was he not calling because he saw me walking on the track with Mark?

Then it occurred to me that maybe he didn't mean he would call on the phone. Come to think of it, he hadn't used the word *call* or *phone.* He had said he'd *talk* to me. Maybe he meant we'd Facebook or email or something. That would be smarter too because if dating was so serious here, she probably wasn't supposed to talk or text boys either. Emails or Facebook accounts could be more private.

On the Academy's website, I opened Magda's email account. Thank goodness for auto-saved passwords. I scanned the recent entries, but they were all school related—teacher emails about assignments, a reminder about an upcoming field trip to see the opera *Aida,* that sort of thing. The school email account was not a major form of kid-to-kid communication.

On Facebook her username and password again filled automatically. A page opened up, and there in the corner was a little sepia photo of Magda in her headband and Layla, her hair straightened, their heads tilted together, smiling. I felt a tinge of guilt. I needed to get right with Layla somehow.

I scanned the last few days of actions. Layla was on today already. In her status line, she informed the world she and Verana were hanging out—a series of just-posted photos showed the two of them wearing big dark sunglasses and making silly faces for the camera. A couple of other familiar faces were online as well but no boys. I went to Magda's "friends" link and scanned for his face. Nothing.

I searched her computer for a Skype account. Nada.

I felt certain What's-His-Name and Magda had—either currently or in the recent past—some kind of relationship, and Magda clearly still had strong feelings about him. The way he'd said he'd be in touch with her later—there was something emotionally charged about the comment. He cared for her too. Could I have read that wrong? I didn't think so.

I listlessly scanned some old messages between Layla and Magda when the word "delete" caught my eye. It was in a message dated three weeks previously from Layla:

I've been trying to reach you all night. Where are you? I wanna talk to you. idk...Magda. This whole thing was exciting at first, but now you two are way too involved. I'm getting scared for you. Where are you? Delete this!

Magda's didn't respond and there were no similar entries. Apparently she also forgot to delete it.

If Magda was supposed to delete that message, I reasoned, it meant the message revealed too much. Magda and someone were way too involved, and it was a secret. So Magda and What's-His-Face had a secret relationship. Maybe Magda didn't want the whole world talking about her and What's-His-Face—like they did about her and Mark. In this world, a relationship was everybody's business.

Then again, her parents had been open to a potential relationship/courtship with Mark. Why wouldn't Magda have pursued that route with What's-His-Name? Maybe she couldn't. Maybe he was Muslim, and her parents wouldn't approve.

Religion could explain everything. If being in love with a Muslim forced them into secrecy, that could be why they acted like they didn't know each other in public but still harbored strong feelings for each other. Magda and What's-His-Name would have to avoid easily-traced contact like the phone calls and texts and resort to whispered comments in the hallway when no one was looking.

So when/where did they meet? Whatever their method, Magda hadn't kept up her end since I shifted, and I had to figure it out soon because What's-His-Name was getting frustrated. "*Why aren't you answering me?*" he had asked. "*Say anything you want—but say something.*"

They could text each other and then delete the texts, but that would be like asking to get caught. All one of them would have to do is leave the phone unattended for a moment and have a text come in while a parent was nearby. Plus I knew from experience that parents get all uptight if you press the delete button as they walk by.

They could meet somewhere discreetly, but his comments didn't make it sound like she wasn't showing up somewhere. It sounded more like she wasn't keeping up her end of a conversation. Besides, even if they had a secret meeting place, they had to communicate when and where they'd meet somehow. Which brought me back again to the computer. They had to "talk" on the computer. But he wasn't on her Facebook account. And social media would be a dumb way to communicate secretly anyway.

Emails that they deleted afterwards? Then there would be at least one email from him waiting for me to read and delete by now.

What if they had a secret Facebook account, separate from Magda's regular one? One just for the two of them? That would actually be outstandingly clever. They could each set up some randomly-named second account, max out the privacy settings, and befriend only each other. You know what? It could work.

For starters, Magda would have to have a different email account to link it to since she used her school account for her regular Facebook. If I was lucky, it would be some generic account like Yahoo or AOL. If I was unlucky, it would be something linked to some obscure Egyptian cable company. I started with *Yahoo.com*. I opened the Yahoo main page but found no autosaved account here. So I tried AOL. Nothing. When I opened *hotmail.com* though, the site recognized my computer and automatically logged me in to an account called *2close2u@hotmail.com*. Bingo! I scanned the account and couldn't find any email entries. It was an account that had been set up but never used. What other possible reason would Magda have to set up an email account and then never use it? I had to be on the right trail.

I entered the email account into Facebook but was disappointed when it didn't autofill a password. Maybe that wasn't weird. She might've declined the autofill option for added privacy. I began trying passwords—Magda. Nah, not weird enough. The weirder it was, the better for a secret account. Which made my chances of stumbling on it really miniscule. I didn't even know his name yet. How about, *secretlove*? Nah, that was corny. I entered in a few dozen random selections based on things I knew about her—her favorite color pink, her little sister's name—but I was losing hope. Then I realized they might choose MySpace instead. Hardly anyone uses MySpace anymore, so that might even be better than Facebook. I went over to that site and tried all the same combinations. Nothing. There were probably a half dozen other even less popular social networking sites out there they could be using. This was as pointless as an umbrella in the desert.

I closed my laptop and made the decision to rejoin reality. Sometimes the best way to work on a problem was to set it aside and let my subconscious fret over it for a while. Right now I would accept help from anywhere I could get it.

I went out to the living room to spend some time with my borrowed family. Magda's dad spoke into his phone without seeing me. "I knew I could count on you," he told someone. "This reform is the best way forward. We can't continue as we have been." He nodded gravely, listening intently to the voice on the other end.

Her mom was back from shopping, so I helped her around the kitchen and tried as much as possible to stick to sous-chef jobs like chopping and mopping. I was afraid she might expect me to know some of her recipes by heart. Following her example, I wrapped grape leaves for her around a mixture of delicious spicy rice and ate heartily while I wrapped.

Then I got ready to work out. I put on a pair of navy gym shorts from school and a plain white T-shirt. I had my hand on the front door when I heard Magda's mom's voice from the kitchen.

"Ahh—excuse me? And just where do you think you're going?" Mom asked, her eyebrows raised in alarm. Over a cutting board of cilantro, her hands paused in mid-chop.

"Er—running?" I said. Really? I wasn't going to be allowed to run?

"Magda, darling, you're not going anywhere in public dressed like that," she said sternly as she returned to chopping. "Honestly, girl, what's the matter with you? People treat you according to how you dress. You know that. What do you think people will think of those short little shorts? That you're a nice modest respectable girl? I think not! You can wear those at school for PE because it's an American school and that's dress code, but that's it," she said. "What's with all this running and working out anyway?" she demanded. Without waiting for an answer she rambled on, "You shouldn't be running at all. It's much too hot. It's the middle of the day! You'll get heat stroke for goodness sake," she said. "Go take a nap. It's Friday afternoon. I'm going to take one myself soon."

Dejectedly, I headed back to the room where Maraya lay curled up on the bottom bed, napping. I collapsed into the desk chair with a thud. Not being able to run was just another setback in a day full of setbacks.

I settled for a homemade workout. As quietly as I could I did high knees, squats, lunges and hefted those cans of beans with every muscle group I could think of. My shoulders and biceps were sore from yesterday, and the way I saw it, that pain was the only sign of real progress I'd made since I got here.

XIII

"So, Friday and Saturday are the weekend, right?" I asked Maraya first thing on Saturday morning.

"Right."

"And no running shorts except for PE, right?"

"Right."

"Anything else I should know?"

She thought about this. "I don't know. No offense, but for someone who's supposed to be smart, you don't know some pretty basic stuff," she paused thoughtfully. She was standing in front of her closet and selected a dark pink dress with smocking.

"Are you dressing up?"

"Just for church. Oh, is that the kind of stuff I need to tell you?"

"I'm afraid so. You see where I come from, the weekend is Saturday and Sunday, church is Sundays, and running shorts are for running—anywhere and anytime. Except maybe church."

"Really? That's so weird," she said as she bent over the bottom of the closet and selected white lace socks and black patent shoes.

I felt a bit like cutting loose today. I was frustrated with all the things Magda wasn't allowed to do—date who she wanted, dress how she wanted—and I wanted to rebel. Her wardrobe wasn't really up to the task, so I chose to express myself with the wildest print in her closest. It was an absolute cacophony of color with splashes of lilac, deep purple, bright yellow and hot pink flowers covering every inch. It was disgusting. It was rebellious. It was a new day, and I was going to embrace it.

No one noticed.

We drove as a family in the family Mercedes. I would've been impressed with a Mercedes in my own garage at home, but here it was just a normal businessman kind of car. A few years old, it had dusty yellow paint and a caramel leather interior. We parked several blocks from the church and walked.

I was curious to see Magda's church after Mark's glowing description. Would it be like the churches in Europe? Something wildly ornate, dripping with gold and marble? It probably wouldn't be anything like my church in Florida—a massive gray-painted concrete building that housed a theatre-quality auditorium.

We turned the corner and the church came into view. From the outside, the Maadi Church of the Holy Virgin was a disappointment. Chipped stucco, painted beige, covered the blocky, square frame. Plopped on top of this foundation stood a very odd series of three beehive-shaped domes, similarly stuccoed and painted. The three domes were lumped together in the middle of an otherwise flat roof, each crowned by a short black iron cross. The expansive Nile River flowed darkly behind it.

As we approached, several people milled about the Nile side, and a set of stairs led down to a shorter, lower porch, nearer the river. A row of small windows dotted the side of the building, each with a window air conditioning unit sticking out. Wires ran up and down the walls here and there then tucked under the roofline. This wiring setup seemed typical of most buildings in Egypt. I guess you can do that in a country that Wikipedia says averages one day of rain a year.

The churchyard buzzed with activity, and we made our way through the courtyard toward the church with a throng of people. The men wore pants and button down shirts; some wore blazers as well. Children in their Saturday best raced underfoot or huddled close to their mothers. The women formed an army of shapeless dresses in vivid colors. The dress I wore to be rebellious today fit right in. People greeted and kissed each other socially as they made their way inside. Probably a thousand men women and children gathered here, and apparently Magda knew absolutely every one of them because I was assailed by kissers.

"How nice to see you!" Magda's mom said as she kissed someone once on each cheek. I followed her example.

"How nice to see you!" I said, as I hugged an old lady with tight gray curls. "How nice to see you!" I said, with a squeeze for a petite girl my age with too-big black glasses. "How nice to see you!" accompanied two cheek kisses for the plump girl with the big teeth.

Our progress was slow.

Massive twenty-foot tall doors, intricately carved with dark wooden latticework, hinted that the church on the inside differed from the one on the outside.

The crowd moved us inside, and as I stepped across the threshold, I stopped in awe of the simple beauty of this massive room. Built from ancient gray stone, the walls loomed roughly four stories high. Rows of gleaming, dark wooden pews filled the room, and the stone floor was worn smooth in the aisles from centuries of use. Two monumental medieval iron chandeliers hung suspended from the tall ceiling. The cool air tasted of dust.

A long row of contemporary stain-glassed windows, just five or six feet high, stretched uninterrupted across the Nile-side length of the church. Were these the ones Mark said reminded him of something Chagall would make? They leant an eclectic air to this ancient space with their modern, clean-lined geometric patterns vaguely resembling palm trees, water and other simple images. Light flowed through the windows and flooded the chamber with splashes of warm gold, purple, blue and red.

Intricate latticework screens, similar to those of the doors, filled the wall behind the pulpit. Above the screens rose twelve golden figures representing the apostles. Still more wall towered above the apostles, with a great black wrought-iron cross in the middle.

The pulpit itself stood a few feet in front of this elaborate backdrop, waist-high and inlaid with gold-veined marble.

The building reflected centuries of worship. Ancient gray stones formed its walls, medieval chandeliers swung slowly above us. Latticework, probably Ottoman Empire, adorned walls and doors and modern stained-glass windows lit the interior. My presence here today was just a flickering moment in the vast expanse of time this church had witnessed.

The congregation separated now, and Magda's dad left us to join the men on one side of the church while her mom, Maraya and I found our way with the ladies to one of the last empty pews on the opposite side.

A low chanting began, and I turned to see the *Baba*—it was a word that popped into Magda's head when she saw the priest—making his way up the center aisle in a slow procession. An entourage of white-robed alter boys, each swinging a golden orb suspended by chains, surrounded the holy man. The orbs swung from side to side as the boys walked and emitted a swirling smoke that filled the room with sweet pungent incense.

Some of the service was vaguely familiar, a bit like a Catholic wedding I once attended. I was young then, but I remember being impressed by two things: Catholic churches were way prettier than mine, and Catholic weddings were interminably long.

This church was way prettier than mine, and I would soon learn that their service made a Catholic wedding look like religion on the fast forward button.

Ritualized prayer dominated the first hour. The *Baba* spoke, and the audience magically responded. I mumbled along, a syllable behind everyone else. The alter boys circled the room chanting in some language even Magda didn't have—maybe Coptic? We kneeled. We stood. We kneeled, we stood, and only every now and then did we—briefly—sit. I saw no fat people here—church was an aerobic workout.

The children stayed with the congregation, and so the noise level in the room grew noticeably louder as the service progressed. No one seemed to care.

An hour stretched into two. What I wouldn't have given for my iPod.

I thought of my own United Methodist church in Florida. My clean-shaven pastor wore jeans and a casual suit jacket. The man at this pulpit came straight out of the Middle Ages. His heavily embroidered white robe scraped the floor, and his head was crowned by a tall white mitre, a pope's hat, which was set on top of a middle-aged face with a long, gray-black frizzy beard. My pastor was miked, and his image projected onto two large screens on either side of the stage. The only technological wizardry here was an old microphone with a long cord that ran openly down one side of the pulpit and along the floor to an outlet in the wall. A lead volcalist, guitar, electric guitar and drums backed up my pastor. This guy had a choir singing hymns. My pastor delivered sermons about charity, faith, hope and love. This guy preached that the devil was everywhere, always looking for a way to break down our defenses and enter into our thoughts and lives. My service was over and done in an hour, no matter what. This one was entering the third hour and still going strong.

At home, my congregation listened politely and quietly to the services, and I suppose most people enjoyed them because they kept coming back, but it's hard to tell. I certainly pretended not to like it, so Mom would have to bribe me to come to church with lunch after at Joey Tomatoes. Here, everyone was politely bored through the ritualized parts of the service, but once the *Baba* began his homily, they watched with rapt attention. The Coptic people cried out in agreement and held their arms up to the heavens at times as they swayed with emotion. At first, I was taken aback by their outpouring of emotion, but after a time I got caught up in the excitement. Like a good concert, it was hard not to get carried away with the crowd even if it wasn't my usual taste in music. An strong and enticing sense of community thrived here, born of centuries of shared faith and devotion.

The four-hour marathon church service wound up with a reconciliation prayer where the *Baba* gave Christ's forgiveness to the people and the people shared Christ's forgiveness with each other by shaking hands.

I've never thought too hard about my own Christianity. I went through the motions, and I believe. I've believed for as long as I can remember. It's not something I've ever really questioned or doubted, but I also never really felt anything I'd call devotion or adoration. I can't say I ever felt God's presence, but I never looked for it either. Here, I was moved by what I had just taken part in. Be it the antiquity of the building or the devoutness of the people, I felt God in this place.

The service ended, and the people rocketed out of their seats. Suddenly, everyone chattered, and the noise echoed through the building multiplying its effect. I saw Layla near the front of the church, but she dashed out, probably to avoid me. Demiana, a girl with ecstatically curly hair who I'd sat with in the cafeteria a couple of times, whispered conspiratorially into the ear of a younger girl I didn't recognize. My algebra teacher shared a photo on his phone with a friend, and they both laughed. More kissing and hugging ensued. A couple of faces I knew from Magda's Facebook friends' photos stood in a corner chatting quietly. I think I may have kissed a couple of strangers. I wonder if they noticed.

Mark was suddenly beside me. How did he just appear like that? I've always been a sucker for a guy in a tie, and today Mark wore a butterscotch shirt and a muted green tie with little silver Coptic crosses on it. A tiny piece of my resolve collapsed again, and I had to embark on some mental retrenching.

"Did you work on your essay yesterday?" he asked, conversationally.

"A little," I said, evasively. He looked at me inquisitively. "Okay, not," I confessed. "Today, I promise, teacher," I said. Maraya had wandered off to play with some friends, and Mom was deep in a clutch of ladies. I found myself walking outside with Mark to the porch overlooking the Nile.

"So tell me, future architect, what year was this church built, anyway?" I asked.

"No one knows, it's been built and rebuilt so many times. Much of what you see is actually surprisingly modern. A major restoration took place in the early 1800s, another in the latter part of that century, and most recently in 1983. It doesn't really matter though, does it? There aren't many churches that can claim to be built on land the Holy Family walked on," he said. The green of his tie drew out flecks of green in his brown eyes that I hadn't noticed before. His cowlick struggled against the gel in his hair, and cowlick had the upper hand.

We strolled along the black iron fence above the river. He gestured down toward the stairs that lead to the Nile. "It's hard to imagine that this is the exact spot where the Holy Family stepped aboard a boat and began their journey to Upper Egypt," he said. "They say Joseph financed the trip using some of the frankincense and myrrh given to Jesus by the three wise men."

We stopped at an iron gate looking down a worn flight of brown stone stairs. At the base of the steps, a path led from the Church yard to the Nile.

I stared at the stairs. Christ had always been a surreal figure. Sort of ghostlike. But here, in this ancient land, he had been real.

"Even the Muslims believe it," he added. I looked at him curiously.

"You know what I mean. Muslims, Jews, and Christians, we all believe in Christ the man," he explained. "We just believe different things about him, right? The Muslims believe everything Christians believe about him, except the part about him being God in human form who died to save mankind. He's just a regular prophet to them. The Jews think he was neither God nor prophet. To them, he was just another rabbi who lived and walked among them. Well, another rabbi who thought he was the Messiah, I guess."

"Kind of funny, isn't it?" I said. "The ones he lived and walked among, the ones he grew up with, were the only ones who didn't believe in him. You'd think he would've convinced the Jews first."

"I know. I guess it's kind of like if one of my cousins was to declare himself the Messiah. I mean, really. I'd be like, '*Sahbey*,'" he said, using a local term for *my friend* that might roughly translate as *dude*, "we shot peas out our noses together at the beach when we were little. You leave your underwear on the floor. You are *so* not the Messiah.' They were just too close to the human in him to see the other part."

I laughed, and then we grew reflective again. "So basically what you're saying is that even though people disagree about *who* Christ was, everyone agrees *that* he was, and that his leather sandals walked these stairs and looked out over these waters," I said and imagined the young Jesus gazing out across this great river, feeling the hot Egyptian sun on his skin and watching the very waters that swirled and eddied darkly below me.

"Pretty much," he said.

I've never been one to be awed by celebrity, but the idea that Jesus in his human form had passed this way gave me goose bumps.

We leaned over the iron railing. The sun at its highest point, all of Egypt lay bare before its scorching gaze. The white sails of Cairo's famous little white sailboats—the tourism websites called them feluccas—darted lithely among the waves of the mighty river and carried tourists and locals across the river as they had for centuries—millennia even.

Without a doubt the widest river I'd ever seen, it wasn't the Nile's scale that impressed. It was its much larger history. To immerse one's hand in the Nile's waters is to insert oneself into the flow of history. Here, Moses had been wrapped as a baby, placed in a basket and floated down to where a princess of the Pharaoh found him. Every pharaoh surveyed the nation from a throne set into the center of a narrow wooden boat and rowed by white-skirted men through the artery of Egypt. Cleopatra sailed this river with Julius Caesar and later Mark Anthony. Napoleon passed these shores, perhaps in a ship with the Rosetta Stone his expedition discovered. It was humbling to add myself as a tiny footnote to all this great history. *Molly was here.* Well, kind of.

I wondered idly if a shifter had interrupted any of those great men or women's lives. Wouldn't that be funny? Look at Cleopatra. I've always thought the Egyptian Queen underwent some kind of weird personality change in the middle of her life. As a young woman, she proved herself one of history's most astute politicians, even winning the favor of Julius Caesar, against all odds, and conniving to have him put her on Egypt's throne. Later on though, it's like she was a different person. After Caesar's death, she had a wildly passionate affair with Mark Antony, who was deemed a traitor to Rome. Does this seem like a good way to further the fortunes of the Egyptian throne?

What if one of those Cleopatra's wasn't really Cleopatra at all, but a shifter? Shifting would explain a lot of irrational stuff in history.

Mark turned around, and leaned with his back to the fence, watching the crowd.

"Your dad seems uncomfortable with his newfound celebrity," he said.

"Celebrity?" I asked, puzzled.

I turned. Magda's dad did seem to be quite the center of things at the far end of the patio. A throng of men bordered him while they laughed and clapped his shoulder. He smiled, but I could see tension in his face. His eyes darted beyond the crowd around him, searching for an escape.

"Well, whatever you want to call it. It is a kind of celebrity though really, isn't it? Being appointed a minister by the President of Egypt—that doesn't happen everyday. Minister Amides. That has a good ring to it. You'd think he'd been crowned Pharaoh or something the way people are fussing over him. How's he dealing with it all?" Mark asked.

I took a moment to digest this. I had just assumed he was some sort of generic businessman. To be honest, I'd been so wrapped up in Magda's life I hadn't noticed him much. A minister? That would make him a sort of advisor to the President of Egypt. Wow.

I searched my mind for something relevant to say to Mark.

"It's been a lot of work for him. He's always on his laptop or on the phone," I said truthfully.

"Do you think he'll be able to make a difference? I mean, don't get me wrong—your dad's a good man. My dad calls him a stealth leader. He works behind the scenes in ways people don't see. He gets things done because he talks sense and people like him. He's not in your face, ya know? And you couldn't ask for a more principled Christian. If anyone can make a difference in government, your dad can. But a lot of people think Christians in the government are basically ignored."

"He's an honorable man," I said thoughtfully. "Where there's an opportunity to do good, he'll make the most of it." An entire sentence of positive words without any actual information in it. Maybe *I* should run for office.

Magda's dad seemed an odd choice for a minister. He wasn't a stereotypical politician— speaking loud opinions or seeking a soapbox for his ideas. Quite the opposite. He spoke very little. When tensions built at home—Maraya dilly-dallying about going to bed or begging incessantly for a play date—Magda's mom was the one who hit the roof. The other day Maraya tried to hide her vegetables in a glass of milk. I think she planned to toss the last half a glass out. Unfortunately, the vegetables were beets, and they turned her milk pink. Magda's mom went nuts, swiped the glass away, and ordered Maraya to her room. Magda's dad intervened and helped her mom cool her temper. After Maraya was out of sight, he even got her to laugh about the pink milk.

"Well," Mark said in response, "it's good knowing there's at least one good, dependable voice for our interests among all those crooks in the government," he said.

"Yeah, right," I muttered, watching Magda's dad continue to squirm.

"Mark, would you excuse me?" I asked without looking at him.

I broke away and made my way apologetically through the throng of men around Minister Amides and whispered into his ear.

"Gentlemen, I'm afraid I must take my leave now," he said formally. He put his arm behind me and guided me from the small of the back the way Mark had the other night. Mom and Maraya saw us leaving, and he gestured to them to join us.

He leaned over me and whispered conspiratorially. "You aren't actually ill at all, are you?" he said.

"Busted," I whispered back.

"Oh, Magda," he sighed. "You are truly an angel sent by God."

We exited the front of the church yard and headed left down a wide street. Scattered park benches on the long, broad sidewalk overlooked the Nile. Horns honked and tires squealed in the street beside us. A two-passenger moped sped by. The passenger in the back held his arms wide around a window-sized pane of glass, which rested on the seat between himself and the driver. Safety wasn't high on anyone's priorities here.

Magda's mother and Maraya lumbered along a few steps behind us and chatted.

After a time, I broke the silence. "Dad, if you're uncomfortable working a crowd, why did you take a position as a government minister?" I asked.

He sighed again and said nothing for a moment. "You have always been a curious girl. I'm not going to tell you I didn't consider saying no when the president called me. But I had more reasons to accept the position than reasons not to," He pushed his black wire glasses back up on his nose.

"I don't like being in the government. Don't misunderstand me. I think most of the men I've worked with in government are good, well-meaning individuals. But they are trying to work within the system as it is, and that means accepting it as it is. I'm not prepared to do that. It was bad enough before I worked in the government, but now? Now I spend all day everyday fighting these, these—" his face reddened, and his right hand formed a fist, "—these idiots. Getting anything done requires the right friends or the right amount of *baksheesh*," he said, using the local term for bribes. "I can spend all day just trying to get people to do the jobs they were hired to do. It drives me crazy!

"It hasn't always been like this. Look around you," he motioned toward a row of crumbling, five and ten-story structures on the opposite side of the road. This is the great Corniche El Nil," he said. The name was emblazoned in Arabic on a street sign opposite us. Unimaginative concrete monstrosities rose above the sidewalk, the sort of things one might expect in an impoverished country. Among these, the decaying edifices of once splendid buildings remained, including a faded yellow apartment house. I imagined how it must've looked when it was new—its paint richly golden, its cornices and moldings whole and its rusted iron banisters black and gleaming.

"Those old buildings among the gray concrete junk are from a time before Nasser, from the early part of the last century when the world's finest architects called Cairo home, and the great minds of that era filled our cafés and debated all the issues of the day. Commerce thrived and Muslims, Christians and Jews lived side by side in harmony. Do you know what they called Cairo then? They called her 'Paris Along the Nile.'"

A young dark-skinned boy stepped in front of us just then. Maybe a little older than Maraya, he wore a faded red t-shirt and pants two inches short for him. He walked backwards a couple of steps then moved to keep pace beside us.

"Hey Mister. Will you buy this sweater?" He held in his arms a worn red sweater with balls of fabric on it from repeated washings. Magda's dad smiled, pulled out an Egyptian pound and handed it to him, then shooed him away. The boy adeptly pocketed the bill and moved in on a couple a few feet away.

Magda's father's voice became agitated again, and the lines of his face tightened in anger. "Now look at what we've become. We're a nation of little boys like that. The Egyptian poor are more poor than ever. More than half of all Egyptians live on just twelve Egyptian pounds a day. Twelve pounds a day, Magda! What can you buy for twelve pounds? A kilo of meat is forty-two pounds!" He threw his hands up in exasperation. Magda's mother had picked up her speed to walk apace with us now and was listening quietly while Maraya skipped ahead.

"Sure, you, your mother and sister and I live in a small apartment, but we are the wealthy here. Most Egyptians live like rats, with a dozen or more people in a single bedroom home. It's all because the government sets out how much owners are allowed to charge for rent. The rates are ridiculously low, so there is no profit in it. No one builds anything new, or fixes anything old. All those great minds firing imaginations in our cafes? Our architects, musicians, composers and writers—all muzzled. Most of them just moved away."

"But there is a greater calling still that lead you to accept the position, is there not, darling?" Magda's mother interjected and slipped her hand into his. Deliciously cool air blew from across the Nile. "Why don't you tell her about that?"

"Yes, yes, of course. We need strong representation to secure the interests of the Coptic people in the government, Magda. We need it, and we need it urgently," he said. Then he waved his hand at me dismissively. "But you know how I feel about this. I don't want to preach to you today."

"No, it's okay. Finish what you were going to say." Magda's father overflowed with information Google couldn't give me.

"It just makes me cry to think of how we were once a model of religious tolerance. For centuries, Muslims and Christians were peaceful. Centuries! And now, in the span of ten years, things have changed precipitously. I want this peace back. So do the vast majority of Muslims I know. But a few radicals who call themselves Muslims are spreading hatred among the poor and uneducated and muddying centuries of religious harmony."

"What do you think caused things to change so suddenly?" I asked.

Magda's father chuckled warmly. "The funny thing is, Magda, I think much of the decline in religious tolerance came about because the president was trying to be tolerant. When the Muslim Brotherhood, with its strong fundamental Islamic beliefs, began to cause trouble in the south, the president banished many of them. A big mistake. Forced out of Egypt, most of them migrated to more radical Muslim countries like Saudi Arabia."

We had stopped at a busy intersection and waited for an opportunity to cross. Magda's father stepped out into traffic, and Magda's mother grabbed Maraya's hand and propelled us out into the street behind him. He motioned to each driver to wait as we moved in front of them. Safely on the other side, we resumed our leisurely pace down a quieter, more residential street.

"In Saudi Arabia and places like that, the radicals learned the strict *Wahhabi* doctrine, and their fundamentalism grew tenfold. When they came home, these newly-emboldened members of the Brotherhood insisted their women bathe in the sea in full burqa," he said, referring to the floor-length veiled gowns that cover the women from head to toe, complete with gloves and little screens over the eyes. Such robes I knew were common in countries like Saudi Arabia, but I had yet to see one in my few days here. "They told their children not to talk to Christians because they viewed Christians as infidels—non-believers. They said it was religiously forbidden for them to talk to Christians. Forbidden where, I ask you?" he waved an arm emphatically. "There is no such text in all of Muslim doctrine. But real people with real bombs believe it. All this has happened in the last ten years. It must be stopped! We Christians have to work together with peaceful Muslims to end this menace. We live in a pivotal time, Magda. Anything could happen."

"Is this why the president appointed you? Does he support your goals?" I asked.

"The international community pressures him to represent his Christian populace. Our numbers have been dwindling. He needed a new Christian, and since we are between elections, he was free to make an appointment of anyone, not necessarily someone elected. I think he chose me, quite frankly, because he thought I was harmless. Does he support my goals? Who doesn't support the goal of peace? As long as it is met on his terms. Defining the terms gets complicated."

"God has called you to this duty, *habibi*," Magda's mom said. "He will give you the strength to do His will," she said.

Magda's father sighed heavily. "I hope so, my darling. I hope so."

He was trapped in a dangerous role, struggling to do what he felt was right in a world that was not of his making. I felt his pain.

XIV

English began at 8 a.m. on Sunday. What's-His-Name sat two rows ahead of me, and I took note of his every breath, of every time he shifted in his seat. Magda's body responded to him like iron to a magnet. I half listened to the too-skinny teacher's Jersey drone while my attention remained riveted on him. It was an impressive feat of mental fitness.

And then, before I knew it, we were arguing.

The teacher called on him. I mean, she actually spoke his name. I finally had a name to attach to all these emotions. Ahmed.

My mind swirling, I didn't hear a word he said. Ahmed is not the world's *most* Muslim name. Muhammad deserves that ribbon, and understandably so since I'd read online that it's tradition to name a first-born after the prophet. There are an awful lot of first-borns out there. Still, Ahmed ranked popular enough that every class I'd been in sported at least one.

So Magda really was in love with a Muslim. My instincts had been right. Chalk one up for the secret relationship theory.

We had begun a new unit on *Romeo and Juliet*. I'd studied it in Florida in eighth grade. It's love at first sight, but their families abhor each other. Love doesn't care, and they risk everything and secretly marry.

Ahmed argued that love and hate are equally capable of causing death, and under the right circumstances, death could be a price worth paying. Both love and hate are powerful themes of the story, and family members pop off left and right because of the feud between the two families.

"Love is an absolute good," he insisted. I savored the way those words dripped from his tongue. "There's nothing that's not worth paying for that prize, even death."

Which is totally bogus.

"No price?" I found myself interjecting. "No price that isn't worth paying for love? That's idealistic nonsense. How much should you really be willing to give up for romantic love? You say you would give your own life. I'd say you could do that, but it wouldn't be heroic, it'd be selfish. Suicide is always selfish. It's about bringing acute pain down on your friends and family just to end your own pain. But that's not the point. Even if you're willing to give your own life, there's a price somewhere that you wouldn't pay for love. How about your family's honor? Or your best friend's life?"

Hmmm. Maybe that isn't the coolest thing to say to your secret love.

The class stared at me. At him. At me. He glared at me too, only he looked like I'd just pulled out my pencil and stabbed him in the eye.

"I mean, don't get me wrong, I'm a true believer in 'love will find a way,'" I recovered, lamely. "There's always a way. But the way comes at a price, and you can't ignore this simple fact. It might be a price like—you can never date anyone else again, ever. That's a pretty normal price to pay for love, but for some people even that's too much. Or it could be, like, death or murder or running away from everyone else you know and love, so you can be together. The question is: what does this particular love cost, and what are both parties willing to pay?"

The one who seemed to be enjoying this most was Ahmed's friend, a boy the teacher called Kamal, who sat next to him. I heard a snicker, glanced over and my eyes met his. I immediately felt a jolt of distaste. Magda hated this short, skinny kid, all bones and a hooked nose. It was all he could do to keep from busting a gut. He was loving this.

"I respect your choice, but it's a choice to put limits on what price you'll pay," Ahmed answered, his words slow and smooth, carefully thought out. "What is it your Bible says? Something about faith, hope and love, and then it says, 'but the greatest of these is love.' True love—not a passing fancy, a crush or an infatuation—but true love is the greatest of all emotions. For those fortunate enough to experience it, I say again, there is no price not worth paying. *Insha'Allah*—God willing—none of us will be asked to pay it, but I *am* willing."

I heard a gentle sigh from across the room. Some young vixen in a rose-colored headscarf, obviously reduced to molten sludge by his words, flashed her inch-long lashes at Ahmed. But his eyes remained on Magda.

The teacher glanced between us, assessing the situation. "Fascinating discussion, people!" she said with a twang. "I think I smell an essay topic here." The class groaned, and several eyes rolled. "But for the moment, let's return to our reading. Act IV, Scene III. Let's see—" she focused in on a boy in the back who was staring intently at some speck on the floor. "Muhammad! Will you begin?" Her words to me were like so much static as I reflected on our conversation, which I think had very little to do with *Romeo and Juliet*.

The class ended, and Ahmed gathered his books up tensely. As he brushed past me, his eyes on some distant point, he whispered with clipped words, "Why aren't you answering me?" And then he was gone.

If my brush with Ahmed wasn't enough drama for one day, Layla was in full passive-aggressive mode with me at lunch. She too brushed past me, this time in the lunch line, and gave me a dirty look when I plopped down purposefully beside her.

"Layla. We need to talk," I said.

She looked at me, wide-eyed with mock shock, her mouth open. "It's a little late for that, don't you think?" she spat. "You went out with Mark on Thursday night, and I had to find out this morning from Michael, who heard it from Marcel, because he and Mark hung out on Friday. But that's not what I'm upset about. What I'm upset about is the fact that you don't give one flying rat's crap about Mark. I have no clue why you would do that to him! You *know* he adores you. You know you're just messing with him. And yet you tease him mercilessly! Is this your idea of fun now? Is boy-catching a new sport? Like your sudden interest in track?"

Her voice grew quieter and more ominous. She leaned in closer, her eyes narrowed. “Maybe this is some kind of twisted game you’re playing for You-Know-Who. Some trick to make him wild. Well, you know what? It’s pretty much working. You’re messing with You-Know-Who too. He calls you *Magnolia*, huh?! He should call you Poison Ivy.”

She picked up her tray, headed to another table, turned her back to me and plunked down.

I sat in stunned silence.

And yet, I wasn’t thinking of Layla or her horrible lecture.

You-Know-Who? Magnolia?

She had given me an idea.

XV

I threw my lunch in my backpack, gathered my computer and my books and hurried into the school courtyard, a small open space surrounded on three sides by school buildings and lined with tall trees. On the fourth side, stood a wooden climbing frame in a bed of sand. Three picnic tables nestled in the middle of the courtyard under the partial shade of the trees. The tables were a favorite place for teachers to sit and watch the lower division kids play, though no one was here now.

I tucked into one of the tables, booted up my computer and started working through all the possible ways Ahmed could communicate with Magda. I now had two new possible passwords, Ahmed and Magnolia. He called her Magnolia. I thought of the magnolia tree growing behind our house in Florida and the creamy, grapefruit-size blossoms with golden centers that burst forth from it every year.

I tried MySpace first. I entered the address for her hotmail account: *2close2u@hotmail.com*. Then I began entering every possible combination of Magnolia and Ahmed. I tried Magnolia. CairoMagnolia. MagnoliaandAhmed. MagnoliaAhmed. Nothing. Nothing.

I tried Facebook and bypassed the automatic settings to login using her hotmail account. Password, M-a-g-n-o-l-i-a, I typed.

My cursor turned into an egg timer, and I held my breath.

The screen filled with text.

I had found their secret meeting place.

A Facebook account. Her profile picture was a surrealist oil painting of a white magnolia flower. His was a photograph of the letter 'A' drawn in the sand. The page displayed no other friends.

An account just for the two of them. Perfect. After they spoke, Magda could just return the account to the previous automatic settings. The entrance to their secret place was hidden. Brilliant!

Sweat dripped from face onto the keyboard as I hunched over my computer in the hot shade and read their first tentative words to each other, written over half a year ago.

Some days they wrote mostly about regular stuff, likes and dislikes, their families, and they shared funny youtube links. The sort of thing I wouldn't have thought twice about writing to a friend at home, boy or girl. But for Magda and Ahmed, because of their culture and religions, every word they shared was a rebellious act.

Over time, their conversations grew intimate.

I want to be with you. I don't care what the world thinks, Ahmed wrote one day, about half way through the entries. *I'd love nothing more than to hold your hand.*

Magda flipped out.

Ahmed that can't ever happen. And not because I don't feel strongly enough about you, not for a second. It's just . . . there's never been an easy time for a Christian/Muslim relationship in this country, but now is harder than ever. My parents would flip out . . . the way they see it, I'd be abandoning them. I can have Muslim friends but not to date or marry . . . not to mention at school our lives would be hell if anyone found out about us . . . I'm not strong enough, Ahmed. . . I love what we have, but I'm not sure I can give you more.

It'd be like abandoning her family? Wasn't that overstating things? But this conversation was repeated in different words every few days.

I'm not sure we should be writing like this, Magda wrote a month previously. *Where can it possibly go?* Then later she waffled, *I can't seem to help myself. I'm not strong enough to move forward with this relationship but not strong enough to resist you either.*

Magnolia, you are what pulls me through each day. I live from one message to the next. I want more than anything to find some secret place to meet with you. One day you'll say your ready. That day will come . . . you know it too. We're destined for each other.

Sometimes the conversation didn't seem to follow sequentially. I guessed they hopped in and out of chat mode as people came and went from the rooms they sat in and typed. I wished I could find some record of their chat conversations, but none remained.

I skimmed to Tuesday, Magda's last day in her own body.

Darn! You're not on anymore, Magda wrote. *I had to leave. My mom came and made me go out and visit w/ Luke and Ariyana:(. They brought the new baby and mom gave her to me to hold so Ariyana could have a break. I have her screaming in one arm while I type this w/ one finger. She's cute, but not cute enough. G2g back out there. I'll write again if I can.*

Ahmed posted the last word that night around 1 a.m.

I guess your magical touch must've got the baby to sleep, and you with her. What I wouldn't give to swap places with that lucky baby! I'm going crazy just seeing you in passing day after day and pretending I hardly know you. Can't wait till you say we can meet???

He never got his answer.

He posted three notes the next day telling her how much he cared for her and that he waited for her next message. In the third one, he apologized if she felt he pushed her too hard to meet and promised to be patient. In the evening, he began to ask why she wasn't writing. By Thursday, his tone began to change.

Saw you with Mark today . . . is there something you want to tell me?

Later: *You looked so frightened to see me today. I've been checking online all night, but you're never there. Now I hear from Marcel that while I've been waiting for you, you've been out on a date with Mark. Tell me it isn't true. I need to hear it from you. What's going on Magnolia?*

Friday, no postings. Saturday, just one.

I know you're reading these, Magnolia. You're breaking my heart. Opening this account and staring into the silence is killing me. If I don't hear from you today, I'll know it's over. I'll delete the account and this will never have happened. You will be free.

I closed my eyes, then opened them and raised my head skyward. The branches of the overhanging trees crossed in the middle of the courtyard. Harsh sunlight pierced their defenses and scattered little blades of light through the courtyard.

This was it. I felt the certainty coarse through my veins and fill me with purpose. I always shifted for a reason, I'd told Maraya. I would have to do or fix something before I could shift back. Now I knew what I had shifted for.

Magda said she didn't have the strength to further the relationship or the strength to leave it. I was going to be the one who decided for her. Cut the cord with Ahmed or follow Magda's heart and challenge the norms of a society I knew almost nothing about. Who was I to make such a decision?

Sitting on the hard bench in the courtyard, I stared at the 'A' drawn in the sand that was Ahmed's profile picture. I felt the heady pull of Magda's love wash over me again. Never in my wildest dreams had I imagined that I could feel this way. It was incredibly right. I would move mountains to keep this love alive for her.

I tore my eyes away from the screen. This wasn't Florida. The consequences of starting a relationship with a Muslim boy in Egypt could be huge. Her family might disown her. Her church and her school friends could reject her. Her father was a government minister, for God's sake. He could be publicly shamed. She would risk everything she cared about if she pursued this love. Was the price worth paying?

But the American in me rebelled against the idea that any culture could stand in the way of a love like this. It wasn't right. Probably hundreds of Coptic/Muslim pairs out there were prevented from being together. Someone had to stand up for what's right.

Should it be Magda? She said she didn't have the strength. Well, I did. This must be what I was here for.

I glanced around the courtyard. Everyone was in class.

I wondered briefly how Magda had been strong enough *not* to do what I was about to do. I poised my fingers over the keyboard.

Drawing a deep breath under the tangled branches of the oaks trees, their limbs a web of foliage, I began to type.

Ahmed, I'm so, so sorry I haven't been writing! I see now what I've put you through. I had so many tests last week I didn't have time to write during school without missing class. The Internet at home isn't working, so I couldn't write there either . . . (I hoped he would think my Internet had been down. Really, I just couldn't navigate through the ether to him—so it wasn't really a lie, was it?). *I should've realized you'd be worried, I'm sorry. I just checked now during lunch, and when I saw what you wrote, well, I'm actually missing bio to write now, and I really shouldn't. I'm not interested in Mark. I needed help with Arabic and he offered. Some people took it the wrong way. I've been very clear with him and I think he understands. I hope you will too. My feelings for you haven't changed. In fact, I've done a lot of thinking lately, and if I'm not too late, I want to meet with you.*

I pressed the send button before I could change my mind.

XVI

I walked to the nurse's office before returning to class and complained of a stomachache. The nurse let me sit in her office for a few minutes until I experienced a startling recovery, and then she gave me the tardy slip I needed for honors biology. Later, I took a test in Spanish class. My body placidly followed the necessary routines through the rest of afternoon classes while competing anxieties ricocheted through my mind. *Magda would be horrified if she knew,* I worried. *Did I really know what I was getting into?* I stressed. *What if the note was too late and he'd already deleted the account?* I wondered. This last angst was among the worst. If the account was deleted, Ahmed and Magda's relationship was over, which would leave me with no theory as to why I had shifted. I needed a problem to solve, so I could hurry up and shift back to Florida before SATs.

Not much point in waiting for Layla. If she did drive me home, it'd be the coldest car in Egypt. I stuck around for awhile, changed into my PE clothes and ran some laps. Up to a pretty consistent three miles now, I didn't feel like throwing up at the end. Progress.

After showering, I headed for the corner with the cabs. The crazy Christian cabbie banged on the top of his car to get my attention, and I headed for him. He might be an oddity, but he had delivered me home safely the last time, so I figured he'd probably do the same again.

"How come you only ride the taxi sometimes?" he said as he pulled out into traffic. The rear windows were open and the air tasted of soot. "You should ride everyday. I would give you a special price."

"Hmmm?" I struggled to bring my mind to the conversation. "Oh. I usually ride with my friend . . . but I may be taking cabs a little more often over the next little while," I said.

"Well, we will have lots of chats then!" he said.

I smiled politely.

"I might be missing for a couple of days next week though," he said gravely.

"Oh." I said.

"You want to know why?" he asked hopefully, his large eyes and silver-framed glasses filling the rearview mirror. On the side of his face was a long white scar that ran from his ear to his cheekbone.

The moment didn't call for a truthful answer, so I replied, "Yes. Why?"

"I got to get a new license," he spat. "That damned government! Last year, it sucked three full days out of my life and my salary, and I'll never get either back. All because they want to leech money from me," he said. He honked his horn while talking and darted across two lanes of traffic.

"I wait in line for three hours, and then I get to the front. It cost me twenty pounds, and they give me a stamp on a form and tell me take it to the other side of the city to another line. I pay another twenty pounds, and they give me another piece of paper and a stamp and send me to another long line in another part of the city. All just to prove I am still a taxi driver!"

I silently vowed never again to complain about the hour I had to spend in the Florida Department of Motor Vehicles to get my driver's license.

"It's like this," he said. "There was a monkey in the jungle, and it saw some tigers running, and a donkey running behind them. The monkey said to the donkey, 'Why are you running?' And it answered, 'because they're arresting all the tigers.' I asked the monkey, 'but why are you running then if they're only arresting tigers?' And the donkey answered, 'because it'll take forever to prove I'm not a tiger.'

He still laughed at his own joke when we drew up alongside my apartment building. I pulled out the fare, with exact change, and thanked him for the ride.

"May God bless you and look after you, little lady," he said to my departing figure. "We Christians, we have to stick together, right? The whole country is going crazy."

I smiled back and nodded as I crossed the street to the front gate of the apartment building.

A woman crossed the sidewalk in front of me as I approached the gate. A white plastic bag hung from her right hand, and a bunch of green leafy carrot tops protruded from the top. She wore a full blue burqa. Long dresses and headscarves were commonplace here, but faces and hands were always exposed. I stared after her in fascination. Every part of her was covered, from her full-length gown to the little perforated veil that covered her face and the white gloves on her hands. What kind of life did she lead, shielded from the world like that? Did she choose to dress this way, or was she forced to by her husband? The thought of such oppression repelled me. Yet how different was Magda? She didn't wear a burqa, yet she was being forced into a different kind of hiding because she loved a boy her culture said she shouldn't. I felt my resolve strengthen. No woman should be made to live her life in hiding. Not the woman in the burqa and not Magda either.

I spoke little during dinner because every time I looked at Magda's mother or father, I imagined their reaction if they knew what Magda planned. Magda's father wanted to see improving relations between Muslim and Christians in Egypt, but I was certain his liberalism didn't extend to his daughter's affections. Magda's mom was a modern woman by local standards, loving and affectionate. Could she really pull away all that love over Magda's choice?

After dinner, I withdrew to my room. Maraya played with a box of little plastic dolls and furniture, which she had spread out across the entire room. I set the computer down on the desk and angled the screen, so her potentially curious eyes wouldn't see. There was nothing. He hadn't written.

I turned my attention to my history project and spent another hour researching Egypt. I opened the files my mother had sent and felt a more familiar type of angst set in as I began my first SAT prep test.

"So, what's it like to be Magda?" Maraya interrupted my thoughts.

"Excuse me?" I said.

"I mean, like, how's it going?" Maraya asked. She seated one of her dolls at a table loaded with bowls of plastic ice cream.

"Oh. Well, pretty good, I guess. She has a lot of good friends. So far, you're the only one who's on to me. You've been really good about keeping my secret. Thanks." I slipped a fingernail into my mouth and then decided to make use of this eight-year-old resource on the floor. "Maraya, can I ask you question?"

"Yeah, sure."

"What would happen if a Coptic girl fell in love with a Muslim boy here?"

"I dunno. It never happens. You're supposed to marry Christian." She placed a second doll at the table and added two plastic soda bottles.

"But what if you didn't?"

"Well, you can't marry if your mom and dad won't let you."

"Oh, I see. But our parents are different, right? They say marry for love."

"Yeah, but everyone knows that Christians always fall in love with Christians, and Muslims always fall in love with Muslims. That's just how it works."

"I see."

"Can you play dolls with me now?" she pleaded, bored with the conversation.

Reluctantly, I left my SAT test, climbed down on the floor and chose a red-haired doll. As sweet as Maraya was, I hate playing dolls, so I was much relieved when Mom announced it was her bedtime. Exhausted from my emotional day, I followed closely behind her.

I brushed out my long hair. Magda's long hair. Darn. I was starting to think of this body as mine. Of this life as mine. A dangerous thing to do, but it often happened after I'd been in a body a few days. I had to try and remain more detached, so I could think clearly.

One last peek at Facebook—nothing. I tucked the computer into my bed. I knew I wasn't going to sleep well until I heard from him, so I figured I'd keep checking.

I slipped into a long, white cotton nightgown and climbed under the covers. I closed my eyes and pictured my real mom—angled blonde bob, blue eyes, laugh lines, always rushing somewhere. I held the picture in my head for a long time. Then I turned the mental page to Gabrielle, her long blonde ponytail, blue eyes, skinny small and lithe, probably in the swimming pool. I had to hold on to these images to remember who I really was.

I might have drifted off; I'm not sure. Maybe it was just the same thoughts twirling around in my head. Maybe it was a dream. Suddenly, I heard a sharp noise.

Thwump.

I tensed, fully awake now. I'd been reading about terrorists online and immediately thought of gunfire. Maraya remained sound asleep, all twisted up in her sheets and lying sideways across the bed.

No more noise. Had I imagined it? I put my head tentatively back down on the pillow.

Thwumpity-thwump.

It was at the window. Something was hitting the window. I slipped out of bed, tiptoed to the window, pulled the curtain ever so slightly aside, and peeked out the corner.

In the darkness I made out a shadowy figure. It must be Ahmed! I slid the second-story window open and felt the warm night air rush in.

"Who is it?"

"Do you have any other secret admirers?" the shadow asked. His voice carried softly.

"Tonight?" I smiled into the darkness, "only you."

"Oh? And on the other nights?"

I gestured broadly to the night sky, "As many as you see stars."

"Then I suppose I'll have to burn the brightest!"

I laughed softly. "Not to worry. You're already like the sun in the midday sky," I said, and added, "Don't go anywhere!"

I slid the window shut. Maraya still slept. Trembling with fear and anticipation, I pulled the nightgown off and grabbed the nearest dress and shoes. My hair fell loose about my shoulders, very un-Egyptian, but I needed to be quick. As an afterthought, I grabbed the lucky bracelet off the dresser on my way out. I wouldn't tempt fate by leaving it behind. I tiptoed through the door and closed it silently behind me. I made my way through the darkened hallways of the apartment into the main lobby then through the front doors and out into the garden.

Where Ahmed waited for me.

There he was—his wavy hair loosely unkept, a hint of five o'clock shadow. His dark skin set off his light honey eyes. My God, he was gorgeous. And he was here. He was really here. And we were alone. I felt a rush of ecstasy.

"Magda," he said, and his voice broke as he took my hand. He drew me in closer. He reached out and touched my hair. "I've never seen your hair down—it's—stunning," he said.

"When you didn't write me back tonight, I thought you'd decided to end it," I whispered.

He looked at me oddly. "How could I write you? Your internet is down."

Crap! I did say that, didn't I?

"Oh—I—it's been fixed. I forgot to mention it."

"We can't stay here," he said urgently, "Come, let's go. I know a place where we'll be safe for a while."

He took my hand and his touch sent shockwaves through my body. He pulled me through the gates of the yard into the street. We climbed into his car, a Mercedes with a beige leather interior, and we sailed through near-empty streets. I felt exhilaration from his nearness but also pure white fear at the immensity of the risk we took. My blood coursed with adrenaline and made me hyper-aware of my surroundings—the touch of his hand, a lingering scent of leather cleaner, the soothing hum of the engine.

Egypt was surreal at this hour. I thought Cairo never slept, but apparently if it gets late enough, it dozes. We sailed over the bridge to Gaza, a street that had been solidly packed with cars last Saturday, but now we could've rollerbladed down the middle of it.

He pulled off the highway and our speed decreased markedly as the roads became narrower and the asphalt rougher. We hadn't spoken yet. I was too nervous for words. Ahmed took a slow, wide berth around an empty cart with a donkey still saddled to it. The donkey startled awake and brayed softly in annoyance as we motored past. We pulled into a quiet spot next to a faded blue concrete four-story building from which I could barely make out the name, J&B Saddlery, printed in English and Arabic.

Ahmed opened the door for me and took my hand again. I was wildly aware of his touch—its warmth, its softness—as he pulled me out of the car. He put his free hand to his lips to remind me to be quiet and opened a side door to the saddlery shop. The scent of straw and leather wafted out to meet us. A horse nickered from a distant stall in the darkness. We tiptoed up four flights of stairs, and he eased open a door onto a wide rooftop patio. Two sides were walled and painted the same faded blue as the rest of the building. The remaining two consisted of a short wall lined with whitewashed cement benches and covered in red and gold tapestry rugs. Worn, white plastic tables with metal fold-out legs and scattered white chairs furnished the space. The dark sky opened above us. Ahmed flicked a switch, and a web of white Christmas lights sprang to life, woven through a metal latticework rooftop. Simple, yet stunning. The night air, warm and comforting, welcomed us.

Beyond the odd nicker from the horses downstairs, it was near silence. Egypt held its tongue and waited for us to speak.

What was I doing?!

"This is my Uncle Abdullah's place," Ahmed voiced softly, motioning for me to sit. "I thought it would be a good place to talk. He has fifteen horses on the bottom floor in the stables. He and his three sons take the tourists horseback riding in the desert across the street there," he said, waving an arm in front of the saddlery shop. I imagined the dark desert sands where he gestured, but all was pitch black with a sprinkling of stars. "Most nights they ride well past sunset, and then they all sit up here and drink tea until midnight or so. Actually, the tourists rarely drink the tea. They prefer to bring the wine they can buy at the corner store down the street. Then they complain it tastes like fermented honey, or something. What do they expect? This isn't the south of France. I mean, I don't think the tourists realize we're strictly forbidden to drink alcohol. I'm rambling, aren't I? Anyway, my point is, it's nearly two o'clock, and my Uncle and my cousins are sound asleep on the second floor. They wouldn't hear a cavalry coming up these stairs at this hour."

What was I doing?!

We lowered ourselves onto a whitewashed bench, overlooking the black desert. I let go of his hand reluctantly. The outer wall of the building formed the back of our bench, and I leaned an arm over the edge—a three-story drop. I wondered if any of his uncle's drunken tourists had ever leaned a little too far and taken a tumble.

We sat awkwardly, side by side, our bodies angled toward each other, untouching. He held his hands together, rubbing a silver ring he wore on his right ring finger.

"What time do your parents get up?"

"Six-fifteen," I said. "I'd like to be in well before that though."

"Of course. If I have you home at quarter to six at the latest, would that be good?"

I thought about it. "That's probably fine," I said. "But let's err on the side of earlier." I popped a fingernail into my mouth unconsciously.

"Magda, I know this is a huge risk, but I don't think it's a mistake," he turned to face me directly, his expression sincere, pleading. "We have something really special. We need to spend time together, to look at each other when we talk and not just at some computer screen. We need to decide what we're going to do about us."

I nodded in agreement. "This is absolute madness, but you're right. We need to find out. That's why I'm here. So what do we do now?"

"We talk, I guess. Let's talk about you. I've read about you on a screen. Now I want to hear it all again from your lips. I want to know why you're so wonderfully different from other girls."

If only he knew how different Magda and I were from other people!

"But first you," I deflected. "Tell me all I should know about you. Tell me about—about your little brother Samir. He's nine, right? That's about the same as my sister, Gabrielle."

"Gabrielle? I thought her name was Maraya."

My face reddened. "I mean Maraya."

"You want to know about Samir? He's nine, and he's a handful, like

I told you. That boy never stops. He has enough energy to power Cairo in a heat wave. When he's bored, it's like the house is a pinball machine and he's the ball. But when he directs that energy—like to his beloved baseball—the kid's amazing.

"Baseball?" I asked. Baseball was an odd thing for an Egyptian kid to love.

"Yeah, I know. Weird, huh? But remember, my dad's last posting was in Washington D.C. We were there nearly five years. That's like practically Samir's whole life. They love baseball there, and if you want to fit in, well, it's easy if you play baseball. Better still if you're good. It's like instant respect. So Dad enrolled us both with a special batting coach. I hated it. No hand-eye coordination. I'm all feet. Soccer's for me. But Samir loved it from the moment he picked up a bat." he said.

"Tell me more about your dad's job," I asked.

"He's a diplomat. Before D.C. we spent two years in Germany and a year in England. The Department of State doesn't like you to spend too many years abroad at once though. I think they're afraid you'll become too much of a foreigner yourself. So we came back here last year. We always left Dad for a couple of months to spend summers here while we lived abroad, but this is the first time in eight years I've lived full-time in Egypt," he said.

"Is that why you hang out with so many foreigners?" I asked. In the cafeteria I'd seen him with a group of tall white kids.

"Do I? Oh, you mean Moe and Marcel. Marcel is Dutch. He's cool. You always know where you stand with him. And Moe, he's not a foreigner. Moe is short for Muhammad. He's pretty light-skinned I guess, but he's one of ours. Maybe those blonde streaks make him look American. Moe lived in California for four years. He's got a total surfer attitude. You can't be stressed around Moe," he laughed.

"You could be stressed around Kamal, though. I really don't get you and Kamal. He seems so different from you. He's like, all hard-edged and intense," I said.

"Kamal is family," Ahmed began. "I know he's got a reputation for being a bad kid, but he isn't really." He reached out with the hand closest to me and gently took mine. Electric shocks raced through me at the point of contact and spread a warm glow through my body. "Kamal's dad is my uncle. His mom died when he was really little. I've never really understood what happened to her. Everyone's really vague about it. She was in and out of hospitals a lot before she died. Anyway, Uncle Radwan was left to raise Kamal alone. I've never heard anyone say anything directly, but I think Uncle Radwan might have some radical ties my father doesn't want to be associated with. He keeps disappearing for months at a time," he said.

"Radical? You mean like terrorism?" I asked, incredulously.

"Not Al Qaeda, but maybe the Muslim Brotherhood. I know the Brotherhood says its renounced violence, and it doesn't have any radical elements anymore, but I don't believe it. How can the Brotherhood be peaceful and still allow a group as violent as the Palestinian Hamas to be an arm of its network? Al Qaeda is as violent a group as there is, and after Osama Bin Laden was killed, it was an Egyptian from the Brotherhood who took over. I haven't noticed any great movement toward peaceful means from Al Qaeda since then, have you?"

I shook my head.

"Anyway, I don't know for sure if Uncle Radwan has ties to the Brotherhood. It's just a rumor, but if you've ever met my uncle, you'd be inclined to believe them. He looks like some wild-eyed, malnourished Osama bin Laden character complete with the long beard. Kamal gets bounced around from family to family when he's gone, and he's lived with us a lot over the years whenever we were in Egypt.

"Until recently, he went to a really bad public school. He hated it. Can't blame him. When they pay teachers less than cab drivers, well, you get what you pay for. All the teachers ever did was make kids memorize things, and then they spent most of the day disciplining the ones who didn't. It didn't help that Kamal's kind of scrawny, a bit of a loner, and everyone thinks his dad's some kind of terrorist. The kids picked on him. He wanted out," he said, and his hand squeezed mine as he spoke.

"His father wasn't about to let him quit school, so you gotta respect how he got himself out. He walked in one day and picked the biggest, baddest guy in the school. We're talking about a kid who was two heads taller than him. A jock. Super popular. With an attitude. He waited for him at the end of the day. There was only one way to leave the school, and that was through the front doors, which passed right in front of the principal's office. He waited for the guy to come to the front doors then he dropped his books and just laid one on him, right in the face. Broke his nose. Right there in front of the principal."

"What about Kamal?" I asked. I couldn't imagine little Kamal fared well.

"Yeah, well, he busted a rib, and his face was pretty smashed up, but he got what he wanted," he continued. "He was kicked out of school, like, instantaneously. We had just moved back to Cairo, and we were seeing a lot of him, so Dad paid to send him to school with me. He had to use every connection he had to get him accepted, but Kamal's a bright kid and scored off the charts on the entrance test, so that helped. Still, with his record, he's totally on probation. One wrong move and he's out."

"Does he live with you guys now?" I asked.

"No. He lives with some cousins on the other side of town. It's a long commute for him every morning, but he doesn't care. He's way happier at our school."

The hours slipped away. Before I knew it, it was nearly four. Maybe we could talk for another half hour. I tried to keep the conversation on him as much as I could, but eventually the conversation came around to Magda's dad.

"He says he remembers when Christians and Muslims lived much more peacefully together than they do today, and he wants to see those times again," I explained.

"Do you feel the same?" he asked.

"Of course!" I retorted sharply.

"And that explains why we're sneaking around—how?" he said, and one eyebrow raised quizzically. "I mean, he's in favor of improving Christian/Muslim relations, right?" He smiled mischievously.

I slipped a fingernail into my mouth and chewed it contemplatively. I was ill-equipped for a battle of religions. "You're kidding, right? I know Dad thinks it's fine and good for Muslims and Christians to hang out and to work together and all that. He's totally cool with me having

Muslim friends, like Aisha. But where boys are concerned, it's a different story. I'm expected to marry a Christian."

I waited for some reaction to the word "marry." Not a cool thing to be bringing up on a first secret date. He didn't seem phased though, and his brow furrowed. "And how do you feel about that?"

I bit my bottom lip as I struggled to find the words to express what I had gleaned from my time here. "It sucks, of course. It's wrong. But it's the reality we live in. Some of it's about religion, of course. In Islam, the only way to heaven is if you believe that Allah is the one true God and Muhammad was his messenger, right?"

He nodded.

"Christians believe that the only way to heaven is through Jesus Christ. Eventually that could be a problem for any couple. Children only make it worse—they can't be raised in both religions, can they? Most of it's not really about religion at all though, is it? I mean a Muslim and a Christian marrying in the States, that's not a big deal," I stumbled, uncertain how Magda would know this. "At least, that's what I've heard. You'd know better than me. But here, if a Muslim converts to Christianity, that's considered treason, right?" I'd read that much online. One newspaper said radical Muslims were pressuring the government to allow the death penalty for leaving Islam. "So that's out. It's usually the Christian who turns Muslim. But I've heard of cases where the Coptic family kidnapped their own daughter to prevent her from converting." Ahmed watched me, intently.

"It shouldn't be like this," I went on. "Your religious beliefs shouldn't be threatened just because of who you fall for. I should be able to believe what I believe, and you should be able to believe what you believe, and we should still be allowed to care about each other, shouldn't we? Why can't we agree to disagree about religion? Mixed couples should be free to work it out in their own way. To, like, take turns going to church one week and the mosque the next, or just do their own thing religiously. Do you ever see something like that happening here?" I said.

"You mean, like, in reality?" he asked then answered himself. "In the real world, it'd be a long hard road to try to live that life in Egypt. That much is true. It's not accepted. But here's what *you're* not accepting—not being together, choosing to pass on what we feel for each other. That carries a heavy price too. Or am I being too forward?"

I thought for a moment. "I'm here, aren't I? I can't ignore my heart. What I feel for you— it's . . . it's overwhelming. It's absolutely wonderful. How can something like this not be a God-given gift?" I paused a moment before adding, "You know, in church last Sun—Saturday, the *Baba* read from the New Testament where Jesus says, 'I came that they (the people) might have *life* and have it to the *full*.' Not, 'I came so that you people could have an okay life,' or even, 'I came so you could live.' I can't ignore the fact that maybe I'm supposed to be with you. My heart is telling me that that's where life to the fullest may be. So maybe I'm not meant to follow the path that everyone else has mapped out for me," I said. He squeezed my hand affectionately as I spoke.

It was time to turn the tables. "We've been talking about what my parents think. What would *your* parents think if they knew you were seeing a Christian girl?"

He laughed, "We're strong Muslims, just like your family is strong Christians. Just like everyone in Egypt is strongly religious, I guess. We have to be passionate about everything in this country, don't we? But I really don't think Muslim families get as upset about mixed marriages as Christians do. Sure, it would be a lot easier to be together if you were Muslim. But would they forbid me to be with you? I don't know. I think most Muslims just look on Christians as— slightly under-informed. My folks would probably enjoy the challenge of trying to 'show you the light.' They would say you already believe in the same God as us. Allah, after all, is just God by another name. You've already found Moses and Abraham and Jesus. You're nearly Muslim already. Now you just need to find Muhammad."

I tensed. "Is that how *you* feel?" I thought our problem would be in figuring out how to coexist with two different religions. Would he want Magda to convert? That was not happening, not on my watch anyway. Magda's religion was not on the table. Maybe I was being naïve in trying to bring these two together.

He must've sensed the change in my demeanor.

"Magda, I don't want you to convert. I don't want you to change a thing about you that you don't want to change. Listen. What if—" he searched for words. "What if religion is really just the language we use to speak to God? I might speak through Muhammad, and you speak through Jesus, but the divine presence we're looking for is one and the same. Whether we bow to face Mecca when we pray, kneel at a pew, or—I dunno—stand on our heads—maybe God doesn't care. Maybe he'd rather that we were united in our love for Him, rather than divided by the words and books we choose to honor him by," he said.

I relaxed a little. "Then I don't think He would have the least bit of problem with a Muslim boy and a Christian girl bringing two different worlds a little closer," I added. A vague, orange glow had crept over the horizon, lifting the veil of darkness before us. There, not more than a mile away, the Great Pyramids of Giza rose from the sands. I stifled a gasp and lifted a hand to my mouth.

"Oh God! They're amazing!" Then a second thought hit me in rapid succession, "And we have to go!" I shot out of the seat.

"It's okay," he said calmly, without rising. "We have five minutes more. We could watch the sunrise here, at least if you want. The ride to your place takes fifteen minutes in afternoon traffic; this is early morning. If we leave at five-thirty, we will have plenty of time before your parents get up at six-fifteen," he said and then saw the panic in my eyes. "Magda, I won't make you late. That would be the end of these meetings, and I'm hoping we will have more. We can have five minutes more to watch the sunrise. But if it makes you too scared, I won't push you."

We had forty-five minutes to make a fifteen-minute ride, and I stood before the Great Pyramids of Egypt, silhouetted against the first fingers of dawn. If I shifted home soon, I might never see them again. I lowered myself nervously back onto the bench, and drank in every detail of the view. I had read about the Pyramids and seen pictures. The largest one was the last remaining of the Seven Wonders of the World, the Great Pyramid of Khufu, flanked by Khafre and Menkaure. Tracing their origins back to 3200 years before Christ, these great pyramids had presided over this view for more than 5200 years.

The pyramids began to emerge in detail from the shadows, revealing individual building blocks of stone, every one taller than a man. Each stone block was the size of a container on a rig. Each was cut and shaped from cliffs on the other side of Nile, lifted across the desert and raised up to be lain in precisely the appropriate spot. A slight error, and the pyramid would collapse.

What would the people who built the pyramids have contributed to our conversation, I wondered. They didn't believe in the God of Christians, Jews and Muslims. They believed in multiple gods. They believed the sun died every night and receded under the Earth to the goddess Nut where it traveled through her womb during the night to be reborn on the opposite side of the Earth each morning.

It sounded ridiculous to modern ears, yet the blood of those ancient Egyptians ran through these veins. Magda's ancestors had believed that. Maybe even Ahmed's. Ahmed reached over and touched my hand lightly.

"You know, wars were fought over gods like Amon and Isis," I said, "the gods these pyramids were built to honor." I felt torn between the majesty of the pyramids and the magnetic pull of his eyes. "And yet no one today believes those gods ever existed. How much time did they waste worshipping non-existent gods? In another thousand years, will anyone worship Jesus or honor Muhammad? Are we as wrong as them?"

Ahmed smiled and swallowed the bait. "God is in everyone," he said. "Whether they choose to find Him or not. I don't think God cares by what name or names you choose to call Him as long as you seek Him. Then he will answer to any name. Even Amon. What language we choose is our own business. The ancients were as right as we both are."

He leaned over and ran his hands through my long loose hair. He pulled me closer, and my world slowed until I felt that my whole life was balanced on the precipice of that very moment.

I have a confession to make. Unless I count a game of spin the bottle in grade eight, I had never really kissed a boy before. In books and movies, girls always look forward to their first kiss but not me. I dreaded it. I mean really—what do I *do* with my lips? How do I move them? How do I breathe? Am I supposed to use my tongue? How can that possibly be a nice thing?

My mom didn't allow me to date until I was sixteen, and since then the few times I did go on dates, I either said goodnight and hopped out of the boy's car before anything could happen, or if he walked me home, I thanked him and dashed inside and slammed the door behind me.

Now that the moment had finally come, I still didn't know what to do, but I felt something that hadn't been there with the other boys. It was some kind of primal desire to be close to him. For once, I didn't dart. I held my ground and closed my eyes.

His lips brushed mine gently. I held still, waiting for him to take the lead. Again, he moved his lips gently across mine. It was sweet and light, and yet it sent powerful waves of delight through my body. I wanted more. More of his touch. More of his warmth. I pressed deeper into the kiss, and then—

Abruptly, he stood. I opened my eyes in surprise, embarrassed. Had I done something wrong?

He was looking down at me, and I could see the fire behind his eyes, too.

He pulled me up gently from my seat.

"It's time for me to get you home before your parents or your sister find you missing." He led me by the hand across the patio toward the door then stopped again. He drew me in close one more time, and my body melted into the firmness of his. In that moment, I felt no fear. I didn't care what the future held as long as it held more of this. And then he pulled me through the door, down the stairs and back to the waiting car.

I dared to look at the clock on the dash. A shiver of fear ran through me. It was five-thirty. The city was awake. Forty-five minutes had seemed like plenty of time a few minutes ago, but now I wasn't so sure. I cringed inwardly as Ahmed touched the brakes for a group of three men in galabeyas who carried prayer mats and crossed the street in front of us.

"Hurry, Ahmed!"

"It's okay. I'll hurry, but don't worry. We'll make it." He gripped the wheel, his eyes riveted on the road.

All-ah hu Ak-bar, came the now familiar call broadcast through streets from each of the city's thousands of mosques. My heart quickened. It was the dawn call to prayer, the first of the five prayer calls that rang through the city daily. *All-ah hu Ak-bar.* God is great, I heard again.

We drove with increasing urgency. I willed the car to go faster. At ten to six we pulled off the main street onto the quiet residential side streets of Maadi, Magda's neighborhood.

Just twenty blocks from Magda's apartment, the car halted. The clock on the dash ticked off ten minutes as we inched down the street until we reached the source of the problem. The wind had toppled a cartload of melons on their way to the morning market, and traffic was being squeezed into a tiny path around the mess as three men worked to clean up. Dawn had turned to daylight. At two minutes to six, we finally sailed past the accident.

Ahmed waited in the car a few houses down until he had seen me through the front doors of the apartment. I slipped off my shoes and padded soundlessly up the stairs. I dashed through the apartment hallway, slowly and quietly unlocked Magda's front door, slipped inside and gently closed and locked it behind me. The muted clicks of the tumbler turning over were like thunder in my ears.

I crept through the darkened hallways of the apartment. I could hear quiet voices and see light under Magda's parents' bedroom door, and my heart pounded so hard in my chest I was afraid they would hear it. I raced on tiptoes past their door and into Magda's bedroom where Maraya lay twisted in her sheets, oblivious.

I willed my heart to slow as I slipped out of my dress into my nightgown and then climbed up into the top bunk. I closed my eyes and sent a silent prayer up. *Oh, God, show me what to do. This is true love, and I am totally lost in it.*

And then the alarm went off.

XVII

Exhaustion would hit later. Right now, pure relief flooded through me. I had made it home safely.

That morning a lightness flourished in my step, tempered only slightly by the guilt I felt when I looked across the breakfast table at Magda's family. I worried also that after our fight yesterday at lunch, Layla might not show up this morning to drive us to school. How would I explain her anger to Magda's parents? How would Maraya and I get to school?

But Layla did show. Sheepishly quiet. As we buckled up, she said solemnly, "Magda, I shouldn't have lashed out at you yesterday. If you like Mark, and Mark likes you, and you want to be together, that's up to you two. I just hope you're being honest with—she glanced into the backseat where Maraya chewed gum and played with her Wee Pets bracelet, "*everyone*, about this."

"Layla," I interjected, "I know this is hard for you to believe. I'm really *not* interested in Mark, not the way you are. He's a really great guy, and I like him, but I think you know he's not where my true interests lie."

"Really?" she said. "Then what were you doing with Mark the other day?"

"It's just what I keep telling everyone," I said. "Arabic."

"Hmmm. I guess. And does *everyone* believe that?" she asked.

"I think it'd be safe to say that—*everything* is going pretty well at the moment," I said. I tried to show her a quiet, confident smile, but my state of bliss was written all over my face. So much for playing my cards close.

She shook her head. "Wow. You're really moving forward with this? You and Ah—," one hand flew up over her mouth. "I hope you know what you're doing. I know I helped make it happen, but it was just a game then. A real relationship is crazy. I get how you feel about him and everything, but this is fire you're playing with now."

"You got that right," I said, my voice thick with double meanings.

The day went by in a wonderful haze. Love is an amazing state.

I actually found myself worrying a little that I might have to leave this body too soon. What if all I had to do was get Ahmed and Magda together? What if I was done? What a crash it would be to come back down to my own body right now. I mean, I still missed my mom and Gabrielle and everything—but I would also lose this really cool emotional state. I was pretty sure that even if I, as red-haired American Molly, were to walk right into the same room as Ahmed after all this, all I would feel is a little nostalgia. The spark was Magda's. I knew in my head this love was hers, not mine, but while I was in her body—well, it was my love too. For the moment.

There would be one definite benefit from this experience when I went home to Florida. I knew now what true love should feel like. I knew what to hold out for. There would be no more wasted time with so-so boys when I got my life back. Somewhere out there was a love like Magda and Ahmed's for me.

When the last bell rang, I gathered all my books into my backpack. I'd sort them out later; I was too tired. I hefted the wieldy sack onto my back and the force of it nearly knocked me off my feet. Moments later, I sped down the road with Layla.

I was tired but not so tired as not to notice when Layla blew right past the turnoff into Maadi.

"What's up?" I asked. "Where are we going?"

"Earth to Magda. Girlfriend, you really are not fully occupying that brain of yours today. It's Monday night so we're heading up the mountain to Verana's youth group."

"Oh, right," I said sheepishly. All I wanted was to get home to bed. Cairo had a mountain? Google hadn't mentioned this.

"Okay, now that I have you alone you're going to have to give me all the juicy scoop. What's going on, really? With you and Ahmed?" she said.

I bit my lip and suppressed a grin. "You—you know how we communicate, right?" I said, probing for her knowledge level.

"Duh. It was my idea, remember?"

"Right. Well, we've gone a step beyond that."

She hit the brakes reflexively. Horns blared. "Mother Mary! You're kidding, right?" she said.

"Not kidding."

"Where? *When*?"

"Last night. A secret place."

She gave a long, low whistle. "Girl, I hope you know what you're doing. If my Dad ever caught me sneaking around with a Muslim boy, he'd beat me senseless and marry me off to the nearest cousin by morning. I know Uncle Cyril is more liberal and is going to let you marry for love and everything, but a Muslim? You know he'd never be okay with that. Magda I love to see you so happy, but I'm scared of where this might go."

"Yeah," I said. "Me too. I can't imagine how this could end well for us together, but I can't imagine how it could end well apart either."

"Having a full set of limbs isn't a factor then?"

"Very funny."

A moment's silence followed, and the scenery gradually began to change. The smooth straight roads gave way to broken asphalt and windy narrow streets. The endless parade of tidy gray homes and storefronts fell into crumbly disrepair. Corrugated tin replaced asphalt roofs. A line of laundry crossed the street a few feet above our heads. Abruptly, the road began to climb.

"I'm really surprised you found the guts to do this. I specialize in guts, but I couldn't date a Muslim. You must really love him."

"Yeah," I said again. "I really do."

"So you're not going to tell me where you guys met?"

"I can't Layla. It's not that I don't trust you; it's just that the stakes are so high."

"I get it. It's okay. But you have to tell me this. Did he kiss you?"

I hoped that Magda's creamy complexion could hide a deep blush better than my own paper-thin skin, but apparently it couldn't. I smiled guiltily.

She shook her head wistfully. "Was it nice?"

"It was every flavor of nice on a single cone. It was delicious. But I only got a taste."

There was a hint of sweetness in the air now. What was it? I sniffed the air, and as the scent grew stronger, I realized suddenly it was putrid, not pleasant.

"Ooo-eeee! Your window is still open girl! What are you thinking? We're on the garbage mountain now. If you puke, you're going to have to clean my car."

"Sorry!" I cried, but the pungent stench already filled the car. I frantically rolled up the window and steeled myself against a growing wave of nausea.

A group of five or six children raced, laughing and shouting, across the street in front of us. In bare feet and threadbare clothes, they chased a red rubber ball. Layla touched the horn in warning, and they dispersed in front of us. The streets, very narrow now, necessitated tight quick turns. The road forked, and Layla forged ahead to the left and nearly plowed into a placid herd of pigs that gathered in the middle of the road and drank from a puddle. She slammed on the breaks and the pigs scattered. "Dang!" she cursed and put an arm across the back of the bench front seat as she craned around backward and reversed back to the fork. "I can't believe I missed that again. I keep doing that. Sorry pigs!" she shouted apologetically as she threw the car back into gear and resumed the treacherous drive up via the other fork in the road.

"How can they *live* like this?" I asked.

"I know. It's disgusting, but it's also kind of amazing when you think about it, isn't it? I mean, all the garbage of Cairo is here. All brought here by the *Zabbaleen,* one donkey cart at a time. Sorting it, bundling it and using every scrap. It's kind of impressive. They must be, like, the world's best recyclers. The pigs and goats eat the food. The paper, plastic and metal they sort, bundle and sell. Nothing's wasted."

I realized then that many of the little storefronts lining the road weren't storefronts at all, but rather storage rooms. Hundreds of neatly stacked bundles of paper wrapped in twine filled one room. Blue-tinted garbage bags of plastic bottles overflowed another.

An old woman in a dusty black, floor-length galabeya, trimmed with gay yellow embroidery, stitched in a plastic lawn chair outside a storefront. Clouds of dust wafted around her as we passed.

"There isn't a scrap of garbage lying around anywhere," I said, disbelieving. The streets, though dusty and wretched, had been swept meticulously with no garbage in sight, save for neat bags and bundles of plastic and paper. Only the pungent cloying stench was everywhere.

"I know, eh? Where do you think the unsorted stuff goes? I've never seen it. Just smelt it. Here where they live, it's as clean as anything."

"No idea."

She threw the wheel sharply to the left, and the car lurched around a corner at high speed. A fresh wave of nausea overwhelmed me, and I turned my complete attention to the road and the need to keep the contents of my last meal safely tucked away.

Then as suddenly as the mountain had begun, it ended. The car sailed up into a great clearing.

Red craggy cliffs bordered one side of the rocky open area. To the right, over the edge of the mountain, sprawled the massive city of Cairo, concrete buildings and roads spreading out chaotically. To the left, the craggy cliffs as its backdrop, stood a perfect little church, its clean yellow lines bathed in late afternoon sunlight, contrasting against the deep shade of a mountain crevice behind it. Two high domes stretched skyward, crowned by Coptic crosses and framing a third, lower dome. The view was breathtaking.

"It's a church!" I blurted out in surprise.

"Okay, hon. Now, I'm really starting to worry about you."

"I mean, I know it's a church. It's just so amazing, isn't it? To find a beautiful church on the top of a garbage hill."

"Yup. Talk about taking lemons and making lemonade right? That's the *Zabbaleen* all right. I suppose it takes a lot of faith to get out of bed in the morning when you live and work here," she said.

We left the car and walked out into the clearing. A light breeze blew across the mountaintop and reduced the stench to a mildly unpleasant sweet odor.

"Why are there only Christians on this mountain? Where are all the Muslims?" I knew I shouldn't have asked as soon as the words were out of my mouth.

"Muslims? *Muslims*? Magda, honey, this is just the last straw. What planet is your brain on? There are no *Muslims* here. This is Mokattam Mountain! It's the Christians who clean up the garbage in Cairo! Now you know that, and I know you know that. So what's going on with you?"

"Hey! Layla! Magda! We're over here!" I recognized Verana's smart, shoulder-length bob as she beckoned us over. Verana was part of Magda's friend group, and I'd glimpsed her in the cafeteria a few times but never spoken to her.

"I just meant, the Muslims are, like, missing out on a great message here," I said as we changed tacks to meet her.

She furrowed her brow. "You're a weird one, Magda," she said and then she shrugged. "I love you, but these days I never know what you're going to say or do next."

Verana waved us into a whitewashed building where a group of about ten girls stood. Most were dark-skinned, slightly dusty girls in plain dresses. I guessed they lived on the mountain. In the middle stood Demiana, her black hair pulled back into a high ponytail that exploded with curls. I smiled at her in greeting, and she waved and smiled back.

"Mr. Elmasry says we're to help with the papermaking today," Verana announced. The sharp cut of her black bob stayed rigid and unmoving despite the light wind that swept across the mountain top. Deftly, she broke us up into groups to work on various projects throughout the facility.

"Magda, you come with me. We're going to the church."

I slipped into place beside her, and we started walking.

"Mr. Elmasry is building a website to get more volunteer tourists up here, and he wants it translated into English for them," she explained. "You and I are the best at English, so I thought this'd be a good thing for us to do."

Volunteer tourists? I opted to hold my tongue this time.

She took me around behind the little yellow church. It turned out it wasn't a church at all but more like a facade. Behind its humble little yellow domes was the most unexpected thing I could have ever imagined. A cave. Not a regular cave like the kind with bears, but a great cavernous cave. It seated, at a glance, probably five thousand—about double what the theater in my hometown of Tampa could hold. It was narrowest at the central pulpit area and then expanded in an ever-broadening semicircle with row upon row of pews. Yellow and gray layers of bare stone formed the cave walls, and bore the marks of chisels. The cool, damp air tasted musty but felt refreshing after the oppressive heat outside.

I tell you the truth, I read carved into the wall near where we stood, *if you have faith as small as a mustard seed, you can say to this mountain, "Move from here to there," and it will move. Nothing will be impossible for you.*

Biblical characters were carved in relief and wore coarse robes tied at the waist. The ceiling wasn't flat. It spread out like an amphitheater, narrow near the pulpit and broad and tall near the edges of the cave. Over the pulpit, Jesus loomed, carved in intricate detail on the cross. Like on the crucifix in Magda's room, blood dripped from the wound in his chest and ran down his forehead crowned with thorns.

Mr. Elmasry, a plump middle aged-man with black plastic glasses, sported a black T-shirt, black jeans and black sandals. He waved to us from a small door off the main cave.

"Ah, Verana, darling," he said as we weaved down the stairs and between the pews to him. "How's the youth group going today? You are such a blessing to His church. What would we do without you?"

"Thank you, sir," she said. "The girls are helping with the paper, like you asked. Magda here is brilliant at English, and she says she can help with your website."

Funny. I didn't remember saying any such thing.

He took us into one of a couple of rooms carved into one of the sidewalls. A small desk that stood against one wall struggled under the weight of a blocky old PC computer with a boxy monitor and a dot-matrix printer. I surveyed the setup doubtfully.

Mr. Elmasry laughed. "Don't worry. Pavli keeps this baby up to date," he slapped the hard drive tower on the table beside the monitor. "Under the hood, it's got all the megs and rams or whatever it is you need to make it work. We need a new printer, I know, but we just don't have the money right now. The marvel is that he can keep that old thing working. It belongs in a museum, doesn't it? You'll be fine. Give me a shout if you need anything," he said as he left.

Verana and I pulled up chairs and began reading. The draft website on the screen had already been roughly translated into English but needed a pretty serious overhaul to be understandable.

"Why are we translating this into English, anyway?" I asked as I skimmed the material.

"It's to try to bring in more volunteer tourists. This website is geared to England, Australia and America. If we could have a dozen volunteers around here most of the time, we could do an awful lot."

"I bet."

"Yeah. We want the text to target Christians. We need it to sound exciting because volunteer tourists are adventurous types. They're people who want to see the world and do good while they're there. Volunteer tourism is already big in India and places like that, so why shouldn't we make it big here? Instead of seeing the pyramids in some tour bus, leaving empty Coke cans and going home, they come here, see how people really live and leave the country a little better than they found it. Good, eh?"

"Cool." I bent over the page.

The site explained that papermaking was one of several businesses in the area that had been set up to give underprivileged Coptic women an opportunity to earn an income. The cash infusion generated a social as well as an economic impact, giving these women more respect within their male-dominated culture and, in some cases, independence. It also increasingly allowed them to send their children to school, rather than putting them to work as soon as they were old enough to do so.

The homemade paper was transformed into greeting cards and other stationary products, which were then sold in Cairo's trendier areas.

I set to work on a boxed article at the left side of the site. It was called "The Miracle of Mokattam." The tenses were jumbled up throughout the article, but the gist of it was this: In the tenth century, the Caliph challenged the Coptic Pope to prove that a man with faith the size of a mustard seed could move a mountain. This was Christ's pledge in the Gospel of Mathew, and to make the challenge interesting, the Caliph said he would kill all the Copts if the Pope failed to meet the challenge.

The Pope prayed, and in his prayers, the Virgin Mary told him to go to the market and look for a one-eyed man carrying on his shoulder a jar of water. He went to the market, and there he found Simon the Tanner, a modest man who had plucked out his own eye because of another verse in Mathew: *If your right eye causes you to sin, gouge it out and throw it away. It is better for you to lose one part of your body than for your whole body to be thrown into hell.*

Simon told the Pope to bring his monks, priests and elders to the mountain where he was to shout, *"O, Lord, have mercy,"* three times and make the sign of the cross over Mokattam mountain each time.

The Pope did as he was told. To the amazement of onlookers, the mountain shifted as they watched. The Coptic people rejoiced, and Simon the Tanner disappeared into the crowd, never to be seen again.

In front of the computer, we went to work. About half an hour later, Verana and I had a product that we felt confidant tourists would find quaint and amusing. We ambled slowly back to the rest of the group.

"I'm really going to miss this place," Verana said.

"I can imagine," I answered, cautiously.

"Don't start," she said sharply. "I already know how you feel. We're just different, you and me. Marriages for love rarely work out."

I held my tongue.

"Besides. I'm sure he'll settle down once he's married. And I'll love Alexandria. I've always wanted to live near a beach."

Silence.

"He's very handsome, you have to admit."

"Yes," I said.

We were at the edge of the group now, and the low, constant whistling of a spring breeze was pierced frequently by the giggling of the girls as they worked.

"It's the right thing to do, Magda."

"Of course." Feeling I needed to fill the conversational void, I added, "Is it all planned out then?"

"The plans of the diligent lead surely to abundance, but everyone who is hasty comes to poverty," she said.

The group was now heavily absorbed in the papermaking process, the scent of vinegar sharp and poignant. Layla stirred a vat of bright red liquid, while one of the local girls poured a clear fluid from a large rusty tin into the vat. The local girl looked to be about twelve, and her black hair was pulled up on both sides into French braids, which met and formed a single braid at the back. Little dusty white silk flowers had been pushed through the braids. A cell phone bulged incongruously from the pocket of her dress. Most of these kids probably didn't have running water, but most of them had phones. I guess kids everywhere are pretty much the same. We long to feel connected.

A fresh wave of exhaustion swept over me, and I closed in on Layla. "D'you think we can get going soon?" I asked.

"Yeah, I guess so," she said, wiping her hands on a heavy, soiled apron. "I've got a ton of homework. Wouldn't hurt to get an early start."

I fell dead asleep within minutes of the car starting. I missed the hair-wrenching turns, the smell, all of it. I just couldn't keep my eyes open. The next thing I knew, Layla shook me by the shoulder.

"Wow, were you ever out. You were, like, the world's most boring best friend ever. You owe me. Again."

I stumbled inside just as dinner was being served. Magda's father said grace, and we picked up our forks. I poked the food around my plate. I did my best to keep my face out of the peppered potatoes.

"Magda, honey, aren't you well?" Magda's mom asked after a couple of moments.

"I'm fine, Mom. I'm just not hungry, and I'm kind of tired."

"It's that mountain," she shook her head. "You're doing God's work there, but that smell always takes away your appetite," she said.

I helped with the dishes after dinner then went straight to the bedroom. Homework, a run, hefting some beans, none of it was happening. I booted up my computer while I changed. There was a note from Florida. Mom said Magda was holding up well in my classes and was actually improving my biology grade, but she couldn't do a French accent and my French teacher Madame Lorraine was getting concerned. My friend Sandra made the lead in the school play which was doubly good—one, because she had an amazing voice and would be great and two, because she'd be too busy to hang with me/Magda for the next few weeks. It's always best for a shifter in my body to be alone with Mom and Gabrielle as much as possible. Fewer things go wrong.

I logged onto Facebook. Ahmed was online already.

Miss you already, where have u been? he asked.

Verana's youth group on the mountain, I answered. *Such an incredible church in the midst of such poverty.*

That church is supposed to be amazing. At the top of a garbage mountain. It's like a flower in the desert, right? There is too much poverty in this country. Christian poverty, Muslim poverty. Poverty knows no religion. It's the root of all Egypt's troubles. Too often it leads to ignorance and violence, not beauty.

Before I could compose an answer, another text line appeared: *How do you keep going? I went home and took a nap.*

I'm falling asleep at the keys.

Get some sleep. Night xoxo

Night xoxo

I set my alarm, so I could get up early to do my homework. If any pebbles rattled my window that night, I missed them.

XVIII

I felt completely renewed after a good night's sleep. Everything was going well. I'd helped Magda make the decision she desperately wanted to make but couldn't. I'd survived and even enjoyed my first kiss, and tasted real love. Now I was ready to shift home.

I spent fifth period study hall in the air-conditioned library, but my mind remained far too occupied to be tempted into the world of Honors Algebra II. I let my fingers wander through my email and then went to Magda's regular Facebook account.

The news feed appeared largely uneventful. A couple of kids prattled on about some new movie; someone posted a group picture of four girls making silly faces at the mall. I recognized Demiana as one of them, her eyes crossed and her arm around one of the other girls.

I found a new friend request and clicked the button to see who it was.

There staring right at me from a photograph was me. Copper-haired me. Molly.

I remembered the photo. Sandra took it at a sleepover at her house a few days before I shifted. It showed my best friend Bethany and me, our faces angled together. The picture was cropped tightly to reveal just our eyes, our smiles and a hint of hair around the edges.

I slammed the computer shut reflexively. Was this even possible? What would happen if we made direct contact? Would we, like, mess with the space-time continuum or something? What should I do?

I decided it would be a disaster to friend Magda. Did I really want her snooping around asking questions about everything I did with her life?

Then I decided it would be dumb not to friend her. She'd be a pretty good resource, after all, when I wasn't sure what to do. She might even have questions to ask me about my own life. Besides, it'd be pretty weird if I didn't answer her request.

Slowly, I opened the laptop again. There I was, staring at me again, asking to friend me.

I clicked on the photo to see my page. I keep my privacy settings high, so without friending me, I couldn't read my own newsfeed. All I could see was my friends list, 440 friends. Cool. The tally was at 438, last I looked. Wait a sec. Who were my new friends?

One was a girl I'd never seen before, and the other was Samuel Abbas. I winced. Really? Samuel? He's not someone I'd normally friend. He's a fairly nondescript guy with dark hair and dark eyes, very quiet, super smart. In bio class, when we exchange marks after a test, no one ever asks Samuel. He always gets 100.

Oh wait—I get it. Dark hair and dark eyes—he's Middle Eastern, isn't he? Is he Egyptian? I racked my brain. Then I remembered. On my birthday once, I brought donut holes to class, and he didn't take one because he was fasting for Ramadan. My friend James teased him that the sun had gone down in Cairo, so he could eat them. Yup, Magda'd found a friend from home.

The clock in the bottom right hand corner of Mozilla Firefox showed I had twenty minutes before my next class.

Without allowing myself to think any further, I pushed the button to friend her.

Then I wandered over to my/Molly's home page.

Before I could start perusing my life, the little chat bubble in the bottom right hand corner of my screen popped to life and announced Molly was online.

Florida is great and everything, but really, you didn't have to shift me. I could've just sprung for a plane ticket like everyone else:)

I typed:

lol. I wish I did this on purpose! This is amazing—being able to talk to you like this. I've never spoken to another shifter. I guess you haven't either, huh?:) Is this is your first time shifting? I had yet to meet another repeat shifter.

You could say that. Bit of a surprise. I managed not to scream until I looked in the mirror.

Bad hair day, huh? I get those a lot, I typed.

lol. . . I love your hair. And your family is really nice! Your little sister makes me miss Maraya.

Ditto. Maraya's a sweetie. Is mom taking you to Disney and everything?

Disney is amazing! Universal too. I love roller coasters. . . and I feel strangely at home in Harry Potter World:)

She was funny. I wondered if we could have been friends in a normal world.

You seem to be adjusting really well, I wrote.

Her tone shifted. *It's getting easier. Molly, this is the hardest thing I've ever done. I'm doing my best but I'm so scared I'm going to say or do something dumb and screw things up for you. Some days I wish I could just stay in bed. And I miss my family so much.*

I know what you're going through. I'm doing my best for you too, k?

When do you think we'll shift back? She asked.

Mom and I had discussed this a couple of years ago. Mom always faced this question from the shifters. She had learned that if she mentioned my theory that I had to fix something in their lives before we could shift back, it made them scared about what was going on in their own lives. It was better to just let them think shifting was random.

I dunno, I answered.

I decided to make use of this connection with Magda. I typed: *Magda, can you tell me about Ahmed?*

The cursor blipped at me for a while.

What do you want to know?

This was kind of awkward. I mean, technically, I was making out with her boyfriend. Wasn't I?

Everything you think I should know. Do you want to be with him?

More than anything. But it's impossible, she replied.

Why not? I mean, I only feel resonances of your emotions, but this love you have, I've never known anything like it. I think this is a once in a lifetime thing. I had no idea I/you could feel this way. if I ever find a love like this in my life, no way is he getting away.

Do you really feel all my emotions when I'm/you're with him?

Knocked me off my feet the first time your emotions hit me. Literally, I fell. Magda, I've shifted before. Not much as a teen, I admit, but enough that I think I can say this kind of love isn't an everyday thing.

Really?

Really.

I miss him, she wrote. *Is he ok?*

He's fine, I typed. *You really should fight for this.*

I want to more than anything, but I would have to give up everything. My family, my friends, everything. Too many Coptic girls have ruined their lives this way.

You could just pass on this kind of love? What if you never find another love like this?

Another silence.

It's impossible. You have American values—love will conquer all and nevermind everything else. My everything else is very important to me too.

Oops. Guilty. I guess I had kind of blundered in that way. I knew there was a price to be paid for this love. I had to remember that the question wasn't whether or not I was willing to pay the price—it was whether or not Magda was willing.

Molly, be careful k? Don't do anything crazy.

This was not the time to mention that we'd shared a secret rendezvous. I was going to have to tell her someday, but if I told her now, she'd panic and try to persuade me not to do it again. Letting her direct her life from Florida wasn't the answer. If she had all the answers, I wouldn't be here. My job was to get the two of them together long term, and I was going to have to do it my own way. I had no idea how, but neither did she.

It was time to gather up my books.

So if I could find a way for you and Ahmed to be together and not lose everything else, would you let me make it happen?

You're a shifter, not a magician. You know exactly how much I'd love it, but Molly, please don't try. I've got too much at stake. It's impossible.

Got it. Gotta run

I closed the browser and powered down.

I hate the word impossible.

XIX

For the next few days, I ran at school everyday and lifted my cans at home. I volunteered at the cave church again. I wrote to Magda daily. I didn't get another chance to chat live with her because of the seven-hour time difference and because Magda in Florida only gets one study hall every tenth school day. When she was home in the evenings, it was the middle of the night in Egypt, and when I was home in the evenings in Cairo, she was in school. Or at the beach, as it turned out. Lucky. My body spent a lot more time at the beach than I ever did. And why did everyone in my body have to learn for the first time that redheads burn in the sun?

I avoided talking to Magda about what was going on with Ahmed. I felt horrible for not being more open with her, but I was here to bring Ahmed and Magda together and doing so involved taking risks Magda was afraid to take. If she approved of my methods, she'd have tried them herself. I hoped to be like a surgeon operating on her life—she didn't need to watch the gory details of my work in the O.R. to appreciate the results. I wished I was more confident in my own surgical abilities, but I would do the best I could.

Instead, I grilled her about the other people in her life and learned as much as I could.

Layla's the best, she wrote one day. *She's my cousin and my—like you say here—my BFF. When I'm feeling down she's guaranteed to pick me up. But if I ever need advice, Demiana has a knack for seeing through the murk, then telling it like it is. It isn't necessarily what I want to hear, but always what I need to hear. She's had a tough go at life. Her mom had her out of wedlock and is raising her alone. I gather that'd no big deal in America, but in Egypt its hugely shameful. She's at the academy on scholarship. She must've blown their socks off on the tests to overcome her background. Anyway, her advice is golden.* I tucked that away for future reference.

I can tell you hate Kamal, I said. *What's up with that?*

He's a religious bigot, she wrote. *The whole school knows his uncle is anti-Christian. He always gives me dirty looks in the hallway and tosses out provocative anti-Christian comments in class. Nothing that could ever get him in trouble, just testing the edges of what he can get away with. He's begging for a fight,* she said. *It's the only thing that worries me about Ahmed. I don't get why they're always together. You are who your friends are, right?*

While Magda and I exchanged a daily note, Ahmed and I wrote each other every spare moment and chatted constantly online. At night, I got so I would wake at the slightest noise—the twists and turns of Maraya or the noise of the air conditioner coming on or off. I was always on alert for the pebbles on my window. Ten days after our first *rendezvouz*, they came again. And five days after that. Four days after that. He tried to email if he was coming, but that didn't always work out. One time his father stayed up too late, and he had to cancel. Another time a track meet was cancelled, and Ahmed appeared unexpectedly.

Always we went to the same rooftop. I began to think of the pyramids as our own personal backdrop. We spoke of everything. We spoke of politics, and war. We dissected the lives of Fatima and Mark and Layla, Marcel, Moe and just about everyone else. We didn't shy away from touchier subjects. I could ask him anything. Was this my love? Or Magda's? It was becoming harder and harder to tell the difference.

He sat opposite me, rubbing his silver ring, a crescent and moon on a black background. I reached over and held his hand in mine and examined the ring. "Why the crescent and moon, anyway?" I asked, touching it. It was warm from his fingers. "I mean, I know it's a Muslim symbol, but I don't know what it represents in Islam."

"It's like your cross." He gently held my wrist and fingered one of the cross charms on my bracelet. "To lots of Muslims, the star represents the five pillars of Islam, but if you look up the history of the crescent and moon, it's actually just a pagan symbol. The Ottoman Empire adopted it as a symbol, and it's been seen as Muslim ever since."

"What are the five pillars again?"

"The five things we have to do." He held out a hand and ticked them off. "First, there's the creed, which says, "There is no God but Allah, and Muhammad is his prophet". Second, there's the daily prayers. Third is fasting during Ramadan. Fourth is almsgiving, which is basically charity. And fifth, we have to make the *hajj*, a pilgrimage to Mecca, once in our lifetime, if we can."

Islam was a demanding religion. "I've always wondered about the prayers. Do you have to do the prayers during prayer call? I hear the calls all through the city, but not everyone drops down and prays every time. Thank God, I suppose, since many of you are driving," I laughed.

"No, it's like a reminder. You hear the call, and you go if you can. It's five times a day, starting at sun up. If you can't go when you hear the call, you just go later when you have a minute. Though I admit sometimes they do pile up."

"Do *you* always do it?"

"Pretty much. Sometimes I just do quick recitations when I'm in a hurry, but if I have time, I turn myself over to Allah for a few minutes. Especially at night. I find it calms me. Puts things in perspective. I've been praying a lot about you and me lately."

"You have?"

"I'm sure you have, too."

"Yeah." I lied. I couldn't meet his eyes. I cast my eyes down in an attempt to look pensive. I probably should pray more. That's what Magda would do, right? And I was Christian too. Praying just wasn't something I often thought to do, outside of church.

"I've never had the nerve to ask this. How come in Islam women have to cover up and men don't? Is that something in the Koran?"

He laughed. "Well, I guess because men are weak, and women are strong," he laughed. "You tempt us constantly with your hair and your curves, but you seem to be immune from temptation no matter how much we pump our biceps," he sighed with feigned exasperation. "But seriously, lots of Muslim women choose not to wear the hijab," he said, using the local word for a headscarf. "My mother doesn't wear it. It's a choice. Mom says as long as she wears her hair conservatively and dresses modestly, she interprets the Koran in an appropriate, contemporary way. Other women take the Koran more literally."

He reached over and ran his hands through Magda's long silken hair. "When I look at your hair, I see what they mean," he said, smiling. "How you can ever have a moment free from the eyes of men with hair like yours, I'll never know," he said.

My eyes widened—would he want Magda to cover her hair one day? That was *so* not happening. I loved her hair.

"No—I'd never want you to cover yours!" he said, reading my mind. "I want all the men to be jealous of me," he laughed. "Besides, it's your choice, not mine."

"Is it always the woman's choice?"

"Of course! Well, I guess I shouldn't say that. Among the vast majority of *educated* Muslims around the world, it's the woman's choice. But there are those radicals in every country, especially places like Pakistan and Afghanistan, where the men treat the women like animals and make them wear the hijab or even the burqa. Their kind make up less than one percent of all Muslims, but I know from when we lived in Washington that lots of people in the States think all Muslim women are forced to wear the headscarf by their husbands and fathers. It's just not true."

On our next night alone, I confronted him about Kamal.

"He's always shooting me dirty looks. Does he know about us? Is that why he hates me? Because he's jealous? Or does he hate all Christians equally? I mean, how can you hang with someone like him?"

"Kamal's a good guy he's just pretty confused," he said. "You gotta remember what he's been through. His father, my Uncle Radwan, was never the same after his wife died. He neglected Kamal, stayed up late, went away for long weekends with his new friends and left Kamal with family.

"Eventually, the trips turned from long weekends into weeks. He never said what he was doing, but there were hints. I remember overhearing a huge fight between him and my father because he thought Dad should force my mom to wear the hijab, things like that."

"Where do you think he was going? Saudi Arabia or Pakistan or something?" I asked. I thought of what Magda's dad had said about the doctrines that radicals learned abroad.

"We don't know for sure," he said. "Anyway, as Kamal got older, he started to change. He's always been an emotional firecracker. I guess he started looking for a cause to get fired up about. He could've turned to my father as a role model, or to any of his other uncles, but in his father's cause, he saw the chance to be a warrior.

"Two summers ago, Kamal left before the whole public school thing I told you about. He went abroad with his father. Nothing we could say or do could make him stay—not without closing his eyes and ears to us forever.

"I still don't know anything about what happened that summer. He was gone two long months. Then suddenly, he was back. The doorbell rang one August morning and there he stood. He never spoke of where he went or what happened, but he was changed. He's not a warrior anymore. He still has a temper and likes to provoke people, but that's just his way. Wherever he was and whatever happened, I think he made the right decisions. Now when his father's in town, Kamal refuses to see him. He never even talks about him." Then he added, with emphasis, "Nor do we."

"Of course," I replied.

Those four nights on the rooftop were bliss. The pebbles came always around two when everyone was fast asleep. At my request, Ahmed always brought me back before five. I didn't want any more close calls like the first time.

The terror I felt that first night when I snuck out of the house and into his car gradually lessened into something more like nervousness. Our dates seemed less risky because we were getting away with them.

Over those four nights, the feel of his hand in mine and his touch on my face became wonderfully familiar. We spoke of a thousand things, and sometimes we spoke of nothing at all, but just as many words passed between us. Only one topic did we actively avoid: we never spoke of the future beyond our next meeting. We never spoke of the consequences of denying our parents' wishes—of what our classmates would do or say if they knew about us. We didn't talk about running away. We lived for that time in a sweet bubble of denial as the flickering wonder of our new love grew day by day more steadfast and timeless and as constant as the moon over the pyramids.

With each meeting, we kissed. The awkwardness of that first kiss passed and in its place grew something deeper, warmer and more urgent. Each kiss lasted longer than the one before. Our bodies wanted more.

I guess we should've known that love is a physical addiction as well as emotional. The times in between our visits became harder to bear. Talking on Facebook, while it cooled the flames a little, was becoming less and less satisfying.

That's how we got ourselves in trouble.

XX

We neared the end of *Romeo and Juliet* in English class. The lovestruck pair had been secretly married, and Juliet was about to take the poison that would simulate her death.

Ahmed and I took more risks. We brushed past each other in the hallways and pretended it was accidental, just to feel close. I turned my head a little to peek at him behind me in class, and his eyes met and held mine. It was an exciting game. We thought no one noticed.

As we left English class, he pushed past me. "Behind the PE equipment lockers, twelve o'clock," he said under his breath. Then the throng of kids and backpacks and computers swallowed him.

Layla reminded me that Ahmed and I courted danger by meeting together in person again and again. I knew she was right. Now he wanted to see me in school. Meeting him here was a very bad idea; I knew it with every fiber of my being. I also knew without the slightest doubt that I was going.

The dirty, gray padlocked PE equipment lockers spanned a twenty-foot long wall. They stored tennis rackets, basketballs and other athletic equipment at the far end of a multi-purpose asphalt court. Twelve o'clock was right after the lunch bell. Everyone would have put their equipment away and cleared the PE fields and the asphalt. No one would be there until next period.

But it was only 10:45 a.m., and I had to get through PE before our meeting. In my month in Magda's body I had never let up on my workout regime and had taught Magda's muscles all the lessons that four years of varsity track experience in Florida had taught me. When the lessons moved from my short-term memory into her muscle memory, all I had to do was build her strength. Within a brief time, Magda's form had become pretty darn flawless. To anyone paying attention, she showed meteoric improvement.

Maybe if our meeting hadn't been the same day I finally beat Fatima in the one hundred meter hurdles, things would've been different.

It was a regular race like any other race in the PE unit, nothing special. Not to anyone else, anyway. The sky was unbroken blue, and the sun beat down on us. I still didn't have the stamina to touch Fatima in the longer races. She had amazing quads that gave her bursts in a straight sprint, but Magda's body had a long-legged gait like a gazelle that gave her an edge in the hurdles.

I hunkered down at the starting line. We formed a perfect chorus line, six runners all crouched low in matching navy shorts and gray PE shirts. Our bright white running shoes stood out on the dusty red track. I took the inside lane—Fatima two lanes over. I had no idea who else was racing. All I cared about was whipping Fatima's butt. Maybe losing would teach the scorpion goddess a little humility.

The gun went off, and I gave everything I had to the starting sprint, but she was still ahead when we hit the first hurdle. I focused on keeping my lead leg up. Then I just felt the rhythm of the hurdles flow through me, and with each jump I edged further ahead until we were abreast.

By the last jump, I was five feet ahead. Cheers of "Go, Magda!" erupted from the dozen kids who had tuned in to watch the race. Few of them realized how far Magda had come in just over a month.

I knew the straightaway at the end would be my challenge because Fatima's sprint was still faster, so I spent every ounce of strength I had. I resisted the urge to look back to see where she was, but I could see her in my periphery, gaining.

I went over the final line about six inches ahead of Fatima. Layla, Aisha and Demiana nearly knocked me over as they ran up and hugged me and squealed with joy. Mark stood behind them and smiled.

It felt good to beat her. I glanced over to see Fatima walking off the run alone. Baysaan came up beside her and tried to put an arm around her, but she shrugged it off. Even as I watched Fatima sulk off the field, it never occurred to me that making her eat a little dust could be anything but great news for Magda. Kids would talk about this for a long time. I thought Magda'd thank me.

Coach Robert's came over. "Hey, Magda! What an amazing run! I'm impressed. You really seem to have a natural ability on the hurdles. You ever think about joining the team?"

"Really?"

"Come talk to me after school. My office."

Would Magda want to join the varsity team? I mean, really, how cool is that? Wouldn't anyone? I wondered if I should talk to her online before I joined the team. Just in case.

And then it was time to change. I raced through the shower, elated. I threw on my uniform, spritzed myself with perfume and a minty mouth spray. I slammed my locker shut, hustled top speed back outdoors and hung a left toward the PE fields. They were deserted. I checked behind me. No one. I crossed the asphalt. As I approached the lockers, I looked back one last time to make sure no one watched. I gasped as a hand reached out and grabbed me and yanked me behind the lockers.

"Ahmed!" I laughed as he pulled me in close. The musky scent of his body so near was intoxicating, and I fell into his now familiar arms with delight. He wasted little time with words.

"I missed you so much!" Ahmed said breathlessly.

"You just saw me two periods ago!" I laughed between kisses.

"It was too long!"

"Oh, Ahmed, the more I get of you, the more I want."

"*Carpe Diem*!" he said.

"What?"

"It means, seize the day, remember?" He kissed me long and hard this time, and I felt his firm chest press against me. The world around me faded away, and all I could think of was the burning need to get as close to him as physically possible. Ahmed broke the kiss and chastised me, "Now get back to class, you!"

He kissed me one more time, and as I leaned into it, I heard the faint but distinctive electronic *click* of a cell phone camera. I broke free from his embrace and turned toward the sound.

Halfway back to the school, cell phone in hand, Fatima sprinted.

Ahmed pulled himself together first and ran after Fatima. He shouted for her to stop, but she raced toward the school. I stayed, half hidden behind the PE lockers. I know I should've raced after her, but my head wasn't screwed on yet. Weeks of sneaking around had instilled in me an instinct not to be seen with Ahmed.

But when I looked out from behind the equipment lockers, I saw him slamming his fist against the brick wall beside the entrance to the girls' locker room. Panic welled up inside me.

I didn't know what I was going to do when I found her. Wrestle the phone from her and delete the photo? Persuade her? Threaten her? Ahmed didn't say anything when I ran past him. He looked at me and at the door. I went in.

I braced myself for confrontation, but she wasn't there. She had left through the door at the other end of the locker room, the one leading back into the school hallways.

I burst through the hallway door. The deserted hallways were silent. There was no sign of her. With a sinking feeling, I realized we were too late.

I raced back through the locker room and outside to where I'd left Ahmed. Still there, he leaned against the wall, both his hands limp in his gray pants pockets.

"I'm so sorry, Magda," he said, his voice barely above a whisper.

"I guess we were playing with fire," I said softly.

He glanced both ways before taking my hand in his. "Whatever happens from here, I'll stand beside you," he said.

I nodded, holding back tears of panic. He leaned forward and kissed me gently on the cheek. I pulled back and looked once more into those molten honey eyes.

Then we went our separate ways.

Blackmail, I decided as I trudged to my locker to gather my books for history class, would be best. If she were to blackmail us—promise to keep the photo to herself in exchange for—what could she want? Money? I didn't know. Blackmail made no sense; she was rich. But blackmail was the least of all the awful things I could think of that she could do.

Blackmail would buy us time to talk to our families and friends. If she were to email that photo or just text it everywhere . . . God. I felt my face flush at the thought. I had rushed into Magda's life with my American ideals about love and look what was happening. Now their love would be forced into the spotlight under the most disastrous imaginable circumstances. My heart did an impression of a dive bomber and crash landed in pieces at my feet.

Then, selfishly, I remembered that if I couldn't fix this, I couldn't shift back. What if I never shifted back? Images of Mom and Gabrielle flickered through my mind, and my gut contracted in panic. A sudden wave of nausea swept over me.

I walked into history class with my head bowed. How could I have let this happen? I *knew* better!

The teacher hadn't arrived yet. I was greeted in the classroom by a low buzz of conversation, and when I looked up, a dozen eyes met mine. It wasn't just eye contact though—they had that wide-eyed look people get when they're craning their necks to gawk at a car accident or watch a fight in the hallway. They're wondering if they'll see blood.

There is cell phone speed, which is instantaneous, and there is word of mouth, which is faster. Fatima must've sent the photo to her entire friend list within seventeen seconds of taking it. A phone or two were probably whipped out right away. Those people sent it to their friends, and word of mouth took over. Now everyone was looking at their phones and staring at me.

A Muslim/Christian romance in Egypt. A kiss in a society where such things are taboo. A government minister's daughter. A diplomat's son.

XXI

If embarrassment could be measured in degrees, I ran a raging fever. The blood rushed to my face, and I struggled to keep tears at bay. Unable to endure the stares a minute longer, I grabbed the books I had just set on my desk, threw them into my backpack and rushed out of the class. I heard someone call out after me, but I was beyond reason.

I went to my locker, randomly threw as many books in my backpack as I could and started for the front doors.

The blazing sun hit me as I burst outside. The steps of the school—normally bustling with kids—were eerily quiet at this time of day. I could feel my phone vibrating in my pocket. I reached down without looking at it and switched it off.

I wished I could be anyone else at that moment. Any of those drivers going past the street in front of the school. If only I could be that lady over there with the screaming baby. She leaned over to strap an infant into a car seat. To be that soldier on the street corner, standing and watching traffic mindlessly. Oh, to be anyone but me.

Okay, anyone but me, Molly. I had totally screwed Magda's life up now. Lucky for her she wasn't here to witness it.

I had to stop such negative thinking. My purpose was to bring Ahmed and Magda together. This much I had achieved. They were closer than I had ever imagined possible, but I hadn't shifted back. That meant I wasn't done. Apparently, I was going to face the far more difficult task of gaining acceptance for their relationship in their communities. I had no idea how to begin, but I was pretty sure that a photo of the two of them kissing spread all over the Internet was not the best way to start an unbiased conversation about a Christian/Muslim romance.

I made my way to the taxi stop on the corner. School wouldn't let out for hours, so the drivers weren't expecting any fares from that direction. I threw myself into the backseat of the front taxi. The driver, leaning against a corner fence and smoking a cigarette, dropped his cigarette, crushed it with his foot, and then rushed over to his cab and climbed behind the wheel.

"Where to?"

Where to indeed. I hadn't a clue. I couldn't go home. I wasn't sure what time Magda's mom got home, and I wasn't ready to face her yet. I needed time to think. I couldn't stay here. All my friends were in school.

"The mall," I said. The eternal refuge of emotional women everywhere. A chance to get lost in the crowd. A safe place to think about what would come next.

I didn't know this driver. I think he sensed I didn't want to talk. Like the Christian cabbie, his cab too was over-decorated but with a Muslim theme. A red carpet draped across the dash with golden crescents and moons woven into it, and golden tassels hung down. A plastic hand-shaped symbol, with an eye etched onto it, dangled from a beaded chain around the rearview mirror. I'd seen these around—they were called the *hamsa*, or "the hand of Fatima," and were meant as a superstitious defense against the evil eye. The irony of this symbol was not lost on me. For me, Fatima was my problem, not my defense.

We were at the mall in a matter of minutes—the streets were less congested in the middle of the school day. Not having negotiated the price in advance and not having the focus to haggle, I overpaid the driver generously. He pocketed the money quickly and pulled away into traffic just as fast—no doubt in case I'd overpaid him by accident.

I pushed through the throngs of shoppers and made my way to the lowest floor, to the food court. The sweet apple smell of *hookahs* filled the mall. How could people eat in a place that smelled of sickly-sweet smoke? I sat down and pulled out my computer. While I waited for it to boot up, I confronted my phone.

Eight messages.

The first was from Fatima. I sighed heavily. I looked heavenward for support and clicked on it.

There was the photo. Our bodies pressed together. Ahmed gently cupped the back of my head in his hand, the other hand disappeared behind my waist. My head tilted up to his. Our eyes were closed. The image was painstakingly clear.

There was no accompanying text. But then again, the picture said enough. The identity of both of us was clear from the photo. Ahmed's face showed more than mine, but my wavy hair and headband were identifying characteristics, and the curve of my face was confirmation. My lucky bracelet sparkled on my wrist and contrasted brightly against the black of his belt.

I glanced at the list of recipients; she must've sent the photo to her entire contact list.

Next was a message from Facebook that informed me I had been tagged in a photo.

A text from Layla.

You've really done it this time, girlfriend.

Several messages I deleted quickly. Some girl whose name didn't ring a bell called me a slut. Two guys asked me for the next date behind the lockers, and one was quite graphic about what he'd like to do to me if I would go out with him.

There was a message from Demiana, the girl Magda said always spoke her mind.

Whoa! Magda in love! If one of us was to wind up in a spot like this, I thought it'd be me, not you, she wrote. Then in a separate text: *Do you mind if I go after Mark?*

Aisha wrote saying, *Are you okay?* and nothing more.

I hadn't counted on any support at all. I had two friends, maybe three, who may not have completely abandoned me.

Well, I wasn't going to find any support at home.

My computer blinked at me. I tried to open my web browser to get on Facebook. Maybe Ahmed would have some brilliant way out of this.

But of course, I couldn't get on Facebook. The mall had no Internet connection.

I flipped my computer shut again and decided to wander until it was a normal time to go home.

What was the worst they could do? Ground me for the rest of high school. Send me to some all-girls boarding school. Would they beat me in a culture like this? Magda's father seemed too patient and caring to hit his daughter. He wasn't the impulsive sort. But then, I hadn't seen him truly angry yet.

I thought wistfully of my own father. I never knew him well. He worked in pharmaceutical sales and was only home on weekends. Even on weekends, he worked a lot. But he had tried to be a good Dad. I remember dancing around the living room with him once to the song "Butterfly Kisses" when I was three. I remember swimming in the pool with him after he went for a run on Saturday mornings. I was nine when the driver of a ten-wheeler in Houston fell asleep at the wheel and crossed the median. The big truck hit his rental car head on. That was so long ago. I hadn't had a dad for a long time. I wasn't really sure what normal Dad behavior was.

I was going to have to face home eventually. I would take what they dished out, but I made one other decision. I wasn't giving up on Ahmed. I still believed I was supposed to bring Ahmed and Magda together somehow. I couldn't have been brought here just to humiliate her. I couldn't promise never to see Ahmed again, and I was pretty sure that wasn't going to fly well at all.

XXII

The Coptic community is as close as one second is to another. Magda's mom knew of the picture within minutes of my friends finding out. I imagine the photo was probably sent to some shared family email inbox, and any good Coptic mom who saw it would immediately call Magda's mom to make sure that justice was dealt.

When I came home, Magda's mother sat at the kitchen table, her hands neatly folded in her lap, head down, unmoving. Her face was blotchy and red from crying.

I dropped my backpack and went to sit silently in a chair near her.

She composed herself and lifted her eyes to mine.

"Of all the children in all our family—of all your cousins and second cousins—Magda, I never thought it would be you who would bring shame on this family." Her voice shook with repressed rage.

I kept my head down and didn't answer.

She was silent again. "You will have no more privileges. You will leave this house for school and church."

I nodded.

"Give me your phone."

I placed my phone on the table.

"How did this happen? How did you communicate with this boy? Or do you kiss all the boys behind the lockers?" she spat, her voice growing coarser and more shrill as she spoke.

"No, Mom, I—"

"Magda, how could you do this! He is a *Muslim* boy. He will never be able to be a part of our family. He will try to make you a Muslim.

Then you will be stolen from our family! Stolen! Do you truly want this? Have you any idea the consequences of chasing a Muslim boy?" She paused to catch her breath, than continued on, only slightly calmer.

"There are so many things wrong with what you did today. Do you understand what you have done? What are your marriage prospects now? Will Mark or any other good Christian boy ever look at you again? You were *kissing* him. Like a common slut! If you had chosen a *Christian* boy, your reputation might never recover. But a Muslim?" The tears had begun to flow as she spoke.

"And your father," she said, almost quietly. "In our community, he has been shamed. In the government, they will ask how he can run a department when he cannot run a home."

Her words stung like alcohol on a fresh wound. I felt strongly that Ahmed and Magda must chart a course together, but I didn't want to hurt anyone, least of all Magda's dad.

"Speak now, Magda, tell me how you did this behind my back."

I had taken some time in wandering the mall to compose my response. I chose a strategy of partial information. My biggest fear had been that she wouldn't let me speak at all.

"Mom, I care for him more than I have ever cared about anyone or anything in my life—short of you and Father and Maraya, of course," I began.

Her breath caught and her eyes rolled heavenward. The tears began again, but she held her silence and allowed me to continue.

"He came to this school at the beginning of last year. His father's a diplomat. They've lived all over the world, even the United States," I said, hoping that at least his good pedigree would win him some favor. Her gaze remained rigid, locked on some unseen speck on the refrigerator door.

"He's warm and kind, and I can have wonderful, deep conversations with him about everything and anything. He listens to my opinion. We disagree a lot, but it never seems to matter. Just the talking is fun. Mom, we're good together. There has never been anyone but him.

"I never meant to kiss him. I know it's wrong to give myself to a boy like that. I know I'm too young. I didn't mean for that to happen. And I promise you; he's never done anything more than kiss me. But Mother, when you care for someone so much, how do you resist?"

I saw some fleeting emotion pass over her face. A crack in her armor. Then the wall of anger slammed back in place.

"The best way to avoid touching the boys," she said, her voice edged with steel, "is to *stay apart!*" I bowed my head in defeat.

"Now," she continued. "Tell me how you managed to have this relationship and all these *deep chats*," her voice dripped with sarcasm.

"We set up a secret Facebook page. I used a different name and password. He and I could talk there, and no one else could read what we wrote," I said. "No one knew about it but us."

"In this very house, under this very roof, you wrote him, night after night." She began softly and her voice escalated with emotion. "Good God in heaven," she said, and her eyes rolled up again. "What have I done to deserve such a daughter?"

"Mother, I didn't know what else to do. I know it's okay for a Muslim boy and Christian girl to hang out in public places and just be friends, but I was afraid that our attraction to each other would show, and I knew you wouldn't approve. If you found out, you would keep us apart." I ignored the *hrmph* of agreement that came from across the table.

"We chose to stay apart as a general rule, in case we might say or do something stupid. But it got harder and harder. We stole moments in the back of the library and places like that. It was dumb. And Mom, there weren't many kisses. It's not really about the kisses at all. It never was," I said.

"And it never will be again. Leave your computer on the table," she said in a commanding tone. "Give me your passwords," she shoved a paper and pen at me. "Then go to your room. I'll let you know when you can come out again."

I began scribbling down passwords. If only there had been a chance to delete all those posted conversations with Ahmed! Most of our chats had been live and the settings had been adjusted so they left no record, but Ahmed and Magda/I had also left a lot of messages for each other. Messages that had shown me in no uncertain terms how Magda and

Ahmed felt about each other. Now all of that would be laid before Magda's mother's eyes.

If the real Magda in Florida had any idea what I'd done, she'd reach through the miles of time and distance that separated us and kill me.

I thought about apologizing again, but the lines of her face tensed, and her right eye twitched. I decided she was barely holding it together, so I picked up my backpack and all but ran down the hall to Magda's room and closed the door behind me.

Some hours later, I heard a short wrapping on my door. I opened it and found my computer on the floor, along with a plate of food and a glass of water.

It felt like a prison sentence. I couldn't think of food. I heard the heavy fall of Magda's father's shoes in the kitchen. No sign just yet of Maraya. I picked up the water and the computer and closed the door.

I booted up the laptop and found both my Facebook accounts had both been deleted. I'd lost my link to the real Magda too. Not that I could face her now. I settled down and tried to do some homework, but I couldn't concentrate.

Around nine, Magda's father knocked. I opened the door with dread and retreated to sit on the bottom bunk, my eyes lowered. I felt ill. He sat on the bed beside me. For a moment, he said nothing at all.

"Magda, do you love him?"

I hadn't expected this opening. I thought he would be talking about punishment. Dare I hope that he could be reasoned with?

"Oh, yes, Dad! I love him more than I ever thought possible. I know you'd rather that I loved Mark, but Dad, I can't help it, and you said I should marry for love," I babbled urgently. "Just because he's Muslim—"

"Magda, Magda. Hold on. The fact that he's Muslim doesn't mean he's not a fine boy," he said. "I want to be sure you understand that your mother and I think there are many fine Muslim boys out there. And girls, and ladies and men as well. I work with many of them. They're no different than any other group of people anywhere. And your mother and I want you to marry for love, if you can find it, so that's not the issue either."

After my conversation with Mom at the kitchen table, I wouldn't have thought so.

"To me, it's not even particularly the religious aspect of it," he continued. "Though your mother would disagree with me here. In John 14:6, Jesus says, "no one comes to the Father except through me". Muslims don't believe Jesus was divine, so she thinks if you aren't Christian, you aren't going to heaven. For your mother, this is a fight over your mortal soul, and it's not a fight she's willing to lose."

"But Dad, I wouldn't ever convert—"

"Hear me out. I was going to say, that's your mother's position. Me, I'm not so sure. This world is full of different religions. I'm not egotistical enough to think we are the only ones who have it right just because that's what I grew up learning as opposed to what someone else grew up learning," he said.

"My main objection—other than kissing, which frankly surprises me from you—my main objection is that you're not thinking through the consequences of this choice. Friendship between Muslims and Christians is a wonderful thing and I encourage it both in my work and in my home, but marriage is a completely different thing. Maybe you do love this boy. That wouldn't make you the first Coptic girl to fall for a Muslim boy. It happened to the daughter of a friend mine about ten years ago. Her name was Hannah, and she begged and begged her father to let her marry a young Muslim named Radwan. My friend refused. As a result, his Hannah ran away one night and came back the next morning a married woman.

"Hannah's parents did not disown her, despite how she shamed them. After a time, they even invited the couple over. Hannah swore to her parents she would never convert. She and Radwan would share everything, she said, even their religion. Well, it didn't work out that way.

"Radwan never attended church, obviously. We all knew he could never become Christian. For a Muslim to leave Islam for Christianity in Egypt is treason. I read in *Al-Ahram* the other day that most Egyptians believe Muslims who renounce their faith should be given the death penalty," he shook his head sadly. "The death penalty! God help us.

"Radwan clearly couldn't convert. He couldn't spend time with his new Christian family in their church or religious functions; even that was too dangerous. There is no place for a Muslim in Coptic Cairo. The reverse, however, is not true. Christians are more than welcome to attend Muslim functions.

"So Hannah was drawn into that other world. She attended Radwan's mosque to be with his family. They accepted her with open arms, and she felt comfortable with them. The women invited her to their prayer groups and social functions. She made dozens of wonderful new friends. I'm not trying to tell you it was a trap or a conspiracy; they were good people and they wanted to welcome her. Hannah's family would've welcomed Radwan into the Christian faith if it were only possible. It's the way things are. There was only one faith they could follow together.

"The basic principles taught in the Koran—charity, love, faith in God—they aren't so different from what our church preaches. Three years later she became pregnant. Shortly after that, she converted. Her new Muslim friends and family rejoiced.

"When she made this decision, Magda, doors opened for her, but every time a new door opens another closes. Hannah didn't understand that she couldn't have it both ways. Once you become a Muslim, you can't ever be fully a part of the Coptic community again. Her friends and family still loved her just as much, but think about it. She couldn't come to church anymore. She was a Muslim now, so her beloved church became a dangerous place for her. She couldn't attend religious functions. All she could do to keep up with her childhood friends was visit them in their homes, and she did so. Some embraced her. But Magda, honey, many more did not. We have no laws declaring it treason when someone leaves the Coptic faith, but many Copts see it that way just the same. She had denounced Christ as her Savior. For many Copts, that's unforgivable. They would say, "it is better never to have seen the light, than to see it and turn it away". Some people openly called her names. Some did so behind her back. She felt cast out."

He paused and I opened my mouth to argue, but he held up a hand to silence me.

"Let me finish my story. Church—its services, picnics, celebrations, youth groups, all the family and friends she had there—was once the center of Hannah's life. Now that chapter of her life was closed. Christmas, Easter, and Palm Sunday—she could no longer celebrate them. She fasted for Ramadan with his family and feasted on the *Eid*. In time, only a few of her closest friends and family continued to visit her for tea. Those visits are now all that remains of the life she knew. Her Christian family won't enter a mosque, so they can't visit her and her growing family in her new world. Hannah's father is heartbroken. His grandchildren are Muslim and celebrate throughout the year with their Muslim grandparents. They hardly know him.

"Magda, once you leave the church, you leave your mother and me. You leave Maraya, Layla, Demiana, everyone. We would visit, but our lives would be separate. We wouldn't celebrate holidays together. We wouldn't pray together. God forbid you ever truly needed us. What if your husband became abusive or embraced some orthodox branch of Islam that mistreats their women? You cannot know now what life will deal you. If the marriage didn't work out, who would you turn to? Sure, your mom and I would be there for you, but you couldn't become a Copt again. You can't come back. Magda, I could never give my blessing to a marriage between you and a Muslim. To do such a thing—it would be like giving away my own right arm."

"But Dad, you don't understand. I would never *leave*. I'm Christian and don't ever want to be anything else. Ahmed doesn't want me to convert. He said so! Dad, he's different. He's lived in America, and he says two different religions *can* live together under the same roof. It happens all the time. It's harder, but it's possible."

"You may think that now. And maybe it's true. But don't underestimate the pressure you'll face. You may think you can go to mosque with him on Friday and to church yourself on Saturday. Maybe for a while you will. But eventually, you'll have children. They can't be full participants in both religions. This boy, Ahmed? His family and community will put enormous pressure on him to raise his children Muslim. Even if he could find it in his heart to let them participate in Christian holidays, I'm not sure he would be allowed to. I've never heard of such a thing. No, you must choose. It's not just a husband you are choosing; it's a community. Magda, this is the most important decision you will ever make."

I hated what he was saying, but he spoke to Magda's heart. I remembered the words Magda had written to me on Facebook: *I would have to give up everything . . . my family, my friends, everything. Too many Coptic girls have ruined their lives this way.* Hannah's fate is exactly what Magda feared.

Dad stood and drew up to his full height. "Magda, you are to stay away from this boy. Not so much as a word to him in the hallways. You are thinking with your heart, and not your head. If you are apart, you will have time to reflect, and let your head rule your heart again," he said.

He turned his back to me and began pacing. "Then we must deal with the matter of your kissing him. That behavior is—" He struggled for composure for the first time in this conversation. His face hardened, and he chose his words carefully before continuing, "simply not acceptable. Perhaps we've been watching too much TV. You are not some sleazy girl in an American sitcom," he said. His fists clenched as he spoke. "Your reputation has been dealt a very serious blow, Magda. You will not be given the opportunity to do it again." I nodded.

"And finally there's the matter of school. Principal Richards has called a meeting of the Honor Council to decide whether or not you and Ahmed should be expelled. I'll do what I can to convince them you're sorry, and it won't happen again. In the meantime, your mother and I are evaluating other options for your schooling. A change of schools might be best for you anyway. For the time being, you will go directly to and from school. You may not go to youth group; you may not run after school. No trips to the mall, nothing. Your school requires you to have a computer and to use it for your homework, but I will tolerate no social networking. Your computer must appear on the kitchen table for charging when you finish your homework. Oh, and your phone is gone. All this is for the foreseeable future. Is that understood?"

I kept my eyes on the floor and said nothing.

He paused in the doorway and said awkwardly, "Good night, Magda."

I looked up at him, with tears in my eyes. "I'm sorry, Daddy," I said. "I'm sorry I've shamed you."

"I'm sorry too, Magda," he said, and the door closed softly behind him.

XXIII

A barely constrained Maraya bounded into the room just before ten o'clock.

"So what did you *do*?" she burst out. "Mom and Dad said it's a boy issue and you made a bad decision and you need some time to think it over and I'm too young to understand, but it's gotta be pretty bad 'cause you didn't even come to dinner and besides, I'm *not* too little, so what'd you *do*?"

"Yeah, I'm in pretty bad trouble," I said. "I guess you may as well know since everyone else does. I kissed a boy. And someone took a picture. Mom and Dad are mad cause I kissed him. And they're even madder 'cause he's Muslim."

"Wooow," she blew the word out slowly. Then her brow furrowed. "Why'd you do *that*?"

"I guess it was a bad idea," I said, ever mindful of her Coptic education. "The kissing part anyway. But I did it because I really like him."

"Are you, like, in *love*?" She spoke the word in exactly the same tone of distaste she reserved for cauliflower.

"Yeah, honey, I think maybe I am," I said, truthfully.

She digested this idea for a moment.

"Is Magda in love with him too?" she asked.

"Magda is very much in love with him. Now it looks like we might both be expelled. I'm not doing a very good job, am I?'

Silence. And then, "I dunno. In a way, it's like Mom and Dad all over again."

"It is?"

"Yeah, you know. Er, well, you don't know. But Magda does. Anyway, Mom and Dad fell in love but Grandma and Grandpa didn't like it, because they said Dad wasn't right for Mom. They were both Christian and everything—it's just that Grandma and Grandpa didn't like Dad's family. See, we never met Dad's parents before they died and cousin Anne says it's cause Grandpa Amides was a drunk. He beat Grandma an' everything. She says Grandpa Amides never got a job or nothing, and they had no money. So Mom wasn't allowed to marry him. He didn't have money for a dowry anyway—"

"A dowry? They still use dowries here?" I interjected.

She looked at me like an idiot. "Well, yeah. I mean, not everyone does it anymore, but they did in the olden days, like then. Anyway, Mom loved him *so* much that she went on a hunger strike for twelve days till Grandpa's heart broke, and he said Dad could earn his own dowry. Dad worked two jobs and saved up to get the old stationary shop. It took him three years, but he did it, and they got married. Isn't that like the greatest story ever?"

It really was. That might explain Dad's gentle approach. He knew how it felt to love someone he's not supposed to love. He had worked years to earn the right to be with Mom openly. I understood Mom's fury less. She had launched a hunger strike to get her parents to listen to her, and now she had turned into her own parents.

Then I remembered the chink in her armor I thought I glimpsed when we were in the kitchen, and I said how hard it was not to touch him. For the first time all day, I felt a trickle of hope that maybe Magda's family could someday be persuaded to accept a love that had grown—like a flower in the crack of sidewalk—where it wasn't supposed to.

I thought about the untouched plate I had left outside my room. Would Magda's parents think I was on a hunger strike?

Maraya broke my train of thought with the very question I had so deftly avoided from Magda's parents. "So are you going to see him again?"

"I haven't really figured out what I'm gonna do," I said, choosing words that conveyed some truth.

"I won't tell Mom and Dad if you leave in the night again, I promise," she said with glee.

"Again?" I nearly choked.

"The pebbles woke me up. Don't worry. I didn't say anything. If you were Magda, I'd have told on you. But I made a promise, and Mom says you must always keep your promises. I promised I wouldn't tell about you being Molly inside of Magda. Magda never snuck out, so I figured this had something to do with shifting. That makes it part of our secret, right? Course now that I know what you were really doing was—"

I interjected before she could finish that thought. "Maraya, you did great. You were right— when I snuck out, that was definitely part of our shifting secret, and I'm really proud of you for not saying anything. I still don't want your parents to know about those meetings, okay? This is all part of what I have to do to be able to get your sister back again."

"Are you almost done?"

"No, honey. I thought I was. But now I'm pretty sure I'm just beginning."

XXIV

Breakfast was a cold affair. The steam that rose from our plates of pita and *fuul*—a warm fava bean paste mixed with chick peas—did nothing to thaw Magda's parents. They went about their business mechanically. I sensed a bit of relief when I took breakfast though. If anyone was going to go on a hunger strike, it would have to be the real Magda. I didn't have the stamina for it.

Layla arrived promptly at seven a.m., a big purple bow tied in her hair and a co-ordinating purple scarf knotted at her neck.

"Good morning, Uncle Cyril. Good morning, Aunt Ireney," she said formally.

"Good morning Layla," they responded coolly.

As soon as the apartment door closed behind us, she stopped me, put an arm on either shoulder and looked me up and down.

"Well, all your limbs seem to be present. Both ears. Nothing missing? That's something. So out with it. Tell everything. What happened?"

I summarized the events of the previous evening. "I'm grounded. From now until eternity. No phone. No Facebook. No Ahmed, obviously. Nothing but school and church," I said, "And even the school part is in question. We could get kicked out. Principal Richards is going to bring it to the Honors Council for a decision." Maybe after I faced Magda's peers today, changing schools would sound like a good thing.

"That's it? You got off easy! Just for kissing a boy, my dad would've beat me and had me married off to some second cousin by morning. I can't imagine what he'd do if the guy I picked was Muslim."

"Yeah. I guess I'm just lucky," I said without enthusiasm.

"Well, everyone's talking about you, I'll tell you that," she said, as she eased herself behind the wheel. Maraya and I climbed into the car.

"I'll bet," I said, listlessly.

"Have you been looking on Faceb—," she caught herself. "Right. Well, I swear the entire school was on last night. Except you. Everyone's taking sides."

"Sides?" I asked. Were they betting on the outcome of our relationship? Or how much blood Dad would spill?

"Yeah! You guys are stirring up a real hornet's nest. Most the kids think a Muslim and a Christian relationship can't work. The divide's just too big. A bunch of freshman girls say kissing any boy makes you a slu—" she caught herself again, "was wrong, and they think that's the main issue because it was so, so—"

"I *get* it," I interjected.

"Oh, God, I'm sorry. I'm really screwing up, aren't I? Well, anyway, I just thought you should know that some of us think you should be allowed to be together. In other countries, different cultures marry, and those couples find ways to make it work. In America, I hear mixed religion couples celebrate both Christmas and Ramadan. I mean, why does our generation have to do things the same as the last generation? Don't they keep telling us in school to become the change we want to see?"

I agreed wholeheartedly, but I doubted that would be the reception at school today.

"You *do* love him, don't you?"

"Like you love fashion accessories."

"Whoa," she said with mock awe. "Okay. No beating around the bush there," she said, and the three inches of gold bangles tinkled on her wrist as she drove. She gave me a sidelong glance. "So, you and Mark...it's definitely not on?"

Now it was becoming clear. So much for "becoming the change we want to see" and all that high talk. If I was throwing Mark back into the pool, she would love my relationship with Ahmed. Whether he was a Muslim or a rhinoceros.

"*Mark and I* was about exactly what I told you it was about. Arabic, okay? Besides, do you really think he'd want anything to do with me after finding that photo on his phone?"

"Great! I mean, fine. Well, you know what I think. I think if you love him, then you should make this work, like *Romeo and Juliet*."

"That didn't end so well."

"We'll write you a better ending then."

"How am I going to make this work anyway when I can't write or see him?" I asked.

"You're the one who told the whole English class that you were a true believer in 'love will find a way,'" she said in a singsong voice as she sidled into a parking space and pocketed the keys.

Each foot weighed a hundred pounds as I took the first step onto the stairs that lead to the front doors. At least a couple dozen kids in white tops and gray bottoms milled about. Some meandered up the stairs while others stood still in chatty little groupings. Heads turned in my direction, and the low conversational buzz was replaced by a spreading silence.

Eyes bored into me. Before any words were spoken, repugnance lurked in their stares. A tall senior with a ponytail came up from behind me and mumbled, "whore," as she walked past. From a group of girls in a circle, "slut." When I looked in their direction, their eyes held mine. I turned away.

"Geez!" said Layla under her breath as we topped the stairs.

I wasn't three feet inside the doors before some short, stocky black-haired guy I'd never seen before brushed past me and pinched my butt. I turned in shock and he mimicked my reaction to his buddies, laughing and winking. I felt suddenly nauseous. This is what I had done to Magda's life. Layla grabbed my arm and propelled me forward in the direction of the lockers.

I braced myself as Layla and I walked past a group of four British and American freshmen, but they continued their conversation without glancing up. The whispers and the looks came from the local kids, both Muslim and Copt. The foreigners seemed uninterested in the whole spectacle the Egyptians made of a mixed-religion romance. I suppose it made sense. Back home, a Muslim/Christian relationship was just a mild oddity. Not really anyone's business.

"Thanks for walking those stairs with me, Layla," I said. "It would've been worse alone."

Her fingers twirled her combination lock. "Hey, you're my cousin. I'm not going to dump you and run. I don't like this whole situation, but I'll stand with you."

Verana zeroed in on me before I could reply. Her arms were wrapped tightly around a binder.

"We won't be needing your help at the youth group anymore, Magda," she spat. "It's a resource group for girls who choose to lead *Christian* lives," she said and was gone before I could formulate a retort.

A few people stuck close to me. Layla, Demiana and Aisha were on my side. British Fiona tucked in beside me and put an arm around me on the way into English class.

"Stiff upper lip, girl," she said, half-jokingly. "It's just the news of the day. It'll pass." And she brushed past me into the English classroom.

Ahmed was already here, near the doorway, talking to a Muslim girl I vaguely knew. I fought back a pang of jealousy—why was he talking to her? Had he already moved on? Found a good Muslim girl? I stopped the thought before it could go any further.

As we passed, we looked at each other. He smiled encouragingly at me, and in that smile all my worries evaporated like dew in the morning sun. He took his seat, and the girl he had been talking to drew up beside me and whispered softly in my ear, "Sit in the third row from the door, fifth desk."

I tried to mask my surprise. I hastened to the desk. Now what? A couple of crosses and moons had been carved into the blonde wooden desktop by years of pens. Reluctantly, I slipped my hand inside the desk. Nobody ever put anything inside these desks except old gum, which we were not allowed to chew in school. My fingers touched a book.

I pulled it out. A small worn paperback anthology of favorite poems by Robert Frost. I flipped the book over for clues. Nothing. Then I noticed a page turned over.

Page 184 contained the poem, "The Road Not Taken," by Robert Frost. It was about man standing at the fork in a path in the woods, trying to decide whether to choose the path that so many others had taken, or the unbroken path. He chose the latter, and was never sorry for it.

The last stanza read:

I shall be telling this with a sigh
Somewhere ages and ages hence:
Two roads diverged in a wood, and I,
I took the one less traveled by,
And that has made all the difference.

This poem expressed exactly what I wanted for Magda. I was leading her down a different path—a path unworn by others that ultimately promised her a more rewarding life.

A very small note was penciled at the bottom of the page. *FB: "your. ahmed." Talk to you soon. I'll stay up all night till I hear from you.*

He had created a new Facebook account. How simple! How perfect!

I took my eraser out and carefully erased the note then slipped the book into my backpack.

Love would find a way.

I lay in bed that night, waiting patiently until long after I heard the soft thud of Magda's parents' bedroom door close. The hint of light from their room across the hall glowed dimly under my bedroom door. Eventually, the light extinguished silently, and I felt my heart rate accelerate. The risk of getting caught now was higher than ever because they watched me closely. The consequences of disobeying Magda's parents again would be catastrophic. Yet the consequences of doing nothing were, for Magda and me, more terrible. I needed to bring Ahmed and Magda together, so we could both shift back. SAT exams were only a couple of weeks away. My own future was on the line as well.

I waited until midnight, a half hour after the hallway went dark. Maraya breathed softly below me. I crept down the ladder and crossed to the door. I turned the knob gently and slowly with both hands then inched it open and tiptoed barefoot to the kitchen table where my computer lay, lined up beside Magda's mom and dad's phones. Quietly, I liberated my computer, snuck back down the hall and passed noiselessly through the door. I climbed the ladder into bed. I set the computer on the edge of the bed, so its light would hit the wall. I tried to dim it further with a careful arrangement of pillows and blankets. I didn't want the light showing under the crack in the door.

As an afterthought, I slipped back down to the ground and opened a drawer, pulled out a handful of T-shirts, and lay them down across the crack under the door. This would hide the light better and also muffle tapping noises from the keyboard. Then back up to the bed, and still, just to be sure, I half-draped the computer with blankets.

It only took a moment to create a new account. I searched your.ahmed. There was only one. The profile photo was a picture of the pyramids at sunrise. I friend-requested him. About a nanosecond later, he accepted.

I'm sorry I put you through this, he wrote.

I am just as at fault as you are! You didn't do anything I didn't do myself, I responded and waited.

Is your father angry? came the reply.

Yes . . . and disappointed. I think that hurts worse. He doesn't know you though. To him its about the kissing, and he's afraid I might fall in love and leave my faith and my community. Mom is more afraid I could convert. She thinks that would damn my soul.

I would never ask you to convert, and I would never ask you to leave your community or family. The words appeared so suddenly on my screen they startled me.

I know. But if we stay together, we'll have to make some decisions someday, I wrote. A quick tap and the words were sent.

The response was again immediate. *IF we stay together?* Then a moment later, *None of this changes how I feel about you. I want to be with you. No matter what. Have you changed how you feel about me?* he typed.

His words were like an elixir. I let them wash over me. My self-esteem was at an all-time low, so I could've easily believed that he would just walk away from this.

Not for a second, I wrote and then paused. *What did your parents say?*

My parents would rather you were Muslim, but they never say that in words. What they're mad at me for is having shamed you and your family. They want me to apologize to your father. Do you think he'd let me?

Wow. It would take a lot of courage to do that.

I don't think you should really try communicating with him right now. I'm doing my best to avoid them both as much as I can myself, I responded.

After a pause, *I really want to see you,* he wrote.

Me too, I answered, truthfully.

The cursor blinked at me and kept pace with the rhythm of my heart. The blue/gray screen glowed eerily in the dark room.

I don't want to get you in trouble, but I'd love to steal you away again. I can't help myself. Do you think . . . tomorrow at 1 a.m.? he wrote.

Absolutely not. My heart pounded. How could he even imagine it? The risks were unfathomable. If we got caught again, Magda's father might very well marry her off to a cousin. Magda would be miserable, and so would I. Heck it might just be me—Molly—living my life with that cousin, if I never shifted back.

I needed to make Magda's parents see reason. I needed a plan. Maybe I could find some precedent—some other mixed-religion couple somewhere in history that had made a relationship like this work. Then we could plead our case to them. Or should we run away and return married, like Romeo and Juliet? Personally, I wanted to just run away with Ahmed and live in America or Australia or England. But I knew Magda wasn't willing to give up her friends and family.

The screen waited for me.

No. I'm sorry. We can't keep doing this. It's slow but certain suicide, I wrote. *Just sneaking down to get this computer nearly gave me a heart attack, and I still have to sneak it back. How are we ever going to be safely together?*

I have an idea. I want to discuss it with you.

Couldn't we just discuss options right now online?

Magda, I can't discuss what I want to discuss with you on the computer. You'll understand once I talk to you, but we need to meet. Just one more time

I can delete everything you send me. What can it possibly be that you want to say that you cant say here?

I can't discuss it here. Only in person. We did it so many times. We can do it once more.

No. I'm sorry, Ahmed, but absolutely not. I'm scared. The only thing my parents don't know about is our late night meetings. If they knew about them I'd be married off to one of those pimply boys at church already.

That's what I'm afraid of too, came the reply.

Give it some time. Let things cool off, I said. *We'll figure something out.*

I don't know if we have time Magda. But I cant force you. Think it over.

Good night Ahmed

Good night Magda xoxo

Xoxo. I ran my fingers over the letters on the screen.

I closed the computer and pushed the blankets and pillows aside. I crept down, carefully returned the shirts to the drawer, then soundlessly slipped down the hallway to return my computer to its prison sentence. When I finally returned to bed and drew the covers up to my neck, sleep was a long time coming. I dreamt the anxious dream about Gabrielle again.

The dream had changed. Now, the whole time we were in the pool, clouds moved in quickly, like rapid time-release photography, forming a broad semi-circular pattern. I knew those formations. When I was a little girl, four hurricanes passed through Florida in one summer. Each time, my mother hastily pulled all the plants into the house, threw the patio furniture into the pool and rechecked a closet in the middle of the house that was stocked with emergency supplies. Mom tried to mask her fear by playing games and singing songs with Gabrielle and me while the winds blew, but panic lurked behind her eyes. I saw it when the wind threw itself at the living room picture window over and over again and pummeled the front door till the hinges squeaked in agony. Then, during a game of Candyland, a strong gust shook the window, the glass shuddered and her head swiveled in alarm. I realized with sudden clarity that she couldn't protect us from this. In that moment, the winds stripped my mother of her strength and protection, and fear swept into my soul. I have been afraid of the wind ever since.

The circle formation of clouds in my dream accelerated, the mid-afternoon sky darkened ominously and the winds picked up. I knew Gabrielle was about to go missing, and I was helpless to suggest we leave the pool. I had to watch the dream play out.

The scene of me running down the street was the same though the cans of beans were gone. As the panic closed in on my chest anew, and I chased the van down the windy street, the clouds moved slowly in front of the sun and extinguished it like a total eclipse. The day turned into night. I knew the end had come.

XXV

I made up a hundred ways to kill Fatima. Then I decided death wasn't good enough. I imagined that she broke both her legs in track one day, and somehow I was the only one there, and she begged me to help her. I would only come to her aid if she told everyone she Photoshopped the photo.

Then I fantasized that her father tragically lost his job and couldn't afford to send her to private school anymore. Or he got a job somewhere far off like Zimbabwe, and they had to move. Her meticulously clean fingernails would always be filthy, and the other kids would all speak a different language and think she was a freak.

Finally, I gave up thinking of these unlikely scenarios, and let my imagination run to the wildly ridiculous. I imagined I trapped her in a sauna, with the door locked. The sauna was made of hot metal. Suspended in the middle of a volcano about to erupt. On the sun.

In reality, of course, I did nothing. When I passed Fatima in the hallway, I just looked the other way and forged past her as quickly as I could. If any of my dwindling supply of friends were with me, I took care to be always engaged in some conversation—any conversation—to look like I didn't even notice her going by. But I did. Every fiber of my being was repulsed when she walked by. I noticed everything about her, without looking.

Today she had adorned her uniform with several strings of gold necklace and a half dozen gold bangles rattled on her right arm. She wore a navy designer scarf with squares of beige. An image of her running, phone in hand, flashed through my mind. It was the same scarf she'd worn that day.

She was always laughing. This whole situation seemed to have brought her some kind of fame. She and Baysaan and another cohort walked together. Baysaan didn't look at me, but turned and spoke to Fatima just loudly enough to be overheard. I'm not sure what all she said, but the name "Make-out Magda" echoed clearly through the halls. Fatima looked at me for a reaction as I passed; her face turned up in a wicked smile. I gave her nothing.

It wasn't just the Muslim kids who were having a laugh at my expense. One group of Copts led by Verana called me Merry Magda—a reference to Mary Magdalene from the Bible. She's the one who overcame a sinful life as a prostitute through Jesus' forgiveness. They were just calling me a slut.

School was rapidly becoming torture.

Sometimes, kids Magda barely knew singled me out. Right after I turned the corner on Fatima, one of the American boys pushed up close to me and said under his breath, his lips brushing my ear, "Hey Magda, wanna go sneak a kiss somewhere?" And when he pulled away to the chorus of guffaws from his buddies, he shouted loudly after me, "What, don't you like the Christian boys?" He whistled as I hurried by. "Such a shame," he added, mockingly.

Most of the foreigners, though, warily kept their distance and watched.

"Magda, it was just a snog. You really shouldn't get fussed about it," Fiona tried to counsel me on the way to bio class. "I think Ahmed's a catch. I'm totally jealous!"

Fiona had such porcelain white skin it was almost translucent, and with her white-blonde hair and the light yellow she wore as her signature color, she was so pale I sometimes felt like I could put my hand right through her. Just as the unrelenting Cairo sun had failed to alter the color of her skin; the local culture had also failed to penetrate that smooth white exterior.

"Fiona, you just don't get it. This isn't London. A 'snog' around here can ruin your reputation—not just at school but with the adults too, and they have a lot to say in our culture about who their children marry. A bad reputation can mean that when it's time for me to marry, no good young men will be willing to consider me," I said.

"You aren't serious, are you? Isn't that some backwoods thing in the countryside or something? Are your parents really going to pick your husband?" she asked, incredulously.

"I'm dead serious. Not so much among the Copts, and you're right, not so much in the city anymore as it used to be. But Coptic families are still very close, and even when they say we can marry for love—like my parents do—they put limits on what kinds of guys we're allowed to fall in love with."

"So, like, your parents might not let you marry Ahmed if you chose to?" she asked, still absorbing.

"Like, duh! Aren't you listening? Fiona, I've lost my phone and my laptop and been put on house arrest for the foreseeable future. I'm not allowed to see Ahmed under any circumstances. We both might get expelled. And a few hundred pairs of eyes in this school would gladly tell my parents if they saw me so much as talk to him. Marry him? I'm not even allowed to *think* about him!"

Foreigners sure could be dense about how things worked around here.

Fiona was quiet a moment as we walked into class. She threw her backpack over the seat of a desk, and I took the desk behind her. She sat down, flipped around backwards and whispered conspiratorially, "So are you going to see him again?"

I slipped a fingernail into my mouth and weighed my answer. I glanced around the room to make sure no one listened.

"Maybe." I couldn't help but smile a little guiltily. Fiona grinned.

Fiona and Demiana joined me for lunch. Fiona spooned her applesauce and swallowed it soundlessly. A group of girls at the next table whispered as soon as we took our seats.

"Don't pay attention to them," Fiona said after a moment. She rolled her eyes toward the girls without turning her head. "They're just jealous."

"Yeah, that's me. Miss Popularity," I replied.

"You know, you could play this anyway you want," Demiana said. Her long curly hair was particularly explosive today.

"What?" I asked.

"Well, you can be the victim. You can let everyone walk all over you, call you names, stuff like that. You can regret what you did. Do you regret what you did?" she asked.

"No," I said truthfully. "I mean—I regret what happened because of what I did. But being with Ahmed? I don't regret that at all."

"Then hold your head up. Be a vigilante. Fight for the right to fall in love with whomever you want," she said.

"I want to. I want to more than anything." Magda had said to trust her judgment. "But this isn't a normal war. If I hold my head up, it will just be cut off."

"Magda, you're totally right. You're like David taking on Goliath, only you're not God's chosen one, and Goliath is the whole of Egyptian culture. You can't win."

"Well, that was blunt."

"Well, it's true. If winning means that you and Ahmed end up in a happy little house with little mixed-religion children going to mosque on Friday and church on Saturday, that's not going to happen. You can't win. But if you set your sights lower, maybe you and he can work out some kind of compromise with the world. Egypt is changing every generation. The whole Middle East is re-inventing itself. If Egypt is your Goliath, well, Goliath looks older and weaker than he did in biblical times. If you throw a few stones and keep your head, you might make an impact. It's a huge risk, but your chances are probably better now than at any time in history. One thing's for sure, if you don't take Goliath on, and you continue to sneak moments with Ahmed behind the PE lockers, you'll be married off pretty soon, and it'll all be over."

"Okay, Demiana. That sounds great in theory. But how does that work in practice? Where do I find these magical stones to throw and who exactly do I chuck them at? I mean, really, do I just stand up and announce to everyone that Ahmed and I are together? Is that what we're talking about? If I do, my parents either marry me off or put me in a different school. What have I accomplished then?" I asked.

"You're being too literal. We're talking figuratively here," Demiana conceded. "We have to figure out how to translate the strategy into practice." She took a spoonful of beans and chewed thoughtfully.

"Speaking of throwing stones, is it true what they say about what you did to Fatima?" Fiona asked Demiana.

My head darted between the two of them. "Wait. What? Demiana, what did you do to Fatima?"

Demiana glared at Fiona. "Nothing."

"That's not what I heard."

"I didn't do anything. She called you Merry Magda. Then she tripped. Call it karma."

"You didn't," I said.

"I absolutely didn't. A girl could get expelled for that."

"Or lose her scholarship."

"Yeah. That too."

"Was she hurt?"

"Just a bruise."

"Geez, Demiana. She's gonna kill you."

"Magda, I'm not stupid. She tripped at the mall. Me and a group of friends from the tenement I live in, we were hanging out there. I may have mentioned that Fatima is the school bully. Then she fell. She talks a big story, but she's a princess. I think she'll keep her distance from me. If not, well, let her try. I'll get her expelled."

"Demiana, that was really dumb. You shouldn't be taking risks like that with your scholarship."

"Who the heck are you to talk about risks I should or shouldn't take? Like you're the Queen of Prudence?" She wiped her face with a napkin and crumpled it on her plate. "Fatima isn't the issue anymore though. Your problem is that you're in love with a Muslim." She pushed her plate away, grabbed a lock of her ecstatically curly hair and wound it around her finger. "How about if you guys get married first and negotiate later?"

"I can't do that, Demiana," I said. There were limits on how far I'd go with Magda's life. I wasn't going to have her come back married. "Besides, I'm only seventeen."

"Lots of girls get married at sixteen or seventeen, Magda," Demiana said.

Fiona's eyes grew wide. "They do?"

"Yeah," Demiana answered. "Around here it's pretty normal. Parents like to marry their kids off young, before—you know—accidents happen. Not as much with kids like us who are going on to college, but it still happens. Look at Verana. She and Peter have been engaged since they were twelve."

I didn't want to think about Verana. "Well, I'm getting an education," I said. "I want to go to London for med school. I just can't think about marriage yet."

"What about Ahmed?" Demiana asked. "Where does he want to go to school? Cause if it's London, you guys could be together over there and then take your time before getting married. You told me once that your uncle in London—the one you're supposed to live with when you go there—you said he's more English than Egyptian. He might give you more freedom than you have here. I bet you guys'd be able to study together in the library. You might even get to walk together in the streets where no one knows the two of you. I'm sure you could even find a way to go for dinner together and the movies, even if it's with a group. Wouldn't that be something?"

That was the closest thing I'd heard to a reasonable strategy. The only problem was I didn't know where he planned to go to school. I had never asked.

"That would be something," I agreed. "He's not sure yet where he'll study though," I fudged.

"He'd better decide soon," Fiona added. "We're in eleventh grade."

"I know," I said.

"Nothing you guys choose will be easy, Magda." Demiana said.

We finished lunch without further progress.

After lunch, I muddled through my classes, trying to concentrate on the material as best I could. I saw Mark in Arabic class, but he didn't meet my eyes. Knowing I wouldn't be able to rely on him for any more help with Arabic, I paid extra attention to the teacher. I was surprised at the end of class to find Mark walking alongside me.

"So you really like Ahmed, huh?" he queried. He had a wounded puppy look about him. I felt awful. I hadn't stopped to think how the photo affected him. Most of the school thought he and I were becoming an item before all this happened. It must've made him look like a loser to his friends. The girl he was playing gets discovered making out with another guy.

I looked at him sheepishly. "I'm sorry, Mark. I never meant to lead you on. You're a really nice guy. I'm sorry if you've been hurt in this."

"Oh, I'm fine," he said, defensively. "You weren't leading me on really. I mean, you made it pretty clear. I just wasn't listening." He paused for a bit. "You really like him then?"

"Yeah. I do," I said.

"So I can't, like, break both his legs to win you back?" He tried a smile, his eyes hopeful.

I laughed. "No, Mark, please don't break both of his legs."

He hung his head low. "Well, best of luck with Ahmed. Let me know if you change your mind," he said, and he turned with an awkward half smile and went the other way.

I guess moments like this really show you who the good guys are. For the umpteenth time in recent history, I felt like a jerk.

I had to go home by taxi again. Layla had plans to go shopping after school with Aisha and Demiana, and I was grounded. I rounded the corner and faced the row of cabbies. The Coptic cabbie grinned his disarming, nearly toothless smile at me.

He always seemed to be here when I came to the corner, and I was kind of starting to think of him as my driver. I hopped in.

"You know," he said, "you have a good name."

"Magda?"

"Magda. That's a good Biblical name," he said. I winced inwardly. He was referring to Mary Magdalene. "My name is from the Bible too. Simon."

"Saint Peter used to be called Simon," I remembered aloud.

He nodded enthusiastically. "Yes, yes. That is one of the good Simons in our religion. My favorite is Simon the Tanner." Simon the Tanner was the guy who moved Mokattam mountain with his faith. And plucked out his own eye rather than give in to the temptation of what he saw. Not really my kind of role model.

He pulled out into traffic. "My cab stinks of smoke, right? Does it bother you? I have this sign right here," he pointed to a plastic sign that was duct-taped to the back of the seat in front of me. It showed a cigarette and a big red "X" through it. "But it doesn't matter. This old man yesterday, he just lights up any old way right in my cab."

"It's okay—I don't mind," I said. But clearly it was not okay. He shook his head emphatically.

"I don't believe this country anymore," he continued. "We're all idiots, running around with our mobile phones and our cigarettes," he said. "Praise God, you don't smoke, do you?"

I shook my head. Traffic was at a standstill, so this could go on a while. "No cell phone either?" I shook my head again. Not by choice.

"Thanks to God, a little bit of sanity in a pretty head. You are a good girl. I can tell. Pure and straight. Not like everybody else. You promise me you'll stay that way."

He didn't wait for an answer. "Not like all these other people." He took both hands off the wheel to gesture with his arms at all the people. "They are all running around these people with their cell phones and their cigarettes, and they barely have money to feed their families!"

"Me, I have a phone," he pointed to a clip on the visor where a silver flip phone hung. "It's a curse. My regulars call it. Sometimes my mother calls for me to get her something. But some people in my cab, all they do is talk and text on the phone and then, God forbid, they smoke in it too.

"Everywhere you look, tell me what do you see?" Again, he didn't wait for an answer. Both hands came off the wheel again and he waved them around in exasperation.

What did he mean? People? Cars? Smog?

"Ads," he said.

My eyes picked out the jumble of protruding bulletin boards, the ads painted on every exposed wall.

"And for what? For cell phones. For tobacco. On the radio and the TV—the same thing. Day and night. It's the devil's art. Beautiful pictures tempting people to ruin."

The traffic surged forward again.

"Knowing we have good kids like you in the world, that keeps me going, you know?" his eyes framed in silver glasses searched for mine in the mirror. "Maybe you'll be president one day. A Coptic lady president, wouldn't that be something?" he laughed heartily as if this were an outrageous prospect. "You'd pull down all the ads for me, wouldn't you? So I can see the sky? And ban the stinking cigarettes, so I can breathe God's clean air. Would you do that for me?"

"I might just surprise you one day," I said. He smiled, taking this as agreement. The cab pulled up to my corner, and I gave him his five pounds. I noticed the nicotine stains on his six teeth as he smiled and took the money.

"You're a good girl. You stay out of trouble, now, you hear?" I heard him say as he drove off.

That was pretty much my main objective.

I puttered in the kitchen with Mom that night and tried to earn my way back to her good side. As hot as the Egyptian sun was outside—that's how cold that kitchen was inside. It promised to be a long night. I carefully folded the little grape leaves around the spiced rice while she salted and sampled the fish. The TV droned on in the background, and Dad sat on the overstuffed gold chair, his computer in his lap. He stared at it blankly, not touching the keys. The TV was on. A commercial exhorted the virtues of a new Jeep Cherokee as it zipped along American mountain roads. Why that would make anyone want to buy one to stand still in Egyptian traffic was beyond me, but I guess the advertising people knew what they were doing because American off-road vehicles cluttered Cairo's roads.

The news came on, and I heard Dad swear under his breath. I wiped my hands on the dishtowel and rounded the corner.

"—in the Church of St. Barbara. Today's attempted bombing was the second plot to blow up a Coptic Church to be unraveled by police this year . . ."

"What!? Dad—seriously?" I asked. It was what Mark had feared. The bomb threats on Christian churches were becoming real.

"Shhhh! Shhhh!" Dad said and wagged his finger at me urgently and turned back to the TV.

". . . officials are blaming the Muslim Brotherhood, but the Brotherhood denies responsibility for the bomb plots," the anchorman pronounced gravely, in his gray suit and greasy, slicked-back hair.

"Coptic Christians are tightening security around many churches to prevent further attempts," he said, and the screen switched to an interview with a bishop who explained that the government allows them to post soldiers in front of each church, but that congregations have also taken 24-hour surveillance into their own hands by posting civilian security guards in many of the city's key churches.

The video clip ended, and the anchor began a report on some new pollution emissions controls being implemented. Dad flicked the TV off.

"Oh my gosh, Dad! This is horrible! Someone could get killed. What about *our* church? Are we doing anything? How will Muslims and Christians ever get along again after a church bombing?" I said.

"If the Muslim Brotherhood is behind this, I'd hate to think what they could do to Muslim/Christian relations in Egypt," he said, sadly.

"Do you really think they could be planting bombs in our churches like terrorists?"

"No, but also yes. Remember, the Muslim Brotherhood is a sort-of political party, sort-of terrorist group," he said. He saw my confused look and added, "I know, I know, only in Egypt does this kind of logic work. It gets worse. For a while the Brotherhood was both democratically elected and outlawed—at the same time. How's that for sense? Nowadays, the Brotherhood is a growing political powerhouse. Officially, the party renounced violence, and most of its members prefer the path of peace. But some members have at times behaved like terrorists, and they are pushing the party toward more violence. Some question whether or not the party has control over them."

"Will they get arrested if they're caught?" I asked.

"Certainly, if they're caught. Probably a few of the usual suspects are being rounded up right now, just to send them a message. I don't like this. Already the first bomb attempt has caused trouble within the government. This second one makes it harder to argue that it's just one nutcase out there trying to make a point," he said.

"Do you think the Brotherhood did it?" I asked.

"Me?" he said, scratching his chin thoughtfully. "I hope not, but I don't really know. It'd just be one more sign that the peaceful majority in the party can't control the radical fringes. Whether they did it or not, the Brotherhood'll be working hard to make sure they don't take the wrap for this."

"Why would the radicals within the party stay hidden? I mean if they're anti-Christian enough to bomb us, why wouldn't they stand behind their actions?" I asked.

"Politics," he answered. "The radicals within the Brotherhood would like all us Christians to convert or leave Egypt, but they have to be careful about attacking us. In other parts of the world, Christians are a major force—America for example. An attack on Christians here could provoke the ire of the Americans," he said. "Egypt gets a lot of financial aid from the Americans. No one wants to see that end.

"More importantly, it would be poor politics for the Brotherhood as a whole to stand by and allow such attacks. It doesn't want to be associated with radical Islamists at all. The radicals are a small minority, and the Brotherhood, like the vast majority of Muslims, would prefer to distance themselves from them. To most Muslims, we Copts are family. We've been living together for millennia. We put up with each other like some bunch of crazy cousins. Every Muslim knows a handful of good Christians. We grow up together; our families have picnics with each other— though we mix only socially and not maritally," he looked at me meaningfully. "We may not see eye to eye on a lot of issues, but a fundamental level of respect exists there," he said.

"Then why don't the majority of Egypt's Muslims stand up for us when we're attacked?" I asked.

Dad sighed. "They do, and they don't. That double answer again. It would be unfair to argue that most Egyptians ignore our plight. You saw the news today. The government has stationed security forces outside of churches. But you also saw that our people didn't think it was enough and added their own forces. We are a minority, Magda, and we are under attack. Of course, we would like more protection."

After a moment he added, "As always, these things are muddy. Have you considered that it may not be a Muslim or Muslim group at all that's setting off these bombs?" he asked.

"What?"

"It's not only the Muslims who know how to make a bomb," he said. "And an attack on the Christians of Egypt would be seen by much of the world as an attack on all Christians. There are those who would love to create a situation that would cause the Americans or the Europeans to get involved in our politics, demanding greater democracy or sniffing around for human rights violations. However ill thought-out that train of thought might be, it cannot be discounted.

Then he shifted gears. "Nor can we discount the idea that you are supposed to be doing your homework. Don't you have exams coming up? So you can apply to American schools as your backup? The SABs or something?"

"The SATs? Yeah. I did all the prep tests, but it wouldn't hurt to go over them again," I said. Magda had completed all of her prep tests, and American universities were only her fallback option. I still had work to do.

The conversation with Dad played out in my head the rest of the evening. I'd never lived anywhere where I might feel threatened, except in Florida by hurricanes. As much as the great winds terrified me, they came with at least twenty-four hours warning and left no murky issues of blame and retribution.

I went to my room, spent an hour on my SAT prep tests and finished my homework. I had a test in Arabic tomorrow, and I was worried about it. I pulled open my Arabic notes and read them again, but the words stayed on the page and didn't penetrate my mind.

The night passed interminably slowly. Arabic can make an evening do that.

Maraya went to bed at ten, as usual. I stayed up till eleven and then climbed into bed as usual, turned out the lights, as usual. I wasn't going to risk sneaking out into the kitchen for my computer again. I stared at the ceiling, feeling very alone. I watched little cones of light appear, flare out and then vanish with each passing car from the street outside. I heard the ticking of the alarm clock on the table beside Magda's bunk, the distant hum of traffic, a horn honking.

When I closed my eyes, my mind wandered aimlessly through all my anxieties. I may have just begun to drift when I heard a familiar sound at the window.

Thwumpity-thwump.

I tensed. It couldn't be. He wouldn't.

Thwumpity-thwump.

He would.

I crept down the ladder, flew to the window and pushed it open as quietly as I could. He stood silhouetted by the light of a streetlamp.

"Are you completely nuts?" I whispered angrily.

"Only about you."

"Ahmed, get out of here! You'll wake someone!"

"It's two in the morning. Your parents are sound asleep, like always. Come with me. Just this once. I promise I won't ask it of you again. Not unless you want to."

I hesitated. He detected weakness.

"I won't stop throwing pebbles till you come."

"You darn well will!"

"Try me," he drew back his throwing arm.

"Ahmed Najjar, I hate you!"

"No, you don't," I could hear the smile in his voice.

"No," I whispered angrily. "Just—just stay there. Don't make a noise. Don't move an inch. Understand?"

He held a hand over his mouth then put his hands in the air in surrender.

I closed the window. Maraya breathed slowly and rhythmically. I tiptoed to the closet and slipped on some black flats and a scarlet dress. My eyes caught on a white a scarf neatly folded on a hanger, and I grabbed it and tucked it into a pocket. I made my way to the door. The latch made a little click as it released. The noise felt like a bomb in the quiet room. I paused again and waited to hear the resumption of Maraya's gentle breathing.

"Where are you going, Molly?" a soft voice asked.

I was a rabbit, caught in the headlights of an oncoming car, unable to move. I released the latch and slid the door shut again.

"Are you going to see him again?" she asked.

I thought about lying then looked down at my red dress. My only hope was in her ability to keep a secret.

"I have to. This is part of our secret again, kay? If Mom and Dad find out, I'll be in even more trouble than I am already, but this is something I really have to do."

"Why do you have to do it?" she asked, rubbing her eyes.

My heart raced. I didn't have time to reason with her.

"Well, it's hard to explain, and I can't really talk about it now because I have to meet him right away. If you can try really hard not to say anything at all about this, I'll take you for ice cream after church this Saturday. Double chocolate. On me. I'll explain everything then." Bribery. An age-old trick.

She looked perplexed at first. How had this chocolate ice cream moment dropped out of heaven? Then her eyes lit up, and her face froze in a silly smile of delight. "Yay!" she said. Her back went rigid, and she flopped back down onto the bed and feigned very loud snoring.

Close enough.

I opened the door more quickly this time and slipped out. I stayed to the edge of the walls, where the floorboards creaked less. Quickly, noiselessly, I slipped through the front door of the apartment. I smoothed my dress down and tried to walk confidently down the hall and out the front door. As soon as I stepped outside, a gust of wind caught my dress and lifted it, briefly revealing more than a smidge of one of Magda's shapely legs.

Ahmed poked his head out from behind a bush near the gate in time to smile at the fleeting vision. I blushed, and he motioned for me to come. He wore jeans and a black T-shirt that matched his dark, tousled hair. He took my hand and pulled me onto the street. I slipped my other hand in my pocket and pulled out the white scarf. I let go of his hand, wrapped the scarf over my hair and tied it tightly under my chin. We became just another Muslim couple on the quiet suburban streets.

He grinned.

"Nice scarf. So you've decided to join Islam? I rejoice in your decision!" he held his free hands up to the sky and motioned with it upwards dramatically, "Muhammad rejoices in heaven!"

I punched him in the ribs, half in anger, half in jest. He knew better than to tease me about converting.

"Ooof! Now wait a second. Nice Muslim girls don't hit their boyfriends," he said.

Boyfriend? I liked the sound of that. We'd never really tried on the boyfriend/girlfriend titles.

"Are we boyfriend and girlfriend now?" I asked.

His eyes gleamed, like a wolf ready to swallow me up in a single bite. He released my hand and reached his arm around to rest on my hip and pulled me close.

"After what we've been through for each other?" he said. "I wouldn't go through this for Kamal, you know."

He didn't get the laugh he hoped for. I was still angry he had tricked me into being here. He opened the passenger door for me.

"Ahmed, no. Whatever you have to say to me, say it here. We can't do this again."

"Magda, think about it. We are in more danger here than anywhere else. Everyone knows you here. One sleepless neighbor glances out his window and your parents will hear about it. The sooner we get away from here the better. Just give me an hour."

Reluctantly, I slipped into the car. He walked around the car and sat down lightly in the driver's seat.

"Maybe we could just pull over somewhere near here," I suggested.

"And have the police stop to investigate? Or someone recognize my car? We need to leave the neighborhood. Uncle Abdullah's place as close as anything and we've been safe there before."

As we merged onto the major street, the traffic picked up. The effort of dodging in and out of lanes took Ahmed's attention. The tapping of horns mixed with the rhythm of music floating from the shops and cafes. I knew Cairo's nights intimately now. Her streets were less busy than they had been in late afternoon, but men and women were still out shopping and walking. The wind was strong tonight, and their galibeyas swirled about them. I saw no signs of drunkenness, even at this hour. The people of Cairo ambled along the streets soberly celebrating the end of another day's work. In an hour or so, her streets would grow quiet. It never ceased to amaze me how alive this city was at this time of night. Even the crowds of Manhattan would be thin by now.

As we crossed the expansive 6th of October Bridge, the wind across the Nile buffeted the car, and Ahmed gripped the steering wheel.

"Ahmed, I'm scared," I said.

He knew I wasn't talking about the wind though that frightened me also.

"I know."

"If we get caught this time, it's going to be even worse."

"We're not going to get caught. Fatima's in bed, okay?" he said and smiled nervously.

I wasn't in a joking mood.

"I'm sorry. I don't mean to be flip. I need this one night with you. You'll understand," he said.

"This had better be good."

"I'm hoping it will be."

We were silent a moment.

"Have the kids at school been hard on you?" I asked.

He looked at me, curiously.

"I think it's easier for a guy," he said. "I mean," he gave a nervous smile, "it hardly makes you a social pariah to be caught kissing the prettiest girl in Cairo behind the PE lockers."

Great. So he was the conquering hero, and I was the social train wreck. I kept my head turned out over the Nile, a dark expanse of nothingness outlined in lights.

"Magda," he said, sensing my sudden coldness. He reached a hand to take mine as he drove. "I'm not playing the macho card, okay? I mean, I'm taking your reputation very seriously. I've already told at least a dozen guys that tried to congratulate me or just slap me on the back that if they say anything mean about you, I'll crack their heads open, and I meant it, okay?"

I think I was supposed to be reassured by this.

"Just a little maiming is all I ask," I said. "No need to overdo it. Besides, I have Demiana to protect me."

He laughed. "She's something, isn't she?" I nodded silently.

His voice took on a serious tone again. "Listen, Magda. To the guys, you see, this was, like, just a kiss. Yeah, some of the guys don't get why I'd pick a Christian girl, but they're narrow-minded anyway. And they've never gotten to know *you*."

I felt my blood pressure rising. "They don't get why you'd like a Christian girl? Are we so inferior that we're not worthy of their respect? Or are we just easier? Is that it?"

"Magda, you know that's not true," he said, his brow furrowing. "No one thinks Christian girls are inferior, and I've never heard anyone say they're easy. More the opposite: they're impossible. Christian girls are off-limits to Muslim guys. Period. Everyone knows that Coptic families don't let their daughters marry Muslims. The guys aren't mad at me or anything. They just think I'm wasting my time."

I stayed quiet and looked out over the last of the cold dark water as the bridge came over solid ground again. Kids could be awful. They had been awful to me. Ahmed wasn't the one I should be mad at.

"I guess girls aren't so easygoing about these things," he added. "What are they saying to you, anyway?"

"Let's see," I said and began counting my fingers. "I've got Makeout Magda," I ticked off one finger, "Slut, sleeze, loose, and one of the British kids called me a trollop. I'm not sure what that means, but I can guess cause of the way he—" my lips curled in disgust, "leered." I ticked off the fifth finger then flopped my hands down in defeat. "I've had about twenty requests for a date behind the PE lockers. I'm grounded for life. I've had all my privileges revoked. We're both waiting to hear if we're expelled, and I'm a major disappointment to my family. Oh, and I'm out with you again, which means I'm insane," I threw my hands up in the air. "That's all I can think of at the moment." My voice cracked with emotion. I fought back tears.

"Magda, I'm so, so, so sorry." The road turned bumpy. We were getting close.

"It's just so unfair," I said, struggling to regain composure. "You're the hero, and I'm the—the—slut. Your friends pat you on the back, and mine desert me. It's such a double standard," I shook my head. "We never should have kissed behind the lockers. It was dumb."

He looked at me, lines of worry furrowing his brow.

"Well, it was dumb to get caught," I said, smiling just a little, despite myself.

Ahmed grinned complicity.

"Stupid Fatima," I added.

"Yeah, well, she's a spoiled brat anyway. Some poor guy's going to have to marry her for her money one day. She'll probably follow him around with a camera all day trying to catch him with another woman," he said, with a smirk.

We pulled up to the stables and parked.

"I was going to suggest we go for a walk in the desert tonight," he said, "but I think it's too windy. Every time we open our mouths, we'd get a mouthful of sand out there. Then again, all we'd be able to do is kiss . . ." He started to drag me toward the black desert.

"Forget it!" I said, laughing, and pulled from his grip and slipped through the side door of the stable. Ahmed followed, with feigned disappointment.

"Bummer," he said. "I played that wrong, didn't I?"

"Guys, you're all the same!" I laughed.

We made our way up the stairs. I pulled off my scarf and let my hair fall loose about my shoulders. We sat in the same spot as before. It was quiet here, out of the wind. Our little oasis. Ahmed leaned his back against one of the whitewashed walls. For a moment, I forgot about the serious nature of our meeting tonight. He put his hands on my shoulders and drew me close, so my back rested against his broad chest. I relaxed into the warmth of his body. I could feel his breath on my neck. I let my head fall on his shoulder, and our cheeks touched. His five o'clock shadow scratched me. Something urgent stirred inside me. He kissed my neck and sighed my name—I mean Magda's. Abruptly I pulled away from him.

"Magda—" he said. "I'm sorry, I—"

"It's okay," I said. I couldn't tell him I was frightened by my own body and how easily it was seduced. "Let's just talk, okay?"

"We'll just talk," he said soothingly and touched the bench for me to come closer again. Carefully, I did. He reached out and entwined a length of Magda's long hair around his finger. "May I do this?" he inquired innocently. "It would be a shame to have you so near me and not touch you at all," he said.

It seemed a reasonable compromise.

"Ahmed, how can we ever make this work? Dad says that whenever a Muslim boy falls in love with a Coptic girl, she ends up converting. He says Muslims can't convert because that's like treason. And neither of us converting isn't an answer because neither community accepts going to church on Saturday and mosque on Friday—especially when there are children. Ahmed, I don't think it's right that I should have to convert."

"Magda. You don't have to convert. I don't want you to change your hair, or your eyes, or your body or your faith. Your religion is a big part of who you are, and I respect that. I don't want you to change a thing about you."

"Really? You think we could make it work without one of us converting?"

"I think we can. It won't be easy, but the inconvenience of two religions in one relationship is a price I'm willing to pay," he smiled, recalling our argument in English class.

I snuggled closer to him. "Demiana says we should take on Egyptian society. Fight for the right for Christians and Muslims to be together peacefully."

"Muslims pray for that everyday," he said.

"What?" I asked.

"Didn't you know that?" he said. "The five prayers begin and end by praying for peace for the entire family of Abraham—Jews, Christians and Muslims," he said.

"It does?" I asked.

"Mmm hmmm. Muhammad was just the last in a series of twenty-five messengers and prophets, starting with Adam and including Moses and Jesus. We believe that Judaism, Christianity and Islam are three forms of one religion, which was the religion of the prophet Abraham," he said.

"So you believe in the Jewish Torah and the Gospels, just like us."

"Islam is just another version of Judaism and Christianity," he said.

"Wait a second. If that's true, how come Muslims everywhere are attacking Christians?"

"Okay, stop right there," he said sharply, and I sat up. "If we're going to be together—and we're going to be together—you have to understand this. Those guys call themselves Muslims, but they aren't true Muslims. Nowhere in the Koran does it say kill, and you shall be rewarded," Ahmed said. "And I don't think there are any informed, educated Muslims who believe that. It's the poor, the uneducated and the vulnerable who fall victim to that kind of crazy thinking," he said.

"What about Kamal and his father?"

"I don't, for a minute, think Kamal is like that. Other than Samir, Kamal is the closest family I've got. If he was some heartless terrorist, I'd know. As for Uncle Radwan, well, he was—vulnerable I guess."

"It can't just be the poor and uneducated. What about those guys who flew into the World Trade Center in New York? They were educated. Muhammad Ahta—that was his name, right? He flew one of the planes into the towers. He was from Cairo. He had a degree from a university here and another from Germany."

"I'll grant you that. Ahta was educated. Osama bin Laden was educated too," he conceded. "The leaders have education and money. Let me put it another way. A small group of wealthy educated people have used their skills and resources to recruit an army from among the poor and uneducated. They've cherry-picked phrases from the scriptures and reinterpreted them to support their cause. They call it Islam, but no other Muslims recognize it. They're raising an army to support their own twisted political agenda."

"What about jihad—holy war—isn't that from the Koran?" I challenged.

"That's a perfect example. Jihad means two things. Mostly, it's about the struggle we all face within ourselves to become a better Muslim. But it's also the idea of a holy war to defend the faith from mortal danger. How could the attack on the trade center be a jihad? Islam faced no mortal danger from New York on September 11, 2001. But it's more than that. Al Qaeda justifies the attack as a *jihad against infidels,* non-believers. That makes no sense. By Islam's definition, Christians and Jews are 'people of the book.' It's like I said, we all believe most of the same things. Christians and Jews aren't non-believers, they're—I dunno—half believers, I guess. But Muslims definitely don't consider them infidels."

I digested this. We were protected from the wind where we sat, but it whipped between the buildings. It made me feel vulnerable, like a sapling the wind might bend and break if it chose. He took both my hands in his.

"Magda, I want to be with you always, not just now, and not in secrecy. I'll take the secrecy if it's all I can have, but I'm in love with you, and I don't think God wants something as wonderful as this to be a secret," he said.

"Ahmed—I'm in love with you too. I want to be with you more than anything. I just don't know how we can make it happen. I stand to lose everything. My friends, my family, my school. My dad could even lose his job."

"I realize this is a lot harder for you than for me," he said.

"So what do we do?"

"That's why I had to talk with you in person today. I couldn't say this on a computer," he said. He gripped my hand tightly, looked down, drew a breath and then met my eyes. "Magda, will you marry me?"

Whoa. My eyes lit, and my heart soared instantly. This is what Magda wanted more than anything—I knew it in my/her heart. Then reason kicked in, and my smile faded. She wanted to marry Ahmed but not under any circumstances. She wouldn't be willing to give up her friends and family to have him. I was a long ways from solving this problem for her. Besides, getting married has to be one of the greatest moments in a girl's life. What if I we didn't shift back before the ceremony began? Could I take that moment away from her? No, I'd brought Magda this far, but marriage was a line I couldn't cross. It wasn't a decision I could make for her.

His face lit with mine then fell again in unison with mine. I hurried to restore his lost confidence.

"Ahmed, Ahmed—I *do* want to marry you." His eyes met mine tentatively. "I want to marry you more than anything I've ever wanted," I said, knowing I was speaking from Magda's heart. I touched his chin and lifted it, so we faced each other squarely. "I *will* marry you," I said firmly. "Just not yet. Not like this. Not in secrecy and scandal. Not with the chance my family could disown me.

"But maybe there is a way we could be together and give them time to get used to the idea. What if you came to London to study with me after graduation? We could be together then without the prying eyes of our family and community. We could eat together in cafes and go to shows. We could hold hands in the hallways at university. Wouldn't that be something?" I said.

"I didn't know you wanted to go to London. I knew you wanted to study medicine, but I guess I just assumed you'd study here."

"I've always wanted to study medicine there. I could become a good doctor here, but I think I could be a great doctor with all that I'd learn there," I said. "Ahmed, we could spend time together in England, and let things cool off here. If we married after our studies, we'd be adults, and our parents might be better able to accept that we know what we're doing. Maybe we could even have a civil wedding in Egypt and invite all of our friends and family. Worst case, if my family still stands against our marriage, we could marry in London and give everyone at home time to adjust to the idea that we are married before we came back. But we would come back. I could never leave Egypt forever," I said.

Ahmed sighed. "It's true what they say. Once you have drunk the waters of the Nile, you will always return. It's fate," he said.

"Are there any schools in London on your shortlist?"

"Well, I was planning to study here though I did sometimes dream of studying economics at Stanford in America before I met you. Now that you mention it, the London School of Economics is prestigious. A degree from there would be a great start. You know, that's not a bad idea. It may be a really good idea." He let the idea percolate then shook his head. "But Magda,

I'm afraid that day might never come. What if between now and then your parents decide to marry you to someone else?"

"They haven't threatened that yet," I said. "And if they don't catch us together again, they probably won't. We probably shouldn't take any more risks though. If they caught us tonight, they would make sure we never saw each other again," I said, glancing at my watch. I would give him his hour, but then I wanted to get home. "I can tell you this much though, I would sneak off to marry you before I'd let them marry me to someone else."

I wasn't planning to marry anyone while I was in this body, but if I were forced to choose, I would choose Ahmed. "Still, assuming we can both get into schools in London, we still have a year and a half to get through," I said. Studying together abroad was a hopeful solution, but just setting up such a plan might not be enough to make me shift. No way was I going to stay in this body for a year and a half to see this through.

"Is there anything you can think of that would help us warm our families up to each other? Let's start with my family, since it's the biggest obstacle. My mother went on a hunger strike for twelve days to get her parents to open up to the idea of letting her marry Dad," I said.

"I would never ask it of you," Ahmed said. "Remember your mother thinks this is a battle over your soul. She may not give up easily." He shook his head. "To be honest, Magda, I think until we're married, your parents won't discuss this with us. Any attempt to open a conversation will only make them suspect we might sneak off and get married. Once they suspect that, they'll make sure we never see or speak to each other again. I think we have to act before they suspect."

He was right, but it didn't matter. Magda wouldn't marry him while I was in her body—not unless we were desperate. I would steer as far from a quick marriage as I could. Where he saw two options—marry now or marry later—I saw only one.

"I get what you're saying," I conceded to his logic. "I need some time to think this through."

"I will give you all the time you need, Magda. While you think, I'll look into the London School of Economics. I'll also investigate our options should you agree to marry quickly. I think I know someone who would marry us. If things go badly, we will need to move fast, and I want to be ready."

I nodded in agreement. "In the meantime, though, we have to play it safe. No more secret meetings. No contact at all. Just our Facebook account, and even that we should use sparingly. Our lives together may depend on it. Oh—and our parents shouldn't find out we are both applying to schools in the same country." I thought of my near miss with Maraya on my way out the door. Our secret wasn't completely our own as it was.

"Staying away from you is the hardest thing you could ever ask me," he said. "But you're completely right."

I turned and snuggled my back into his chest again, intensely aware that these could be our last moments together alone.

A silence stretched between us. I wanted this moment to last forever, but his hour had nearly ended. The wind picked up. What had been a low whistle between buildings escalated to an intermittent wail.

"I'll never get used to *khamsin* season," he said, moving the conversation to safer ground.

I searched my brain. What was a khamsin? The word sounded Arabic, but Magda's brain wasn't telling me what it meant. Maybe that meant I didn't have a word for it in English?

"What?" I asked, pretending I hadn't heard him.

"Khamsin season. You know—the sand storms. It's early yet for a big one, I know, but all this sand reminds me of the big one last year. Where were you when it hit?" he asked.

Where would Magda have been?

"We were in town," I ventured vaguely.

"Us too," he said. "I was swimming at the club, and it came totally out of nowhere. One minute the sky was clear and the day was hot then the wind picked up suddenly, and I heard someone shouting. I looked up and saw a monster wall of red-black sand in the west. Everyone started running around, gathering up their things and making for their cars.

"We got home about ten minutes before it hit, *Alhamdulillah*," he said, meaning "thank God." "My Mom and I ran around shoving towels under all the doors and window sills to keep the sand out. It worked a little, but the whole world was sooty and gritty for days after," he said. "How many people died? Do you remember?" he asked.

"No," I said, truthfully.

"It must've been dozens. I forget the final count. It's here in the desert that it's the worst," he said. I know Uncle Abdullah had a panic attack getting all his tourists and their horses back in," he said. "But you're probably used to these storms," he said. "I've been away too much."

"You never get used to them," I said, assuming that was probably true.

I glanced at my watch. It was 3:00 a.m. We had to go.

He pulled me up, and drew me in close. He touched a hand lovingly to my face and leaned down. The wind tossed my hair and tugged at my dress, wrapping around him as we shared a slow, gentle kiss.

"There will be many more, Magda, I promise," he said softly.

I nodded, fighting back tears. God willing, Ahmed and the real Magda would share more kisses like this, and their love would grow with the years. For me this was probably my last moment under the heady spell of Magda's love. If I'd done my job and put Magda's life on the right course, I would shift soon. If I didn't shift, it would mean that I hadn't found a way for these two to be together. Either way, this would be our last kiss.

We descended the stairs briskly. The sweaty smell of horses filled my nostrils as we hit the bottom steps and opened the door. We stepped outside and the wind grabbed us. It pulled hard at the steering as Ahmed drove across the expansive 6th of October Bridge. But the arteries of the city lay open in the pre-dawn hours, and we made good time. Ahmed parked a block away.

We dared not risk a parting kiss. I squeezed his hand as I left him and moved silently through the gate. As I passed through the main doors to the building, I pulled the scarf from my hair and tucked back into a pocket. I slipped off my shoes and raced silently up the stairs and down the hall to Magda's apartment door. I slid the key in and slowly turned the tumblers, cringing with every click they made as they fell into place. The door squeaked slightly as I opened and closed it.

It was not yet four o'clock, and no lights shined under the bedroom doors. I crept down the hallway and opened the bedroom door carefully, closing it behind me. Relief washed over me as I pulled off the scarlet dress and put it in the closet. I climbed the ladder and slipped into my nightgown and under the covers.

I felt a tear slide down my cheek in the quiet room. I closed my eyes, and this time sleep took me gladly into its dark embrace.

XXVI

I found the first one right after the Arabic. Magda's mom had given me my cell phone that morning for use only at school, so she could contact me if she needed to during school hours.

The phone vibrated in my pocket as I pushed through the crowded hallway during break. I had one new text message from an unknown number.

Repent or He will punish you.`

An involuntary chill moved through my body.

Who would send something like this? Could it be Fatima? Or Verana? Was one of them actually threatening me? And what did the message mean? Punish me how? It had to be about the photo. No one had hated Magda enough to send something like this until I came along and screwed up her life.

I closed the phone quickly. Would the person who left the message be watching for my reaction? All I saw was the usual hustle and bustle of kids late for class. No one's eyes locked onto mine or turned away.

My heart pounding, I put my phone away and went to my next class. What else could I do?

At lunch, I showed the message to Layla.

"Geez, Magda! It sounds like someone wants to *kill* you!"

"I know. I'm pretty freaked out about it," I said.

"Magda, this is serious. What are you going to do?" she asked.

"About what?" asked Demiana, as she sat down beside us. Her curly black hair was down again today. I think I could see a headband in the curls somewhere, but I wasn't sure.

Layla snatched the phone out of my hand and put it in Demiana's. "Look at her text messages," she said.

Demiana flicked the phone on and hit the messages button. Her face turned white.

"Yikes, Magda—that's totally creepy! Who do you think sent it?"

"Maybe it's Fatima," Layla said.

"I don't know. Even she wouldn't go that far. Would she?" I said.

"You have to tell your dad about this, Magda. Maybe he can help you figure out where it came from," Demiana said.

"It's just a prank," I said, with conviction I didn't feel. "It doesn't mean anything."

"It *could* just be a prank," Demiana demurred. "But what if it isn't?"

Yeah. What if. I buried my face in my bag of potato chips and shrugged.

That evening when I got home, I breezed into the kitchen, kissed Mom, and headed to the fridge. There was some tahini left over from last night's dinner and some bread. I spooned the tahini onto a plate absent-mindedly and piled some bread up beside it.

"When will Dad be home tonight?" I asked. His schedule was pretty unpredictable, and I still needed to decide if I should show him the message. The temperature in the house had warmed up just enough that I could talk and even laugh with Magda's parents sometimes. Right when our family was beginning to heal, this text message could slice open the wound.

"He's on business in Alexandria until next week, honey," Magda's mom said.

Oh shoot. I hadn't even said goodbye. Magda would've said goodbye.

Briefly, I toyed with the idea of telling Magda's mom about the texts, but I decided it would worry her, and without Dad's calming influence, she would definitely want to keep me even closer to home. She'd already given me my cell phone for day use. I really missed working out after school and hoped to ask if I could stay late to run.

I had to return the phone to her after school hours, so I decided to just delete the message and forget about it. The text was probably just from some crackpot anyway. I opened the phone to delete the message before I returned it. Three more texts, all exactly the same, waited for me:

Repent or He will punish you.

I deleted them all before handing the phone to her.

By Thursday I'd had more than twenty of these messages, and I was freaked out.

"Have you had any more of those messages?" Demiana asked in the hallway.

I had decided to keep the lid on this. If this was a prankster, he or she would be waiting for my reaction. If I admitted that I was getting these messages, then I was giving whoever was sending them a victory. And whoever it was, was almost certainly in this school somewhere. Maybe even watching me right now and delighting in the dark circles under my eyes. Fatima? Verana? Kamal?

"Nothing more from that number, thank God," I said, truthfully. Every message was from a different number. How could anyone have access to so many different phones? Or was it more than one person?

Repent or He will punish you.

Five messages waited for me on my phone Saturday morning. I'm not sure why I kept checking. Like a mosquito drawn to a flame, I was mesmerized by my own tormenter.

We went to church. Magda's dad's conference continued through next week, and he had decided to use the weekend in Alexandria to catch up with his second cousin. People here had so much family. The Molly in me was a little jealous. Hardly anyone had family in my hometown of Tampa. Tampa barely existed before air conditioning became cheap in the 80s. Then the city exploded as people from all over the country swarmed in for the sand, beaches and work, leaving their extended families behind.

Here in Egypt, everyone was born in Cairo. Everyone knew everyone in his or her community, and it was just assumed that you'd know each other until one of you died. So God forbid if you screwed up like I did. Everyone knew about it, and no one got to start over.

Today was my first day at church since Fatima's photo. Mom, Maraya and I entered the churchyard and heads swiveled in my direction. I tried to bury myself in my cell phone—of all things.

Bing! My phone registered a new text message.

Have you repented yet? my phone demanded of me.

Anger boiled up inside of me, and at that moment, it spilled over. I'd had enough. I was tired of being scared.

I hit reply then jabbed my finger into my phone and typed the words, *NO! HAVE YOU?!* I hit send before I could think it over.

"Hey, Magda!" came a voice. I turned to see a girl, maybe fourteen or so, with scraggly, unbrushed hair and a big smile. She came close and gave me a friendly squeeze.

"So is it true you're seeing a *Muslim* boy?" she said. A half dozen ears cocked in our direction and waited for my reply.

"Yeah, it's pretty much true," I said. "Everything you've heard."

"Then do you love him?" Whoa. Talk about direct.

I was painfully aware of the other listening ears. Everything I said would be on a direct playback loop to Magda's mom. I sighed.

"Yes, I do," I answered simply. How could I lie? Things were not going to get better when Mom got wind of that.

"Neat." She said and disappeared into the crowd.

Even here, pockets of resistance.

The ceremonies that had been beautiful and exotic the first time I witnessed them dragged on in endless tedium today. I bent my head and spent a few minutes asking God for guidance. He offered me none today. I was tired from several nights of poor sleep. I wanted to go back to Magda's bedroom and rest. I shifted around uncomfortably in my seat. It was well past noon when church let out, and I looked forward to some enforced quiet time at home.

"I'm sorry, honey, but you know every first Saturday of the month I have to stay for my Women's Bible Study class," Mom said. I was going to have stay here until she finished?

"How about if I take Maraya for ice cream?" I asked.

"Honey, you know the ice cream shop is blocks from here, and you're grounded," she said, sternly.

"Mom, I'm with Maraya. I won't even buy one for myself. I just want to do it for her," I said, going for the parental heartstrings. I hung my head low and added, "I've been kind of a pain to be around lately, and I'm trying to make it up to her. My own money."

"Well—" she hesitated. I detected weakness and went in for the kill.

"If you let me go right now, I can be there and back by 1:30, no problem," I said.

Her lips held a straight line as she debated her decision. "Straight back now, you hear? If I get wind that you stopped anywhere else on the way, you'll never leave the house again, understood?"

"Understood."

She dug through her purse and reluctantly tossed me the keys. Keys? It hadn't occurred to me I would have to drive. I'd sworn I'd never drive here. Well, today *was* Saturday, and the traffic on the way here had been light. Magda's mom's car was a stick shift, and I'd grown up driving a stick shift on my Mom's car at home. No more excuses. I could do this.

My ice cream date with Maraya would be my first outing away from church or school since I'd been grounded, not counting the stables, and it would probably be my last for a while once she learned I'd said I was still in love with Ahmed within hearing of half the church. I began preparing a mental defense as I searched for Maraya. *I was only telling the truth. She could keep me away from Ahmed, but she couldn't change how I felt.* Words like those were more of an entrenchment than a defense. I needed something better.

Three new messages on my phone. I knew whom they would be from. I resisted the urge to check them and put the phone back in my pocket. I wasn't sure I was supposed to have the phone this morning since it wasn't a school day, but I figured church was similar to school. If Magda's mother minded or even noticed, she didn't say anything.

Maraya ran through the crowds playing tag with some other girls. I called her over to tell her about the ice cream. She whooped with joy and did a little happy dance.

"Double chocolate chip—oh, and can we get one of the new gelatos? They're way better than regular ice cream. They don't have chocolate chips though," her face turned solemn. Then she perked up again. "Maybe I'll try the pistachio this time! Or should I get the lemon? The lemon was soooo good. What should I pick?" she asked.

"We'll get you a scoop of each. How about that?" I said.

She looked up at me in wonder. "Wow. You can go out with Ahmed as much as you want, and I promise I'll never say any—" I clapped my hand over her mouth and then tried to cover the move with a forced laugh.

"Shh!!" I said urgently, my eyes wide with meaning. "You mustn't say silly things like that," I pretend giggled. I looked around furtively. The crowd had thinned, and I don't think anyone noticed.

Having arrived a little late, we had parked a ways from the church. Not that it had mattered since church always started late anyway. Nothing in Egypt ran on time. Except school. School was the great world equalizer. Always on time, everywhere—the one thing all students wished would run late.

The streets grew narrower and quieter as we got further from church. After about ten minutes of walking, I threw my hands up in the air. Wasn't this the street where we'd left the car? Or was it the next one? When we arrived, I had been so engrossed in my own worries that I hadn't paid much attention to where we parked.

"Maraya, do you remember where we parked?" I asked.

She paused, taking inventory of her surroundings, apparently for the first time. "Yes," she said confidently. "It's over here." She led the way one more street up and another over. Nothing.

She stood still, looking around, a finger on her chin. "Maybe that was where we parked last week," she said. The streets were surprisingly quiet here, so close to the main drag. Just the odd stranger loitered along the sidewalks.

"Let's try walking up three more streets, and if we don't see it, we'll go back and ask Mom," I said.

"Okay," Maraya agreed brightly. Do eight-year-olds ever get worried?

Maybe I was just being paranoid. A short, bulky man in an ill-fitting gray suit lingered over a newspaper a ways behind us. I turned back, but the moment I did, he slipped the newspaper under his arm and disappeared down a small side street.

Surely, these threatening text messages were making my imagination run wild.

"Listen, let's just head back," I said, trying to cover my sudden bout of nerves.

I took a right turn, to keep clear of the strange man. We walked swiftly down a small sidewalk, lined with parked cars. As we approached a small red van parked along the road, I glanced up into its reflective rear windows, and the same short man strode purposefully toward us in the reflection. The hairs on the back of my neck rose.

This feeling was *just not right*. I wasn't being paranoid. And even if I was, I'd rather be paranoid than sorry. I grabbed Maraya's hand and started to run.

"Ow!" Maraya protested. "What are you doing? That hurts!"

"Run, Maraya," I said, "Don't ask questions, just move!" I dragged her around another corner in the general direction of the church, and there, thank God, I saw our car just three cars up.

I let go of Maraya's hand to fumble for the keys in my purse while we ran and heard a car door slamming and an engine roar to life behind us. I didn't pause to look up.

"Magda, you're scaring me!" Maraya said. Her eyes were frozen in fear and beginning to well with tears.

"It's okay, Maraya, just stay calm. I think that man who was behind us is a bad man. I'm going to get us out of here."

At last I found the key and turned it in the passenger lock. I threw the passenger door open and pushed Maraya in then ran around to my side. There were no power locks, so I had to fumble with the key again. The door gave way, and I looked in the rear view mirror to see the dingy red van accelerating down the street toward us.

"I'm not allowed in the front seat!" Maraya cried. "I'll get in trouble!"

I threw the car in gear and lurched into reverse, ramming straight into the car behind. This had better be the real deal, I thought ironically, or Magda's mom's going to kill me for doing this to the car.

I put it in drive, yanked the steering wheel toward the street, and the car leaped out of the parking spot. I slammed it into second, then third, and soon we were roaring down the street. The van was right on my tail. Its windshield was dark, with a strip of reflective coating across the top, so I couldn't see more than a shadow at the wheel. I prayed that no one would step into the street ahead of me and slammed it into fourth before careening out onto the main street about five blocks away from of the church.

Tires squealed as I turned the corner into traffic. Our little car was more agile and allowed me to get a couple of car lengths ahead. The van followed, but as always in Egypt, if there is a car length between two cars in traffic, a car is soon to occupy it. A green Jeep Cherokee separated us. My heart pounding, I looked in my rearview mirror and saw flashes of red as the van darted from side to side behind the Jeep, looking for an opportunity to pass.

Where should I go? *Forward*! a voice in my head shouted. I obeyed.

"Put your seatbelt on," I said firmly to Maraya. "Never mind about the front seat. Do it now!"

She reached across and put her seatbelt on, not taking her wide eyes off the street. I raced between cars and laid my hands on the horn at every turn. The van kept pace turn for turn. *Oh my God, how could I have brought Maraya into this!* I would never forgive myself if anything happened to her.

I reached into my pocket for my phone and opened the screen. I had another new text message. I ignored it. I fumbled through my favorites list. Who should I call for help? Who could help me here?

With no one else to call, I hit the number for Dad. The phone rang three times. "I'm sorry I can't come to the phone right now," I heard. I flipped it shut. I hit redial.

"Please, Dad, please," I whispered under my breath as I threaded through the traffic. And then for good measure, "Please God, let him answer."

The phone clicked over again, "I'm sorry I can't—" I flipped the phone shut fiercely and swore under my breath.

There was one other person I could call.

I saw the sharp turn to the right that would loop and take us up onto 6th of October Bridge. I slowed for a moment, waiting for the van to catch up and be right on my tail. Then, at the last possible second, I yanked the wheel to the right and took the exit onto the Bridge.

I heard a cacophony of horns, and I looked up to see that the van had reacted behind me and taken the turn too wide. The van was on the narrow shoulder of the road and tried to merge into traffic on the exit. Its sudden swerve from the road had toppled a cyclist with a box of produce on the back of his bike, and tomatoes and oranges lay everywhere. The disgruntled biker waved his fists and swore at the van.

I pushed the speakerphone button and passed the phone to Maraya. "Dial this number for me," I ordered her.

With trembling fingers, she pushed the numbers as I called them out. They were numbers I had never dialed but had committed to memory.

I was in the right lane, nearest the edge of the bridge. Beneath us, the vast expanse of the Nile surged—its edges dotted with serene little white falukas, taking passengers up and down the river. A narrow raised sidewalk and chest-high, green-painted metal fence were all that separated us from the powerful river below. I was stuck behind a slow moving black and white taxi. I laid my hand on the horn and tried to move out into the left lane, but a blue Nissan with a dented passenger door blocked me. A quick survey of the rearview mirror showed the van had entered traffic again and gained on me.

The phone rang agonizingly slowly. One ring. Two rings. Three rings. An answering machine. "Hey. Ahmed here. I can't come to the—" the voicemail announced.

"Try it again!" I shouted. The left lane opened a bit, and I ducked in behind the Nissan, but it had pulled abreast of a taxi and slowed. I darted from right to left and honked at the two cars in front of me, but my desperate honk just seemed to blend into the everyday patchwork of sounds and sights in Cairo, and the two cars, if they witnessed my panic, showed no evidence of it. The van was right behind me now, and as I dodged to the right, the van took advantage and pulled beside me on my left.

I was trapped between the red van and the edge of the bridge. Time slowed. I watched in horror as the vehicle began to move toward me and prepared a direct hit from the side. A shiny black Nissan tucked in directly behind me. I had nowhere to go. I tightened my grip on the wheel with my left hand, braced myself and threw my right hand across Maraya. I pressed her into the seat and shouted, "Hold on!"

The car shuddered as the van slammed into the driver's side door, and I swerved toward the edge of the bridge. I yanked the wheel to the left to counter his force, but it was no good. The impact pushed me up over the sidewalk and a sickening clang rang out as the car hit the metal fence. The fence held strong, and as I rebounded from the impact, my wheels gained traction, and I was able to swerve back into traffic. I couldn't believe we were still on the bridge.

"Are you okay?" I asked Maraya, taking my eyes off the road just long enough to see her silent, tear-stained face staring straight ahead.

"I think so," she said, in a small voice. The phone in her hands was ringing again—once, twice . . .

The van was still beside me and winding up for another hit. The cars in front of me reacted to the metal-on-metal noise—not a normal sound even in Cairo. The white sedan in front of me accelerated, which gave me an opportunity to pull ahead out of the range of the van for the moment. The van locked in behind me.

I heard the click of a phone and then a familiar voice, "Hello? Magda? Is that you?"

"Ahmed!" I shouted. We had left the Nile behind us, and traffic was being forced into a wide arc to the right that looped around and exited under the bridge. A space opened up on my left, and I darted into the opening, moving into the far left lane as the curve tightened. The van followed me move for move.

"Ahmed! I'm on 6th of October Bridge, and some crazy man in a van is trying to drive me off the road!" I shouted at the phone in Maraya's hands.

I watched the speedometer top 50 mph, a rare sight in Cairo traffic, just as I pulled into the curve. Suddenly I was fast approaching a slow-moving, battered pick-up. A man in a dirty gray-blue galabeya sat in the back of the truck, his arm draped loosely around a goat. Man and goat stared at me in wide-eyed horror as I tried to brake. The wheels of the car had already started to lose traction, and the brakes made them lock. The car began to slide sideways out of control.

"Magda? Who is it? Who's trying to run you off the—" were the last words I heard. The car continued its flight sideways through the black guard rail on the edge of the ramp.

I remember seeing the blue sky fill the entirety of the windshield and thinking briefly how lovely and smog-free the day was.

And then everything went black.

XXVII

I was at home in Florida and drove down the highway with the top down in Mom's 1975 Triumph Spitfire. I loved that car, I learned to drive stick shift in it. Mom was beside me and she laughed, her hair caught up in a scarf that trailed behind her in the wind. The afternoon was hot, but the breeze cut the heat. I felt like a wild stallion galloping in a vast open field.

I remember thinking that Mom shouldn't be laughing because the situation wasn't funny. It wasn't funny at all. I shouldn't be here. I wanted to be here—I liked it here, but I shouldn't be here now. There was somewhere else I needed to be.

I heard a voice. From where? It was disembodied. It didn't belong here. Was I going mad, hearing voices? The sound was low and quiet, urgent. A man's voice then a woman's too.

The Spitfire faded away, and as I slowly opened my eyes, Florida disappeared, replaced by a dingy white hospital room. The voices grew louder, and I could make out some words.

". . . just needs more rest, *Pasha*," The nurse said, using an old-fashioned Egyptian form of address for a respected male. "Her injuries are . . . come round . . ." I couldn't make out her words. I heard the shuffle of footsteps leaving.

Magda's dad. I was Magda. I was in Egypt. There was a boy, a wonderful boy, and the pyramids, and—where was I?

"Dad," I croaked from the bed. I delved through my memories to remember why I was here.

Dad rushed to the side of the bed.

"Magda, baby, oh, praise God! We have been so worried," he reached down and kissed my hand, pressed it to his cheek then kissed it again.

I struggled through the fog of my mind. "I thought you were in Alexandria? Why—"

And then it all came back to me in a rush like a herd of stampeding buffalo. The van. The collision on the bridge, the blue sky...

"Oh, God," I tried to sit up and a burst of sharp pain shot through my chest. I collapsed onto the bed and gasped for breath.

"Shhh, shhh, darling. Don't move. You've fractured a rib. Banged your head. You're going to be sore for quite a while," he said soothingly, "It's important that you rest."

"Maraya! Where's Maraya? Oh, God, is Maraya okay?" Panic rose up in my throat like bile.

He was silent a moment, and his eyes evaded mine.

"Dad, what happened!" I shouted. "She's okay, isn't she? Dad? Dad!" I shot up in bed. The pain was excruciating. Stars appeared in my vision, and blackness crept in near the edges and pulled me in.

"Breathe, Magda baby, breathe!" He put his hands on my shoulders and pressed me back down onto the bed.

My chest relaxed again, and I inhaled. The world calmed, and the black edges receded.

"Don't do that! You must rest. Everything's going to be fine. Your sister's going to be fine," his eyes darted away as he said it. He lied.

"Dad, you tell me how hurt she is," I said in a tone that I hoped allowed no argument.

He watched me and debated.

"I can tell you're lying. Tell me the truth, or I'll walk out of here and find her," I said.

"Okay, okay. Baby, her injuries were more severe. She's in another room with your mother. They're giving her the best possible care."

OhGodohGodohGod, NO!

"But she's going to be okay? Isn't she?" My voice was shrill.

"God willing, she will be fine. But you must worry about yourself for the moment."

"I'm not going to worry about myself right now! Tell me what's happened to Maraya!"

He sat down on the edge of the bed.

"She has a ruptured spleen and is in surgery now. We'll know more shortly," he said. His face was drawn with worry. Dark circles blackened his eyes.

Confused, I struggled to process this. "What's a ruptured spleen? What does that mean? Will she be okay?"

He sighed heavily and explained. "Your spleen is on the left side of your abdomen. It helps you fight infections and filters out old and damaged red blood cells. It makes some kinds of white blood cells," he said and leaned over to take my hand in his.

"It's nice to have one, but if she loses it, her body will compensate. The problem isn't so much that she might lose her spleen. The problem is that a ruptured spleen causes a lot of internal bleeding. She has lost a lot of blood, Magda," he said.

I lay back, absorbing this. Everything was going madly, impossibly wrong. I was sure I was sent here to fix things for Magda. How could Maraya being seriously injured or worse be part of the plan? I was a total and complete screwup. The real Magda would never forgive me. I didn't deserve to be forgiven. Magda was right to keep her distance from Ahmed in the first place. None of this would have ever happened if I hadn't shifted.

I thought of sweet little Maraya, those big brown eyes and those insanely long lashes. I remembered the day we played dolls together. How well she had kept my secret. I saw her eyes frozen in fear in those last moments we had together. I thought of her, somewhere in this hospital on an operating table, her body ripped open and her life's blood flowing freely. Tears formed and tricked down my cheeks.

"Oh, Maraya, baby," I told the ceiling, "I am so sorry! This is all my fault! How can I have done this to you!" The tears turned to sobs, which hurt my ribs and made my head throb, but I couldn't stop the sobs from coming. I gasped for breath through the pain.

"Magda!" Magda's dad's voice cut through my tears. His voice was suddenly firm, his manner changed. "This is *not* your fault. Police at the accident said someone tried to run *you* off the road! I don't understand how or why, but this is not your fault. This is the fault of whoever did this to you." he said. He stood now beside the bed, his eyes penetrating and intense.

Startled by his sternness, the tears shut off. I had been wallowing in self-pity. Self-pity never helps.

"We must stay positive and pray for her quick recovery," he said. Dad squeezed my hand. I nodded obediently.

The nurse returned. She wore a pale pink hospital pantsuit with long sleeves, her dark hair tucked under a scarf of tiny purple flowers.

"She's awake! Alhamdulilah. Are you in pain, my darling?" she asked and then before I could answer, "You will be in pain for several days, I should think, while that rib heals."

"I'm doing okay," I said tentatively to her back. She already bustled around, opened curtains and checked readouts on the machines hooked up to me.

She placed a paper cup beside me with some pills. "These will help," she said. For a nurse, she didn't seem terribly interested in how I felt. And then she was gone again.

Quizzically, I looked at Dad.

He shrugged. "We have a great shortage of nurses," he said, apologetically. "Your mother and I were able to get you a private room, but they have so few nurses in this hospital, and they are all over-worked. I could hire one of the British nurses. They're supposed to be very good—"

"Dad, I don't need a nurse. I'll be fine," I said. "I don't need a private room, either. I'd be fine with roommates. It doesn't matter." Eyeing the pills suspiciously, I decided the pain justified them. I chased them down with some bottled water on my bedside table.

He wrinkled his nose in distaste. "No, we can't have that. It's hard enough to keep the private rooms clean. You're in a public hospital I'm afraid, and hygiene is a real problem, but Maraya's condition was urgent. She needed the closest hospital, not the closest decent one. Your mother gave this room a thorough cleaning as soon as we could get someone to bring her cleaning supplies. We'd move you to a better hospital, but it's too soon to move Maraya, and we want you two together."

"Dad, it's okay, I'm fine."

"If you're feeling better now, darling, the police would like to talk to you. Are you well enough? We are very anxious to find who did this to you. Several witnesses saw a red van trying to run you off the road. Have you any idea who did this to you or why?" he asked.

Where to start?

"Dad, I have no idea who did this. I wish I could tell you. . . but I'm pretty sure it has to do with this whole business with Ahmed," I admitted.

"Are you sure?" I looked in his eyes and saw a different kind of worry behind them. Suddenly, I understood. He thought this happened because of his new ministerial post. He thought this was his fault.

"Dad, I doubt this has anything to do with you or job. This is my own doing."

"Tell me from the beginning," he said, tonelessly.

I told him about the threatening texts, and my belief that they had to do with my seeing Ahmed.

"Why didn't you show the messages to your mother or me?" he asked, his brow furrowed.

"I wasn't really sure this was different than any of the other stuff going on at school. I thought it was just Fatima or someone like that. And I knew that if I told you or mom you'd be concerned, and I'd never get any of my freedoms back. You'd want to keep an even closer eye on me," I said.

"You were right about that," he said.

"Actually, I almost told you right after the first one came because I was pretty creeped out. But my timing was bad—it was the day you left for Alexandria. Which reminds me—aren't you supposed to be in Alexandria?" I asked.

"Magda, I've had plenty of time to drive home from Alexandria. It's been a full day since the accident. You took a serious blow to the head. You've been unconscious, sleeping all that time," he said.

My eyes grew wide. Time had stood still for me. I assumed everything had just happened a couple of hours ago.

"How did you—find out and everything?"

He sighed and looked me in the eye. "Ahmed called me," he said.

My mind raced. Ahmed? Then I remembered—the phone calls in the car. Right before the crash the call had connected, and I'd heard Ahmed's voice. He must've heard the collision.

"He called you?" I said. Oh, God. So much for keeping a low profile about our relationship.

"He said he spoke to you right before he heard a crash, and then the phone went dead. He wasn't able to get a connection again, and he was worried," he said.

"Dad—I—I mean," I stuttered, "I know I'm not supposed to call him and everything, but I—" my eyes must've reflected my panic.

"Shhh, shhhh," he rubbed my arm soothingly and shook his head, "I saw the two missed calls on my own phone. I'm so sorry, honey. I was on another line; I had no idea. But you calling Ahmed is the least of our worries now. He did the right thing. I got straight into the car and started making phone calls to the police and the hospitals. Within a few minutes, the police were able to identify your mom's car at the scene of the crash. Your mom met you and Maraya at the hospital as you arrived," he said.

My thoughts turned to Magda's mom. I was supposed to have just gone for ice cream, and now look at what I'd done to her baby. Both her babies.

"How's Mom?" I ventured tentatively.

"She's with Maraya," he said. "She's waiting outside the operating room for news. It could be a while before we know anything definitive. But she keeps coming back here to check on you too, so I'm sure she'll be here soon."

Hearing an approach, I listened for the click of Mom's sensible heels, but I knew immediately it wasn't her. The footsteps bore the distinctive clunk of soldiers' boots. In walked two uniformed policemen.

They marched purposefully into the room. Their posture rigid, their expressions stern. They wore woolen berets, black long-sleeved uniforms and pants over heavy black leather boots. Badges with the golden eagle of Saladin, a national emblem, stood out on their left shoulders. A standard-issue assault rifle lay draped across their backs. I knew in my head that these men were here to help, but I stiffened in fear nonetheless. Such men are not the sort of people one ever wants to see at one's bedside. Instinctively, I felt threatened.

When the men entered, Dad stood, shook their hands and welcomed them formally. They greeted him as "Mr. Minister."

"May we ask a few questions of your daughter, sir, now that she's awake?" the gray-speckled mustached one asked.

"Of course," Dad said, waving them to my bedside.

I struggled to sit up and Dad adjusted a pillow behind my back. I coughed, and they waited until I caught my breath again.

"Miss, would you please describe for us the man or men who pursued you," the gray mustache began, and the younger man flipped open a little leather-bound notebook then took out a pencil.

"I only saw one man. He wasn't tall," I said, gathering my thoughts. How do you describe someone in a culture where everyone had brown eyes, dark complexions and black or gray hair? "Maybe medium build. Older. Gray hair."

The young man wrote something down. "Solidly gray?"

"Yes, I think so."

"Can you recall his clothing?" he prompted.

"A gray suit," I paused, slipping a thumbnail into my mouth while I thought. "There was something odd about it. The suit I mean. Maybe it was just that it didn't fit right," I struggled. Then I shrugged in defeat. "That's it; that's all. I didn't get a really good look at him, and when I try to see him again in my mind—I'm just not sure. He may have had a mustache. I'm just not sure."

I was able to give a more thorough description of the van, but I was pretty sure others would've already provided that.

"Can you think of any reason anyone would target you this way?" the gray mustache asked.

Magda's father nodded sternly. Reluctantly, I told them about the photo. They kept their faces remarkably deadpan, for which I was grateful. I said that I'd made a good many enemies at school, but I didn't think anyone would try to kill me over it. Besides, it was an old man who was chasing me, not a kid.

They were very concerned when I told them about the text messages. I looked dumbly at my bedside table as if my phone would somehow be there. "My phone—?"

Dad, who had taken a step into the background, stepped forward again. "The phone was not among the things collected at the scene of the accident," he said. "We think it was probably thrown clear, or perhaps it's in the car somewhere. They told us the car was being towed to a garage but was most likely totaled. I can give you the name of the garage if you like," he added.

"That would be helpful," the gray mustache said then turned to me again.

I really wasn't giving them much to go on, but it was all I had.

"Do you have any idea who might've done this?" I asked, hopefully.

"It's too early to say just now," he said vaguely, "but *Insha'Allah* we will find him," he said. "This type of criminal never remains hidden for long."

The younger man flipped shut his notebook. The officers both thanked me and shook Magda's dad's hand before leaving.

"Dad, who do *you* think would do such a thing?" I said.

"It's hard to say, Magda. You do understand that photo of yours went completely viral," he said. I stared at him blankly. He sat down on the edge of the bed. "Magda, honey, if you take a close look at the photo, everything is there. Your bracelet with all the crosses on it is glinting in the sunlight. Ahmed is wearing a silver ring with the Islamic crescent and moon on it. It was all over Facebook and was tagged with your names. Lots of people don't adjust their privacy settings, so now when your name is Googled, the photo comes up. We're trying to get the web servers to remove it, but it's already been picked up by an anti-Muslim Christian blogger and a number of very offensive Muslim extremist websites. I'm afraid you and Ahmed have unwittingly become poster children for extremists of both religions. These crazies see you two as the unclean mixing of religions—a portrait of a society gone very much off track," he said.

Until now, it had never occurred to me that the ramifications of my actions could go beyond Magda's social life.

"The fundamental Christians see you as a traitor to your faith. The radical Muslims see you as an infidel; a threat to their way of life."

"*Me*? A traitor? A threatening infidel? I'm a seventeen-year-old girl with good study habits who wears a headband. And now they're out to get me? What are we talking, like, Al Qaeda? Muslim Brotherhood? This is crazy!"

"No group has come forward to claim responsibility. And running you off the road isn't the usual modus operandi for those groups. Bombing our house would've been a more traditional—"

"Traditional?" Breathing was getting difficult again.

"Traditional approach *for their kind,*" he repeated. "Or bombing our church would've been even more typical. The man or men who attacked you might have planned to hide a bomb at the church, but you surprised them by leaving early and forced them to consider another approach," he said.

"Magda," he said, and his manner turned cold and professional. "There's something you should understand. What you and Ahmed did was irresponsible, but it does *not* justify this attack. This is a whole different thing. Whoever did this to you and Maraya? We will find them. I will use every contact at my disposal. I will call in every favor that is owed me. I will find this man and see that justice is dealt."

"I believe you will, Dad," I said. I lay my head back on the pillow, which forced my breathing to return to normal.

A slight movement in the hallway caught my eye. A soldier in a camouflage uniform adjusted his stance outside my doorway. His back was against the wall and hands behind his back, so I could just see a shoulder, a bit of pant leg and one of his boots through the doorway.

Magda's father spoke. "That's the other reason you have a private room. He'll be with you until this matter is over."

XXVIII

"Magda?" I felt a gentle tug on my shoulder. Then a whisper, closer to my ear, "Magnolia?"

I was dreaming. Or was I? My eyes flew open. "Shhhh!" Ahmed whispered urgently, a finger to his mouth. Hidden from the view of the door, he crouched low between the bed and the exterior wall.

"How did you get in here?" I whispered. "There's a guard—" I motioned frantically toward the door, open just a crack. But the guard was not at his post.

"Shhhh! It's okay, baby," he whispered, soothingly. "I know. I wasn't expecting *him*. I waited more than an hour. I almost went home, but I got lucky. Even soldiers have to go to the bathroom every now and then. We only have a couple of seconds."

"You're nuts! What are you doing here? How did you get in here?"

At the open window, a curtain caught in the breeze and flipped outside. We must be on the first floor, I thought.

"You've got to get out of here! If you get caught, it'll ruin everything!" I whispered.

"Shhh. I know. I just had to see you. Magda, I heard the crash. For a while I thought you were dead."

I reached out a hand to touch him. Even in the dark I could make out his honey-colored eyes. Crouching low, he put his hand in mine and kissed it. Then I remembered.

"Ahmed, they think Maraya might not make it!" I said, my voice wavering.

"I know. We are praying for her too. But Magda—" his eyes grew fierce and his jaw set. "Magda, I swear to you, with every inch of my being, I *swear* to you that I will find whoever did this to you and to Maraya, and I will hunt him down and kill him."

"Ahmed, don't! If you found this guy and hurt him, you're the first one the police would look for. That would make everything so much worse. Ahmed, you have to get out of here. You said we shouldn't take any more stupid risks!"

"I just had to see you. I don't know what I'd do if anything happened to you. I love you."

"I love you too. And I'm not dead. Now go!"

He made his way to the window and stepped over the ledge. Just before he disappeared, he mouthed the words, "lock—the—window——this—time—kay?"

I nodded, and as suddenly as he came, he was gone, a ghost in the Egyptian night.

XXIX

Magda's parents let me visit Maraya before I left the hospital the next day. She lay motionless in the big white bed in her white nightgown on the white sheets in the white-walled room. The only color in the room was the red sac of blood and the thin red tube that led into her tiny arm. The doctors had removed her spleen. They told us her body would, in time, learn to compensate for the missing organ. She was still bleeding far too heavily.

I nodded to Mom, with her red-rimmed eyes, sitting in a corner chair. She hadn't been home since the accident. Her normally tight bun was loose, and little strands of hair floated softly about her face.

She beckoned to me and pulled me down into her arms. I squeezed into the oversized chair, partly on the chair and partly on her. I wrapped my arms around her.

"Magda, darling, I thank God you're okay. I can't believe how much evil is in this world." She kissed my forehead. "Now we must pray with all our hearts for Maraya. You haven't been praying enough lately. You need to pray. You'll do that, won't you?"

"Yes, Mama. I'll pray as hard as I can." Her head fit naturally in the groove between my head and shoulder. We stayed like that a moment, then I looked up and saw Magda's father waiting in the doorway. He gestured toward the door.

I left Mom in the chair and paused on my way out to take Maraya's limp little hand in mine. The big eyelashes lay closed. Tears streamed down my face. It shouldn't be her in the bed. It shouldn't even be Magda. It should be me, Molly. I'm the one who blew into Magda's life like a great black khamsin and forced all my Western values about love on her world like whirling walls of sand upon the city.

The tears flowed freely, and soon I was choking back sobs, and my chest strained against the bandages wrapped around my ribcage.

As I stared at her frail form, my sorrow shifted channels and turned to anger. I may have screwed up, but I didn't deserve this punishment. One man was responsible for putting Maraya in this bed. A man in a gray suit who wanted to kill Magda for a single kiss. I felt anger at him—anger at a world where two people could love each other so perfectly, but that love could be twisted into so much horror. And for what reason? We all worshipped the same God.

Finally, my anger turned on God. How could He let this happen? How could He put Maraya, a complete innocent, here? And what possible purpose could her death serve? Why did He make me shift anyway? What was the point of all these different religions? What a messed up, confused world we lived in.

I squeezed Maraya's little hand and whispered, so only she could hear, "You get better, Maraya, do you hear me? You get better, and I swear we'll find the man who did this to you." The rage burned brightly inside me. "And I will bring your real sister back to you. I promise. You just get better." It was a command, not a request. I kissed her cold, bloodless cheek. "Besides," I said softly. "I still owe you gelato."

Magda's dad still stood in the doorway and solemnly watched. He came and pulled me gently away from her. Then Dad, myself, and the soldier who had failed to catch the visitor in my room last night, went home.

Magda's father told me the soldier's name, but I couldn't remember it. It was something that started with a "B." He was a young man, in his early twenties, perhaps, who rarely spoke. He had a large jaw with a terrible underbite which gave him the look of a pit bull. I decided to call him Butch. I didn't want to get to know him.

Butch didn't drive home with us. I don't know how he got there, but he left at the same time we did and was already home when we got there. He stood outside the apartment gate with his broad stance and arms crossed behind his back. Magda's father nodded to him.

He followed us through the gate. I wondered if he was going to come watch us eat our lunch, but when we went inside, he stayed in the hallway with his back to the door.

It should've been a relief to step through the doors of the apartment and to see Magda's bedroom again, but the sight of the empty bottom bunk filled me with dread. This room, without Maraya, became a place of sorrow. I sat on the edge of her unmade bed and stared at her dolls. She'd cleaned a few of them up recently, but a combination ice cream parlor/playground still lay spread out in front of the night table, alongside a shopping mall for pets near the dresser.

My life was spinning out of control, and I felt powerless to stop it.

Magda's father, on the other hand, worked doggedly. He was on the phone constantly, massaging his networks, trying to find out what person or organization was behind this attack. He leapt from one call to the next. He said his contacts were sympathetic, but no one knew anything. He went through the government offices and made appointments where necessary and sometimes just walked in on members elected through the Muslim Brotherhood. Most listened sympathetically. A few expressed outrage when he barged in on them. None of them gave him useful information. They claimed the Brotherhood had nothing to do with the attack.

"Maybe I'm going about this the wrong way," he mused a couple of days later as we sat at the kitchen table drinking mint tea. "The Muslim Brotherhood is a fractured entity. It is unified in its goal but not in its methods. The men I know, the ones who were elected to government office, they favor a traditional, gentle approach to achieve the changes they want. They work through people's hearts and intentions. Such people don't even acknowledge that the radical elements of the party exist, but we all know they do. The radicals operate on their own, without formal party approval. They say that to lead the Brotherhood is like riding an unbroken stallion at the head of a parade through downtown Cairo." He drummed his fingers on the tabletop thoughtfully.

I nodded sympathetically.

"I need contact with the radicals directly," he said emphatically, setting his teacup down so forcefully it splattered the table. He wiped it up with his finger while he spoke. "But how? The last people who would ever give me contact with the radical Brotherhood are the elected officials. These are the same men who claim the radicals don't exist," he said, dejectedly. "And what of the radical splinter groups that come and go like the khamsin, keeping their origins hidden in distant lands? How can a Christian government minister possibly hope to open dialogue with them? I am at my wit's end."

I chewed a nail as I listened.

"Perhaps, you need a Muslim to nose around and ask your questions," I ventured.

He pondered that. "You have a point. While it's true that most Muslims despise the terrorists for not being true Muslims, the reverse doesn't apply; the terrorists see themselves as one with all Muslims. They might speak more openly to someone they perceive as a brother in Islam. I need someone with broader contacts within the government, someone whose reach is international in scope. Someone motivated to help us."

I knew of one person who fit this description to the last syllable, but Magda's father wasn't going to like the idea.

"I don't know, Magda," Dad said reluctantly when I voiced the idea. "I don't know Mr. Najjar personally. There are other men who know me better and might be willing to do me this favor."

"Dad," I pleaded, "Ahmed's father works in the most international parts of the government. He has ears where domestic politicians don't. And," I paused to frame my words carefully, then finally just blurted it out, "he has a brother whom everyone suspects works *with* radical elements."

"You've chosen an interesting family to become entangled with," he said grimly.

"Mr. Najjar's not like his brother Radwan, Dad. Radwan is an embarrassment to their family, but they still have contact with him because they're more or less raising his son for him. If there is anyone with the connections to find out who might be behind these attacks, it's Mr. Najjar. We have to try. I think he'd do it—if not for us, then because Ahmed would want him to."

Magda's father shook his head in resignation. "Give me some time to think on it."

I had to rest a few days before I could go back to school. Magda's dad came and went from the house. He visited Maraya and went to work.

Butch continued to be a near constant presence at the front door. Occasionally, he wandered the outside of the building and kept guard, in his way. Twice, another soldier took his place—a twin more or less, minus the underbite. I suppose Butch needed to sleep sometimes.

I spent most of my time resting in Maraya's bed because the ladder to the upper bunk was painful to climb. Sleep was difficult. When I closed my eyes, my mind tripped over itself competing against images of Maraya's pale frame in the hospital bed, the man wearing the ill-fitting suit walking briskly down a Cairo street and the red van accelerating into me on the 6th of October Bridge.

I tried to keep busy. When Dad left, I booted up the computer. I used it for schoolwork like I was supposed to, but I also used it to keep my mind occupied. I found some Pilates exercises from a website. I'd heard that Pilates was originally designed for bed-bound patients. Apparently, those patients didn't have broken ribs. Almost every exercise involved using your core muscles, right around the ribcage. In the end, I was able to do girl pushups and squats.

Evening approached and Dad wasn't home yet. I checked watch and realized that Ahmed could be home from school and track. I opened our Facebook page.

You home yet? I'm dying of boredom alone in this house.

Want me to come cuddle you? Came the reply.

I'd laugh but you might be serious. The cursor blinked.

So how are you feeling?

Rib hurts. Mostly just worried about Maraya.

Any news?

Nothing. I feel angry, Ahmed. What kind of God would do this to her? She's innocent. I waited for a response. *Do you ever question your faith?* I asked.

Sometimes...especially after 9/11. We were in Washington. I was pretty little but I remember asking Mom how Allah could let all those people die.

You were in Washington when that plane crashed into the Pentagon? And the Twin Towers? That must've been horrible! Were you frightened?

I didn't understand much, he answered, *but I remember my mothers fear. The day after the bombing I was eating eggs at the kitchen table when all of a sudden she shoved me and Samir out the door and we were in the car racing through the streets.*

Why? I asked.

I had no clue. Samir was just a baby maybe a year old. Mom strapped him in and made me feed him his bottle. I'd never done that before. Milk ran all down his face and into his little blue pajamas. It was sticky and I thought I was going to get in trouble for making a mess. She never noticed. I could see her from behind—she was shaking.

What was she afraid of?

She thought the Americans would turn on the Muslims like they did on the Japanese after the bombing of Pearl Harbor in World War II. She thought they might target the embassy where Dad worked. She told me later that when Dad left for work he forgot his phone. That's what triggered the race across town.

I don't get it, I wrote. *She was upset just because he left his phone?*

She had this idea that if he had his phone he would be safe. When we got to the embassy we found Dad at work in his office on his computer and drinking coffee. He gave me a cookie from the office kitchen. He hugged Mom a lot.

I only know a couple of Muslims in the States, I typed. *I never thought about how scary it must've been for them.* I realized my mistake as soon as I hit return. I wanted to dive into the laptop and pull the words back.

What Muslims do you know there? Came the reply.

I mean—I only know a couple of Muslims who have lived in the States, I corrected. Quick, deflect: *Were you ever persecuted there?*

Me? I was too little. I remember a friend of ours though, Dr. Assaf. He was a dentist. Always brought us sugar-free lollipops when he came to the house. I heard him tell my Dad that he'd had patients tell him flat out they couldn't see him anymore cause he was Muslim. He moved back to Egypt that winter. We nearly moved too.

Moved home?

back to Egypt. It was a couple of weeks after the World Trade Center, and Dad came home saying it was time to send us home where he could be sure we were safe. It was mom who convinced him to stay. She said we had to stay to be the true face of Islam in America. 'We must show the Americans we are not like those animals,' she said.

I'd like to meet your mother one day, I wrote. *I think I'd like her.*

She's a strong woman. Like you. I paused, formulating a response, when a new question appeared.

You asked me if I had ever doubted my faith. Are you questioning yours?

Sometimes I think if there was a God He wouldn't stand by and let such horrible things happen to good people...other days I look at the brilliant design of the electrons and protons in an atom or the ingenuity of the body and I think there must be a God. This can't all have come to be through a series of accidents. I waited for his response.

I don't think It's an accident that we've come together, either, Muslim and Christian, brought together by God, Ahmed wrote. *We're like Romeo and Juliet, a spark meant to reunite our families.*

I don't feel like much of a spark right now. More like a wet blanket:)

But speaking of uniting families, I continued, *you're not going to believe this. There's a chance—probably a slim one—that my dad may call your dad...* and I told him about the conversation I'd had with Magda's father.

Interesting...let me

The message ended mid-sentence.

gtg, he typed.

And he was gone.

I leaned back in the kitchen chair, alone with the ticking of the clock on the wall. I spent some time Googling aimlessly, researching the Muslim Brotherhood, Al Qaeda, and looking in vain for a face I'd barely seen, a man wearing a bad suit.

XXX

On the couch, Magda's dad sat rigid and proper, legs uncrossed, both hands in a death grip on a cup of Turkish coffee. I positioned myself beside him, rocket straight, legs crossed at the ankles, hands clasped in my lap.

Across from us, on an opposing couch, sat Hassan Najjar, Ahmed's father, his own Turkish coffee cradled in his hands. Ahmed pulled a dining room chair in to join the group.

The room was warmly decorated with a rich red carpet woven with geometric patterns of gold, burgundy and navy. No paintings adorned the white walls, but an elaborate three-part wooden latticework screen served as a room divider between living and dining room. A silver plate on a stand dressed an end table, with a star and crescent moon hammered into it.

Ahmed and I carefully avoided each other's gaze for the sake of other eyes on us.

It wasn't my father or me who brought this meeting into being—it was Mr. Najjar. He had called my father at work and invited him to the Najjar home to discuss how he could be of help to him. The result was this very uncomfortable meeting.

Mr. Najjar bore the figure of a man accustomed to rich dinners and long meetings. He had Ahmed's angular good looks, made softer in the details by age, and his hairline receded slightly. The wave in his hair mimicked his son's but was neatly combed whereas Ahmed's fell in an untidy jumble. Clean-shaven, he wore a deep gold suit with a light blue shirt and coordinating tie. The ring finger of his right hand bore the same crescent moon ring that Ahmed wore.

Mrs. Najjar bustled back and forth from the kitchen with another woman, probably a maid, setting out little cookies and bite-sized cakes beside the Turkish coffee on a table of in-laid marble.

I had expected Mrs. Najjar to be a slight woman, a beauty perhaps, shy and a step behind her husband—the perfect Arabic diplomat's wife. She was nothing of the sort. A rather plump woman, just over five feet tall, her features were plain—neither angular nor soft. Her hair, only touched with gray, was pulled back softly into a clip at the back of her head. As soon as we arrived at the door, she had put an arm possessively around me while expressing words of sympathy and concern for Maraya and led me into the formal sitting room.

"Please," Mr. Najjar said as soon as we were all seated. "Tell us of Maraya. Such a tragedy. Has her condition improved?" Mr. Najjar's use of Arabic was stilted and old-fashioned, befitting a formal level of respect. I understood, but my ear was unaccustomed to it.

Magda's father's head bowed sadly. "Regrettably, sir, it has not. But many thanks for your concern. God willing we shall have good news soon."

"Insha'Allah, Insha'Allah, soon," Mr. Najjar nodded gravely. "Our prayers are with her every day, five times a day."

"That's very kind of you. Every prayer helps."

"Indeed it does," Mr. Najjar agreed.

The two fathers behaved like distant relatives visiting for a few hours as if Ahmed and I were barely-acquainted cousins.

"Mr. Amides," Mr Najjar said as he set down his coffee and leaned forwards. "I am very troubled by your most unfortunate circumstances. More troubled than I can say. Your family's pain is our pain," he said, glancing knowingly at his son and then smiling at me. "We wish to support you. Tell me, how may I be of service?" he inquired.

"I must find the man who attacked my daughters on that bridge," my father answered. His eyes were dark and swollen from lack of sleep. "I see two possibilities. It may be someone who feels threatened by my position as minister. This could be anyone. It could be a man I may have offended by some position I've taken in the past or the present. It could be an ordinary citizen or member of a religions group that doesn't approve of Christians in government. Chasing this line of thinking is like chasing fireflies in the night sky. Magda, however, believes strongly it is someone who is religiously motivated to keep our children apart. The texts she has received support this line of thinking. Such a one would be fanatically religious. He could be known to other radicals. I have spent the days since the car accident approaching everyone I know with connections to the more radical elements of our great nation. God has blessed me with broad access to the halls of governing, but no one has a message for me," he sighed and placed his coffee cup on the table. I have no idea who would do this to my family."

Mr. Najjar leaned back against the coach and rubbed his chin thoughtfully.

"It is unconscionable, Mr. Amides, that anyone should seek to bring animosity between our two peoples. The strife of these past few years is not mine. I am one with the generations that came before, through all the centuries when Christian and Muslim lived together in peace and relative harmony. Mr. Amides, you and I are brothers. Any attack against the Coptic people is an attack against all of Egypt."

"A noble statement, sir, and we accept your assistance gratefully." My father's stilted manner betrayed his discomfort with this situation.

"You should know, then, that I have been asking these questions already, out of *my own interest*," Mr. Najjar said, looking pointedly at Ahmed as he spoke the last three words.

"I have various contacts, I'm sure you know, many of them formal, and many, not so. It is my job to speak for our government abroad, but even more so, to listen for our government, and what I hear is not always what I want to hear. But in this respect, I am the ear to many factions."

Did he refer to his diplomatic contacts or his brother, Kamal's father?

He leaned forward now, his hands clasped together. "Mr. Amides, I have researched the matter thoroughly, and I'm afraid what I have to say is not what you want to hear. I can inform you without any doubt whatsoever, that neither the Muslim Brotherhood nor Al Qaeda nor any of their kindred organizations of which I am aware, lay claim to any part in this terrible attack." His eyes bore into Magda's father's, their meaning clear. Do not ask any more questions.

"I see," my father replied. His lips drew tight. "If I am to disregard those possibilities completely, it would be helpful to understand the source. May I ask how you know of their innocence with such confidence?"

An uncomfortable silence ensued, but Mr. Najjar's gaze never left my father's face. "I would not allow the word innocence to grace the same sentence as the people of whom we speak, Mr. Amides. These men are a brutal sort. With every drop of my blood, I detest what they do and how they think. Such men are primitive tribal warriors, not men of Allah. They are victims of poverty and ignorance framed and shaped into the image of wickedness. And yet they are a growing political force, and we must deal with them.

"I believe the road to change is formed on the bedrock of communication. And so I listen and convey. Communication is the purest essence of my work as a diplomat. Rest assured, my sources are very knowledgeable and are in a position to know if such an act were sanctioned within those organizations. You need look no further, sir. They spoke with the utmost confidence, and I see no motive for them to lie. Such men are more likely to claim acts for which they are not responsible than to deny acts for which they are. They see themselves as the weapons of righteousness, and they prefer not to let those weapons rest."

My father's expression deflated. "Then who is after my daughters?"

"Your daughter, Mr. Amides. Maraya was most certainly an innocent bystander. And I would like very much to know who he is. In fact, I would like to know for another reason as well. Because if this madman isn't after your daughter through one of these known organizations, then we are dealing with a wild card. If the affection between my son and your daughter has angered him to the point of violence, we cannot say that my son is safe either."

All eyes swiveled to Ahmed. His hands flew into the air in mock surrender.

"But Dad, I haven't received any threats," he said.

"I know, but neither of you are safe until this matter has been brought to a conclusion," he said. His words hung in the air.

Magda's father drained his coffee and stood to leave. I mimicked his actions and prepared to follow.

"May I have a word with you in private, Mr. Najjar?" Magda's father asked.

"Why certainly," Mr Najjar replied warmly and gestured him down a hallway. Magda's father shadowed him. I glimpsed a set of opaque French doors at the end of the hall and behind them a wooden desk and a high-back leather chair set against a backdrop of bookshelves. The two men stepped inside.

Mrs. Najjar, Ahmed and I remained standing awkwardly on the threshold of departure. We looked at each other uncertainly. For the first time since we arrived, I was able to make direct eye contact with Ahmed. I shrugged nervously.

Mrs. Najjar set about seating us again.

"So, my dear," she addressed me. "Will you be able to return to school soon?"

"Thank you for asking," I said. I hadn't spoken since this meeting began, and I struggled to find as many formal Arabic words as I could to throw into my sentences. "I'm thinking perhaps I'll return tomorrow. My ribs make movement painful, but I can't bear to stay home alone anymore," I said.

"I see. I suppose I'd feel the same. When troubles are plenty, one's own mind can be a minefield," she said. I nodded solemnly.

"Would you like more coffee while we wait?" she asked softly.

"Oh, no, I—" my eyes caught Ahmed's, whose expression reflected surprise. He held my gaze and nodded very slightly and emphatically in my direction.

"Well, actually, that would be most kind of you," I said. Only as Mrs. Najjar gathered up the coffee pot and bustled out to the kitchen did I realize what had happened. Mrs. Najjar had purposely affected a small opportunity for us to be together.

"I can't believe we're alone," I whispered. "Surely, she doesn't approve of me?"

"I've told you before, Magnolia," Ahmed said. "My parents would probably prefer I chose a Muslim girlfriend, but I think they also recognize that, in many other ways, you're all the things they would want for me. I know we'll always face challenges as a couple in Egypt, but they would accept you. The biggest obstacle will never be my family, but yours."

"You make it sound like my parents are backwards—" I began, defensively. They may have been my current jailors, but I understood what they tried to protect.

"Not for a minute. Your people are a minority in Egypt. They protect their own, especially the beautiful and clever ones," he said.

My cheeks colored. Just then we heard the exaggerated clinking of dishes in the kitchen, a broad hint that someone was returning. We had seconds to finish our conversation. Something weighed heavily on my mind.

"What about Kamal. Do you trust Kamal?" I asked.

His eyebrows rose. "With my life. Why?"

"Put it together, Ahmed. He hates me. He wants us apart. He has connections."

"Not in a million years. He's not his father, Magda. Once he flirted with his father's path, but he was a kid then, and he rejected it. You can't be as close to a guy as we are and not know him. He can be a first class jerk at times, but that's a long way from a murderer."

"Well . . . so now . . ." Mrs. Najjar said brightly from the kitchen before rounding the corner into view, her arms laden with a tray of fresh coffee. "They say we might be getting a storm soon," she said as she laid the tray gingerly on the coffee table.

It took me a moment to process she was indeed talking about the weather.

"Oh?" I pictured a dreaded khamsin, armed with hundreds of pounds of sand capable of enveloping a city in minutes. What more could God throw at me? "When?"

"Oh, well, dear, you know they never can predict these things accurately. But the conditions are ripe—that's what they're saying," she said. "And the winds of late are more ardent, don't you think?"

We had only taken our first sip of coffee when Magda's father and Mr. Najjar, with grave faces, emerged from the study. I gulped the hot liquid down and stood again to leave.

At the door, Mr. and Mrs. Najjar promised to pray for Maraya, and Magda's father thanked them both. Mr. Najjar held the door open for Magda's father first and then for me. As I brushed past Mr. Najjar, he said softly for my ears, "May it be God's will that the next generation bring peace where ours has failed."

I smiled softly and chose the words I think Magda would have chosen.

"God's will be done."

If I wasn't being chased by a madman and terrified for Magda's sister's life, I would have felt like skipping through a meadow on a sunny day. I had just seen Ahmed, walked in his home and I think passed inspection with his parents. It was a confusing time.

The car ride with Magda's father was quiet. I didn't dare ask what Mr. Najjar and he had spoken about. Dad would tell me if he wanted me to know. We stopped and grabbed a bite to eat at a smoky corner café then climbed back in the car. We were on our way to the church where the *Baba* had arranged a special prayer service for friends and family to pray for Maraya's recovery.

"We must try all that is in our power in this world, but ultimately, all of our lives are in God's hands," Magda's mother had explained on the phone that morning when she told me about the 6 p.m. service. "Never underestimate the power of prayer, Magda. The doctors are doing what they can. Now we must do everything we can."

The church was cold and empty without the Saturday crowds. Our footsteps echoed. About three dozen people gathered in the center of the vast stone sanctuary and spoke in hushed voices. I recognized a few of them from last weekend. Layla and Demiana chatted quietly near the pulpit. Mark stood beside a slightly shorter, older version of himself in a navy suit. I nodded to Mark, and he nodded back.

I held Dad's arm and let him lead me in. Seated in the front pew, Mom's face was deeply lined and without color. A group of women milled around her sympathetically, and the *Baba* stood among them as he listened and nodded gravely.

Dad strode purposefully into the group and shook the *Baba's* hand in the two of his. The *Baba* moved closer and pat him sympathetically on the back.

Someone stood, freeing the spot beside Mom, and Dad slid in. Without Dad at my side, the women circled around me and began to hug and kiss me and tell me to be strong. Magda's parents sat, clasping hands. Her head slid into the crook of his neck, her eyes downcast. Her body shook. He held her sobbing frame.

The *Baba* moved to the pulpit, and the rest of us obediently began to look for seats in the pews. Fifty people gathered now, and more trickled in. Magda's mother looked up, her eyes wet and red-rimmed, and she gestured for me to sit on her other side. I did.

"Oh, Magda, baby," she said.

"She's going to be fine, Mom," I said, firmly.

"Yes, God willing," she sniffed. "She's going to be fine."

"For when two or three come together," the *Baba's* voice boomed, "there I am with them. Matthew eighteen, verse twenty. Today, Holy Father, we gather in your name to pray for our beloved child, Maraya Amides."

A hush settled over the room.

"Let us pray."

Heads bowed.

"Lord Jesus Christ, Good Shepherd of the sheep, you gather the lambs in your arms and carry them in your bosom. We commend to your loving care the child, Maraya Amides. Relieve her pain, guard her from all danger, restore to her your gifts of gladness and strength and raise her up to a life of service to you."

Someone began whispering behind me. Softly at first, then with growing insistence.

"Give strength to her parents, Cyril and Ireney Amides, and her sister, Magda Amides, in this, their hour of need."

The whispering became urgent, and heads began to turn.

"Heavenly Father, giver of life and death—"

"Father, forgive me, but . . ." a man in a well-tailored navy suit interjected in a voice accustomed to authority. Mark's father. "These are troubling times for Coptic churches or I would not interrupt. When I sat in this pew, my foot struck a black backpack. It looks very similar to the ones we have all seen on the news in other Coptic churches around the city. Perhaps I am overly cautious—it is a common bag. Does it belong to someone here?"

A couple of gasps reverberated around the room as the meaning of his question sank in. Then silence again, a collective holding of breath, punctuated by the ever present hum of traffic and horns from the traffic outside.

"Does anyone belong to the black bag under Mr. Ideodaniach's pew?" the *Baba* repeated, his gaze combing the crowd. More people had joined our group. Some eighty people scanned the room nervously.

Nothing.

"Mr. Ideodaniach, I'm sure it would be reasonable to gently open the zipper on the backpack and put our imaginations to rest," he said firmly.

Mark's father obeyed. He put both hands around the pack and gently eased it out from under the pew. He grasped the zipper and began to pull it slowly up and over in an arc. As he pulled the zipper down, the fabric of the bag fell open to reveal four steel pipes, sealed on either end, a small black box and a length of brown wire.

"Lord Jesus, Mary, Mother of God," Mr. Ideodaniach breathed.

Until that instant, no one had moved. Beyond the craning of a neck or two, time stood still until the moment of revelation.

In that second, the room erupted in a clamor of screams. The magnificent acoustics of the church amplified and projected the sound, which gave eighty the voice of eight hundred.

People all around me fled. They grabbed their little ones and ran for the church's main doors. Others, sitting in the pews nearest the Nile, headed for the side door. I watched, frozen in disbelief.

A bomb?

Magda's mom, so frail and weak a moment ago, took me by the shoulders and pushed me forcibly toward the side doors. I stumbled along, looking back, to where Mr. Ideodaniach stood with the *Baba* and a couple of other men, huddled over the backpack, consulting. They straightened up, and a man in a blue shirt with his back to me grabbed the backpack. Then I was pushed by the throngs into the still-hot Egyptian early evening where we were met by a blazing, red-orange sun poised for its fiery decent upon the city.

The patio where Mark and I had stood and talked quietly after the service just a few weeks ago filled rapidly with about thirty wild-eyed parishioners. As one, the crowd turned in shock as a man burst through the doors behind us, the backpack over his shoulder. He ran through the crowd to the black wrought-iron fence overlooking the river. There, he stopped, crouched low with the backpack behind him and then with both arms swung it in a wide ascending arc behind him and released it powerfully skyward.

The black pack arched gracefully up. From where I stood at the back of the crowd, nearest the church, it rose heavenward only a few feet until it paused in the middle of the angry sun. And then the sky cracked open. The sound didn't register as a noise but as a direct searing pain in the ears. In slow motion I saw the sun's rays painted over by blinding hurtful pelting rays of light and fire, perforated by shards of black.

A second later the destruction radiated outwards from the source. The man who had hurled the backpack was thrown back first. His body was lifted off the ground; his head turned toward us as he flew. I recognized Mark's face.

The hot blast reached me, propelled my body backwards then slammed it down on the concrete floor.

XXXI

Ahmed and Kamal lingered over french fries and chocolate shakes at a table in McDonald's. A busy street coursed in front of them. Across from restaurant stood an empty commercial lot strewn with dirt, weeds and garbage. Had there been a view of the horizon, the two young men would've been just in time to see the first golden-orange rays of the sunset wash gently over the city.

Here in the suburbs, the buildings crowded out the horizon, and Ahmed and Kamal saw only an empty lot as it grew dimmer. A TV in the corner of the restaurant blared the news— just another voice in the room.

Their PE uniforms were still damp, clinging to their bodies. They were in no hurry. After the meeting with Magda and her father, Ahmed had jumped into the car and raced to a mandatory track practice. Now he and Kamal relaxed before heading home to do homework. Kamal was spending the last two weeks of track season at the Najjar house to eliminate the long commute during the heavy practices.

"We should get going," Ahmed said finally. "Dad told me to lay low until this guy gets caught. I know he's being paranoid, but we should probably head back."

"You mean you could seriously be in trouble with your dad because we stopped for fries?" Kamal asked.

"I don't know. Maybe it wouldn't matter, but we should go."

They had just started packing up their trays when the noise level in the room suddenly went down, and heads turned to the TV.

"... just moments ago," the news anchor said. His square, clean-shaven face and tidy short-cropped hair faced earnestly into the camera. "The blast took place at the Maadi Church of the Holy Virgin on Corniche el Nil. Police and ambulances are on the scene. There appear to be multiple injuries, but no word of fatalities at this time. Victims are being transported to El Salaam Hospital. We will keep you posted as more news reaches us. In world soccer today, Brazil took on ..."

"Ahmed, *sahbey*," Kamal said, "wasn't that Magda's church?"

"Geez, yeah. That's crazy. Why would anyone attack a church on a regular weeknight?" Ahmed asked, popping a French fry in his mouth. "You don't suppose any of her family might've been there? That's all she needs right now."

"Uh, Ahmed," Kamal said tentatively, "I think *she* might've been there."

"What?" Ahmed's head shot up. "No way. I just saw her, like, a couple of hours ago. She's fine."

"No, I think she might've been there. I heard Demiana and some of the others talking about going there tonight for a special prayer service for Magda's little sister."

Ahmed jumped out of his chair with Kamal trailing behind.

They climbed into Mr. Najjar's Mercedes, the same one that Ahmed drove to and from their secret meetings. The car shuddered as the doors slammed shut. Ahmed threw the car into reverse then raced through the gears as he screeched out of the lot and into traffic, his hand on the horn. Kamal was pasted to the back of his seat, gripping the dash, eyes wide.

"You're not gonna help anybody if you don't get us there in one piece!" Kamal said.

Ahmed ignored him and blasted his horn again as he swerved into the next lane of traffic.

Abruptly, Ahmed let out a scream of pain and pulled his hand off the stick shift to clutch the calf of his driving leg protectively. Something hard and small went flying, and Ahmed's head hit the roof of the car as he jumped.

"What the—?" Kamal cried.

"Something just bit me!" Ahmed's head bobbed between his leg and the road.

Kamal's eyes searched the car for the source of the bite.

He froze. "Pull over, man," he said in a low voice that left no room for discussion. "And don't move a muscle you don't have to." Ahmed followed Kamal's gaze. On the seat between them, a pale yellow scorpion gathered its feet underneath it, tail raised high.

"My backpack! Throw my backpack on it!" Ahmed whispered urgently. Without taking his eyes off the scorpion, Kamal slowly reached into the backseat, grabbed Ahmed's red and gray backpack with one arm then dropped it on the insect. Instinctively, they both leaned back toward the doors of the car and put as much distance as possible between themselves and the aggravated creature between them. Ahmed still held the wheel in his left hand, his attention torn between the road and the seat.

Both boys watched in astonishment as two more scorpions crawled out of a side pocket of the backpack. Pale creatures, the color and translucence of amber, they scurried across the pack and onto the seat. Their tails raised high in alarm.

With one long blast of the horn, Ahmed threw the car across two lanes of traffic toward the sidewalk. A small parking space appeared between two cars—just big enough for Ahmed to squeeze into. But not at the speed he was going. He flew into the opening and the front of the Mercedes buried itself in the tail end of a parked cab. Both boys were propelled forward by the impact and then backwards into their seats. As soon the car came to a stop, they flung the doors open, shot out and slammed the doors behind them. They stood, panting, staring at the car.

"You okay?" Kamal asked as he caught his breath and waited for Ahmed to make his way around the back side of the car onto the sidewalk.

Ahmed clutched his right leg as he lurched toward Kamal. "At first it was like a sting, but now—now it's something else—" His jaw tightened, and he grimaced.

A bearded, old man ran out of a nearby store front. "What do you two crazy boys think you're doing?" he shouted, his arms flailing angrily at Ahmed and Kamal and the car. His hair was wrapped in a scarf that used to be white, and his blue galabeya flapped about him as he waved. "You boys drive like idiots! That's my cab you hit!" He held his head in his hands then threw them skyward, "That's my livelihood! What am I going to do?!" he cried.

Kamal bent over Ahmed to examine the bite, but Ahmed couldn't seem to peel his hands off it.

"Sorry about your cab, sahbey," Kamal said, still trying to examine the puncture. "But there are scorpions in that car. One bit my friend. Is there a doctor around here?" He scanned the gathering crowd.

The man paid no attention to his words. "I have a wife and three children! That cab is all I had to support them. What am I going to do?"

Kamal stared at him in disbelief. "Old man. My friend's been stung by a scorpion. Forget about your stupid cab for a minute. We need to get him to a hospital."

The word scorpions seemed to sink in, and his rant changed direction. "Allah help us! Scorpions! Shaytan's creatures!" he drew back from the car as if the vehicle itself might bite him.

Ahmed tried to stand on the bitten leg. His face screwed up in pain when he put weight on the leg, and he had to reach out and put a hand on the car for support.

The man sized up Ahmed and then at Kamal. He came closer and peered through the windows into the car. He stared into the front seat and rubbed his chin thoughtfully then stepped back. He was quiet for a moment.

"Two blocks up. The hospital. You were almost there. Here, you help him on that side, I got this side." The two men put their arms under Ahmed's for support and crossed the street in the direction of the hospital.

"Thanks," Kamal said as they walked, "Sorry about your cab, really, we'll—"

"Piece of crap. Let Allah look after it a while. I've done enough for it. And if He doesn't watch it, then Shaytan will get the man who tries to steal it. We will look after your friend," he said.

They quickened their pace to a kind of modified hop as they pushed their way along the wide sidewalk of El Corniche el Nil. With three of them moving together, their progress was quick. Soon Kamal could see the six stories of the white concrete hospital looming ahead through the gathering dark.

Sweat broke out on Ahmed's brow, and his breathing grew ragged.

"Hang in there, sahbey," Kamal told him, "we're almost there."

They were less than a block from the hospital. A man in green scrubs stood outside a door, his frame illuminated by the neon sign that announced the ambulance entrance. He smoked a cigarette, which he tossed aside and stepped on as the threesome approached. "What've you got?" he asked as he caught up with them. The taxi driver panted, and the man in scrubs relieved the cabbie by easing his arm under Ahmed's.

"Scorpion sting," Kamal said. He slipped a few bills into the tech's hand to ensure Ahmed was seen promptly.

The man put the money in his pocket without acknowledging it. "Let's get him inside." He directed the three men toward the emergency entrance and shouted for assistance as they went. They hobbled along a white hallway and into a larger room with several curtained beds, most of which were occupied. Friends, family, nurses, techs and doctors crossed paths in the central area. The tech helped settle Ahmed onto a bed with graying sheets and pulled the curtain around him and then left. Ahmed lay on the bed, his pulse racing, his eyes closed against the pain.

A large clock on the wall ticked off the time. A paint roller had run through the numbers on the clock and erased three through seven, which made it difficult to judge the time. The cabbie stood with his back to Ahmed and Kamal and spoke into a cell phone. A woman in pink scrubs and black flip flops entered the room and asked Kamal for Ahmed's insurance information. Ahmed couldn't make out the details of the conversation, but angry words were exchanged. Kamal slipped a bill into the woman's hand, and the information suddenly appeared to be in order.

"That better be the last bribe I've gotta pay," Kamal said to Ahmed, after she left. "That was my last pound. You're running up a tab, cousin."

"You know I'm good for it," Ahmed replied. "We don't have to bribe the doctor do we?"

"No!" Kamal said, glancing over to make sure the cabbie wasn't listening. "Only the ones earning starvation wages. Doctors'll take your last pound, but they're totally open and honest about it."

Several minutes later, a middle-aged man with small, round gold glasses and a white lab coat whisked the curtain open. A cat tried to dart in with him, and he kicked it out with a black leather shoe as he sealed the curtain behind him. The cat hissed before scurrying off down the hall.

"I'm Dr. Faoud, and you must be Ahmed," said the doctor, examining a clipboard, "Now, what have we here?"

"It's just a bug bite," Ahmed said. His breath came in short gasps now.

"Scorpion," Kamal clarified.

The doctor raised his eyebrows. "Where's the puncture?" he demanded. Ahmed pointed to his right leg. His swollen thigh stretched the fabric of his pants taught.

"Can you remove your pants?"

"No way."

The doctor produced a pair of scissors from a shelf under a metal table beside the bed and proceeded to tear the pant leg open.

"How long ago?" He asked as he cut and tore at the pant leg.

"I dunno," Kamal looked at the driver for support. "Maybe forty minutes? Forty-five? We walked here from just a few blocks down. Then your little nurse back there held us up with a bunch of useless bloody paperwork," he spat.

The doctor ignored his outburst. "You shouldn't have made him walk. It spreads the poison." The pant leg torn open, Ahmed's leg lay exposed. The bite was on the middle of his quad, and the entire upper leg was swollen. Most of the swelling was in an area defined by a clear red ring, the circumference of a grapefruit, with a black bruise inside.

"Forty minutes might not be too long, depending on the scorpion that bit him. "Do you have the scorpion?"

Kamal looked at him incredulously. "No, you know what? I didn't stop and get a bowl and a cutting board and capture the thing before we *rushed to the hospital—*"

"It was a Deathstalker," the cabbie interjected calmly, from where he stood near the curtain wall.

The doctor gave a low whistle. "That's a goodie. Are you sure?"

"Pale desert yellow scorpion, about this big," he said, holding his fingers up to show about two inches between thumb and forefinger. "Seen 'em before, just not in the city," he said.

"They were in his backpack," Kamal added.

The doctor pushed the gurney alongside a bed. The tech appeared again and helped him lift Ahmed onto the bed. Ahmed groaned. His eyes swimming with pain, rolled back in his head.

"Either you kids have been playing picnic with your backpack deep in the desert, or one of your friends has a nasty sense of humor," the doctor said grimly as he examined the puncture.

"Deathstalker," Kamal said. "That's like an exaggeration, right?"

"Deadliest venom out there. I don't see those little guys' bites but once or twice a year. They don't like the city. If they're here, it's because someone brought them here. They prefer to hide in the desert sands," he said.

"Is he going to be okay?" Kamal asked.

"Allah is watching over you boys. This venom is about the most painful out there, and if Ahmed here had waited too long before coming to the hospital, things would be much, much worse. A good antidote exists for this venom, made by a German pharmaceutical company. There's little call for it, so I'm pretty sure we have it in stock." He gave instructions to the tech who had just returned with cold compresses which he laid on the puncture site. Ahmed tensed as he applied them. "The compress will slow the spread of the poison until we can get him hooked up to an IV with the antidote."

Ahmed eased himself back on the bed, his hands clamped to the steel bed frame.

"Hang in there, big guy," Kamal said to Ahmed. "You're gonna be okay."

"Good," said Ahmed. His face dripped with sweat. "Cause this bed is the last place I want to be. Kamal, sahbey, you gotta go out there and find Magda. This is El Salaam Hospital. She could be right out there somewhere. Make sure she's okay," he said, panting. "Please?"

"I'm not going anywhere till they get this magic potion stuff in you and working," Kamal said. "I'm also going to call your parents. After that, I'll do what you want."

Ahmed swore and screwed up his face as a new shot of pain raced through his body. The tech returned with an IV and began setting it up.

"The anti-venom is in the IV," the doctor explained. "It'll be in your system soon, and if your friend here was right about the type of scorpion, the anti-venom will bond with the venom and neutralize it."

"How fast?" Ahmed gasped.

"You'll be up and around tomorrow, assuming no side effects," he said.

"Tomorrow?" Ahmed cried.

"Now you lie back right now, young man," the doctor said sternly. "You're not helping, spiking your blood pressure like that. You've got to keep calm, slow your blood down. Nothing in the world is so important that it can't wait a day," he said. He turned to a tray and pulled out a short needle.

"I'm going to administer an EpiPen for your breathing, and you'll be feeling a lot better in a few minutes. But you'll need to stay put until we're sure the anti-venom has trapped all the venom. Even after you start to feel better, you don't want to be wandering around with any of that stuff still circulating in your system. Left unchecked, the Deathstalker's poison is associated with all kinds of side effects, including paralysis and circulatory failure.

"*What* failure?" Ahmed asked.

"Sahbey," Kamal clarified. "You're stayin' put. If you get up too soon the doctor says you'll have a heart attack."

Ahmed looked down helplessly at his right leg, black and swollen, covered in a large green compress. His right arm was tethered to an IV pole. A wave of pain tore through his leg again and spread to his hip. He sank back into the bed, drew a long shaky breath and closed his eyes, beaten.

XXXII

The black veil lifted. My head spun. I could've been anywhere, at home in bed—mine or Magda's—at school. But I was in an unlikely place. I was at Magda's church. Why? I shook my head, and the events of the last few minutes began to fall into place like the pieces of a puzzle. I was on the deck of the church, Nile side. Sirens wailed in the distance, and the air tasted of smoke. A muted whimpering emanated from somewhere behind me. Twenty or more bodies lay scattered about, some sprawled and unmoving, some sitting, all covered with a fine black ash.

Craning my neck hurt mildly. My already fractured ribs ached agonizingly every time my lungs expanded. I looked down at myself—I too was coated in a fine black ash. I wiped my forehead, and my hand came away with a soft, chalk-like dust that clung to my fingertips.

Someone next to me screamed. It began as a low moaning and escalated into warbling high-pitched notes of hysteria, broken by fits of sobbing. It was Magda's mom.

She sat on the ground, legs underneath her, her bun collapsed, so her hair hung down past her shoulders. Tears cut multiple paths through the soot on her face. Dad had one arm around her and whispered consolingly in her ear.

I picked myself up and staggered over, sat down opposite Dad and put an arm around Mom. The screaming stopped abruptly. She looked at me in shock, jolted back from the brink of insanity.

"Mom, Mom, shhhhh," I cooed. "We're all right. The three of us are all right," her body swayed, her muscles rigid.

"Magda, thank God, you're all right," she said. She wrapped her arms around and Dad and I, bringing us into a three-way embrace.

"Are you both all right?" Dad asked.

"I'm fine, Dad."

"Yes, yes, habibi, thanks to God, I'm all right," Magda's mom said, pulling herself away. "I'll be fine," she sniffed, petting down her clothes and pulling her hair back.

Dr. Amides stood up, wiped her eyes on her sleeve and began to triage. Most of these people were related to her, but she surveyed them clinically. She worked her way over to a young girl about Maraya's age who lay with her leg at an unnatural angle. She checked the girl for other injuries and advised her not to move the leg until help arrived. She moved on.

Following her example, I stood and surveyed the wounded. The worst injuries seemed to be near the river, and I worked my way there. I helped an old man rise so he could limp back into the church. More and more people stood and began to hobble away.

"Ireney!" a voice called near the Nile side of the deck. "Ireney, over here! Hurry!"

I turned in the direction of the voice. I recognized Mark's father bent over the body of a young man. The last piece of the puzzle fell into place.

I sprinted across the deck into the midst of a small group of people gathered around Mark. I wondered fleetingly how much worse this scene would've been if he hadn't done what he did. The people and the building he loved so much—all of them might have been lost.

He was conscious but not moving. He' been thrown straight back, probably thirty feet, and landed on his back. Dr. Amides ordered everyone to stand away. Carefully, she moved her hands up and down his body. She paused over a couple of ribs and pressed her ear to his chest. His eyes were open, unfocused. I worked my way to the front of the crowd, most of whom alternately praised and fretted over him. His breath came in long broken gasps.

Dr Amides sat up. "Mark, baby, can you wiggle your toes for me?" His eyes seemed to focus a little, and he did so.

"Good, good. Now your fingers," she said. He obliged.

I maneuvered myself into his line of vision. He offered up a weak smile.

I shook my head in admiration. "You're amazing," I said.

He drew a ragged breath. His voice came out a raspy whisper, "I've always wanted," he paused, filling his lungs, "to hear you say that," again a pause. "But better—when I could move."

He was teasing me. I felt a hand on my shoulder then and saw Layla. She must've just arrived—her clothes weren't covered in soot. She put one hand on my shoulder, slid in next to me, then turned to Mark. Her eyes filled with tears.

I took my queue. This wasn't my place. I slid back out of the way. A half dozen emergency personnel in black pants and white shirts poured through the doors, and within moments one of them was at Mark's head and another at his feet. The two men jointly lifted him onto a spinal board. Mark's father and Layla walked alongside him as they made their way through the church to a waiting ambulance.

Little by little, the building cleared. Medical staff examined the injured, and either told them to go home or instructed them to go to the hospital. Those who escaped the blast unscathed returned to their cars. A half dozen reporters picked through the scene, and a television reporter in a corner of the church interviewed *the Baba*. His white robes, heavily streaked with ash, glowed eerily under the bright lights of the cameras.

I made my way back out to the now-empty church patio. In the failing light, the once-clean, gray stone deck was trampled black. Footprints filled the church near the Nile doors. No visible structural damage marred the building, yet the wounds brought about this night were deep. The wrought iron fence over which Mark had propelled the bomb stood unmarred. The wail of ambulance sirens faded as they took away the six most seriously wounded. Mark, with his spinal issues, was the most critical though a five-year-old boy was also in serious condition after falling into the Nile waters and nearly drowning.

I stood on tiptoe to peer over the fence and down the steep, stony shore to where it disappeared beneath the darkening waters. In the dim light, I couldn't make out any fragments of the frightful backpack that had wrought such destruction.

Magda's mother came up from behind and put an arm around my shoulder.

"It's time to go, darling. We'll go to the hospital in Dad's car and let the doctors there check us over," she said.

"But Mom, I'm fine. I just need a shower. Are you okay?" I asked.

"Yes, yes, I think so. But we'd better let them have a good look at all us, just in case."

"Can't you just look us over?" I asked.

"Not really, honey. A good doctor never treats herself or her family. We can't be objective."

I nodded and turned to leave with her. El Salaam Hospital was not far, and it's where we would've gone after the service anyway since Maraya was there.

I had only once before been to an ER, three years ago when Gabrielle stepped on broken glass and needed stitches. This hospital was nothing like that Tampa hospital with its clean quiet waiting room, its long white hallway leading to a sterile ER full of gleaming equipment and its quick and efficient staff.

Here in Cairo, friends and family of the injured came and went between the waiting room and ER at will as they talked loudly and dragged sticky-fingered children. Nurses and techs scurried about with an air of overworked impatience, and a matted orange cat walked nimbly through the legs of a cart laden with medications. The walls were covered in black scuff marks, and a puddle of dirty water lay in a the middle of the chipped linoleum floor. A nurse in pink scrubs trudged through it with her black flip flops, her eyes on a clipboard. She looked down in frustration, stepped aside and shook her foot, then walked on leaving a trail of dirty prints.

I left Magda's parents in the waiting room and cut through the ER in search of a restroom to wash my hands and face. I passed a row of beds, some curtained closed, and ducked out of the way of a tech pushing an IV pole.

When I threw open the door to the ladies' room, I was immediately accosted by the stench. I froze in the doorway. From where I stood I saw three stalls, all standing open. I let go of the door and stepped tentatively in. Two of the toilets were clogged. The third overflowed. Human waste clung to the rim of the bowl, and a steady stream of yellow-tinged water flowed over the seatless edge and ran in a crooked path to the rusted drain in the center of the room. Scraps of saturated toilet paper lay strewn about among mucky footprints. The two enamel sinks were heavily chipped and filthy.

Now I understood why Magda's mom's first act on the day Maraya and I were sent here was to clean. I understood why Magda's dad had spoken of hiring a British nurse, and why Magda's mom rarely left Maraya's side. I shuddered at the thought of leaving Maraya in such filth and imagined re-used needles and sub-standard medication from unreliable sources. In Maraya's case, still bleeding internally, the hospital was a necessary evil. In our case, I really couldn't see how we wouldn't be better off going home right now.

I turned straight around without washing my face and walked briskly back to the waiting room where Magda's parents still sat.

Dad was seated in a red vinyl chair in the unairconditioned waiting room. His phone rang as I approached. He squinted at his cell. His brow furrowed as he got up and headed for the front doors. My chest constricted—was it bad news about Maraya? Mom broke away from a conversation to follow him outside. I made a move to go with them, but Dad waved me away. He pushed the door open and walked outside. I sat down in the chair he had vacated. The orange cat appeared and rubbed against my legs sympathetically.

Moments later they returned.

"Is it Maraya?"

"What?" he responded. "It's not Maraya. It's just—it's nothing. A call from work."

We waited half an hour in the sweltering waiting room before a disinterested nurse called us to the desk. As soon as she learned that Magda's mother was a doctor, her manner improved. She apologized for the wait and blamed the sudden influx of wounded. Within minutes, we were settled together in a curtained examination room, and not long after that, an amiable middle-aged doctor appeared with round gold glasses. He asked questions about our injuries and one by one examined us before declaring us fit enough to go home.

We left the ER and went straight upstairs to check on Maraya in intensive care. Her frail little body lay motionless in the big bed. Magda's mom headed to the nurses station and asked to change Maraya's IV. She returned with a small cart, washed her hands carefully in a sink fixed to the wall of Maraya's room, opened a sealed package with a needle and proceeded to insert a fresh IV bag. I'm sure the nurses in Tampa would've been astounded at a mother hooking her own child to an IV, doctor or not, but here the nurses showed no reaction at all. Perhaps they appreciated the help.

Staying wasn't an option. We were covered in black soot, our clothing stained and torn. Mom sagged, and reluctantly agreed to go home, shower and change. She pledged to return later for Maraya.

We were home by ten. I stood in the shower for twenty minutes and let the hot water pour over me as I willed it to wash away the horrible events of the evening. Finally, when the water began to cool, I got out. I wrapped myself in a towel and opened the door, immersing the hallway in steam.

"Magda?"

Magda's dad buckled his belt in the front hall.

"I'm going to take your mother back to the hospital. I'll be back in an hour. There's something you should know though," he said, slipping his suit jacket over his shoulders. "Ahmed was in the emergency room tonight too," he said. His words landed like little bombs at my feet. "He's okay—he's going to be fine. It was a—a bite. A scorpion bite. The doctor administered an anti-venom, and he's going to be in observation overnight."

I stood there, stunned.

"Was that the phone call you took at the hospital? The one where you went outside?"

"Yes. Yes, it was."

"You said it was work."

"I didn't want to worry you."

My face turned crimson.

"Wait. Let me get this right," I said. "We could visit Mark in the ER. We could offer support and encouragement. But when Ahmed is injured, you keep me away."

"You can't compare the two," he said firmly. "Mark was with us in the church. Mark saved our lives. Mark is—is—"

"One of *us*?" I added, in feigned helpfulness.

"Magda, I don't have the energy for this now. It's not about us and them. Ahmed had his own friends and family there. He didn't need us, and we have enough on our plate already."

"No," I said. "*You* have enough on your plate. You know that I care for him, and you don't approve, so you chose to lie to me about that phone call. Didn't he call you right after the accident? He didn't have to do that. Didn't his father help us try to find my attacker? Ahmed might not have saved our lives like Mark did, but he's been there for me, and for you."

I had crossed a line.

"That's quite enough. Ahmed is not your boyfriend. You have no rights where he is concerned. None at all. The matter is closed. We'll deal with your attitude later," he scooped his keys off the hall table.

"I—I–" I stopped myself short, uncertain how to retort without getting into the small matter of my own web of lies. He was my boyfriend. And making Magda's father angry now wasn't going to help anything. I willed myself to calm down.

"It was just a scorpion bite?" I asked, more calmly and with an attempt at sweetness. Scorpion bites weren't uncommon in parts of the States and usually aren't serious. They were painful and warranted a trip to the doctor's office or ER. Ahmed was healthy and strong—he should be fine. "How bad was it? Was it a little one?" I asked. I had heard once that it's the littlest one that carry the deadliest venom.

Agitated, Magda's dad combed the apartment for his phone. "I don't know how big it was. It was a nasty one though. He was lucky to be so near a hospital with the right anti-venom."

"A scorpion bite? Right now? With all that's going on? This is totally weird." Then I looked at him again, my head tilted in curiosity. "How did you find out about this anyway? Who called you?"

Magda's mom was in the foyer too now and zipped up an overstuffed black vinyl bag.

He turned to face me.

"Mr. Najjar called me. I guess—" he was struggling for words. He sighed in defeat. "Magda, there have been threats on Ahmed as well."

"What?"

"I reactivated your phone. It's in my bedroom. It's a new one actually, but just the same as the old one. I hooked it up to your old number, so I could monitor any incoming texts from the guy who's chasing you. I hoped for a lead, but all I got was the same craziness he'd been sending all along. Well, a few days ago the texts began threatening Ahmed too. That's what I spoke to Mr. Najjar about in the other room today. He needed to know direct threats were being made on Ahmed's life too." He bent over his briefcase, emptying its contents onto the floor. "Aha!" he said at last and victoriously pulled out his phone.

"Dad, I want to come with you to the hospital."

"I think not. You will stay here in this apartment, and when I return, I expect I'll find you in bed asleep. I'll be back in an hour," he called over his shoulder as Mom opened the door and they both stepped outside.

The door shut behind him, and the key turned in the lock. I ran to the computer on the kitchen table. It booted up, and I went straight to our secret site. My mind raced. I was agitated, tired, and uncertain. I was scared for Maraya, scared for Ahmed, scared for Magda, scared for my own life and scared for my sanity. How long could I keep up this double life?

Magda's dad said plenty of Ahmed's friends and family had come to the hospital for him. Surely, someone had brought him a toothbrush and his computer. I needed to know that he was okay. Why a scorpion? How? Nothing made sense.

A status update waited for me.

Magda, are you okay? I heard about the bombing, and I need to know you're fine. I'm tired, but I'll stay online as long as I can.

I looked at my watch. It was nearly eleven. A glance at my screen showed his Facebook page was still open.

Are you ok? I typed in the chat box. *Dad told me what happened.* Five minutes passed with no response. I got up for a glass of water and nibbled nervously on a flatbread. Why wasn't he answering? Had he taken a turn for the worse? I was about to give up and power down when a new message line appeared.

Better. No pain now.

Are you alone?

Yes, hamdullah. The entire Najjar clan was in here a couple hours ago. Mom is staying but she's in the hallway talking to the nurses . . . I'm exhausted. Now what about you?

I'm fine, I answered. *Home now. Was it really a scorpion?*

Yeah. Stupid bug packs a wicked punch.

How'd it happen?

It was in my backpack . . . I figure your crazy man did it when me and Kamal were in McDonalds. He had plenty of time. My backpack was in the backseat and I never lock the car.

You mean you were bit in the car? Were you driving?

Yeah.

Geez, I responded.

Tell me what happened at the church.

I recounted the evening for him.

Layla, Demiana, Aisha and Moe were here earlier. They told me some of it. Mark's a true hero. They're doing a lot of tests on him I hear. No news yet. I'll try to visit him tomorrow morning.

Layla, Demiana, Aisha, Moe . . . All our friends got to visit Ahmed except me.

Ahmed, I wish I could've visited you. Dad only just told me about you when I got home.

I never expected your dad to let you visit me. I'm the one who should feel bad. I knew you were in the hospital but they wouldn't let me go to you.

Of course not! You wouldn't have got to see me anyway, I was with dad the whole time.

My fingers paused over the keyboard.

Here's what I don't get, I typed. *If this is some kind of Islamic terrorist, I get why he's after me. I'm the infidel, right? But why would he go after you?*

The screen glowed at me, silent. I waited.

Yeah, well I've been wondering about that too.

More silence.

Maybe he doesn't hate Christians so much as he hates Christians and Muslims mixing, he typed.

Maybe, I thought. *He needs to get his own life.*

After a moment, I added, *Did it hurt a lot?*

When I came in it was a hundred knives all digging into my flesh at once. It's just an ache now.

A pause.

When can you leave?

I can't even get up to go to the bathroom right now. In this place maybe that's a blessing. They want to observe me till morning. Then insha'Allah I'm going to school, he typed.

You are? You have like the world's most perfect excuse for skipping!

Well, you told my mom you might be going back tomorrow. I need to see you. You're the only medicine I need.

I dunno Ahmed . . . I'm exhausted from tonight.

Then rest now. But come to school tomorrow. We have English.

Of course, I couldn't say no. He was my medicine too.

XXXIII

At six-thirty in the morning, I walked into Magda's parents bedroom, picked up my phone and texted Layla to pick me up for school. It wasn't a very Magda-like thing to do. I was mad at Dad. The Najjar's had done everything they could to help us, and Dad still wouldn't even tell me Ahmed was seriously hurt until I was safely home with my armed guard. The Molly in me felt reckless and ready to take a few risks.

Of course, it would've been a lot braver had there been a reasonable chance he'd see me do it—he was down the hall and around the corner in the kitchen bent over his laptop and eating toast. Since Magda's mom spent so much time with Maraya at the hospital, toast was pretty much it for our meals. I scanned previous text messages on the phone, and my stomach rolled over.

For He did not call on us to be impure but to live a holy life.

His kingdom is at hand, Repent!

Overcome with the blood of the lamb.

Repent ye therefore, that your sins may be blotted out.

Do not be yoked together with unbelievers. For what do righteousness and wickedness have in common?

Repent or pay the price.

There is none among you with whom there is not a companion from amongst the jinn!

Fight and slay the infidels!

My tormenter—actually, it was *our* tormentor now; Ahmed and I had found something we could really share—had become a lot more wordy. All the messages were still from different numbers, and again

I wondered if we were making a mistake looking for just one man, the man I'd seen in the red van.

What was a jinn?

I entered the kitchen.

"School today?" Dad asked, in surprise.

"Yeah. I can't just sit here anymore."

"Hmm. I suppose."

I looked at the paper he was reading.

"Can I see the front section?" I asked.

He considered for a moment then handed it over.

I would've thought the bombing of a church would be the main headline the next morning. Instead, it appeared as a little teaser line on the left side of the page under the fold: *Twelve wounded in church bombing,* the headline read. *Details on page ten.*

I flipped the pages. There was a picture of the outside of the church—not even a recent photo but one taken on some other sunny day. All those reporters swarming the scene taking pictures, and the newspaper ran a file photo?

Twelve people were rushed to El Salaam Hospital yesterday, and two were in critical care after a bomb hidden in a backpack exploded in the Church of the Holy Virgin on Corniche el Nil.

The bomb was discovered during a special prayer service being held for eight-year-old Maraya Amides who has been in hospital fighting for her life since Saturday when she was pulled from the scene of a car crash.

No one has claimed responsibility for the bomb, but sources near police say they are close to making an arrest. The suspect has no known links to existing Muslim fundamentalist groups and was probably acting alone, the sources say.

I looked up. "He has no links to other groups? He was acting alone? They know who it is?"

"Of course not, Magda darling. The police these days are—well, they're all monkeys. Their chatter is all skin and no banana," he said, waving an arm dismissively. "They just want to sound like they're hot on the trail—like they're taking it seriously."

"If they're trying to show they're taking it seriously, then why is the bombing of a church on page ten?" I asked.

"That's not the police's doing. That's the newspaper, *Al Jeezerah*. It's government run, and the government doesn't want this to be a fundamentalist movement. They can't hide it— everyone knows about it. So they minimize it. They're saying, 'It's no big deal. It's just one crazy man, and we're on it.'"

Brrrrriiiing! Brrrriiing!

I opened the door and there stood Layla. Her hair was tucked back in a simple ponytail, and she wore her plain white uniform shirt and gray skirt with no accessories. She must've been rushed this morning. I picked up my laptop and backpack and headed for the door.

"Magda?" Dad called before I could leave. "I'm going to tell Burhan to pick you up right outside the school as soon as the last bell rings. This is no time for you to be wandering the city alone. Understood?"

Burhan? Oh, he meant Butch, my soldier. "Understood."

I followed Layla to the car. The day was hot and cloudless like everyday, yet something was different. A dingy, orange cast filled the western sky. The air felt thick and cottony, and noise of distant traffic was oddly muted. No birds chirped in the trees nearby.

"Is that what I think it is?" I said, looking at the western sky.

"Khamsin?" Layla asked. "Could be. I know my Mom's running around putting towels under all the windows and drawers just in case it hits while we're all out today. I'm hoping it does because I've got a wicked algebra test, and I'm not ready. My luck, it'll just blow itself out in the desert and that'll be that," she lamented.

"You think we'd get out of school?" I asked as I opened the passenger door. I bit my tongue. That was a dumb question—something Magda would've known. But Layla didn't seem to notice.

"Hey, we can hope!" she said, as she squeezed in behind the wheel.

The car felt empty without Maraya, and when we arrived, the kids at school felt distant. I didn't get any cutting comments or pinches today. News of the bombing had spread, and my situation was no longer comical or gossipy. Kids stared at me in the hallways and then looked away when I approached. I didn't care. These people didn't have a sister in critical care or a crazy man who tried to run them off the road, bomb their church or put scorpions in their boyfriend's car. We no longer had anything in common.

I had come back to school too soon. I wanted to be at Maraya's bedside. Even more I wanted, selfishly, to be back home in my own school in Florida with my own friends and my own everyday problems, like persuading my Mom to buy me a MacBook laptop, getting out of cleaning Kiwi's birdcage or helping Sandra decide if she should break up with Kevin or not. The real Magda should be at Maraya's side holding her hand, not me. But then again, Magda wouldn't have gotten into this mess. This was my mess, and I had to fix it. Somehow.

I sat in the back of the English class and tried to be invisible. I felt listless, exhausted, sore. Worry and pain were a constant wrench. I was being selfish—coming just to see Ahmed. I belonged at the hospital with Maraya. Maybe Dad would let me visit her after school.

Ahmed walked into class just as the bell rang, his gait slow and careful, with a marked limp. His face was pale, and his honey eyes looked tired and dark, but they lit up when he saw me, and he grinned openly. Caught off guard by this brazenly public smile, I smiled slightly and lowered my gaze. His forwardness was unexpected and not something we had agreed to.

We had a sub. A thin, gray-haired man in a gray three-piece suit, he held a pair of reading glasses in one hand and tapped them annoyingly on his book as he walked.

He was either a sadist or the only one in the school who didn't know what was going on in my life. We were reading the final act of *Romeo and Juliet*, and when he saw me trying to blend in with the walls, he chose me to read the part of Juliet.

He continued his tapping and looked around the room for his Romeo. The boys in the room shuffled uncomfortably, suddenly interested in the dirt in the grout of the tiles near their desks, their pencil leads, their shoelaces.

To the shock of the room, a hand raised. It was Ahmed. I heard a couple of stifled gasps, and some low chuckles.

"Excellent, young man!" the teacher said, surprised but pleased to have a volunteer.

We were near the end of the story. Juliet had swallowed a poison to feign her own death, and now she lay unconscious in the family crypt, alone with a frantic Romeo.

Eyes, look your last! Ahmed read for Romeo, and his baritone voice rolled over the syllables as he caressed them with sincerity and inflection.

Arms, take your last embrace! and, lips,
O you, the doors of breath, seal with a righteous kiss
A dateless bargain to engrossing death!

Ahmed's head drooped as his character lapsed unconscious. The class, silent as the Sphinx, looked between him and me as he read. The only sound was the tinkle of my lucky bracelet as I lifted the book to read.

What's here? A cup, closed in my true love's hand? I felt twenty-some pairs of eyes lock on me. Petrified, I needed to see this through. Summoning my courage, I read with conviction:

Poison, I see, hath been his timeless end:
O churl! Drunk all, and left no friendly drop
To help me after? I will kiss thy lips;
Haply some poison yet doth hang on them,
To make die with a restorative.

The scene paused for Juliet to kiss her Romeo, and I heard Fiona's voice whisper audibly, "Go for it, Magda! Kiss him!" I looked up at the teacher who didn't appear to hear. He was so wrapped up in the story that he motioned me to continue. My face flushed.

Thy lips are warm, I read. A loud snicker escaped someone in the back of the class.

Oh happy dagger, This is thy sheath.
There rust, and let me die.

Juliet plunged the dagger into her breast and died.

Grateful that my character, quite dead, had no more lines, I sank bank into my desk.

The other actors in the class carried on until the last lines were read and the student body, as one, closed the book. The sub pulled out a tissue and blew his nose then picked up a red dry erase pen and wrote on the board in large letters, "Were Romeo and Juliet's parents responsible for their deaths?"

Only the sub had no knowledge of the irony of asking this particular question at this particular moment. He taught on blithely and debated the issue with himself before informing us that our regular teacher had assigned the question as an essay, due Thursday. The class became quiet again.

The lessons of the story echoed in my head. Two lovers dared to love when their parents didn't approve. Two lovers had to give their lives before their families saw their own folly. Only after the pair died did the families recognize in the couple the one shining chance the two communities had of finding love in the midst of such tragedy. The lesson came too late. Were their families to blame for their deaths? Of course, they were. They were to blame for creating and perpetuating the whole situation. But Romeo and Juliet were to blame also. They didn't have to accept the world they were born into. They never once tried to be a voice for the peace they sought. Instead they chose to hide their love and run away.

Maybe we should excuse Romeo and Juliet for being so young. They were fourteen. They were born into their families' bad history. They had no experience of life. At seventeen I was much older, yet I was completely inexperienced in the ways of modern Cairo. Then it occurred to me that I had one key advantage over Juliet. For Juliet, every challenge she faced was new. I had read this story before.

How could Ahmed and I avoid their sorry fate? Suicide would not be our final act, but many other possible tragic endings could yet be written in. If this love ended in tragedy, would Ahmed and Magda's loss make a difference to anyone but them (and me, of course)? Would society change? It was possible, but not likely. Theirs would be just one more in a string of deaths tied up in the region's ongoing struggle with religious fanaticism.

Was there still time to choose a different path?

I definitely shouldn't have come to school today. My ribs ached with every breath. I was mentally fragile after the bombing and obsessively worried about Maraya. A madman was still out there trying to hurt Ahmed and I. While I was relieved to see Ahmed was recovering well from the bite, I was also angry with him. We had just agreed not to take risks. Now was a lousy time to flaunt our feelings for each other. I knew what he was doing. He was expressing his feelings in a way that the whole school could see but that would be clean in the eyes of our elders: a school dramatization in a class full of kids under the eyes of a teacher. He had done no wrong. I appreciated his motives, but his timing sucked.

I gathered up my things and pushed out into the throngs of kids already in the hallway. Kamal's thin frame kept pace with me.

He said softly, "Magda, I know the Brotherhood isn't the group doing these things." I stared at him, stunned. He glanced briefly at me and continued. "I'm not the monster you think I am."

"How do you know? About the Brotherhood?" I asked, shocked that he would admit to any ties with radical fundamentalists.

"I just know," he said, his eyes evading mine.

I stared at him unblinkingly. "You— just—know."

He squirmed uncomfortably and rubbed the side of his long hooked nose. "Yeah. Well," he stammered. "Look, don't say anything, 'kay?" he pleaded. He scanned the kids moving alongside us, but no one was close enough to hear. "All right. I know through my father's friends. Not only do they say they have nothing to do with this, they say it's not in their interest. They say killing Copts would unite the world against Egypt's Muslims. No one in the Brotherhood would do this. It wouldn't help the—their cause."

I took note of his word choice. He called the Brotherhood's interest *their* interest, then switched to *ours*. He spoke of *the* cause—then quickly corrected it to *theirs*. Whatever Ahmed thought, Kamal was either still aligned with the radical elements of the Brotherhood and was pretending not to be, or he stood at the crossroads.

Either way, he had been asking questions on my and Ahmed's behalf. Perhaps he was not my enemy. Not today, anyway.

My eyes narrowed. "Then who is doing it?"

He bowed his head. "No one knows. Some of the Brothers think the Army of Islam may be responsible for the bombing. They're not taking credit, but they've expressed approval. They're the ones publicly accused of bombing that church in Alexandria on New Year's Eve a while back. They didn't take credit for that either, but a lot of people think they did it. As for the van that chased you off the road, and the scorpions that got Ahmed, that's really not the way any of these organizations work."

"Who is the Army of Islam?" I asked.

"They're a Palestinian group who—"

"Palestinian?" I groaned. "Now I'm being attacked by Palestinians?"

Kids on either side began to slow and stare.

"Magda, it's not about you. Don't you *get* it at all?" He glanced around, embarrassed.

I stopped dead in the middle of the crowded highway, turned and glared at him. "My sister is in the hospital fighting for her life, my rib is fractured and sends shooting pains through my body when I breathe, I watched my church get bombed yesterday and my—" for the first time in public I voiced the word, "my *boyfriend* was attacked and could've died yesterday, Kamal. I *get* it." I spat.

I turned to leave, then whipped back around to face him. "But you know what? It *is* about me. It's about Christians and terrorists, but it's also about me, my family and Ahmed and his." I glanced around and then leaned in and lowered my voice menacingly. "What I want to know is how you come off knowing this much about our attacker when you've supposedly abandoned any ties to that sort of thing since you started hanging with the Najjars, and they started paying for your schooling."

"What the—?" Confusion clouded his expression then his eyes hardened and his thin lips formed a thin angry line. "I don't like what you're insinuating. I'm in this too. Ahmed is my cousin, and it was me who dragged him to the damned hospital yesterday and practically restrained him there because he was trying to get out of bed to see if you were okay. And you know what? I was just trying to help you out with this information. But fine, you don't want any help? Have it your way."

He stormed off and disappeared into the slipstream of kids heading to their next classes.

My shoulders sagged, and my books weighed a hundred pounds. I let my backpack slip off my shoulders onto the floor. Was he just trying to help? Maybe he was; maybe he didn't deserve my attack. But he wasn't giving me any real information. He had just told me what everyone else was saying—that no one knew who was behind this.

I closed my eyes and felt hysteria mounting inside me. It was like a kettle screeching in my mind, and if I didn't take it off the burner, it was going to explode. I needed to remove myself from everything, right now.

I stood in the intersection of two hallways, my pink backpack at my feet and my English books in my arms. One hallway led to my next class. Another led to the front doors. The walls began to close in. Kids swirled around me. Everything spun. This small decision—which direction to go—paralyzed me. I stood frozen, my mouth gaping.

I don't recall making a decision at all. I picked up my backpack and marched out the front doors. Immediately, a gritty wind lashed me across the face. I squinted through a beige haze to the street in front of me. An empty tin can clanked and rolled haphazardly down the street. My first breath in tasted of sand, and I snapped my mouth shut. I closed my eyes, and for a moment I was back in Florida. A hurricane bore down upon the city. A window shuddered. Fear darkened my mother's eyes. Maybe I should go back inside the school. But I couldn't go back and face Kamal, or Ahmed, or anyone else right now. A sand storm, I consoled myself, wasn't nearly as deadly as a hurricane. It was nothing but a big sandy cloud and a stiff wind. Layla would be thrilled. I wouldn't be surprised if school let out soon.

I turned left, walked to the cab stand. I glanced down the line of cabs for my regular driver but visibility was poor and I didn't see him. I climbed quickly into the backseat of the first cab in line. The driver, who'd been huddling with the other drivers against the ten-foot-tall cement fence that bordered the school, stamped out a cigarette and slid behind the wheel.

"Whew! Allah's angry today!" he said and turned his key in the ignition. "Where you going? You okay, Miss?" his face filled the rearview mirror.

I lay my head on the back of the seat and closed my eyes. The panic subsided, and his words penetrated.

"Miss?"

"El Salaam Hospital, please."

XXXIV

Ahmed entered the hallway well behind Magda and walked briskly toward her. He was nearly caught up when he noticed Kamal beside her. He slowed his pace to watch. She leaned forward and spoke angrily at him, her words swallowed by the hubbub of the hallway. Kamal shouted something back at her then turned sharply and came back down the hallway, straight into Ahmed.

Kamal's face registered surprise, then his expression quickly cleared. He nodded at Ahmed and started to move past.

Ahmed reached out and grabbed his thin arm. Kamal instinctively pulled back, but Ahmed whispered in a low and menacing voice, "Kamal, you tell me what you said to her."

"I—I—it was nothing," he said and tried to pull free. Ahmed's grip tightened and his eyes probed Kamal's intensely. Then he looked back down the hallway. Magda stood in a trance, her backpack at her feet, kids moving past her in every direction.

"You're lying," he said viciously, drawing him closer. "Now you tell me what you said to her."

"Ahmed, damn it, you're getting all bent out of shape over nothing," Kamal retorted angrily. "Get your damn hands off me," he said and tore his arm free from Ahmed's grasp.

Ahmed looked back down the hallway. Magda was gone. "You're coming with me, cousin," Ahmed said. He put an arm behind Kamal and shoved him.

"All right, all right, just keep your hands off me," Kamal said. He shook himself away and kept pace reluctantly.

Ahmed hurried to the center of the hall where Magda had just stood. "Where'd she go?" he said as much to the hallway as to Kamal.

"I dunno. She probably just went to class. What's with you? When did you become her guard dog?" Kamal's face was a mixture of anger and confusion.

"Kamal, you don't understand. We're not playing some stupid game. Someone is trying to kill her. If anything happens, and I find out you had anything to do with it, so help me—"

Ahmed caught a fleeting glimpse of pink backpack near the front doors and took off after it. Kamal followed.

"Get a grip, Ahmed," Kamal called out behind him. "She's got a *guard*. That girl is the safest girl in the school. No one's trying anything after what happened."

"Look around you, Kamal. Do you see a guard? There's no guard here. He guards the house. She's supposed to be safe in the school. But if she leaves the school, she's not safe," he pushed his way to the front doors. "She's just watched half her family get hit by a bomb intended for her. Her sister's dying, and she's mad with worry. She's not thinking straight."

They burst through the doors and into a wall of wind. Instinctively, their hands moved to protect their eyes. The wind gusted, and Ahmed braced himself against it. A cloudy orange haze obscured the street. Squinting, he looked in the direction of the cab stand just in time to see the vague figure of Magda plunge into the backseat of the lead taxi.

"Damn!" Ahmed swore. He took off after the cab at a run. Kamal followed.

But the taxi was gone.

"Come on!" Ahmed called. The two boys ran full tilt to the taxi stand and bowled into the six drivers who were pressed up close to the school fence against the wind and not about to let nature cheat them of a fare.

"Patience, patience—" one of the drivers chastised the boys, but then another interrupted, "Never mind, Hassan, you can see these boys are in a hurry." He put an arm around Ahmed and pointed him into his cab. "My taxi looks very old, but it has an engine that would turn the American Space Shuttle green with envy," he said. "I will take you where you need to go."

He jogged around front and climbed behind the wheel. "Where to?"

Ahmed and Kamal looked at each other. Magda's cab was long gone.

"I can only think of two places she would go," Ahmed said. "Either the hospital or home." Then, before Kamal could answer, Ahmed shouted, "El Salaam Hospital, Corniche el Nil. Quickly."

The taxi lurched into reverse and then bolted into traffic. The driver pushed the accelerator to the floor. The old cab shook and wobbled in protest, and what its mediocre engine lacked in performance, the driver attempted to make up for in enthusiasm as he bobbed and weaved through traffic.

Ahmed kept his eyes on the road, scanning the sea of black and white cabs in search of one with a girl in a black ponytail. "Now you gonna tell me what you said to her?" he asked Kamal.

Kamal squirmed in his seat and looked uncomfortably out the window. "I told her they didn't do it."

Ahmed absorbed the fact that his best friend still had contact with those crazies. Did he really know his cousin at all? Anger battled in his mind with an even more unwelcome emotion—what was it? Gratitude. It would've been easier to just be mad. He had hoped/prayed/believed that Kamal had closed that door completely. He hadn't. But he had used what he had to help Magda. And to help him.

Ahmed said nothing. Just then the cab made a sharp turn to the right, off the road and into a small strip of shops.

"What the—?" Ahmed said, incredulously. "What are you *doing*?"

The driver pulled into a gas station.

"It's Allah's will!" the driver said apologetically, gesturing at the gas gauge of the old cab. "What can I do? If I don't fill her up now, we're gonna be stuck in the middle of the road! It'll only take a second—you just wait, I'll have you there in no time. No one else drives as fast me. I'll have you—"

But as soon as the car rolled to a stop Ahmed was out the door. "I don't believe this!" he shouted. The wind had picked up sharply, and a plastic bag inflated with wind tumbled down the street in front of him. An angry red-brown cloud crouched menacingly over the horizon. Khamsin. Their eyes tucked low against the sting of the wind, they raced toward the street.

"Hey!" the cabbie shouted after them. "My fare! You didn't pay my fare!"

"You didn't take us anywhere!" shouted Ahmed as he ran down the street scanning for another cab, Kamal hurrying beside him.

Only in Cairo, Ahmed mumbled, and waved his arms at a passing taxi.

Three lanes deep in traffic, another cabbie waved them in. They darted through the slow-moving traffic and clambered aboard as they pulled their backpacks beside them. They slammed the doors quickly, so this driver wouldn't hear the cries of the other cabbie who was wading into traffic waving his fists and shouting, "Hey! Thieves! My fare!"

"To El Salaam hospital," Ahmed cried. The driver's response was lost in the shrieks of the wind and the tinny wails of the music on the car radio. The cab lurched forward in traffic.

XXXV

I felt a little more in control by the time I got to the hospital. The hysteria was gone, replaced by numbness.

I hadn't negotiated with the cabbie for a fare, so I guessed at what it should be, added a couple of pounds, pressed it into the driver's hand and stepped out. The wind pulled at me and tried to knock me off my feet. The gray smog of the city mixed with the red-beige fog of sand obliterated both the sky and the horizon. I fought the wind to the front entrance of the hospital, stepped inside and relished the sudden quiet.

I took the stairs up one flight to intensive care and entered Maraya's room. Mom dozed on an overstuffed chair in the corner.

Maraya was still and small, adrift in a sea of blinking lights and buttons. I slid my warm hand into her pale, cool one. I stood like that for a while.

I walked to Magda's mother, leaned down and put a hand to her cheek. She looked so frail. She stirred, startled, and peered anxiously over at Maraya. I shook my head.

"Can I bring you anything?" I asked.

She was quiet a moment. "You could bring some of her books," she said. She pointed to two books on Maraya's bedside. "I've been reading her these, but I've read them both twice. If she hears me, she must be sick of them. Bring me the Lemony Snicket books on her shelves. She started the series just last week, and I think she liked them," she said.

"She's going to get better, Mom, I know it," I said, trying to impart a confidence I didn't feel. I had no idea whether Maraya would get better or not. I could only hope.

She nodded. "I know," she said.

"I'll be back."

If Mom noticed I was there before school let out, she didn't let on.

I kissed my fingers and touched them to Maraya's forehead. Then, on impulse, I unclasped Magda's lucky bracelet and slipped it onto Maraya's limp cool wrist.

"You need this more than I do," I whispered.

The wind met me eagerly, shrieking and tugging at my clothes. I held my skirt down with one hand and walked numbly to the street in front of the hospital. Before I could head toward the taxi stand, a cab pulled up in the ambulance lane. The backseat was empty. I stepped in and told the driver to take me home.

"I know where you live, Magda," the man said, smiling. It was that Christian cabbie from the school. It was good to see a familiar face, but I hoped he wouldn't have a rant for me today. I didn't feel up to listening.

He must've judged my mood because he didn't so much as comment on the weather. I let my head fall back against the seat and closed my eyes. The lull of the cab starting and stopping through traffic was soporific.

I must've drifted off because I woke to the sudden coolness of a damp cloth being pressed to my face. It smelled faintly sweet, like honey, but with something vaguely rotten behind it. My eyes flew open. I couldn't remember where I was. I gasped reflexively—a sharp intake of breath.

The gasp was a mistake. The world spun out of control. My last image was the bulging eyes of the cabbie behind his silver frames, leaning over into the back seat, his hand pressed against my face.

XXXVI

Ahmed and Kamal bumped along in the taxi on the Corniche el Nil. The cab flew in and out of potholes and careened around corners as the driver zigged and zagged through traffic. At midday, the streets should've been filled with people, but only a few remained, walking purposefully with their heads bowed into the wind. The wind raced up and down every street, howled at every door and clawed at every window. Ahmed's Uncle Abudullah would have brought in all the tourists, and the pyramids would be closed to visitors. The desert was not the place to be in a khamsin. There, the winds ran free and wild, whipping the sand into frenzied funnels. In the city the winds were frustrated, constantly running up against shops and apartments, regrouping to charge again.

"She's probably just gone to the hospital or gone home," Kamal said. "She'll be fine."

Ten minutes later, they pulled up to the hospital. Ahmed told Kamal to hold the cab while he ran inside. He took the stairs to intensive care two at a time.

Ahmed bounded breathlessly past nurses and doctors then rounded the corner into Maraya's room.

Maraya lay on the bed, unmoving. Magda's mother looked up at him, startled. She stared at him a moment—she'd never actually met Ahmed, only seen one unwelcome photo. A light of recognition dawned, and she recoiled slightly.

"Dr. Amides?" Ahmed said, breathlessly.

"Ahmed—I presume?"

"I'm terribly sorry to bother you, ma'am." He said nervously. "Some—others—are looking for Magda, and we thought she might be here. Have you seen her?"

"Ahmed, I really don't think my daughter's whereabouts are any of your business."

This was not at all how he might have hoped his first introduction to Magda's mother would go. "Dr. Amides, I mean you no disrespect. She left school early today, and I don't think she's well. I—we're worried about her. She doesn't have her phone, so we can't contact her. I thought I'd check if she was here. But I see she's not here. I'm sorry to have bothered you."

He turned to leave.

"Ahmed." He swiveled back obediently.

"I think everyone would be better off if you two would concern yourselves less with each other. A lot less."

Rebuked, he nodded demurely. As he turned to leave, his eyes lit on a familiar bracelet on Maraya's arm. He looked again. It was definitely Magda's bracelet. The one that jingled when she moved and had filled the quiet English room with its music while she read the part of Juliet. He felt a surge of hope.

He exited the room, gently closed the door, and ran again. He launched himself down the stairs, and passed nurses laden with trays and an old lady working her way methodically up with a cane.

Kamal braced himself against the cab, watching a row of palm trees across the street bent double in the wind. He looked up expectantly when Ahmed approached.

"She was here. She must've just left. Did you see anything?"

"What? Like I would've just stood here and watched her go?"

"Whatever," Ahmed said tersely. Then, more to himself than to Kamal, he mumbled, "She was here, but she's gone. That means she probably left before we got here. Let's go talk to those cabbies over there. See if they can tell us anything."

Kamal shrugged and motioned their driver to wait. They hurried to the taxi stand at the corner. A row of taxis lined the street, all of them empty. Their eyes scoured the area looking for the drivers.

He rounded the corner just beyond the cabs and there, inside a doorway, a group of four drivers huddled and smoked cigarettes out of the wind's reach.

He pulled out a couple of bills and held them up as an offering for information. "We're looking for a girl. She's wearing a school uniform, gray skirt and white shirt. Did any of you see her? It's important."

They looked from one to the other and shrugged collectively.

"Nope," said the first man in a blue checked button-down shirt with a thick graying mustache. "Last fare we had was maybe ten minutes ago. Muhammad took 'em. I think it was a family, wasn't it, boys?" he said, blowing out a puff of smoke, his eyes on Ahmed's money.

"Yeah, I saw 'em," the youngest one said, pushing his wire-rimmed glasses up on his face. "Father, mother and a little girl, like five years old or so. There's been no one since."

"Nope," they echoed.

"'Kay. Thanks," Ahmed replied, dejectedly.

"Oh, wait," the elder cabbie said. "there was that joker who ripped past us and nabbed someone up there."

"What?" Ahmed said.

"Yeah. If you wanna fare, you gotta do your time here. 'Bout five minutes ago, this idiot just blew on past us like we wasn't here. He tore up there, and someone got in. We were gonna take a strip out of 'im and send him to the end of the line, but by the time I ran over he was gone. Never saw who got in. They'd already took off when I got there."

Ahmed nodded. It was the only possibility.

"Did you notice anything about the cab? Or about the guy?"

"Never saw the guy. He didn't get out of the cab. Looked like a regular cab. Older'n mine," he said, gesturing to the first cab in line. The front bumper was dented and lower on one side than the other, a big crack ran down the passenger-side front window, and an entire panel above the front wheel was held together with duct tape. "There was some stickers 'n stuff on the back of it though. Crosses and Jesus stuff. And a huge gold box of tissues in the back window—don't know how he could see out."

"Which way did it go?"

"South," he pointed across traffic to the opposite side. "He screeched out o' here like the jinns themselves were on his tail. Probably were. Then again I guess if he's Copt, he don't believe in jinns, so it must'a been somethin' else that scared him," he snickered at his own humor.

"Thanks," Ahmed pressed the cash into the man's hand then turned and ran with Kamal back into the fog.

"That's it?" Kamal said as they ran. "You're all excited about a Jesus cab? We're looking for a snowflake in a damn sandstorm."

"Not really. She was just here, and I can only think of a handful of places she would go," Ahmed replied as they stepped into their cab. "We can still find her." Then to the cab driver, "South on Corniche el Nil. Head for Maadi. Road 208." It was Magda's address.

"Keep your eyes open for another cab," he said to the cabbie.

The driver snorted. "Another cab? That's all you got? There's one," he said pointing out the window. "There's another one. This is easy. There's one." Tiring of his joke, the driver shrugged his shoulders and gestured with two upturned hands at the traffic around him. "Every second car in Cairo's a cab," he said. "Besides, in case you didn't notice, there's a khamsin comin'. Can't see more'n ten cars anyway."

Ahmed ignored him. "It's a Christian cab. Jesus stickers and crosses all over it. Just tell us if you see it."

The driver shook his head in disgust.

Fifteen minutes brought them to the front of Magda's building. Ahmed jumped out while Kamal waited in the running cab. Ahmed returned moments later, his shoulders hunched, his expression defeated. "She's not there. No one answered. I climbed the fence in the yard to look in her window. She's not in her room. The guard isn't even there," he said.

Kamal swore. "What're we gonna do now?"

Ahmed picked up his phone and stared at it for several seconds. Then he dialed.

"Hello?" a thick voice answered.

"Mr. Amides? This is Ahmed Najjar, sir. I'm sorry to bother you again, but I thought you should know. Magda was at school a few moments ago, and I saw her leave. She shouldn't be on her own with that madman on the loose. I checked the hospital and she'd just been there. I'm at your house now, but she's not here."

There was silence. "She left the school early? You're sure?" he said.

"Yes, sir. I don't know for certain, but she may have got into a cab after visiting Maraya at the hospital. Some of the other cabbies say another cab cut to the front of the line and picked someone up, but they don't know who. Other than that, they hadn't had a fare in a while that could've been her."

"Thank you for calling, Ahmed. I'll take it from here."

"Sir?"

"Yes, Ahmed?"

"Is there anything I can do?"

Another pause. "No. I'll have the headmaster check the school. And I'll call Burhan. He'll be at the school waiting to pick her up. I asked him to take her home today. I'm sure we'll find her."

"Burhan, sir?"

"Burhan—the soldier we hired to watch over her."

"Oh. Okay. Would you please let me know if you find her? Or if there's anything I can do?" Ahmed said.

The response turned cool. "Thank you for calling, Ahmed. You did the right thing to let me know. I'll take care of it. God willing, she just stopped for some groceries on her way home or returned to the school. As for you, you know this man is after you too. You'd better get home. Your father will be worried." He hung up.

"The Cairo American Academy," Ahmed directed the driver.

The cab didn't move.

"You boys gonna be able to pay this fare? I'm not gonna be drivin' around half the day then find out you boys got no allowance. This is a lot of driving, and any sane man'd be home out of this wind with his wife and kids by now anyway," he said.

Ahmed pulled out a fifty-pound note and gave it to the driver. "Go."

The driver hit the gas.

"Ahmed, this is crazy," Kamal said bitterly. "We *know* she's not at the school. She just left there cause she couldn't handle it. We'd be better off just randomly driving the streets."

"I know she's not at school," replied Ahmed. "But the last one to talk to her aside from her mom was the cabbie who took her from school to the hospital. Maybe she said something to him. I know it's a long shot."

"Duh," Kamal agreed.

"Listen, you got any better ideas?"

Kamal drew his lips into a tight line. He looked away. "No."

They pulled up to the cab line outside the school. Classes had let out. Students poured out into the street and held tightly to books and bags against the wind. The drivers were distracted and intent on fares.

"Hey, did any of you guys see a tall girl take a fare here this afternoon?" he shouted over the screeching wind. "Name's Magda Amides. She gets cabs here sometimes. She's about five-foot-seven, wears her hair in a ponytail—"

"Eh? What's that?" a fat balding man near the back of the group asked.

"Tall girl, five-seven, pretty, pink backpack and matching laptop case, ponytail, wears a dangly bracelet with lots of crosses. Named Magda Amides. Gets a cab here a lot. You guys know her?" he shouted, cupping his mouth with his hands to be heard over the wind.

"Yeah, sure, we know her," another driver stepped forward, younger in a red button-down shirt. "That's Simon's girl. He's thinks that girl's got wings and farts halos. Been takin' her the past few weeks whenever she comes. Whenever he sees her, he pays off the lead cab to get out o' the way so he can get her," he said. "Nice extra cash for us."

Ahmed's brow furrowed. "He does?"

"Yup. You'd think she was his daughter. I dunno. Them Christians stick together ya know? We let 'em have her. Most the time."

"Did he take her this afternoon?"

"This afternoon? Nope. Samir took her today. He was at the front of the line, 'n Simon was at the back. I bet Simon was set to get her after school, but she came out way early today— 'round one this afternoon. Anyway, Samir don't think it's right, Simon always coppin' the fare, and he's had words with Simon about it. So today when she came out so early and just plopped down in his cab, he grabbed the fare 'fore Simon could do a thing. Oooeee!," he laughed. "You should'a seen ol' Simon! He was so mad he nearly popped a tooth. Screeched out'a here after them like he was on a mission for Shaytan. Don't know what he was gonna do—she was already in the car. Didn't see neither of 'em since."

"What does Simon look like?"

"I dunno. Mid forties maybe. 'Bout the same size as me. Not as good lookin'," he smiled, baring nicotine-stained teeth. "Grey hair, not too much of it. Hardly no teeth. Says he used to be a *Zabbaleen*, but he don't stink too much," he laughed.

"A *Zabbaleen*?"

"Yup. Still lives on that mountain with all the garbage. He used to haul garbage in a cart till his back went out."

"What's his cab like?"

"You know, black and white. Only his is covered with crosses and the Virgin Mary and Jesus and stuff. Even got stickers on the bumper."

Ahmed thought about this for a moment. "Gold tissue box in the back?"

"Yeah! I think so. Yeah, that's right."

"You know his license?"

"His license? Heck, no! I know his teeth and his bad breath, but I don't know my own dang license," he laughed. "Who does?"

"Thanks," Ahmed said, clapping the man on the back and tucking a bill into his hand. "You've been a big help." He darted back to Kamal and dialed, his phone already in his hand.

"Mr. Amides?"

"Ahmed." His voice was tight, distant.

"I may have a lead, sir."

"O-kay."

Ahmed told Magda's father what he knew.

A heavy sigh answered him. "That's not the kind of news I was hoping for. She should've been home by now even if she stopped along the way," he sounded tense and anxious. "All right. I'm not taking any chances. I'm going to get an APB put on that cab."

"Uh—Mr. Amides? My dad has done that sort of thing before. He was an officer in the army before he joined the diplomatic corps. He could get it done."

"I suppose." Mr. Amides agreed reluctantly.

"I'll call him right away," Ahmed was about to hang up when Mr. Amides interjected.

"No, Ahmed," he said firmly. "I think the call to your father should come from me. Let me grab a pen." There were fumbling noises on the line. "Now. Describe the cab for me one more time."

Ahmed did so.

"All right, thank you. Now you go home and wait there. The last thing we need is for you to go missing as well."

"I understand," he said, choosing his words carefully. Magda's father hung up.

"He told me to go home," Ahmed said to Kamal.

"We're not going home, are we?"

"It's a long shot," Ahmed said. "But I have an idea where they might be. Pray to Allah I'm wrong."

XXXVII

Darkness—a sensation of falling. I tumbled down a deep black hole. Falling for a thousand years. Faces blowing past—Gabrielle and Maraya, Ahmed and Mark, my own eyes obscured with strands of strawberry-blonde hair, each face whipping in and out of focus—there and then torn away before I could reach out to touch it.

Abruptly, my mind cleared. My eyes blinked open. I made out the figure of a man standing over me in the darkness of a small room. Slowly, he came into focus. He leered at me through silver-framed glasses, a broad grin over six broken, nicotine-stained teeth, a scar on his right cheek. His face glowed with sweat, and he wheezed. Each breath stank like rotten fish. He wore a button-down white shirt with yellow sweat-stained underarms, a sleeveless undershirt visible beneath it. At the collar hung a large silver cross.

I jerked away. I was laid out on a table, legs and hips bound to it with rows of thin plastic rope, my hands tied together at my waist. I pulled desperately at the bonds, but they didn't give. I kicked to free my legs, but the rope held solidly.

I suppose I should've screamed, fought and bit or whatever I could do, but panic hadn't set in yet. I saw everything as if from a distance. Maybe it was the chloroform or the shock or just denial. Was I dreaming? This simply couldn't be happening. Not to me. Not to Magda. It made no sense. We were looking for a Muslim terrorist. This guy was Christian. Why would a Christian target Magda?

He turned away, reached into an unfinished wooden chest against a wall and scooped out handful after handful of candles. Tall ones, short ones, mostly white but a few muted blues and greens. Dozens of them. This felt like something out of a movie. My mind slowly cleared, and I realized the horror of my situation. I started to shake, and I pulled harder at my bonds.

With roughly-chiseled walls of stone, this place was more of a small cave than a room. A faintly rancid sweet smell reached my nostrils, and I knew where I was. Mokattam Mountain. The only furniture was the narrow table I lay on and three rough wooden chests, one of which blocked the door. Along one wall hung a row of hooks draped with silk ceremonial vestments of red and gold and white. The room appeared to be some kind of storage area or perhaps a wardrobe room for priests. The one wooden door, to my right where I lay, had a small opening in it. The only light in the room came through that paneless window, along with a hint of a breeze. A much bigger wind whined from some distant place and cried to get in.

I found my voice. "What is this?"

He showed no sign of hearing me. He reached into the chest again and this time brought out a handful of photos. They were black and white enlargements; 5x7s and 8x10s. They looked worn and old, but as he began fixing them to the walls, I saw they couldn't be. They were all recent photos of Magda. I saw me/Magda in the cafeteria with Layla. Magda walking out of the school with Aisha and Demiana. Some were from Facebook. Then he revealed an 8x10 of Ahmed and Magda—the infamous photo of our stolen kiss.

"What are you doing? Are you some kind of terrorist?"

He didn't answer. He stood the candles up and fitted them into little tarnished brass stands. He placed them carefully on the floor near the walls and on the chests as he worked his way around the room.

"What are you going to do to me?" I begged. Tears of panic threatened to spill from my eyes.

"You have nothing to fear, Magda," he said gently, without turning around.

He took a tall blue candle and lit it with a disposable lighter. Then he began touching the wicks of the other candles, thus multiplying the flame. The ones near the window flickered when the breeze blew in. He lit his way around the room then paused as he straightened his back painfully. He glanced over his shoulder at me. I couldn't read his expression. It wasn't anger. It was soft. Kind?

The tears streamed down my face now. "What do you want of me? I thought you were Christian. I'm Christian too! Why would you want to hurt me?"

He turned to face me, his expression a mask of surprise. "Magda, I'm not here to hurt you. This is *far* harder on *me* than it is on you. Your pain will be little. But it must be done. And the rewards will be—" His eyes searched the ceiling for the word. "Unfathomable." He smiled, his head cocked benevolently.

"Magda, my darling," he said with an angelic smile, "I'm going to save your immortal soul."

I twisted and turned. The thin plasticized rope cut into the flesh of my wrists and ankles.

"You're insane! Let me go!" I screamed.

"You were such a lamb. Pure and chaste," he said sadly without pausing from his lighting. "I watched over you for many months. You were everything a good Christ-loving girl should be, like the daughter I once had."

"If I'm like your daughter, then why am I tied up on this table?" I retorted furiously and then immediately regretted my words. I struggled against the plastic bonds and blood trickled from wrists and ankles. "This makes no sense!"

"Of course, it does! What good man wouldn't help you, Magda? You've gone down the wrong path," he said. He shook his head sadly. "God tried to warn you. He gave you a thousand chances to repent. I know because he did it through me. He sent so many texts, to help you, but you wouldn't listen."

"I *am* sorry for your sister's injuries," he added with feeling as he lit another candle. "I didn't want to hurt her. It was God's will—His last attempt to wake you up. He really has been patient." He turned to look at me again. "Magda—there is no path to heaven but through Jesus Christ, our Lord. You *know* this. And yet you can't stop yourself from seeing that boy, hearing the words of the devil through him. Brick by brick, word by word, he builds a wall between you and Christ. If I don't stop you, you will someday mix your pure Christian blood with his heathen blood," he spat the last words out.

His breath a raspy hiss, he made an effort to calm himself. When he spoke again, it was with resignation. "It's not all your fault. You were born a daughter of Eve, a temple of original sin. The Bible says the flesh is weak, so the flesh of woman is weakest. It's up to me to stop you now, so you can never consummate this sin."

He lit candles under the photo of the kiss. Then he reached up and tore it off the wall. He held it in his hands. Revulsion spread across his features. He took the candle and touched the flickering flame to the photo. The flame licked at it. The paper caught, and the bottom edge began to curl. He held the top corner of the print lightly and watched the flame eat Ahmed and me. He dropped the burning photo, and it drifted to the floor where he stomped it out with his grayed running shoes until the flames were gone. He bent down and resumed lighting the remaining candles.

I craned my head on the table and stared at the remnants of the photo on the floor. I remembered the horrible texts.

Repent or He will punish you!

"I can repent!" I said, seizing on the magic word. "I'm sorry! I'm really, really sorry!" I said.

"No, you aren't," he said, his back still turned. "You'll say anything now. Anyway, it's far too late for that. If you haven't repented yet, you're not able to. Not sincerely. You are like the moth drawn to this flame," he gestured to the candle. "Bent on your own destruction. Don't worry. I will help you. I cannot save you from yourself, but I can save something far more important. I can save your soul." He had nearly completed lighting the candles now.

"How—exactly—will you do that?" I asked in a small voice.

"First, we will pray, you and I. You will confess and accept His forgiveness for the sins you have committed with your body and your heart," he said. "Then, with your soul cleansed, I will release it, so you can find your rightful place in heaven." Abruptly, his voice turned low and venomous. "That's what those filthy Muslims don't understand. They think that by setting off bombs, they kill infidels and guarantee themselves a place in paradise. That's not how it works! They ignore the Old Testament, a holy book for them too, so it's no excuse saying they don't believe it. They kill ruthlessly—innocents and guilty alike—and then kill themselves. All of this violates the sixth commandment, *Thou shalt not kill.* The Bible says suicide is a sin. Suicide is far *worse* than murder, because it's a final act, and can't be repented. It doesn't guarantee a place in heaven, but in hell."

As quickly as he'd angered, he grew calm, "Ahh, I don't cry for them."

"What about murdering me? Isn't that breaking the— the—"

"Sixth commandment?" he replied, helpfully. "Magda," he scolded, "surely you know your commandments by now. You haven't missed a day at church."

He was silent a moment and appeared to forget my question. "Do you know my name?" he asked suddenly.

I scoured my mind. Maybe if I remembered his name it would create an opening—a chance to talk him out of this. Had he mentioned it? I pictured his eyes in the rearview mirror and tried to replay the conversations we'd had. His name, his name. It was something Biblical, I was sure of that. Samuel? No. Wait!

"Simon! Your name is Simon."

"Good. I am Simon. Simon Abraham, actually. I am Simon, like the humble Simon the Tanner, who moved Mokattam to prove to the Caliph and the world that faith the size of a mustard seed can move a mountain. I am also Abraham, like the Abraham of the Old Testament, sent by God to sacrifice his son to prove his faith. Do you remember the story?"

I was pretty sure Magda knew it better than me. God told Abraham to sacrifice his own son Isaac. Abraham dutifully climbed the mountain with his son and prepared a fire for the sacrifice. Oh, God—is that what Simon was doing now? Preparing a fire to sacrifice me? It wasn't until Abraham had tied down his son and raised the dagger to make the final sacrifice that God stopped his hand, congratulated him on the strength of his faith and provided him with a lamb to take instead.

Now I understood. He was saving my "purity" by cleansing my soul and then sacrificing me while I was sinless. He wasn't murdering me—he was sacrificing me to God.

XXXVIII

Ahmed and Kamal climbed back into the waiting cab.

"Mokattam Mountain," Ahmed instructed the driver. "The cave churches—whatever they're called. There's another twenty in it for you if you make it in under fifteen."

The driver hit the accelerator, and the cab lurched forward into traffic.

"Why are we going there? And in the middle of a sandstorm?" Kamal asked.

"The driver's from there. He could take her anywhere on the mountain, but there's this huge church on top. Magda told me about it after she went to a youth group there one time. My plan is to head for it first. With that APB out, the army will be everywhere that's anywhere, but they don't consider Mokattam to be anywhere. They're not going to have any men patrolling around there. And no one's going to be sending choppers out looking in this khamsin either, so if he's up there, it's the perfect hiding place."

"That and you'd have to be completely insane to go up that mountain in a sandstorm," Kamal said. "Which means, since he's insane, he probably is up there. And it means you're insane for following him. What's your plan if we actually do find them there?"

"Yeah, well, I'm working on that."

Kamal shook his head and looked out the window. They were about five minutes into traffic. The cab lurched left and right through the yellow-red fog of sand that filled streets. Their ears were inundated with noise from all directions—the howling wind, the Arabic radio station that blasted away in the cab and the constant punctuation of the cab's horn. The storm had lightened traffic, and despite the poor visibility, the cabbie made good time.

Ahmed's phone vibrated. His father's number.

"Ahmed, I just had a call from Mr. Amides. What's going on? Is everything okay?"

"I'm fine, Dad—but Dad, I really have a bad feeling about Magda. That crazy guy is still out there, and she leaves school in the middle of the day, alone. No one can find her. I don't like it."

"I know. I don't either, Son. We've got the whole city out looking, and we will find her. He can't hide a cab like that for long. Now, the last thing I need is for you to be out in this storm alone looking for a lunatic. He's after you too. You get yourself home to where I know you're safe. Let the army handle this, understand?"

"Yes, Dad. I understand. Don't worry about me. Have you been able to learn anything?"

"We've identified the cab. It's owned by a Simon Abraham. We don't know much about him. He's got a clean record as a cabbie, and so far nothing else has shown up to identify him as a troublemaker," he said. "It's not going to be easy to find him in this storm, but the Egyptian army is on every street corner in this city. The army will find that cab."

"That's good news," Ahmed said. "Dad, one more thing. The cabbies told me he was a Zabbaleen. I wonder if someone should check Mokattam Mountain for her."

"That's a good thought. I'll see what I can do about sending someone up there. Now what about you, Ahmed? Are you and Kamal together?"

"He's right beside me," Ahmed replied.

"Are you home yet?"

"Not yet, Father," he said, again with the careful wording.

"Go straight home and call me when you get there," his father commanded.

Ahmed drew a deep breath. "Dad, I'm not a child to be protected anymore. I'm a man. This is my girlfriend. I love her, Dad. I want to marry her someday if she'll have me. I can't just go home and sit on the couch and pretend this isn't happening. I need to do something. You have to let me help," he pleaded.

"Ahmed, that's out of the question. Man or child isn't the issue. Putting yourself in the equation right now adds a whole new element of risk. I want you and Kamal to go straight home right now. There will be no discussion."

"But Dad—"

"No—discussion." The line went dead. The cab began the sharp upward climb that marked the beginning of the mountain. The windows were tightly rolled up against the wind, but he and Kamal both automatically double-checked them as the first sweet acrid whiff of air penetrated the cab. The driver did the same.

The sharp twists and turns of the mountain were never meant to be taken at such a speed, and certainly not with these winds. The cab whipped around a corner and nearly drove straight into a startled goat in the middle of the road. Ahmed and Kamal were both thrown into the front seat as the driver lay on the brakes to avoid it. Unhurt, the goat ran off. Still, the cabbie didn't slow down.

A few turns later, they approached a fork in the road, and it was impossible to see which fork was the main road. The cab swung to the left then slammed on the breaks for a herd of pigs that squealed and scattered before the car. Again, Ahmed and Kamal pulled their faces out of the cab's plastic upholstery, only to be thrown back into their seats as the cab slammed into reverse out of the side street and tried the other fork in the road.

"I guess he wants to earn a big tip," Kamal whispered to Ahmed under his breath.

"He'll get it," Ahmed replied beneath the roar of the engine.

The cab accelerated up the hill again and a fresh waft of putrid odors penetrated the cab.

Ahmed's phone rang.

"Ahmed?"

"Marcel?"

"Ahmed! Are you on Facebook?"

"Er—No. Why?"

"There's like this massive manhunt on for Magda. The whole city is looking for her. You didn't know?"

"Yeah, Marcel, I know. I didn't know *you* knew."

"How could I not know? It's all over the Internet. Where are you? It's crazy noisy on your end. You aren't out in that storm are you?"

"Marcel, this isn't a good time to talk."

"Oh? *Verdomme*! I mean, sorry. I guess you're in the loop, then. Just wanted to make sure you're okay. You saw that they found the cab they put the APB out on, right?"

The cab lurched and Ahmed nearly dropped the phone. "What?"

"The cab. On the APB. It says here there've been a half dozen credible sightings, and the army thinks it's found the cab near Tahrir Square," he said, naming the famous central square of the city.

"Are you sure?"

"Hey. It's on the Internet. That means it's true, right?" he joked. "Seriously, where are you Ahmed?"

"I'm looking for her, Marcel. Yes, I'm out in the storm. I gotta find her! Kamal's with me. We'll be fine. Just let me know if you learn anything else, 'kay?"

"I'm on it, buddy. You shouldn't be out there, but I'd probably do the same thing if it was my girl. Have strength. I'll be in touch." he said and hung up.

"What was that?" Kamal asked. "What'd Marcel say?"

"I don't get it. He says the army found the cab in Tahrir Square. That's like the most public place in the whole city. It's packed with people day and night. Why would our man kidnap Magda and take her there? It has to be a mistake."

The car reached the top of the mountain. The smell was still there, but it was dialed down several notches when the wind whipped freely across the mountaintop. Visibility was about five feet. The wind howled and shook the cab. Neither horizon nor sky was visible. The little cab was enveloped in a cloud of sand.

"You boys are crazy to be up here in this wind! We're all crazy! I should be home by the TV with my wife and children!" the driver said.

"Drive around the area," Ahmed ordered him. "Please. I'll give you another twenty pounds when we get home. If I'm right, the cab we're looking for is parked around here somewhere."

"Twenty pounds? You have to pay me lots for this. Like—" he paused, calculating. "Like a hundred pounds!" he said. "At least!" he added to strengthen the argument.

"A hundred!" Ahmed began to argue. "Listen, my father will pay you well when we get home. But please, drive around the area."

"Drive around the area," the driver repeated emphatically. "Crazy boys," he put the car in first and began a slow crawl around the edge of the clearing. Once every minute or two, a sharp gust blew across the mountaintop and they could see, just for an instant. It was in such a moment that Ahmed spotted a black and white cab in the distance.

"There!" he shouted, pointing. But the sand obscured it again.

"Where?" said the driver. "I don't see nothing!"

"Just drive where I'm pointing. I'm sure I saw it."

The car made it's way slowly, and then suddenly, the cab appeared, parked in front of them. The back bumper was covered in stickers with crosses. One faded sticker, barely legible, read in Arabic, "Jesus Saves."

A gold tissue box stood in the middle of the back window.

"This is it," Ahmed said.

"Whoa," Kamal said. He got out first. He took a deep breath. Sand caught in his throat, and he coughed to clear it. Bracing his slim figure against the wind, he fought his way to the parked cab and peered inside. Ahmed emerged from the cab. The sand assaulted his eyes, and he squinted and tried to take in their surroundings. He could just make out several buildings around them—probably chapels. It was impossible to tell where the cave churches were. She could be anywhere.

"What you want me to do?" the cabbie shouted from inside the cab. "It's not safe in these winds! I don't know how long I can wait. I got to get home to my family," he said.

"Just wait a couple of minutes more," Ahmed said.

"Ahmed!" Kamal said urgently. "Get over here!"

Kamal pointed in the window.

Magda's pink backpack and laptop lay on the floor of the backseat.

The breeze cleared the sand for a moment, and they saw the opening of a cave directly in front of the cab. "Over there," Ahmed said, pointing to the cave. They both ran.

"Hey!" the cabbie shouted after them. "You gotta pay me for this! I ain't gonna wait forever!"

"You'll get your hundred pounds!" Ahmed shouted.

They ducked into the entrance of the cave. The wind died suddenly. Below them the massive hand-carved cave-cathedral sprawled out, hundreds of pews arranged in a semicircle cut through with staircases leading down to a central main sanctuary. A monolithic carved crucifix towered over the pulpit.

"You check there," Ahmed ordered in a whisper, indicating a couple of doors off the sides of the cave. "I'll check the doors behind the sanctuary,"

Both boys raced to their destinations, taking the steps two at a time.

Ahmed ran down the aisle between the pews until he reached the sanctuary. Behind the pulpit were three doors. He slowed when he saw flickering light through the open window in the middle door. He moved swiftly to one side of the doors and began working his way toward the light, carefully ducking under the dark window of the first door as he passed it.

He came to the middle window, crouched down low and then slowly raised his head until he could see in. The room was awash in candlelight. Directly in front of him, stood a balding little man in a white undershirt and gray pants, his back to Ahmed. The candlelight glinted off something metal in his hands, which were raised high above a table in the middle of the room.

Strapped to the table lay Magda, a cloth stuffed in her mouth, her long wavy hair beneath her flowing out in all directions.

XXXIX

I did the only rational thing under the circumstances. I filled my lungs with air and screamed. The noise erupted from deep within me, a primal thing that drew all my resources and concentrated them into a single shrill, outpouring of sound. The scream pierced the cool damp cave air and competed in strength and fury with the shrieks of the khamsin that raged outside. My lungs emptied. I gasped and arched my back and felt the rush of air pouring back in when I was stunned by a sudden blow to the head. Within seconds, the cabbie stuffed a cloth in my mouth. I recognized with disgust his own stained undershirt. Half the wadded up cloth filled my mouth, while the other half he carefully tied around my head to hold it in place.

"Such a shame," he said as he tied the cloth, his anger barely controlled now. "How are you going to confess if you can't talk?" He reached down and pulled a dagger from his sock. The silver blade gleamed in the candlelight. The hilt was a marble-inlaid Coptic cross in mother of pearl. He pressed the blade against my neck.

"You're just going to have to nod, okay?" he said. I nodded vigorously.

"Our Father in heaven," he spoke, his eyes heavenward. "I, Magda Amides, do confess the weakness of my flesh," he looked down at me, and I nodded again, wide-eyed.

"I detest all my sins, for you are worthy and deserving of all my love," he said. I nodded, not about to miss a beat.

"Forgive me for turning my eyes from you and from the path of righteousness." More head bobbing. His eyes turned heavenward.

"And by your grace, in the name of the Lord Jesus Christ, I commend my soul to you, through your humble servant Simon Abraham," he said. I stared at him then vigorously shook my head with a muffled, *NO!*

Like the Abraham of old, he prepared to sacrifice. His eyes scoured the ceiling as if waiting for God to still his hand—to speak out and tell him not to act. I closed my own eyes and prayed for a lamb to offer itself up in my place.

In that single instant while he paused, knife raised, a thousand thoughts went through my head. I wondered if I —Molly—was going to die. What happens if you are in someone else's body when you die? Maybe I would die in Magda's body, and she would live on in mine. Or Magda's body's death would force us to shift again and to sort things out in the final act. It was hard to say which ending I preferred.

I heard a loud crack—was this the moment of my death? My eyes flew open. Someone had thrown open the door. The wooden chest that had been pushed up against the door was propelled into the room. Simon twisted around, re-directing the dagger toward the intruder. Ahmed rushed directly at the balding little man, reached for Simon's wrists and combined his youthful strength with his weight to pin Simon to the wall. Candles scattered and rolled in their midst. The air gushed out of Simon's lungs as he hit the wall, and Ahmed used the advantage to pry the dagger out of his hand and then turned and threw it across the room.

With Ahmed's back briefly turned, Simon launched himself at Ahmed and undercut him hard in the ribs. Time stood still. Ahmed gasped and staggered backward, dazed. Simon roared with righteous fury. He swung his fist hard into Ahmed's ribcage, again and again. I gasped and tried to call out, but the cloth in my mouth rendered me mute. Ahmed stumbled back under the force of the blows. Then, using his head like a battering a ram, he propelled himself forward into Simon's chest. He slammed Simon into the wall, stunned him with a blow to the head and then threw his weight behind a kick to Simon's ribs.

I heard the distinctive crack as one of Simon's ribs snapped. Ahmed moved in closer and pounded him hard in the chest with his fists. Simon, unable to resist the onslaught, crouched to protect his ribcage. Ahmed threw one last punch with all his weight into the side of Simon's head, and Simon's eyes rolled up before he went down with a thud amongst scattered vestments and candles.

Ahmed stared at Simon's collapsed frame.

"Nmph!" I croaked through the cloth. He looked at me, then back at Simon. Ahmed retrieved the dagger and ran to me. Simon moaned lowly. He wouldn't be any trouble for the next few seconds. Then I saw it. "Nmph!! SHI-YR! SHI-YR!" I screamed, my eyes wild.

"Magda, I am so sorry," he whispered as he threw off the gag.

"Fire! Ahmed, fire!" I shouted. Flames flickered and danced over a white vestment. The fabric twisted, melted and turned black while the fire grew brighter. Vestments had fallen and been kicked throughout the little room in the fight. Ahmed stamped at the white vestment, but the flames resisted him. All around the room fallen candles licked at the clothing. Simon lay unconscious in a corner, his curled up frame half on top of a smoldering red robe.

Ahmed abandoned his efforts and ran back to me.

"We have to get out of here. Are you okay?" he asked as he frantically cut at the rope with the dagger and began unwrapping it.

"Yes. I'm fine. Hurry!" I cried. It took several seconds to work through the rope and several more to loosen the dozen-odd coils around my waist. Ahmed sawed vigorously at the twine that held my arms.

One by one the garments around the room caught fire until the room around us was ablaze. Smoke clung to the ceiling in a thickening layer. As I came vertical, the last of the drug left my system and gave adrenalin free reign of my body. Everything intensified. The heat of the fire scorched my skin, and the smoke burned my nostrils.

He cut the last of the fibers and raised his head just in time to catch a sudden motion as Simon vaulted over the wooden chest and out the door in one fluid motion.

"He's mine!" came Kamal's war cry from outside the room, and I heard footsteps running up the stairs.

Ahmed threw down the twine then reached and picked me up in his arms. With one foot, he pushed the burning chest out of the way, and we squeezed out the doorway, slamming the door shut behind us. Our lungs filled with the cool clean cathedral air.

"Can you make it out of here by yourself?" he asked urgently, setting me down gently on the alter.

"Yes, Ahmed. Be careful! He's insane!" I said.

"This ends today," he said, and took off up the stairs.

"Ahmed!!" I cried. But he was already gone.

I stood unsteadily. My legs held. Adrenalin masked the pain in my ribs. I walked tentatively toward the steps as Ahmed raced up the last stairs at the mouth of the great cave and disappeared into the wall of sand.

I had to go after them.

XL

"Get him Kamal!" Ahmed shouted ahead of him, as the red winds swallowed Kamal's lithe figure. Simon was nowhere in sight.

Ahmed crested the stairs, and the biting sand hit him head on. With the khamsin in full force, he couldn't see more than a couple of feet ahead. The wind whipped first in one direction then rushed in ferociously from another. It was impossible to tell where the next blow would come from. Each gust nearly toppled him. Ahmed stood with his legs wide apart, braced, one arm out in front of him and one above his eyes to protect them from the stinging sand. He was almost completely blind. Simon would know this hilltop intimately, but Ahmed did not. Instinct told him to head to where Simon had left his cab, but then he heard shouting in the direction of the road that led down the mountain. He hesitated, torn between the two choices. He followed the noise.

Ahmed fought the wind, his hands held out in front of him, lifting his feet high so as not to trip over unseen obstacles. Tense and alert, he knew that Simon could be just feet away from him, yet completely hidden. The old man could jump him at any moment.

Hearing no sound but the constant shriek of the wind, he made his way toward the road that opened into the clearing. Abruptly, he broke his stride and narrowly avoided a form lying prostrate on the ground, face down. Kamal.

He fell to his knees and rolled the body over. Kamal was conscious, his eyes wide with pain. At first Ahmed saw nothing wrong with him, but then he looked down to where Kamal's blood-soaked hands clutched his gut.

"I don't know where the knife came from," Kamal gasped. "I had him down, Ahmed. I had him down! He pulled a dagger, and he got me. You gotta stop him, sahbey. He went back that way. Go!" he pointed a bloody hand in the direction Ahmed had come from.

"Kamal, I can't! You're bleeding—"

"Oh, yes, you *can*! The army's on its way, sahbey. I called your dad as soon as I heard you in that room," he winced and curled up tighter. "Just get me off the road here, and I'll be fine till they come. He went back that way, on foot, and he's still got a knife. You gotta get him before he hides. If he gets away, he's just going to keep hunting you guys."

Ahmed gently half-dragged, half-carried Kamal to the side of the road. "Are you sure, sahbey?"

"Go! Just go, damn it!" Kamal said.

An engine revved nearby, and an instant later a black-and-white car flew over the spot where Kamal had lain just seconds before. Directly behind it ran a gazelle-like figure, her dark hair streaming behind her.

"Magda!" Ahmed shouted and took off in pursuit.

XLI

I took the stairs gently at first then with confidence. My legs obeyed. Adrenalin surged through me. I began to jog them. I ran headfirst into the wall of sand. Then I froze. The red winds whipped at me and thrashed my skirt and blouse. Near hurricane force now, all my childhood fears flooded back. An internal battle between fear and courage raged for control of my mind and body.

Mark Twain once said that if you do the thing you fear most, the death of fear is certain. I opened my eyes. I couldn't see more than a few feet, so I focused my adrenalin-enriched senses on listening. All I could hear was the screech of the incessant wind taunting me, threatening me. I breathed in a lungful of sandy air and choked back a cough. The last thing I needed to do was give away my position. I heard a noise coming from the road that entered the clearing and moved in that direction then heard the distinctive click-rev of an engine starting up behind me.

Headlights briefly penetrated the haze, and an engine accelerated. The car cut across my path in the direction of the road that led out of the clearing.

I don't know if I actually voiced a scream, but "*No!*" burned through every layer of my consciousness. I focused on the vehicle's taillights and ran.

The cab crossed the broad clearing, and its taillights blinked out of sight as it dipped sharply downwards and began the long zigzag descent down the mountain.

I kept my eyes on the spot where I'd last seen it and made for that place. When I reached the spot, I could just make out the taillights about ten yards ahead. I kept my eyes on the road and navigated the dips and rocks while my peripheral vision tracked the bouncing red taillights. I ran at top speed over the rough and pot-holed dirt road. One moment the wind was at my back propelling me to speeds I could barely control, the next instant it ran headlong into my face. It felt like the dream again. I was chasing the van with Maraya in it, and no matter how hard I ran, I couldn't seem to get anywhere. The red lights flickered and faded into the fog ahead.

Still I kept on. This was my only chance to help make right what I had made wrong. I was not letting this monster get away to hunt another day. A few hundred yards down the road I heard the footsteps of someone else running behind me and gaining. I didn't have to look to know who it was.

"Run, Magda!" he shouted, "Run for all you're worth!"

And so I did.

I ran with every skill I had. When a goat stepped into the street to stare after the fleeing car, I was going too fast to break my stride and zig around it. Without a thought, I launched into the air, straightened my right leg out in front of me, raised a hooked left leg beside me and hurdled it.

The cab slowed and lay on the horn for some unseen obstacle. I gained a few yards before the taillights disappeared to the right. I reached the spot where they vanished and saw them again, below and to the right.

I kept up like this, vaulting obstacles and recklessly racing down steep hills. The road dipped sharply downward at one point, and I lost my footing and skidded down several feet on my backside. Ahmed appeared, grabbed my arm and pulled me up, and we continued on side by side with no more caution than before.

The taillights were a little further away each time we turned a corner, and I gave the chase everything I had. This was the race of my life.

The white lights of an oncoming truck pierced the fog, illuminating the narrow road in front.

The truck swerved and flashed its lights. Brakes screeched, but the collision was inevitable. The cab was going too fast, and it plowed straight into the truck with the ear-splitting clash of metal-on-metal.

Ahmed and I couldn't stop. The wind was at our back, and the momentum of the mountain pushed us downward at breakneck speed. The taxi was melded to the side of the truck, and the two vehicles slid backward down the hill as one. We were nearly on top of them when Ahmed threw himself into me, and we tumbled sideways and rolled on top of each other until we came to a rest, bruised and battered at the side of the road.

Flames erupted from the hood of the truck. We lay where we had fallen, just holding each other and watching the fire progress from the truck to lick the hood of the cab. A man in a soldier's uniform tumbled out of the driver's side door of the truck and took off down the mountain. There was no movement from the cab.

The wind pushed the flames violently from side to side, but the flames fought back. Each time I thought the wind and sand had doused the flames, the flames shot up again in another place. Then just when I thought the wind had won, a great explosion cracked through the air, and fire engulfed the wreckage. A wave of heat rolled over us. It passed, and we stood and watched, mesmerized, as the whirling, whipping fire fed ravenously on the metal beneath it.

I was vaguely aware of people now. They streamed out of the homes and businesses as they struggled through the wind and carried pots and buckets of water to throw on the fire. Others gathered up handfuls of sand where it collected along the road and threw it on the flames.

Tears streamed down my face, and Ahmed pulled me closer. He ran his hands through my hair and kissed my forehead. I closed my eyes and felt myself let go. My tears were not the tears of movie stars, but the kind of wracking violent tears of release that come with snot and blubbering. I fought for a while to contain them, but this was their moment. I must've been like that two or three minutes, and he just held me through it all.

That's how they found us.

XLII

The next day, the city of Cairo began the task of cleaning up after the khamsin. Few of the city's houses were sealed well enough to resist the desert sands, no matter how many dish towels and pillowcases were stuffed in the cracks under doors and windowsills. A thick coat of red dust had to be lifted off tabletops and cabinets. All the windows needed to be washed, the beds laundered, the floors mopped.

The hospital was one of the few places that withstood the sand-laden winds well, at least on the upper floors where the windows were permanently sealed a result of too many suicidal patients jumping. From where we stood in the dust-free hospital room, the skies were clear and innocent as if yesterday had never happened.

"You were just standing there, watching Simon burn, when the army arrived?" Kamal asked, from the bed. His mid-section was wrapped solidly in bandages from armpit to waist. The doctors said the wound had missed all internal organs. They gave him twenty-five stitches—a number he seemed quite proud of. He had lost a lot of blood, and the doctors kept him for observation.

"Pretty much," Ahmed said. "The truck he hit was an army truck—it was nearest the mountain when your call came in—and first to answer it. More army jeeps and other cars arrived within a couple of minutes. Dad and Mr. Amides," he smiled mischievously at me, "were with them."

I blushed at the memory. We had been locked in an embrace when they found us, but we pulled apart when we recognized our dads and took our respective fathers into our arms to assure them we were unhurt. Not even Magda's father, in all the hours since, had said a word about it.

"We sent a car straight up the hill to find you," Ahmed said to Kamal.

Kamal shook his head. "I still can't reckon where Simon pulled that blade from. I had him down and was punching him, and suddenly I had this horrible pain in my stomach, and I couldn't move. He just pushed me off him and ran, and all I could do was watch."

"You were amazing, sahbey," Ahmed said.

I leaned over Kamal from the side of the bed opposite Ahmed, squeezed Kamal's hand and kissed him on the forehead. "Thanks, Kamal," I said. "This wasn't your mess, but you stood by me when I needed you."

Kamal blushed, not an easy feat through his dark skin. "Hey, I had to do what I had to do."

Maraya giggled from her wheelchair in the doorway. "Magda, you're not supposed to kiss *him;* it's the other one!" she said.

I ran over to her and gave her the biggest hug I could without hurting her. She'd gained consciousness yesterday afternoon, shortly after I left the hospital. Magda's mom said she just woke up like it was a regular Saturday morning. She was still weak, and the doctors weren't letting her walk yet, but Magda's dad had hired one of those British nurses to stay by her side, so she could come home to sleep in her own bed tonight.

The room filled up as more visitors arrived to congratulate Kamal on his bravery. Moe sauntered in first, his dark, unkept hair so long he kept sweeping it out of his eyes. Beside him was Marcel, a perfect foil to Moe with his short, white-blonde hair and Dutch milk-and-honey complexion. Layla, freed of her school uniform, arrived in a gold-trimmed purple kimono dress while Demiana wore a simple denim dress with a leather belt.

A pink-clad nurse came to take Maraya back to her room for lunch, and as the nurse pushed her chair out into the hallway, she nearly collided with an oncoming wheelchair.

"Geez, I'm sorry!" Mark apologized to the nurse as he maneuvered past them. "Still getting the hang of my new wheels."

The room erupted into choruses of joy, and Mark was inundated with hugs and well wishes. He showed no sign of injury from the church bombing, but I knew that in addition to two broken ribs and a concussion, he'd bruised his spine, which can be very serious. He'd undergone countless MRIs, CT scans and serial examinations.

"When will you be back in school?" Layla asked. She assumed pride of place at his right shoulder.

"One more week, if I behave myself, they say," he said. "And back to sports in a month."

"You were bloody lucky," Marcel piped in.

"Yeah, well, that's one way of looking at it, I guess," Mark said.

It was Moe who raised a question that hadn't occurred to me. "I get that Simon was the dude who chased you and Maraya off the bridge . . ." he said, addressing me. Then, with a nod toward Ahmed, "And that Simon planted the scorpions in your backpack while you two were at McDonald's, right?" he said. Ahmed and Kamal nodded agreement. "All that makes some crazy twisted sense. But why would a Christian blow up a Christian church? Isn't that like the ultimate blasphemy or something?" he said.

I guess it was kind of odd. But he'd found religious justification to murder already. Was it really that much of a stretch?

"Guys, I can't believe we're having this conversation," Marcel interjected in his Dutch accent. "Don't you guys listen to the news?"

An honest answer? No. But no one said so.

He walked over to the hospital TV, which was suspended by an iron rod from the ceiling opposite the bed. He reached up and switched it on.

He twisted a knob on the TV and flipped the channels and settled on one with a greased-back newscaster in a gray suit and red tie. He turned the sound to a background level while the reader read the day's soccer headlines.

"Everyone knows you guys now. First, it was just a little story about a kiss. But then we had a van almost push another car off the 6th of October Bridge in full view of about a gazillion witnesses, a church bombing, and yesterday—yesterday we had an APB through the whole city of Cairo for a kidnapper, and then a great crash on Mokattam Mountain and an army truck in flames. Now the government is doing a, a—*hoe zeg ja dat?*—a victory dance," he raised his arms and wiggled his hips, "to tell us the great and powerful Egyptian army conquered the enemy."

"Of course, the TV news tell the government's version of the story," he continued. "The real news is on Facebook and the blogs. You guys know the blog *Amir's Mirror*?" More blank stares. "Seriously guys? The blog has, like, four million hits." We looked at each other and shrugged our shoulders. Marcel shook his head in disbelief.

"Anyway, back after the church bombing, when everyone thought it was still Muslim terrorists stalking Magda, Amir blogged about how you're just a couple of dumb kids stupid enough to be in love," he said. "He told his readers they should feel crappy that we live in a world where you two can't be together without death threats.

"Of course that changed after Simon went down yesterday. Some of the army went poking around aiming to pin the whole backpack bomb thing on him, but they couldn't. They got him on the scorpions. He was raising them in the apartment he shares with his mom. He's got a dozen of them in a big aquarium filled with sand rocks. I guess they're really hard to raise since they tend to—*hoe heet dat weer?*—cannibalize each other," Marcel said.

"Many talents, our Simon," Ahmed said.

"Yeah. Anyway, the army talked to the guys at the taxi stand by the school, and it happened that Simon spent that whole afternoon at his regular stand. There're, like, six cabbies who were with him. So they looked a little closer at the bombing, and now they think a Muslim terrorist group did it after all. No one's coming forward to claim it, but they're saying the M.O. was exactly the same as that bomb that didn't go off in the Church of St. Barbara last month."

"Whew...." Moe said. "I'm thinking about watching the news. There's, like, stuff going on in Cairo, isn't there?" he said.

I rolled my eyes. Moe could be an idiot.

"Yeah, whatever Moe," Marcel continued. "Anyway, now Amir's organizing a demonstration. He says the new generation of Egyptians has to stand up for the peaceful view of Islam."

Ahmed and I stared at each other.

"We caused all *that?*" Ahmed said.

"Yeah, well, don't get too full of yourself, sahbey," Moe said. "All you really did was get your head turned by a pretty face. You ain't the first one in history that's happened to. The rest just happened *to* you. Wrong time, wrong place, ya know?"

More true than he knew.

Kamal, the quiet center of the room, had hardly spoken since the others arrived. Now, Mark wheeled closer to the bed.

"Let's not forget Kamal's part in this," he said. "Kamal, you took a dagger for Magda. That's pretty amazing. We may not have given you your due in the past, and if that's true, I'm sorry. You've shown us today what kind of man you are."

Kamal tensed. "Yeah, about that." His eyes toured the room accusingly. "Why did I have to take a knife in the gut for you all to believe in me?"

The room was quiet. Seven pairs of eyes fixed on the black and white tiled floor. Everyone of us, with the exception of Ahmed, had assumed that the son was like the father—it was just a matter of how much so.

"Kamal, sahbey—" said Ahmed.

"Not you, Ahmed. You were the only one who was willing to see the real me. Everyone else here treated me like some kind of terrorist. I think half of you probably even thought I bombed that church somehow. I never did a damn thing to deserve that."

"You're right, Kamal," I said at length. "I heard the stories about your Dad. I thought, you know, you are who you hang with. I'm—"

"See!" Kamal shouted then winced, and his hand flew to his stitches. He continued more softly. "This is what I've had to deal with my whole life. I'm not like him! I've never been like any of them. We don't choose our parents, okay?"

An awkward silence ensued, and then Ahmed asked, "Kamal, what happened that summer when you went with him? The summer you came back alone?"

Kamal's lips formed a tight angry line. "You may as well know. He took me to this hot, dirty, dried-up little village in Pakistan. There was nothing there. No jobs, no running water, no electricity, nothing but a filthy stream and couple of huts. The terrorists, they brainwash the young boys there with these crazy ideas about jihad. It's just—sad."

Murmurs of shock emanated around the room.

"Some of the boys, Ahmed, they're not even twelve. They're little kids! They're like Samir. They'll believe whatever you tell them. They sit in their dirty old galabeyas and learn how to hate and fight in exchange for a full belly. In a few years, they will be men. Bingo. Instant army. The stuff they teach them? It has no basis in Islam! I watched my dad work with these boys for a week until I couldn't take it anymore. I walked twelve hours to a village with a train station and found my own way back here. And then I get here, and you all just assumed I was one of them."

"Kamal," Ahmed said. "Why didn't you just tell us what happened over there as soon as you got back?"

"Because! First, everyone knew about my mom and her affair then my dad—the rumors were bad enough. To confirm them? Like, hey guys, guess what? My dad really *is* a crazy man who helps breed little terrorists. No thanks. Our family suffered enough shame. I wanted them to stay rumors. Probably should've just left it that way."

"You did the right thing to tell us," Moe said. "You shouldn't have to carry a weight like this alone."

Kamal looked at Ahmed. "Your dad knew what happened. He never said anything, but I'm pretty sure he knew where I'd been. 'Member how that summer after I came back, all of a sudden we packed up and went on vacation to the Sinai? To that hotel with the eight swimming pools? I don't think he took us for the pools. 'Member what else we did?"

Ahmed shook his head. "We made some side trips too, didn't we? Like to a monastery or something?"

"St Catherine's Monastery?" Layla asked. "I've been there. It's built on the site where Moses saw the burning bush."

"Oh, yeah. Now I remember," said Ahmed. "I took a picture of the bush. It's supposed to be the same one Moses saw."

"Yeah, well, Uncle Cyril didn't take us there for you to take pictures of a bush," Kamal said tersely. "He wanted to send me a message. He wanted me to see the copy that's there of the Charter of Privileges to Christians."

"The what?" said Layla.

"The Charter of Privileges to Christians. Sometimes it's called the *Achtiname of Muhammad.* It says that Muslims must never destroy a house of the Christian religion. It says Muslims are to fight for Christians. It's signed by the prophet's own hand, may he rest in peace." Then he added coldly, "your Dad was making damn sure I knew what was on it."

"Kamal, sahbey, calm down," Ahmed said. "Dad wasn't testing you or accusing you. He wouldn't do that."

Kamal sighed. "Maybe he didn't mean anything by it. But your dad of all people should've known. It's not guys like me that end up running around with pipe bombs," his eyes flickered unwillingly to Mark.

"What about your dad then? How'd he end up a terrorist?" Marcel asked. All eyes froze on him.

"Geez, Marcel—" Mark began.

Kamal interrupted. "It's okay, Mark. I started this, I may as well finish." All eyes were fixed on him. "My Dad wasn't born like he is. Everything changed about a week after my Mom died when he found out that she'd been sneaking around on him. I suppose he could've felt hurt or betrayed, but it was easier to be furious. The terrorists teach that women are weak and not to be trusted. They are to be locked up, hidden, beaten like animals. By following their teachings, he could be filled with righteous anger instead of pain," he looked around the room again then added, "but I don't see things his way, okay? I'm *not* my dad," he spat.

"Kamal," Mark said. "We're on your side."

"Yeah, I guess." he said.

"No. Kamal," Ahmed said. "Mark's right. We're all on the same side. This Amir guy's right. We've gotta find ways to fight poverty and to show people what Islam is really about. We've gotta quit being victims—quit sitting around waiting for bad stuff to happen. That's what the last generation did, and look where it got us!"

"A revolution!" said Moe. "I'm in! Unless it's nonviolent. Is it nonviolent?"

Ahmed laughed. "Yeah, Moe, I can just see you leading our revolution. What's your weapon of choice? A surfboard?"

"Hey. I've got a lot of scars from surfboards. They're seriously violent in the wrong hands."

"Hey, what about us foreigners?" Marcel interjected. "What's our part in the revolution? We Dutch are fearsome peacekeepers. Do you need any peace keeping?"

"Nah, I think we'll take a conflict-free approach right from the get-go," Ahmed said with a laugh. "No surfboards allowed."

"And us Christians? I'm not sure I get how we fit in. It's supposed to be a Muslim demonstration," Layla said.

"Well, you and all Christians stand side by side with us, of course, since we're fighting a common enemy," he crooked a beckoning finger at me and pointed to the space beside him. "Nice and close preferably."

"Geez, Ahmed," Layla laughed. "This hospital would be, like, half as busy if you'd just love some of us Christians a little less, 'kay?"

Ahmed shrugged her comment off with a smirk.

"Hey, guys. Listen to this. It's about Magda's church," Marcel reached up and adjusted the volume on the TV, so we could all hear.

". . . in preparation for this evening's service," the newscaster read, and the screen behind him showed a long shot of hundreds of people surrounding the Maadi Church of the Holy Virgin and holding up Korans, crosses and Bibles. "Muhammad Husayn has the story. Muhammad?"

"Thank you, Karim," the reporter said as he stood among a crowd of swaying candle-bearers, most of them in pants and T-shirts or button downs. "They're calling it a Circle of Protection, and here's why. This church was the scene of a brutal bombing last Thursday. Witnesses say a young man, whose name is not being released, grabbed a backpack with a pipe bomb and ran out of the church and threw it out onto the banks of the Nile, which prevented a far worse disaster," Several hands slapped down on Mark's shoulders where we watched, and he smiled humbly.

"The back side of the church was blackened and charred. Twelve people, who were gathered here in a peaceful prayer service, were injured. Police are placing the blame for the bombing on Muslim terrorists, and that has many Copts here concerned that they're no longer safe in their own church. The Muslims have formed a Circle of Protection to send a message that they're tired of violence being used against their Christian neighbors and friends," the reporter turned and faced a young twenty-something in a black T-shirt and jeans beside him. "Fouad Alhazred here is one of the protesters who used his website, Facebook page and Twitter to get people out tonight. Mr. Alhazred, why are these people here tonight?"

The camera zoomed in on a clean-cut man holding a candle in one hand and a prayer book in the other. A microphone pressed up to his face. "We are the true Muslims, and our religion stands for peace," he said, "The Christians are our brothers in peace, our friends, and we stand here to protect them in their place of worship." Whoops and shouts of agreement came from a group of young people behind him.

The reporter took back the mic as a group of Christians pushed through the crowd to go inside the church. He swung the microphone around and into the face of one of the men.

"Excuse me, sir," he said, and we all recognized Mark's father, Mr. Ideodaniach. "How does it make you feel to see all these Muslims outside of your church?"

"It does my heart good," he said without hesitation. "It is my hope and prayer that the peace and understanding of today will continue. I know those here today represent the true heart of Islam," he said, "and for these people here tonight I say humbly, *Hamdulillah*—thanks be to God."

"*Hamdulillah,*" repeated the reporter to Mr. Ideodaniach with a nod. "And that just about says it all. Back to you, Karim."

The coverage moved on to show damage from the previous day's storm, and we turned the volume down again.

"So," I looked at Ahmed. "Back to reality, do you think this changes anything for you and me?"

He looked at me intently. "Look at us," he said, glancing around the room. "We're not alone, but we're not chaperoned either," he said.

Moe guffawed, "We can leave, sahbey."

Ahmed smiled. "That's not what I meant, Moe. I meant that our parents aren't here. I don't think that's an accident."

"Wow," said Kamal. "All you gotta do is save a girl's life, and her folks'll let you hang with her in the hospital room. Why didn't you figure that out earlier, Ahmed?"

Ahmed grinned sheepishly, and his eyes penetrated mine. "Cairo wasn't built in a day. It's a start."

XLIII

I stayed home from school another day to be with Maraya, to rest my painful rib cage, and to knit my sanity back together. Butch was gone, and I didn't miss him. I wondered why I hadn't shifted yet. What possible purpose did my being here serve now?

Mom and Dad didn't mention my relationship with Ahmed. They didn't mention the embrace Magda's dad found us in after the accident, and they let me visit Kamal in the hospital knowing Ahmed would be there. These two developments were in themselves nothing short of groundbreaking. I didn't expect them to ever welcome Ahmed with open arms—the challenges of accepting a Muslim in a Coptic Christian family were too huge. But after what Ahmed had done for us—saving my life and helping us catch Simon—the mere fact they no longer openly opposed our relationship meant Ahmed had earned a level of acceptance.

When Magda returned, she would find that everyone knew she and Ahmed were a couple and that the situation was tolerated by her family, some of her friends, and even, to an extent, her community. The way forward would never be easy for Ahmed and Magda, but there was a way forward now that included both her family and Ahmed. She had said this was what she wanted. She had said it was impossible.

It hadn't come without costs. I kissed Maraya's pink cheek where she slept on the bottom bunk. The British nurse Magda's father hired had left a short time ago and would be back at dawn and spend the day with her.

I climbed the ladder to my bunk and found my computer and my new phone, fully charged, laid out on it.

I logged onto my computer and logged onto Magda's regular Facebook page for her. Then I wandered over to Magda's school email, which I almost never checked. There, I discovered, was where the real Magda had looked for me when her Facebook account disappeared. Three separate emails asked what had happened to the account and why I wasn't writing. One email told me about the joys of Clearwater Beach, and the last one apologized for getting a C+ on my last two English essays. She warned me that my French teacher probably wasn't buying the story about me having laryngitis for the last two weeks.

I decided I had some explaining of my own to do. I sat down and spent the rest of the evening writing a very long email telling Magda what I had done and why. I hoped she would forgive me for barging into her peaceful life and making such a mess of things. I prayed she would understand that I had her heart at the time. I made a list of each of her close friends and told her what she would need to know about what happened with each of them in the last few weeks. I concluded by telling her how fascinated I was by the country she called home, and how much I would miss Cairo's passionate people, the sweet Arabic music in the streets, the warm nights near the pyramids, and the mighty Nile that ran through it all. Ahmed had said that once you have drunk the waters of the Nile, you are destined to return. I felt confident now that Magda would return soon, and I hoped that I would to, only next time I'd like to come in my own pasty-white skin.

The next morning, I dressed in my uniform, combed my hair and placed a dull gray headband in it. Maraya, behind me, was just waking up, her hair sticking out in all directions.

I had breakfast in the kitchen and enjoyed bread and eggs and the fact that Magda's mom was back, her sensible heels clicking around the kitchen as she got lunches ready before work. Magda's dad read the paper. Maraya came in, and Magda's mom brushed her hair. She wouldn't be going to school today but maybe next week.

The doorbell rang, and I grabbed my pink backpack off the back of the chair and took off for the door.

I smiled when I saw Layla. She was pushing the uniform code to its limits, as usual. Today, she wore a pink plaid sweater vest over her uniform blouse, set off with pink suede ballet flats. Her hair was combed into two low pigtails.

We were nearly at Layla's car when I felt a drop of rainfall on my arm. Startled, I looked up. In a country that sees at best one day of rain a year, the sky clouded over.

Layla looked up at the same time and let out a whoop. "It's a miracle!" she shouted. "It's raining!"

Giggling, we ducked into the car as the drops began to come faster. It was only a sprinkling, but it put Cairo traffic into a tailspin, and it took half an hour to make the ten-minute drive to school. All along the drive, shopkeepers stood at their windows and watched. Men walked broadly down the streets smiling and laughing as the rain soaked them. Women gathered under awnings in the streets and looked up in fascination while children ran and splashed in the puddles at the side of the road. Not a single umbrella appeared.

The bell had already rung when we arrived at school, but we weren't the only ones late. A few kids lingered outside and enjoyed the rain. Layla and I slowly made our way up the stairs as we let the rain soak us and held our mouths open to catch the drops. They tasted of smog, but once a year wouldn't hurt anyone.

There, on the other side of the broad staircase, was Ahmed, talking and laughing with Moe and Marcel. He looked over at me as he spoke, smiled, and winked openly. I smiled back, touched a hand to my heart, and kept walking. Everything was the same. Nothing was the same.

Ahmed and I had chosen the path less travelled by. It would be a long time before a couple like us could walk side by side through a school in Egypt, and our future together was still uncertain. But it rained in the desert today. Anything could happen.

I looked up once more at the Egyptian sky and a drop of rain landed on my cheek. I smiled. Suddenly, the world around took on a familiar intense white glow. Relief flooded through me.

Abruptly, everything was pitch dark, and I was pressed back hard into some kind of seat. I heard wild giggling beside me and felt myself pitched to the right, then the left, then my stomach did a sudden three-story dive bomb, and I shrieked. Thrown sharply forward, I lurched to a stop.

A light up ahead illuminated the darkness, and I looked beside me—Gabrielle. And in my ears the hum of the Rock'n'Roller Coaster at Hollywood Studios, Disney World.

The ride continued.

About the Author

M. R. Hennecke is a mother of three in Tampa Florida. Canadian born, she has spent her life living in a new city every three years, from Edmonton, to Amsterdam, Mexico to Cairo, Montreal to London.

The plot for *Shifting Sands* was inspired by three years spent in Egypt living and raising a family among the native Egyptians, both Muslim and Copt.

M. Hennecke earned a Bachelor of Journalism and Political Science from Carleton University, spent several years as a speechwriter for Canadian politicians, and had her own company in the Netherlands writing English language communications for a broad range of Dutch companies.

Made in the USA
San Bernardino, CA
07 July 2014